Also by Sharon Sala

THE NEXT BEST DAY

SHARON SALA

sourcebooks
casablanca

Published by Sourcebooks Casablanca, an imprint of Sourcebooks
P.O. Box 4410, Naperville, Illinois 60567-4410
(630) 961-3900
sourcebooks.com

Printed and bound in Canada.
MBP 10 9 8 7 6 5 4 3 2 1

Chapter One

IT WAS SATURDAY IN ALBUQUERQUE. THE FIRST Saturday in February and it was cold. But weather was not an issue for twenty-nine-year-old Katie McGrath. She awakened in a state of absolute bliss, calm and confident in everything this day would bring, because she was getting married.

And she wasn't just gaining a husband. She was getting a family, something she'd never had. She didn't know where she came from, or who her parents were, or if she had any extended family. All she'd ever known was foster care.

She'd come close to getting adopted more than once, but every time, something would happen. Either the couple changed their minds about adopting or decided she wasn't the right fit for their family.

By the time she was twelve, she had a chip on her shoulder and was tired of pretending anyone cared about her. At that point, she was just another half-grown kid in the foster care system, so she made her peace with it and finally aged out.

Once she graduated from high school in Chicago and left the foster care system, she knew exactly what she was going to do. She wanted to be a teacher, and with the help of a couple of grants and working two jobs for four years, she put herself through college.

Coming to Albuquerque to teach, which was where she was now, was also where she met Mark Roman. He was a farm boy from Kansas who had a junior position in a CPA firm, while Katie taught at Saguaro Elementary. Now, three years later, here they were, ready to take that next step in their relationship, and she couldn't be happier.

She was just getting out of the shower when she got a text from Lila Reece, a fellow teacher who'd become her best friend, and today, her maid of honor.

It was a "good morning, good luck, see you at the chapel" kind of message, but it brought reality to the day. It was time to get moving.

After breakfast, Katie loaded up her things, made a quick trip to her hairdresser, then hurried off to the chapel to meet Lila.

Lila was short, blond, and curvy—the opposite of Katie, who was tall with dark shoulder-length hair and the metabolism Lila longed for.

When Katie pulled up in the parking lot, Lila helped carry in the dress and everything that went with it.

"I love your hair!" Lila said, eyeing the smooth, silky strands as they headed inside.

Katie smiled. "Thanks. This style works really well with the veil," she said.

They spent the next couple of hours getting ready in one of the dressing rooms, laughing and talking.

Gordy Thurman, Mark's best man, arrived early, too, and popped in to give her a thumbs-up.

"Hey, Katie, you look beautiful. So do you, Lila," he said.

"Thanks," Katie said. "Is Mark here yet?"

"Not yet, but we both know Mark Roman is never going to be the early bird. He'll be here soon," Gordy said, then waved and went to find the men's dressing room.

The wedding chapel was a popular venue, even though the wedding wasn't going to be a large one.

Just Katie and Mark.

A maid of honor and a best man…and fifty guests.

The florist stopped by the bride's dressing room to drop off flowers, then scurried away.

Katie was listening without comment to Lila's continuous spiel about what a fun weeklong honeymoon she and Mark were going to have at the Bellagio in Vegas.

"You're going to be in the honeymoon suite, living it up. That should warrant enough good luck to do a little gambling while you're there," Lila said.

Katie laughed. "We have a little money put aside for that, too."

They were down to finishing touches when Katie finally sat on a bench so that Lila could fasten the veil to Katie's hair.

Once Lila finished, she eyed the pretty woman before her and sighed.

"You look breathtaking, my friend. Your wedding dress is as elegant as you are. Mark is one very lucky man."

Katie shivered. "I'm the lucky one," she said, then got up, moved to the full-length mirror in the corner of the room, and did a full turn, eyeing herself from front to back. She felt beautiful and loved.

She was still thinking of Mark when her cell phone rang. When she saw it was him, joy bubbled up into her voice.

"Hello, darling. Are you as ready as I am?"

"Um…Katie…I have something to tell you," Mark said.

Katie laughed. "Sorry, but last-minute jitters are not allowed."

"It's not jitters, Katie. I'm so sorry, but I can't marry you."

Katie's knees went out from under her. For a few horror-filled moments, this was her childhood all over again. She reached backward for a chair that wasn't there and sat down on the floor.

"What do you mean, you can't marry me?"

Lila saw her fall and then heard those words coming out of Katie's mouth and gasped, but when she started toward her, Katie held up her hand.

Lila froze in midstep—horrified.

"I can't marry you because I'm already married…to Megan. We eloped to Vegas last night. I'm sorry but—"

Katie went numb. "Megan who?" Then she gasped. "Megan, your boss's daughter, Megan? You married Walt Lanier's daughter? Just like that?"

Mark Roman sighed. "No, not just like that. We've been seeing each other for a while and—"

Katie's voice rose two octaves. "You've been cheating on me and still playing out this wedding lie? When you knew it wasn't going to happen? What kind of a lowlife does that?"

"I know you're—"

Katie interrupted him again. "Oh! Now your unexpected promotion makes sense. Your boss can't have his daughter married to a lowly CPA in the financial department."

"Look, Katie, I'm sorry. I didn't mean to hurt you. It just—"

Tears were rolling down Katie's face, and her heart was pounding so hard she didn't know she was screaming.

"You lie! You don't give a damn about what you just did to me. Just stop talking. I can't believe I was this blind, but I'm beginning to realize how freaking lucky I am to find this out about you now. You are a cheat and a liar, and you just sold your honor and your word for money. You deserve each other."

"I'm sorry... I'm really—"

Katie interrupted him again.

"Not as sorry as you're going to be when you remember everything about today was paid for with your credit card," Katie said, and hung up.

Lila's eyes were wide with unshed tears, and she kept staring at Katie, waiting for the explanation.

Katie looked up. "Mark married his boss's daughter last night. They eloped to Vegas. Our Vegas. Will you help me up? I have to tell the guests."

Lila reached for Katie with both arms and pulled her up and then hugged her so hard.

"I'm so sorry, Katie. I'm stunned. I can't believe he just—"

Katie pushed Lila away and took a deep breath.

"I should have known. I should have known. I have never been enough," she mumbled. "God give me strength."

Then she tore off the veil, tossed it aside, yanked up the front of her skirt with both hands so she wouldn't trip, and strode out of the dressing room.

Gordy had just received the same phone call from Mark and was coming to look for Katie when he saw her storming up the hall toward the sanctuary with Lila running behind her, trying to catch up.

"Katie, I don't know what to—"

She just shook her head and kept walking, unaware Gordy and Lila were behind her. They stopped at the door to the sanctuary, but Katie kept walking down the aisle before stopping at the pulpit and turning around to face the guests.

Her eyes were red and tear-filled, and the splotches on her cheeks were obvious signs she'd been crying. Total humiliation was imminent, but she lifted her chin and met their gaze.

"I have just been informed there will be no wedding today. I'm not getting married. Mark eloped with his boss's daughter last night. They got married in Vegas. Thank you for coming. Please take your gifts home with you when you leave. The wedding food will be going to a homeless shelter."

The communal gasp was so loud Katie felt like it sucked the air from the room, and then the buzzing undertone of shocked whispers began.

She went back up the aisle with her chin up and her head back.

"Worst day of my life," she muttered, and walked back to the dressing room and changed into the clothes she'd arrived in. She left the wedding dress and shoes in a pile on the floor, leaving Lila to contact the caterers to have them pack up the food and take it to a shelter.

Lila kept telling her not to worry, she'd take care of everything and call her tonight, but all Katie could do was thank her and hug her.

She couldn't face the pity.
She couldn't face herself.
She wasn't enough.
She drove home in a daze.

———

Meanwhile, Mark Roman was alternating between being a happy bridegroom and feeling like an asshole, which was fair because he qualified in both categories. When he'd told Megan he had to make the call to Katie and needed some privacy, she'd been more than understanding.

"I totally understand, darling. I have some things to take care of anyway. I'll be back later," she said.

So now he'd made the dreaded call and Megan was still gone, and he was too rattled to go looking for her, which, as it turned out, was for the best because Megan was only two floors down in one of the suites reserved for the big spenders the casinos called whales.

And this particular whale, who went by the name of Craig Buttoni, didn't just gamble with money. He was in the drug game up to his eyeballs, and Megan and her father, Walt, were, in a sense, his employees.

Walt Lanier used his CPA business as a front, while he controlled the flow of cocaine coming in and going out of New Mexico. From time to time, Megan had her own little part in the business, and she'd just fucked it up by getting married to an outsider.

Craig Buttoni was pissed, and when he found out

she was honeymooning in Vegas, he sent her a text she couldn't refuse, demanding her presence in his suite.

The moment she knocked on his door, he opened it, grabbed her hand long enough to look at the size of the ring on her finger, rolled his eyes, and then pulled her into his suite and locked the door.

"Is he making payments on that thing?"

Megan glared. Buttoni was in his late forties, with a bulldog underbite and diamonds in his ears. His eyes were always at half-squint, and she was just a little bit scared of him. She didn't like the comment or the tone of his voice, and snatched her hand back.

"I didn't see you offering anything better," she snapped. "I'm happy. Be happy for me."

Craig liked it when she got feisty, but business was business.

"He's not in the loop. He could cause us trouble," Craig said.

Megan shouted, "You keep your hands off him. If I think he's dangerous to us, I'll just dump him. I got married in Vegas. I can get unmarried here if the need arises."

Craig held up his hands and took a step backward.

"There's a lot riding on your itch for sex. Just making sure we understand each other," he said.

"I can scratch my own itch," Megan said. "I married him because I love him."

Craig threw back his head and laughed. "Okay. But you're the one with the most to lose. He can't suspect anything. If you fuck up, you know my rule for fuckups."

"Yes. You eliminate them," Megan muttered. "I'm

leaving now. Happy roll of the dice," she said, and let herself out.

When Megan got back to the honeymoon suite and saw the look on Mark's face, she knew what she had to do, and it all revolved around getting naked.

———

Katie holed up in her apartment for the entire week that would have been her honeymoon. She slept away the shock, then ate away the rage, and ignored the phone calls from everyone but Lila. Those she took, only to reassure her best friend that she was still kicking. By the time she was ready to go back to Saguaro Elementary, she had her game face on.

It took that week of solitude to remind herself that, in the grand scheme of things, her heart had been broken, but nobody died. She was tougher than some man's lies. She didn't need a man to take care of her. She didn't need anyone. Ever again.

It was time to go back to work. Some would talk behind her back. And some would not. But her first-grade students would not know the depth of her heartbreak. She'd been Miss Katie before and she was still Miss Katie. She would keep their little world safe and secure, and they would know they were loved.

For Katie, it was enough.

———

Six weeks later

Katie was getting ready to walk her class down to the cafeteria for lunch.

"Boys and girls, if you brought your lunch, get it out of your backpack and get in line," she said, and then took a deep breath when two of her six-year-olds suddenly lost their minds, launched at each other, and began wrestling on the floor. "Oh no! Alejandro! Kieran! I'm so sorry, but you forgot the rules. Get up and go to the back of the line."

Alejandro scrambled to his feet, his dark eyes wide with instant distress.

"But, Miss Katie, it's my turn to be leader!" he said.

"I know!" Katie said, keeping the tone of her voice between regret and it's out of my hands. "You and Kieran made bad choices. Now, get to the back of the line and do not look at each other. Do not touch each other. And just to make sure, I'll be watching you to help you not forget again. Allison, you will be leader today."

"Yes, ma'am," the little girl said, and strode to the front of the line like she was walking a runway.

Katie sighed again. Three more hours and Saguaro Elementary would be out for spring break. It was none too soon.

The past weeks had been stressful beyond words. By the time she'd returned to work, everyone knew what had happened. Half of the staff wanted to talk about it. The other half just gave her sad, hangdog looks. It was the students who'd saved her sanity. They didn't know what had happened, and the few who'd asked her if her name had changed were fine when she answered, "No."

But today, the kids were antsy to be gone, too, and Alejandro and Kieran were examples of the lack of focus within the building.

Katie glanced up at the clock again, then nodded at Allison.

"It's time. Lead the way," Katie said, and watched Allison disappear out the door, with the other students in line behind her. Katie stayed toward the back of the line to make sure her little rebels were still there, and up the hall they went.

They were halfway to the cafeteria when they began hearing popping sounds and what sounded like a scream in another part of the building.

Before she could get on her walkie to check in with the office, the principal was on the school intercom, and the panic in her voice was enough to freeze Katie's blood.

"We have an active shooter in the building. Proceed with lockdown procedures immediately."

Katie groaned. She was halfway between her room and the lunchroom so she immediately ran to the nearest classroom, which happened to be Lila's room, and yanked the door open.

Lila was already in lockdown mode and running to lock the door when Katie appeared.

"Lila! We need to shelter with you. We were on our way to the cafeteria. It's too far from our classroom to go back!"

"Get them in here," Lila said, even as she was getting her students on the floor against the far wall, away from the door.

"In here! In here!" Katie cried, and began hurrying her students into the room.

A series of single shots rang out, as if the shooter was picking targets, but the screams she'd been hearing suddenly stopped, and the silence was more terrifying than the screams.

Katie was counting kids as they entered the room, and then realized she was missing two. In a panic, she spun and saw Alejandro back down the hall, lying on the floor with blood pouring from his nose, and Kieran kneeling beside him.

"Oh my God! Lila! Proceed with lockdown. I've got two missing," she cried, and turned and ran.

Lila saw the little boys way down the hall, and Katie running in an all-out sprint to get to them, even as the screams and gunshots were getting louder.

"Hurry, Katie! Hurry!" Lila shouted, and then slammed the door shut and locked it before running back to the students who were now in a state of panic. Some were crying, and some were too scared to move. She had to get them into the safest part of the room and flat on their stomachs. The smaller the target, the harder they were to hit.

For Katie, the slamming door was a relief to hear. Her students were safe. Now all she had to do was get the last two and bring them inside with the rest of her class before it was too late.

———

Alejandro was crying so loudly that he didn't hear his teacher calling to them, but Kieran did. When he heard Katie shouting at them, he looked up and realized the other kids were gone and the hall was empty.

"Get up, Alejandro! Miss Katie said we have to run!" Kieran cried.

At that point Alejandro looked up and realized they'd been left behind.

"Miss Katie…I fell!" he cried as Katie came to a sliding halt in front of them.

"I see, baby, I see," Katie said. "But we have to run now," she said, and grabbed them both by their hands and started back up the hall with them, moving as fast as their legs would take them.

All of a sudden, she heard the sound of running footsteps behind her and panicked.

Oh God, oh God…he's behind us. No time to get into another room. No time. No time.

And then some older students flew past her unattended.

"He got in our room. He shot our teacher," one girl cried as she flew past.

Katie got a firmer grip on the boys and began pulling them as she ran, but the shots were louder now. The shooter was getting closer.

Then out of nowhere, one of the coaches appeared at Katie's side. Their gazes met as he reached down to help her. His hand was on Kieran when a bullet hit him in the back of the head, splattering blood everywhere as he dropped.

Both boys screamed.

"Miss Katie!" Alejandro cried.

The shock of what Kieran had seen was too much as his little legs went out from under him.

Katie yanked Kieran up into her arms and pushed Alejandro in front of her.

"Run, baby, run!" she shouted. "Go to Miss Lila's room. See, the door up ahead! Just run!"

No sooner had she said that when a bullet hit the floor between her feet, and then a second one ripped through her shoulder. It was like being stabbed with fire. She screamed, nearly dropping Kieran, and in a last-ditch effort to save the boys, she grabbed Alejandro and threw herself on top of them.

Kieran was screaming and Alejandro was in shock.

Katie's shoulder was on fire and everything was fading around her.

God, oh God, please don't let them die. She wrapped her arms around the both of them and held them close, whispering.

"Alejandro...Kieran. Don't talk. Don't move. I love you."

More gunshots rang out. She heard a body drop beside her, but she wouldn't look. Couldn't look. And then there were more screams, more shots as Katie took a second shot in her back and everything went black.

Seconds later, police appeared in the hall in front of them and took the shooter down, but the damage was done. Katie was unconscious and bleeding out all over the boys beneath her.

The shooting was all over the news, both locally and nationally.

Thirty-six hours later, of the five adults who had been shot, Katie McGrath was the only one still alive.

One student, a fifth-grade girl, died at the scene, and twelve other students had been shot and transported to hospitals. All but two of the surviving wounded were released within a couple of days, and the last two were due to go home tomorrow.

Only Katie's condition was unknown. Her tenuous hold on life was still wavering, and she had yet to wake up.

———

Four days later

The news was traveling fast throughout the hospital.

Katie McGrath was exhibiting signs of regaining consciousness.

Lila Reece was all the "next of kin" Katie had, and she was on her way to the hospital for her daily visit when she got the call.

She cried the rest of the way there out of relief.

Visiting time was in progress when Lila entered the ICU. She went straight to the nurse's desk to get the update.

"Her heart rate is stronger. Her pulse is steady, and all of her vital signs show signs of waking," the nurse said.

Lila nodded, too emotional to comment, then hurried to Katie's bedside. She clasped Katie's hand and began patting it and rubbing it until she got herself together enough to speak.

"Hey, Katie, honey… It's me, Lila. Can you hear me? You have no idea how many people have been praying for you. Your students have been calling me every day, asking for updates. You saved them. They love you so much. We all do. I'm here. Right here. Nothing to be afraid of anymore."

Katie was trying to wake up, but she couldn't think what to do, or how to move. She heard a familiar voice and was struggling to focus on the words, but they were garbled.

Then she heard her name. Katie! Someone was calling her. She wanted to respond, but it was too hard, so she slid back into the quiet. But the voice wouldn't let her go.

Memories were coming back with the sounds. She'd been running. There was blood. *My students! Where are they?*

She moaned, then someone was holding her hand. She tried to grip the fingers, but moving made everything hurt.

The voice...familiar, but she kept trying to remember what happened.

We were running. Hide. Hide. Hide.

"Her eyelids are fluttering," Lila said.

The nurse nodded.

Lila leaned down near Katie's ear, speaking quietly.

"It's me, Katie. It's Lila. You were so strong for the little ones. They're safe, Katie. They're all safe...and so are you."

A tear ran down the side of Katie's temple.

Lila's eyes welled. "You hear me. I know you hear me."

It took a few seconds for Lila to realize Katie was squeezing her fingers. Ecstatic, she squeezed back.

"Yes, Katie, yes, I'm here. I have to leave now, but I'll be back. You aren't alone, honey. You are not alone."

Visiting time was over and the floor was still bustling with nurses tending patients and doctors coming and going.

Katie's imminent awakening brought her surgeon to the ICU to check her stats, and someone had tipped off the media. They were back out in the hospital parking lot, waiting for her doctor to come out and make a statement regarding her status, because Katie McGrath's welfare had become the city's concern.

Video from the halls of Saguaro Elementary had shown the panic and horror of that day. There were images of teachers and children being shot on the run, and of the shooter coming out of classrooms he'd just shot up.

Parents were traumatized as they watched their children all running for their lives. And then the blessed relief of the arrival of the police, and the shooter being taken down.

The first funeral had come and gone, and three other funerals were imminent for victims. The grief and horror in the city were real.

There was a clip of Katie throwing herself on top of two little boys, and then getting shot in the back, that someone had leaked to the media. It was viewed tens of thousands of times before the administration realized and had it pulled.

The shooter was unknown to the community—a loner who'd been in Albuquerque only three months, and while the authorities were still investigating, his reason for what he'd done had died with him.

There were so many people grieving the people who'd

died, and others coping with wounded children who were going to suffer lasting trauma to their bodies, and both teachers and children were so traumatized by the incident they didn't want to go back to school. They all needed good news, and finding out that Katie McGrath might be waking up was it.

———————

Katie opened her eyes to a nurse and a doctor standing at her bedside.

She recognized being in a hospital, but she was confused about why. She hurt. Had she been in a wreck? What had—?

And then it hit her! The shooting!

"The boys…the boys…" Her voice drifted off, but the doctor knew what she meant.

"Your students are safe."

Tears rolled down the sides of her face. "Died…saw…" she mumbled, and closed her eyes.

"Yes, but you're not one of them. Your wounds were serious, but you're going to heal, and that's what matters. A whole lot of people have been praying for you. They are going to be ecstatic that you finally woke up," he said, and patted her arm.

The words *finally woke up* made her realize she'd been unconscious for a time.

She reached for her mouth. Her lips were dry. The words felt caught in her throat.

"How long…here?" she asked.

"Four days out of surgery," the doctor said. "Welcome back, Katie. Just rest. All you have to do right now is rest

and get well, and I have the pleasure of going out to tell
the media that you're awake."

———————

They moved Katie from the ICU to a private room the
next day, and Lila was right beside her all the way, quietly
celebrating the knowledge that her best friend was still on
this earth. As for Katie, she waited until the nurses finally
left before she began questioning Lila.

"Are my kids all okay?"

"Yes. You saved their lives, Katie," Lila said.

Katie sighed. "Who was the shooter? Why did he do it?"

"A stranger, and as far as I know, his reasons died
with him."

Katie's voice was trembling. "I know Coach Lincoln
died. He was right beside me when it happened. Who else?"

Lila's eyes welled. "Darrin Welsh, the security officer.
Our principal, Mrs. Garza. Ellie Warren, who was one
of the science teachers, and a little girl named Barbie
Thomas—a fifth-grader."

"Oh my God," Katie said, and burst into tears.

Lila held her hand and cried with her. Being a survivor
brought its own level of hell: the guilt of being alive.

Chapter Two

AFTER TEN DAYS IN THE HOSPITAL, KATIE WAS released.

Lila picked her up and took her home, made sure Katie was comfortable, and left to get her some fresh groceries.

Katie was propped up in her bed with a cold drink on the side table and an enormous pile of mail beside her. According to Lila, they were well-wishes from students and their families, as well as get-well wishes from strangers who'd heard about the shooting and her bravery and sent the cards to Katie in care of her school.

She lay there for a bit, staring at the pile of mail, and then closed her eyes, trying to make sense of what she was feeling. After being jilted, she'd slipped back into the old foster-kid mindset, wondering why she was never enough, why there was no one who wanted her, and as she grieved the loss, buried what was left of her dreams in her broken heart. But after she'd gone back to work, the passing days had moved into a maze of repetition that began to feel safe again.

Then the shooting happened, and when she took the first bullet, she was so afraid that she would die before she got the boys to safety. They were all that mattered. Now, knowing all twenty of her students had come through that horror without being shot was all she could have asked for. She would have gladly died to keep them safe, only the sacrifice had not been necessary after all.

There had to be a message in this for her.

Maybe she mattered more than she thought.

She mattered enough to still be breathing.

Her cell phone rang. She glanced at it, let it go to voicemail, and then got up and slowly walked through the rooms of her apartment. They were familiar. Nothing had crossed a boundary here that felt threatening. She'd been alone all her life. She could do this. She could get well here, but going back to bed was the first step. Her legs were shaky as she crawled into bed and began sorting through the pile of mail until she found names she recognized and began with those.

Some were from students she'd had in previous years, some from parents, from staff and teachers at Saguaro Elementary, and many from people across the country. Some of them even had money in them, and all of them were filled with love and prayers.

There was a big manila envelope filled with messages and hand-drawn pictures her students had sent to her. She knew them well enough to read between the lines. They were traumatized by what had happened to them and afraid she was going to die.

Katie was in tears as she put everything back in the manila envelope. Her students wanted to know when she was coming back, and she didn't know if she could. Just the thought of being back in those halls made her nauseous. She was scared to go back, and scared what would happen to her if she didn't. What if she was too messed up to ever work in public again?

She rubbed the heels of her palms against her eyes and leaned back against the pillows, trying to regain her equilibrium as she gave herself a pep talk.

This was her first day home from the hospital.

She was a long way from being healed.

Nobody was pressuring her to do anything, and she had a lot of sick leave built up, so she was still getting paid.

She would figure it out as she went, just like she'd done everything else, only not today. She fell asleep with a pile of letters in her lap and woke up when Lila came back with groceries.

"Hey, honey!" Lila said. "I got that prescription for pain pills filled. Do you need one?"

"Yes," Katie said, and started to get up.

"No, I'll bring it to you," Lila said.

Katie eased back against her pillows as Lila ran to the kitchen, grabbed the sack from the pharmacy, then raced up the hall again.

"Here you go. I'm going to put up your groceries."

"Thanks, Lila," Katie said, and was opening the container when Lila left the room.

Katie could hear Lila banging around in the kitchen and relaxed. Whatever needed doing in there, Lila had it covered.

Katie took a couple of pain pills, and then slid back down in the bed, closed her eyes, and drifted off to sleep.

Lila began by cleaning out the refrigerator, dumping what was bad or out of date, and carrying out the garbage, then putting up the new groceries. When she had finished, she went back to tell Katie she was leaving, only to find her asleep.

She wrote a quick note, turned out the lights, and let herself out of the apartment.

Katie woke sometime later, found the note and food ready to eat in the refrigerator, and once again was so grateful for such a good friend.

She spent the rest of that evening going through the pile of mail. The notes were unexpected and heartwarming, except for one. Even before she opened it, she recognized the writing.

Mark.

She stared at it for a few moments, debating with herself whether she would even open it, then frowned and tore into it, pulled out a standard get-well card with religious notes, and a brief comment about how proud he was of her. She stared at the signature for a moment, wondering what the hell made him think she ever wanted to hear from him again, and then threw the card in the trash.

That night, she dreamed of the shooting and woke up shaking, stumbled to the bathroom and threw up. Afterward, she made her way to the kitchen and got something to drink to settle her stomach. She was standing in the shadows with the glass of Sprite in her hand when she heard sirens in the distance and started shaking. It made her angry that the woman who'd given birth to her had chosen to abandon her in an alley, and that two men—one she'd loved and one she never saw coming—had come close to destroying her.

What the hell am I supposed to be learning from all this crap?

She took a sip of the drink in her hand and then walked to the window and looked out at the city below. The lights of the police car she'd heard were out of sight, but even at this time of night, the streets were still teeming with cars and people. Too many people. Too many loose cannons. She did not feel safe here. Not anymore.

She carried her drink back to the bedroom, took a couple more sips, and then got back in bed and turned on the TV. She finally fell back asleep with a Disney movie playing in the background, and woke up after 9:00 a.m. to find a text from Lila, reminding Katie to message her if she needed anything, and that she was bringing fried chicken and sides in time for her evening meal.

———————

And so Katie's self-imposed isolation and healing began.

They told her to take it easy and rest, and she was trying her best, even though it seemed as if the phone never stopped ringing. She kept wondering how people even got her number and decided someone in the school system had to have given it out. But if she didn't know the name that popped up, she let the call go to voicemail. It was her only defense.

She was mobile, to a degree, but still not released to drive, so she had groceries delivered, and sometimes food delivered, and the only person who came to see her was Lila.

As time passed, her isolation brought home to her how small her circle of real friends was, and she admitted most of that was her fault. She didn't want to be out and about.

However, the faux safety and comfort she felt during the day ended when the sun went down and the lights went out.

Then, the dreams came as she relived the panic, the pain, the horror.

Some nights she woke up screaming.

Some nights she woke up sobbing.

And every night when she went to bed, there was a subconscious fear that she would not wake up at all.

The toll it took on her physically and mentally was becoming obvious. Her clothes were hanging loose on her body now. Her face was thinner. She jumped at the slightest sounds. She was Zooming with a mental-health professional.

She'd survived, but at what cost?

———

Mark and Megan were living the high life. His new job was fulfilling, and while Megan wasn't exactly the homebody he'd expected of a wife, their time together was everything he'd dreamed it would be.

When Mark went to work, he left his wife in bed. And when he came home from work, she always had a beautiful table set and good food ordered in. It didn't even matter that she never cooked and didn't clean. She was pretty, and rich, and good in bed, and he knew she loved him.

And then the shooting happened at Katie's school, and the fantasy he'd been living in began to deflate. As soon as he heard about it, he was in hysterics. He and Megan had their first fight about Katie. He wanted to go to the hospital to see her, and Megan told him if he did, not to come home.

Mark was pleading. He didn't believe her. "But Megan, it doesn't mean anything other than not wanting her to suffer alone."

And then Megan screamed and threw a plate all the way across the room, shattering it against the wall.

"No, Mark! You left her alone when you married me. She is no longer your business, and neither is her life. You're a fucking fool if you think she wants anything to do with you. Don't you understand that she probably hates you? She'll live or she'll die, whether you're there or not."

Mark was in shock. The woman screaming at him was a stranger. He'd never seen this cold, unfeeling side of her, and in that moment, something between them shattered.

He turned around and walked out of the room and didn't come back.

Almost immediately, Megan realized what she'd done and went after him. But it was too late. She saw the shock on his face. The damage was done.

"Look, I'm sorry that felt brutal," she said. "But you aren't seeing this from a woman's viewpoint. You betrayed her. She will hate you forever. And you're betraying me by wanting to rush to her side. How do you think that makes me feel?" she cried.

"Like an insecure bitch?" he asked, and closed the door to their bedroom in her face.

She gasped.

"I won't be talked to like this," Megan screamed. "I'm going to Daddy's to spend the night."

He didn't respond, and he didn't come out. Megan was furious, but at a loss. Instead of following through on her threat, she slept in one of the spare bedrooms and the next morning got into the shower with him and gave him the blow job of his life.

The fight was over.

But neither had forgotten what had been said.

The honeymoon was over, but the marriage was still intact.

———

It was a Tuesday in late May when Katie got an invitation she couldn't ignore. It was from Boyd French, the new principal at Saguaro Elementary, requesting her presence at a special assembly on Friday to honor those who died, and the victims who survived.

The thought of it made her ill. But she needed to know if she could go back to that school and teach again, so she told him yes and didn't tell Lila. She could drive herself there. She could walk into that building on her own. After that, she made no promises, not even to herself.

Friday came in a burst of sunshine in a cloudless sky the color of faded denim, with the Sandia Mountains delineating the space between heaven and earth.

Katie dressed with care, trying to minimize her waif-like appearance by wearing a long, pink-and-green-floral dress with a black background. The hem stopped midway between her knees and ankles, hanging loose on her slender body. The petal-style sleeves were comfortable, and the sweetheart neckline finished off the look. She chose plain black flats and wore her hair pulled back for comfort against the heat of the day, but her hands were shaking as she grabbed a small pink shoulder bag, then dug her car keys out of the bag, slipped on a pair of sunglasses, and headed out the door.

It was just before 1:00 p.m. when she pulled into the school parking lot and, when she got out, fell into step with a small crowd of people entering the building. She kept her head down and got all the way into the office without being stopped.

Michelle Aubry, the school secretary, looked up just as Katie was taking off her sunglasses, and burst into tears.

"Katie! Oh, I'm so glad to see you."

Katie sighed. *This is why I don't go anywhere. Everyone I see reacts like they're seeing a ghost.*

"It's good to see you, too, Michelle. I was summoned to attend an assembly. I assume it's in the gym?"

"Yes. They have a stage set up and the media is here, too, so prepare yourself."

"Oh lord," Katie said, and then a man came out of

the office, saw Katie, and came toward her with his hand outstretched.

"Miss McGrath, I'm Boyd French. Thank you for coming."

Katie shook his hand and smiled. "Katie, please, and it's nice to meet you, sir."

Boyd French shook his head. "Believe me, the honor is mine. It didn't take me long to learn how much you have been missed. I'm not going to pretend this day will be easy for you, but you have no idea how beloved you are here. Your students ask me every day if you're coming back. I think they just need to see your face to know for themselves that you are well."

Katie's gut knotted. Guilt was a hard copilot, and knowing her children wanted her back made her feel sorry for them, and for herself.

"I'm looking forward to seeing them, too," she said.

"Well then, if you're ready, I'll be escorting you to the assembly," Boyd said, and then glanced at Michelle. "Call if you need me."

"Yes, sir," the secretary said, and then waved at Katie as the duo left the office and started down the maze of hallways to get to the gymnasium at the far end of the building complex.

There were dozens of people in the halls, all of them walking toward the gymnasium, chattering with each other and calling out to friends as they passed.

A sudden screech of laughter made Katie jump.

Classroom doors were banging as lagging students hurried to the gym to get into place. To Katie, it sounded like gunfire.

The first time it happened, she gasped, and for a moment she was back in that day, looking for a place to hide.

Boyd saw her turn pale and slipped his hand beneath her elbow.

"I'm sorry. I didn't think," he whispered.

Katie shook her head. "It's okay. Just nerves," she said, then lifted her chin and focused on the cool air from the air-conditioning wafting down the back of her neck.

Boyd wasn't fooled. He'd done two tours in Afghanistan and Iraq, and he knew PTSD when he saw it. Katie McGrath was struggling. Maybe it would be better when they got out of the hall.

"We're almost there," he said quietly.

Katie nodded, blinking back tears. This feeling was awful. She was failing horribly. If she couldn't get down a school hallway, how would she ever be able to teach here again?

And then they reached the gymnasium. The bleachers were packed with students and families. The chairs set up concert-style out on the gym floor were for victims and their families.

Katie assumed she would be sitting there, until the principal led her up on the stage. The moment she started up the steps, she noticed cameramen from local news stations aiming their cameras at her. She was trying to come to terms with being the focus of attention when she heard little voices begin calling out, "Miss Katie! Miss Katie!" and lost it.

She made herself smile as she turned and waved, but she couldn't see the faces for the tears.

Boyd seated Katie next to him, handed her a program, gave her a quick nod, and then moved to the podium.

"Ladies and gentlemen, students, teachers, and members of the media, thank you all for coming. Six weeks ago today, a tragedy occurred here at Saguaro Elementary. A stranger came onto our property and shot his way into the building, causing great sorrow to all of us. This gathering is to honor and commemorate those wounded and those we lost, and thank you for coming."

The big screen above the stage was suddenly awash in color, with the logo of Saguaro Elementary, and as Boyd continued to speak, the images of those he began naming flashed on the screen behind him.

"As you all know by now, we lost our security officer, Darrin Welsh, a valued member of our staff. He'd been with us for almost eight years, and he lost his life in a valiant effort to stop the shooter. Elena Garza, who had been your principal for thirteen years, called the police then ran out of her office into a blaze of gunfire and died. Coach Aaron Lincoln, who had been your soccer coach and history teacher, died trying to save children caught out in the hall.

"Ellie Warren, one of our science teachers, had already turned in her paperwork to retire at the end of this school year, and was shot and died in her classroom. And we lost Barbie Thomas, one of our precious fifth grade students, who was looking forward to moving on to middle school."

The silence within the walls was broken only by the sounds of weeping. Boyd French cleared his throat and continued, and so did the slide show, as he move on to the recognition of each of the twelve students who'd been wounded, and then the last picture was one of Katie.

"All of you…those who were not wounded, and those who were…those who we lost, and those who were saved, are heroes because you did everything right. It was the stranger who did everything wrong. But in the midst of all the tragedy, first-grade teacher Katie McGrath shielded two of her students with her body, took the bullets meant for them, and saved their lives, and for that we come today to also honor Miss McGrath. Katie, would you please come forward?"

Katie stood, her knees shaking. And as she began walking toward the podium, everyone in the gym began chanting her name.

"Katie! Katie! Katie! Katie!"

Boyd held up his hand, then pulled a plaque from a shelf beneath the sound system.

"Katie, on behalf of the Albuquerque public school system and Saguaro Elementary, it is my honor to present this award. It reads: 'To Katie McGrath, for courage, bravery, and sacrifice in the line of fire.'"

He handed it to Katie, who was visibly overwhelmed as she clutched it to her.

"Are you okay to say a few words?" he whispered.

She nodded, then moved to the microphone and took a deep, shaky breath.

"Thank you. This is unexpected, and such an honor. But it feels strange to accept an award for doing the same thing every other teacher here was doing that day. We were all putting ourselves between your children and the danger they were in. Every year, your children, who you entrust to our care, become ours for a little while each day. We work hard to make sure they are learning what matters.

"Some days we want to wring their necks. Some days we are so proud of them for how hard they try. And every day we love them. Enough to die for them, which is what happened here. I don't know why I'm still here, but all I can assume is that I am supposed to be. Again, thank you for this recognition, and thank you for the hundreds of letters and well-wishes that were sent to me."

The audience gave her a standing ovation as she walked back to her chair, wiping tears as she went.

The principal ended the program with a final announcement.

"Earlier this morning, we unveiled five wooden benches on the playground. Each bench has a name etched on it to commemorate a precious life that was lost here. Yes, the names will be reminders of our tragedy, but as time passes, the benches will also come to represent a place to rest from the innocence of play, and for teachers to sit while they watch over your children on the playgrounds. We will not forget.

"Now, this concludes our program. Students, unless your parents are here, you will return to your classes. Parents, if you wish to take your children home with you at this time, they will be excused. Just notify their teachers before you leave with them. And…Katie, I think your class is going back to their room with their parents and teacher in hope that you will stop by to visit with them before you leave."

Katie nodded, but she was sick to her stomach. How in

the hell was she going to get through this without falling apart?

———————

Lila had known nothing about the award, or that Katie was coming to school, and when she saw her walking up on the stage, she could tell by the way she was moving that she was barely holding it together.

Every time in the past few weeks when she'd mentioned coming back to school, Katie had gone silent, and now, seeing her like this, she understood why. It broke her heart to see her best friend so shattered again, but she knew in her gut that Katie McGrath would not be coming back.

She wanted to talk to her, but they both had other agendas. Katie was headed for her old classroom and her students, and Lila had to go back to the classroom with her students. She'd have to call Katie tonight.

———————

"I'll walk you to your classroom," Boyd said. "And if you'll call the office, I'd be honored to escort you back to your car when you're ready to leave."

"I appreciate your company to get me to my room. I'm sure I'll be fine to get myself to the car, but you have been so kind and…understanding."

He offered her his elbow, and she slipped her hand beneath it. Together, they made their way through the exodus of guests. They were about halfway there when

Katie realized where they were and immediately looked down. When she did, she stumbled and would have fallen if the principal hadn't caught her.

"I'm sorry," Katie said. "I just realized where we were. It took me off guard."

"I don't know what you mean," Boyd said.

Katie shuddered and started walking, almost at a run, as if to get away from the area, and Boyd hurried to catch up.

"That's where Coach Lincoln was shot. We were running," Katie said.

"Oh my," Carl said. "I'm sorry. I didn't realize."

Katie shook her head. "It's not your fault. Everything in this building triggers a memory now. It is what it is." And then they were at the door to her room. "I can take it from here," she said. "What's the substitute teacher's name?"

"Um…Abby King," he said.

"Thank you," Katie said. She took a deep breath and knocked, then pushed the door ajar.

There were parents lined up against the walls, and a short, thirtysomething woman wearing a yellow smock and purple pants standing beside the desk. She had a turned-up nose, pink hair, and a pencil stuck behind her ear. She looked like a living, breathing fairy. *How absolutely perfect*, Katie thought, and then smiled.

"May I come in?"

Abby King turned and opened her arms wide like she was going to hug her.

"Yes! Yes! Welcome back!" Abby said.

Katie waved at the parents and barely got the door closed behind her before she was engulfed. Twenty familiar little faces were turned up to her. Hands were touching and petting, and all of them were talking at once. And then she saw Alejandro and Kieran pushing their way through the crowd, and they were crying. When they got to her, they just wrapped their arms around her legs and held on.

Abby King immediately took control of the situation.

"Children, let's give Miss Katie a little room, okay? You will all get a chance to talk to her personally. Each of you find your spot on the floor in the reading circle, and Miss Katie can sit in the teacher chair, okay? Parents can listen in, but I think today is for Miss Katie and her class."

At that point, Katie put her purse and the award aside and dropped to her knees, hugging the boys to her.

"We thought you died," Alejandro said. "I'm sorry I fell down. You came back for us."

Kieran nodded. "You sure can run fast, Miss Katie. Thank you for coming back."

Katie knew if she cried now, everyone in the room would be in tears.

"Of course I went back to get you both, and Alejandro...everyone falls down. It's the getting back up that matters. And we all got up and ran, didn't we? And we're safe now. Okay?"

"Okay," they echoed, and then hugged her again. "We heard you tell us not to talk and not to move, and we did just what you said," Kieran whispered.

"I'm so proud of you for following orders. It was important, wasn't it?" she said.

Alejandro nodded, then reached up and patted her cheek.

"You said you loved us. Just like Mama says when she tucks me in at night."

Katie's eyes welled. "And I do love you. All of you. You are so precious to me. Now. Let's go find our place in the reading circle, okay?"

They took off toward the circle as Katie followed, and then stopped at the desk where Abby King was sitting.

"Thank you, parents, for waiting so I can speak to your babies, and thank you, Ms. King, for letting me disrupt your class."

Abby smiled. "It's your class, too, and I'm just doing what I love. It's a pleasure and an honor to meet you. Now go sit down in your teacher chair and prepare to be grilled."

"Yes," Katie said, and slipped into her seat. For a moment inside that room, with all of the familiar faces of her littles, she almost forgot all of the bad stuff. "Okay, boys and girls, this is the last period before the bell rings, so each of you ask one question, and I will answer. And then if we have more time, you can ask more questions, okay?"

They nodded, and up went their hands.

Katie put hers in her lap so no one would see them shaking.

"I don't want to get mixed up with whose turn it is, so we'll just start here on my right with Dawson," she said.

The little redhead leaned forward. "Did it hurt to get shot?"

Katie's fingers curled a little tighter, but she kept the tone in her voice calm and even.

"Yes. It hurt then, but I don't hurt anymore. Karen, do you have a question for me?" Katie asked.

And so it went, until nineteen questions had been

asked, and details added. When she got to Alejandro, who was the last student sitting on her left, she looked into his big brown eyes and saw fear.

"Alejandro, do you have a question for me?"

He nodded. "Miss Katie…are you coming back? Will you be our teacher again?"

Katie paused, choosing her words carefully without giving anything away.

"Well, as you know, the school year is almost over, so Miss Abby is going to finish out this year with all of you, and I can see from the amazing art on the walls and the happy faces before me that you all really like Miss Abby. Is that right?"

"Yes! We like Miss Abby," they chimed, and Katie flashed Abby a quick thumbs-up.

"So, when you come back to school after summer vacation, you won't be first-graders anymore. You'll be in second grade, and you'll have a new teacher. That's how school works, remember? You had a pre-K teacher. Then a kindergarten teacher. And then there was me, your first-grade teacher, and now Miss Abby. I'm all healed, but I don't have much 'pep in my step' yet, so I won't be back here before you go home for the summer. I'm still taking it easy at home. But I want you to know how much I loved having you in my class. And how much I love each of you, okay? Will you promise me to always listen when Miss Abby tells you something?"

"Yes! Yes! We promise, Miss Katie!" they cried.

Katie laid her hand on the top of Alejandro's head and then looked at the faces of the children before her.

"We all have people who come and go through our lives, but there will always be family and best friends. Now, it's almost time for the last bell to ring, and I know Miss Abby has things for you to do before you go. So I'm going to tell you goodbye, and maybe one day we'll see each other again. Now come give me a hug and go back to your desks."

They got up slowly, almost reverently, and filed past her, hugging her goodbye as they returned to their seats. Alejandro was the last in line, and when he hugged her, he whispered in her ear.

"I will be good. I love you."

"Oh, honey…you are such a good boy. I love you, too."

Katie got up before she burst into tears.

"Thank you, Miss Abby," she said as she picked up her purse and the award, then paused at the doorway before turning around. Everyone was watching her. She waved, and then she was out the door, swallowing back tears.

The hallway was empty, but she could hear clamor behind every door she passed as teachers were winding up another day on the job.

Her footsteps echoed, making her think there was someone behind her, and she kept looking over her shoulder, just to make sure she was still alone.

Her legs were shaking now. Her heart was hammering so fast it was hard to breathe, and it was all she could do not to run. The office was just up ahead, and after that the front exit, and then she'd be clear.

"Oh God…help me, God…just a little bit further," she kept muttering, and then she turned the corner in the hall and saw the office in front of her, and then the front door to her left, and began counting off the steps to freedom.

One, two, three, four, five…ten, eleven, twelve…twenty-one…twenty-two steps! Take a left, Katie.

And she was out the door.

The afternoon heat was sweltering, and she was shaking as if she were freezing.

Shock.

Jesus wept. I am done.

Katie made it to her car, started it up, and drove away as if the devil was on her heels. The farther away she got, the more she began to relax, and the heat of the day began to seep into her bones.

She turned on the air conditioner and put the fan on blast as she moved into the traffic of the city.

It had been her day of reckoning, and she would never come this way again.

Chapter Three

THE MOMENT LILA REECE GOT HOME FROM SCHOOL, SHE called Katie, but it went to voicemail, so she left a message.

"Hey, Katie, it's me. Call me back when you feel like it. I'm home for the evening."

Then she hung up and went to change before settling in with a stack of papers to grade.

———

Katie was on the sofa in the living room, wrapped up in a blanket against the blast of her air conditioner and watching a movie, when the phone rang.

When she saw it was Lila, she let it go to voicemail. She just wasn't in the mood to rehash anything right now. Being back in that school building had taken everything out of her that she'd fought to regain. She didn't know what she was going to do with the rest of her life, but it wouldn't be happening in that building.

Once her movie ended, she called in a DoorDash order at Saggio's Pizza and then, while she was waiting for it to arrive, returned Lila's call.

The phone rang a couple of times, and then Lila picked up.

"Hey, girl," Lila said.

Katie grinned. "Hey, yourself. This is me returning your call. Do you have exciting news for me...like maybe that cute guy who lives down the hall finally asked you out?"

Lila groaned. "Unfortunately that is not the case. But I was hoping I could talk you into going to lunch with me tomorrow. We haven't had a girls' day out since you came home from the hospital, and I think it's time we did."

Katie surprised herself by agreeing. "That sounds like fun. I'd love that. Where and when?"

"Oh yay!" Lila said. "Let's do lunch a little early, say eleven thirty?"

"Works for me," Katie said. "Where are we going?"

"I was thinking Pappadeaux. I'm craving their seafood Cobb salad with shrimp," Lila said.

"Yes! We can get our Cajun on there, for sure! Okay, I'll see you there tomorrow."

Lila hesitated, then had to ask. "One other thing... Are you—"

Katie interrupted. "Yes, I'm fine...now. Yes, it was hard. No. 'Hard' is the wrong word. If I'm honest, it was awful going back. But I needed to see my kids. We all needed closure. They needed to see me alive and walking and talking, and I needed to tell them all goodbye."

"I guessed," Lila said. "So. We'll talk more tomorrow over good food and be grateful for the opportunity."

"Thanks," Katie said.

"For what?" Lila asked.

"For being the best friend I've ever had...for

understanding…and for the invitation. See you tomorrow," Katie said.

"Yes, tomorrow," Lila said, and they both disconnected.

Lila was in tears. She felt her best friend pulling away.

But Katie was at peace. She'd faced a hurdle today, and while she might not have cleared it, it had become painfully obvious to her that she had to reconsider her options.

When Katie woke up the next morning, she stayed motionless a few moments, remembering today she was going somewhere fun with her best friend. She could be honest with Lila about her fears for the future, and maybe get a few good pointers along the way.

Finally, she got up and went to make coffee, then headed for the shower. She had a couple of hours before she was supposed to meet Lila, so she didn't have to rush. She stripped off her pajamas, wound up her hair and clipped it on the top of her head, then turned sideways in front of the full-length mirror to look at the healing wounds on her back.

One was on her shoulder, the other lower down on the other side of her back. Red, slightly puckered, still fragile skin was healing over the gunshots. Neither had an exit wound, which had been the blessing, or the boys might have been shot if the bullets had passed through her to them. But the extent of the surgery to get them out without damaging vital organs had slowed down her recovery.

She grimaced. Thinking about what-ifs was

self-defeating, so she grabbed a washcloth and stepped into the shower. The jets of water hitting her body were warm and welcome, and by the time she got out, she was planning what she was going to wear. The predicted high today was in the 70s—sandals, summer blouse, and slacks weather.

A day for making good memories.

———————

Mark had been cleaning the pool in their backyard all morning so that Megan could swim in it this afternoon, so he was hot and sweaty when he finally went inside. He took off his shoes in the utility room and padded through the house to their bedroom to clean up before he took Megan to lunch.

When he walked into the room, she was pushing a drawer shut in her dresser and jumped a foot when she realized she was no longer alone.

"Oh my God! You scared me. I thought you were still outside," she said.

Mark frowned. "I'm sorry. I'm going to shower, and then I'm taking you to lunch, remember?"

Megan took a deep breath and then smiled. "Yes, I remember. You clean up while I change, and then I'm going to finish that grocery list in the kitchen before we leave."

He nodded and went into the bathroom, turned on the shower, then stripped and got into the stall and grabbed the shampoo.

Megan's heart was still pounding at the close call, and as soon as she was certain he was in the shower, she began pulling open drawers, stripping what was taped there, and stuffing it all into a tote bag. Then she ran through the house and out into the garage and hid the duffel bag beneath a fake floor in the trunk of the car before dashing back inside.

Living a life of lies was harder than she'd expected it to be, but Mark was amazing in bed, loved her to distraction, and except for his continuing guilt about Katie McGrath, they were fine.

Now that she had the drugs and cash hidden, she dressed and then touched up her makeup before coming out.

Mark was half-dressed when he saw her, and the temptation to take off what he'd just put on was strong. But Megan's hair was done and her makeup was on, and he knew once she was primped, she did not like to be messed with.

"You look beautiful, darling," he said. "Where would you like to go for lunch?"

"I'm thinking Pappadeaux. It's been forever since we've been there. Does that sound good to you?" she asked.

"Sounds great," Mark said. "I won't be long."

A few minutes later, they were in the car and on their way across town, chatting about a golf tournament, the fall balloon festival, and what they were going to order.

———

Katie was a little late leaving her apartment, but once she got out of the building, the drive and traffic weren't bad.

She was over halfway to Pappadeaux when her phone rang. She hit her Bluetooth to answer and kept driving.

"Hello?"

"Katie. This is Lila. I had a flat in the driveway. I called an Uber and I'm on the way, but I may be a few minutes late. Go ahead and get a table, and I'll join you when I get there."

"Bummer about the flat. I'll happily get the table and get some appetizers ordered. I'm starving. Do you have any requests?" Katie asked.

"Ooh…either crab cakes or fried calamari?" Lila said.

"You're reading my mind," Katie said. "See you soon," she added, then disconnected, braked for a red light, and then took a left on a green arrow.

A few minutes later, she pulled into the parking lot, glad they'd decided to come a little early because it was already filling up.

She grabbed her purse and got out, put on her sunglasses, and headed for the wafting aromas of Cajun cooking and seafood.

Once she was seated, she ordered fried calamari and iced tea for both of them, then settled back to wait for Lila to arrive.

It didn't take long before Katie saw her come flying through the front door and lifted her hand. Lila saw her, and when she reached the table, paused long enough to give Katie a quick hug, before sliding into the seat across from her.

"Thank you for ordering! Is this tea for me?" she asked.

"Yes, ma'am. Drink away," Katie said.

Lila took a quick sip of the cold drink. "That's nice. Maybe it'll cool down my stress. Lord. A flat."

"At least it happened while you were still home, or you'd be on the side of the freeway somewhere," Katie said.

"True. And AAA was changing out my flat in the drive-way when I left. I'll take it to get fixed when I go home. Now…please tell me you ordered an appetizer already. I'm starving!"

"Fried calamari," Katie said.

"Yes! My fave. You're the best," Lila said.

Katie laughed, unaware the sound had carried across the dining area.

———

Mark Roman was absently listening to Megan's chatter when he heard that laugh. His heart skipped a beat as he looked past his wife's shoulder to where Katie and Lila were sitting and felt the blood draining from his face.

Megan had paused in her conversation and was waiting for Mark to respond when she caught him staring across the room.

"What are you looking at, darling?" she asked, and then turned around to look for herself. Almost immediately, she spotted Katie. "Well, hell. What are the odds?"

Mark sighed. "Yeah, what are the odds?"

"Ignore her," Megan said, and reached for his hand.

Mark frowned. "I feel like I should say something to her. I mean, she nearly died."

Megan glared. "You do *not* go speak to that woman!"

Mark's eyes narrowed. "We've already had this conversation. I will take orders from your father because he's my boss, but I do *not* take orders from my wife."

Megan blinked.

"Well, darling… Of course I did not mean to insult you. I just thought since the acrimony between you is so obvious, it would be in poor taste to disturb her. Especially since it appears she's having a good time with that woman."

"That's Lila, her best friend. They teach together," Mark muttered.

Megan swallowed the anger she was feeling. "Don't blame me if they dump their food on you," she said, and took another bite of her entrée.

Mark frowned. "She would never do anything that crass."

Megan didn't like it that he was defending Katie.

"Don't say I didn't warn you," she snapped, and swallowed the bite whole.

Mark was already regretting the urge, but if he backed down now, Megan would assume he was buckling under to her, so he headed toward the table where Katie and Lila were sitting.

———

The waitress arrived with the appetizer Katie ordered, took their orders for their entrées, and was walking away when Mark suddenly appeared at their table.

Katie was stunned.

Lila was livid.

Because Mark was nervous and uncertain how to begin

such an awkward conversation, he just started talking in a genial, conversational tone.

"Katie, it's good to see you up and about. I just wanted to say what an amazing woman you are, saving those children like you did."

Katie heard him, then looked back down at her plate, popped another bite of calamari into her mouth, and started chewing without responding.

It was all Lila needed to see.

She waved her hand at him as if she were flicking away a fly.

"Get lost, dude. Your opinions and presence are unwelcome here."

Mark frowned. "I'm not speaking to you."

"And Katie isn't speaking to you, so beat it," Lila snapped.

"That's exceedingly rude!" Mark said.

Lila leaned forward, her voice rising. "No. Rude was what you did when you cheated on Katie, then jilted her at the altar and married the skank you were cheating with. You are a lying philanderer and you're in our space. Get lost, and if you think I'm kidding, I'm happy to start a great big fuss right here in the middle of Pappadeaux, and see how long it takes for someone to video it and upload it to their favorite social media sites."

Mark glanced at Katie, who was calmly dunking a piece of fried calamari in rémoulade sauce, then turned on his heel and walked away, well aware of the curious glances he was getting from the people who'd overheard their conversation. He hated to admit it, but Megan had been right, and she was waiting at their table with a smirk on her face.

"The waiter just came with the bill." She pushed it toward him. "Have a seat. You can't run yet."

Mark glared, pulled out a credit card and laid it on top of their tab, then grabbed his cell phone and began checking his texts so he wouldn't have to talk to her.

As for Megan, she'd just seen a side of Mark that made her nervous. He'd defied her. What the hell would he do if he ever found out about the Lanier family's side hustle.

———

Back at their table, Katie swallowed her bite and grinned.

"You rock big time, my friend," she said.

Lila's cheeks were pink, and she was still livid.

"I swear, that man is clueless as hell. The absolute gall of just strolling up and thinking we would be glad to see him."

Katie laughed, and again the sound rang out—all the way across the room to where Mark and Megan were sitting, still waiting for their credit card.

This time, even Megan heard it and wondered if they were laughing at her and Mark. She didn't like thinking she was the butt of anyone's joke, and stood up.

"I'll be waiting in the car," she said, and strode out of Pappadeaux with her head up and her hips swaying.

Several minutes later, Mark followed her out.

Lila had been keeping an eye on them, and once they were gone, she breathed easier.

"Well, Dumb and Dumber are gone, and here comes our food. Yum," she said.

Now that Katie knew she was no longer subject to

Mark and Megan's presence, she relaxed. The rest of their lunch went undisturbed.

They were finishing up their meal when Lila finally broached the subject of Katie's future.

"Are you still going to teach?" she asked.

"Not in that building. I just can't," Katie said.

"Maybe in another school in the system?" Lila asked.

"I don't know, Lila. What I do know is I barely made it out yesterday. I wasn't sure if I was going to throw up or pass out before I got out of there."

Lila's eyes welled.

"I'm so sorry. That just breaks my heart. You're so good at what you do, and I love you to pieces, but at the same time I can't even imagine how you feel. I was standing at the locked door at my room, praying you'd come flying back knocking and shouting for me to let you in, and instead I heard shooting. When one of the bullets hit the door to my room, I hit the floor. I locked you out, and I will never forget that."

Katie pushed her food aside and grabbed Lila's hand.

"You did what you were supposed to do…what I asked you to do! You saved not only your class but mine as well. And I was never going to be able to get the boys back in time. That's why I threw myself on top of them. The shooter caught us out in the open. We're more fortunate than the five who died. And if the worst thing I have to live with is PTSD in school halls, then so be it. I may teach again, or not. I have to support myself, but I was a survivor a long time before this shooting ever happened…a long time before I got jilted. Okay?"

Lila sighed. She knew Katie's history. She got it.

"Yes. Okay. But you have to promise… Whatever you do, wherever you go, we do not lose touch with each other."

"Count on it," Katie said.

———

Mark and Megan's drive home was much quieter than it had been on the way to lunch, and as soon as they got home, Megan received a phone call from her father. They spoke, and as soon as they ended their conversation, she got up.

"I have to run over to Dad's house."

"Want me to go with you?" Mark asked.

Megan's stomach clenched. "No. This is your day off. I have every day off. Why don't you put on your swim trunks and lounge around the pool with something cold to drink? It won't take long and I'll be back to join you in the pool later."

"You sure? I don't mind," Mark said.

Megan threw her arms around his neck and kissed him.

"Yes, I'm sure. You're a darling. You worked hard all morning, and I'm sorry I was cranky. Go enjoy the fruits of your labor."

Then before he could argue further, she got her car keys, blew him a kiss, and hurried out through the kitchen into the garage where her Porsche was parked. She made sure the bag she'd locked up in the trunk earlier was safely stowed and took off in a rush.

It was delivery day at Daddy's, and she had something over eighty thousand dollars in that bag that she'd wanted out of the house.

After dropping Lila back at her apartment, Katie stopped off at a supermarket for groceries, and as she shopped, she thought back over her conversation with Lila. The weight of indecision was gone. Katie was not going to renew her teaching contract in the Albuquerque school system, and just acknowledging that released her from a mountain of guilt.

Within a week, she had turned in her resignation. A few days later, she received a personal letter from the superintendent of schools, thanking her for her years of service and expressing his sympathy for what had happened to her. He assured her that he would give her a glowing recommendation wherever she chose to go and wished her well.

Now that she'd officially resigned, she was free to start looking into other options. She didn't have time to waste in deciding what to do because when her contract ended in June, so would her paychecks.

She began by making lists of jobs other than teaching and researching the qualifications needed. The biggest drawbacks were the pay scales and benefits. The jobs either had a decent wage but no benefits, or basic benefits but lower pay. It was a rude awakening. Between the nightmares at night and the uncertainty of her future, Katie McGrath was scrambling to find a foothold again. It was beginning to look like teaching was still, for her, her best choice, but she had to find a way to get past what had happened to her.

After looking online at Teacher Certification Reciprocity, she easily found out what was required in other states to be certified to teach there, then began ruling out anything farther west than where she was right now or in the northern states.

Then she began looking at job openings in small towns in the rural South. Once she was assured of certification in the states she'd chosen, she applied in rural areas of Texas, Tennessee, Oklahoma, Missouri, and Arkansas, and then settled in to wait for responses, while checking new postings every day for something else that might work for her. Everything about her life was in flux, which meant all options were open until she made a new decision.

Almost every night when she went to bed, she relived the shooting. Even when a dream started off on one subject, it morphed back to the school, and she would wake up in tears or hysterics. Katie's cheeks hollowed out from lack of sleep and weight loss, and the shadows beneath her eyes grew darker.

Emotionally, she was in prison—and she was her own jailer.

———

The first four responses from her applications came from multiple states. One from Arkansas. Two from Texas. One from Missouri. She immediately checked the pay scale to see where they fell within the parameters she needed, went online to research the towns they were in, then checked population and available rental properties before responding. Once the interview times were set up on Zoom, Katie began to feel optimistic.

The first Zoom interview was at 10:00 a.m. the next

day, which happened to be on a Thursday. The open position was for a second-grade teacher in a small town not far
from Hot Springs, Arkansas.

When it began, four people, counting Katie, were
logged into the meeting. An elementary principal and two
teachers were part of the interview committee. They'd
barely made introductions to Katie before the principal,
a man named Forbes, bluntly asked if she was the teacher
from the school shooting in Albuquerque.

Katie was taken aback that the shooting incident, and
not her qualifications, was the first subject of the interview because she had included that as part of her personal
info when she applied.

"Did you not read my application?" she asked.

He frowned. "Yes, I read it, but—"

Katie was stunned. "So, you already know the answer,
and yet you asked it anyway. Why?"

"I just wanted to get a feel for your emotional stability
and—"

The callousness of the offhand comment made Katie's
skin crawl. She cut him off without hesitation.

"Oh, my emotional stability is right where it always
was…intolerant of rudeness and insensitivity. I'm ending
this interview right now because I don't like what I'm feeling about your attitude. It makes me very uncomfortable.
It no longer matters what you think of my qualifications
because I withdraw my application. I have no interest in
associating with your administration."

She disconnected herself, closed the lid on her laptop,
and got up. She was so angry she was shaking. She'd expected

questions about the shooting, but not confrontations just to see if she would throw herself into hysterics.

She was hurt, and disappointed, and struggling not to be discouraged.

The next interview wasn't until right after lunch. It was for a position as a first-grade teacher in an elementary school in a rural school district outside of Shawnee, Oklahoma. But after that first slap in the face, Katie was anxious. To kill some time, she traded her good clothes for shorts, a T-shirt, and running shoes, put on her Fitbit, grabbed her sunglasses, and left her apartment for a run around the neighborhood.

It felt good to be outside as she paused to stretch before taking off at a jog. Within a couple of blocks, she got lost in the impact of foot to concrete, the swish of her clothing as she ran, the sun on her face, the anonymity she felt behind the sunglasses.

But her endurance wasn't back in full force, so she paced herself by jogging a distance and then walking, then repeating the process until she was back her apartment.

Katie was bathed in sweat, but she felt good—like she'd outrun the anger she'd left home with. She stripped, showered, and threw on a robe and went to the kitchen and dug through the fridge for the container of tuna salad she'd made last night. She got some crackers and a glass of iced tea, then turned on the TV and sat down to eat. She'd just taken a bite when she reached for the remote to up the volume on a news conference taking place.

The FBI was finally giving a statement regarding the shooting at Saguaro Elementary and the shooter himself.

Katie quickly turned up the volume and pushed her

food aside to listen to Special Agent Baldwin, who was at the bank of microphones.

"…false name. He was living under the name Wilton Theiry, one of several aliases. His real name was Reuben Wyandotte Hollis, and he was born in Albuquerque in 1977. He was in and out of foster care here from the age of nine until he quit high school a month before he graduated. He had been living a transient life all over the lower half of the States and had been in San Francisco for the past five years. The people we've interviewed who knew him indicated his continuing anger at what he called 'the system,' and said he blamed it for his inability to thrive in society.

"We don't know why he moved back to Albuquerque, or why he chose Saguaro Elementary as a target, but as far as we know, he had no personal connection to anyone there. As for what might have triggered him, it was discovered during his autopsy that he had stage-four liver cancer, so he may have chosen to end his own life this way before cancer did it for him. And like every other mass murderer, he chose people he didn't know to destroy. Finishing up this profile has ended our investigation. Do you have any questions before we end this?" he asked.

Hands went up as he glanced across the crowd of reporters and pointed at one.

The reporter immediately spoke up.

"Agent Baldwin, unfortunately, mass shootings have become almost commonplace now, and I've covered my share. But I've always wondered, why do mass murderers choose strangers? If they're angry with certain people, why aren't they the targets?"

Baldwin didn't hesitate. "Think about it. If they don't have a personal agenda with certain people they want dead, then they choose strangers so they don't know who they're killing. They don't have any guilt or emotional connection to strangers' deaths. Mass murderers are not trying to punish those people they kill. They just want the world to see *them* and *their* purpose…*their agenda.* The dead are just collateral damage. And very few mass murderers expect to survive their personal rampage. They want to die in public. They view themselves as having not been 'seen' in life, but everyone will see them when they go down in a blaze of gunfire."

The questions continued, but Katie was done. She turned off the TV, so angry she was trembling. She knew the horror stories of foster care. She'd lived it. But she'd matured enough to know that there were some people who had turned their loss, grief, and rage into an identity. They took no responsibility for the troubles they had as adults and lived life as eternal victims. Getting cancer must have been what pushed the shooter over the edge.

She stared at the food on the table, then put the lid back on her tuna salad and returned it to the refrigerator. Right now, if she put another bite in her mouth, it was going to come up.

Instead, she took her iced tea out onto the little balcony off her bedroom and sat down in the shade to finish her drink. By the time she was through, her emotions had settled, along with her stomach, and she went back inside to get ready for the next interview.

Thankfully, the interview went well. The principal at that school was a middle-aged man, and the only one

Katie spoke to. He never mentioned the shooting, which was a plus in Katie's eyes. It ended with the same speech about still interviewing applicants, and even if they were not offered the job, they would all be notified when the position was filled.

The next day was a repeat of the same. Two more interviews, these in Texas, both of which were less than promising. She had the feeling these people were going through the motions because that was required, and that someone within the school system was going to be offered the job. She didn't take it personally. That's how the system worked.

A couple more days went by, and Katie was constantly checking for new posts when she noticed one in a little town called Borden's Gap, Tennessee, that sounded promising. The opening was for a first-grade teacher. The pay was at the same scale as what she was receiving. Then she checked for rental properties and quickly discovered the one apartment building in town did not have vacancies, but there were small two- and three-bedroom houses for rent at a lower rate than what she was paying for her one-bedroom. So Katie filled out the application, sent off everything that was requested, and waited to hear back.

She woke up the next morning to a response from one of the schools in Texas stating the position had been filled, and before the day was over, she had another email from the Oklahoma interview with the same message, that the position had been filled.

Lila called her that afternoon and invited herself to Katie's with the promise of bringing dinner.

A couple of hours later, Lila was knocking on the door and came in with a to-go order from their favorite barbecue. Ribs, beans, coleslaw, and hush puppies, and pecan pie for dessert. When Lila began taking containers out of the sack, Katie started laughing.

"Girl, are we supposed to eat all this ourselves?"

Lila shrugged. "We can divide leftovers and won't have to cook tomorrow."

"True," Katie said. She got out plates and napkins and filled glasses with ice and sweet tea, then sat down and began filling their plates.

"So what's been going on?" Lila asked.

"I've been interviewing," Katie said.

Lila stopped, licked barbecue sauce off her thumb and grinned.

"So? Don't stop there. Talk to me."

Katie shrugged. "I ended the first one before it even began."

Lila gasped. "Why?"

"First thing out of his mouth was asking me if I was the same Katie McGrath from the school shooting, when he already knew it because I'd been up-front about it with my personal info when I applied. You know why he asked anyway? To assess my mental condition."

"Are you serious?" Lila said. "That's appalling. I'm sorry."

"I'm over it," Katie said. "I've had a few more interviews. Two have already filled positions since, but I'm still in the running for one or two more, and I just applied to a new place today."

"Where is it located?" Lila asked, then popped a hush puppy in her mouth.

"Rural Tennessee. I'm not looking to teach in big cities again. Going toward small-town America, in rural communities."

"Ooh, that's interesting. Not just a new location, but smaller ones. Good call, Katie girl."

Katie smiled. "I thought so."

They ate their way through the rest of the meal and were dumping scraps and getting out plates for pecan pie when Katie thought about the announcement from the FBI.

"Hey, Lila, did you happen to catch that FBI news conference about the shooter?"

"Yes! I did! Oh my God, Katie. Dying of cancer. Pissed at the world. And decides to shoot up a school? No conscience. No soul."

Katie nodded. "Agreed."

"I have a little bit of news," Lila said as they sat back down with dessert.

Katie looked up, saw the grin on her friend's face, and sighed.

"He finally asked you out, didn't he?"

Lila giggled. "Yes! I've lived on the same floor with that man for over a year, and all he could manage was the occasional conversation about weather while we waited for an elevator."

"So what changed?" Katie asked.

"Ironically, it was the shooting that prompted his concern, then one thing led to another and...well...he asked me out. We had our first date last Saturday, and we're going out again this coming Saturday."

"So? Is he fun and sexy and nice?"

"All of the above," Lila said, and popped a bite of pie into her mouth.

"I'm so happy for you…and it's about time!" Katie said.

"I'm happy for myself," Lila said. "School is out tomorrow. I'm going to sleep in every day next week. Promise you'll keep me updated on your interviews."

Katie nodded. "I will. And you have to keep me updated on the new guy. What's his name again? I forget."

"Jack. Jack Monroe," Lila said.

"I won't forget again," Katie said.

"If you do, I'll just remind you again," Lila said.

"You just like to say his name," Katie said, and laughed at the look on her friend's face.

"Shut up and eat your pie," Lila said.

Chapter Four

Saturday morning, Katie received an email from the school she'd applied to in Borden's Gap, Tennessee. They wanted to interview her and sent a choice of three different times from which she was to choose.

Katie quickly responded, choosing a time on the following Monday. She received acknowledgment and confirmation that they would send her a link.

Happy that she still had irons in the fire, she did her usual Saturday morning cleaning in the apartment, then changed clothes and left to run errands.

About an hour later, she was walking down the concourse in Cottonwood Mall with her purse on her shoulder and carrying a couple of sacks. She was thinking about stopping off at the food court to get something to eat when Mark and Megan Roman walked straight out in front of her from a shop she was passing.

They had to stop to keep from running into her, and it was obvious they were as startled as Katie felt, but she never halted her stride, looking past them as if they weren't there, and kept heading for the food court with them a few yards behind her.

She was irked, even though they had as much right to

be there as she did. Moving away would certainly put an end to this.

When she got to the food court, she went straight to Hot Dog on a Stick and ordered one of those and a lemonade to go with it. As soon as she got her food, she turned around to look for a place to sit and saw a little girl and her family waving her over. It was Trinity, one of her students. She started weaving her way through the tables.

"Sit here, Miss Katie! Sit here!" Trinity cried.

Her parents grinned. "We'd love to have you if you're not already meeting someone else," her mother said.

"I'd love to sit with you. Thank you," Katie said. She took an empty chair from another table and pulled it up.

"I love those!" Trinity said, pointing to Katie's food.

"So do I, and the lemonade, too! Have to have the lemonade to go with it," Katie said, and took a little bite, testing to make sure the corn dog wasn't too hot to eat. "Ooh, I think this needs to cool a bit. So tell me, Trinity. What have you been doing since school is out?"

The little blond was so excited to be eating with her teacher that she couldn't remember, and looked straight at her mother.

"What have we been doing, Mama?"

Katie giggled when Trinity's mother rolled her eyes. "Well, we're going to start swimming lessons soon, and then next month we're all going to Iowa to visit grandparents."

"Yes, that!" Trinity said. "What are you going to do this summer, Miss Katie?"

"It's hard to say right now," Katie said. She picked up the corn dog, dunked it in a little cup of mustard, and took a big bite.

She ate while the little girl talked around every bite in her mouth, until her mother finally stopped her.

"Trin, darling. We don't talk with our mouth full. You need to chew and swallow first, okay?"

She nodded, did as she was told, and then took another bite and started talking again.

Katie laughed. "It takes a while for rules to sink in."

She didn't know that Mark and Megan were, once again, having a meal and listening to Katie's animated voice and the bubble of her laughter carrying across the food court, and she wouldn't have cared if she had.

But Megan didn't like it, and Mark was getting tired of his wife's jealousy.

"She's ruining our day," Megan muttered.

Mark dunked a fry in ketchup and popped it in his mouth. "She who?" he asked.

"Your old girlfriend."

"My old fiancée, and she's not bothering us."

Megan sniffed. "She bothers me."

"I don't suppose she's overly fond of you, either, but she's not making a fuss about it. Do you want some more iced tea? I can get you a refill if—"

Megan shrugged.

Mark waited, and when she said nothing, he just kept eating.

Finally, Megan snapped, "I thought you were going to get me a refill on my tea."

"And I thought you would say those words if you wanted one," Mark said, then stood, picked up her cup, and went back to get it refilled.

Megan frowned. Mark was a good man, and she loved him. But when it came to Katie McGrath, he bowed up like an old rooster and defied everything she said.

She thought she'd done something, taking him from the woman he was going to marry, but she was beginning to wonder if she was the one who'd been used.

Mark came back with her drink.

She flashed him a sweet smile, and then leaned over and kissed his cheek as he sat down.

"I'm sorry I was such a baby. You are the best."

Mark gave her a quick wink. "It's okay, honey. I'll bet you're getting tired. I need to get you home. You can relax in the pool while I finish up a quick job for your dad."

She pouted. "You have to work on Saturday?"

"I work when Daddy says," he reminded her.

And when they got up later to leave, they both realized that sometime during their squabble, Katie McGrath had departed from the food court and was already on her way home.

Megan was fine with the fact.

Mark was still living with guilt at what he'd done. And he already knew that while he'd chosen Megan and the money over Katie and love, somewhere down the years he would likely live to regret it.

Katie was antsy all weekend. Another job she'd applied for had been filled and she was online making sure she didn't miss any new postings. Then she went to bed stressed about finding a new position and started dreaming about walking her students to the lunchroom. Part of her knew she was dreaming but she couldn't pull herself out of it, and when Coach Lincoln ran up beside her, she kept trying to tell him to get down but she couldn't get it said fast enough, and so again she watched him die and woke up screaming.

Within moments, someone was knocking at her door and calling out her name.

"Oh lord," Katie groaned, then threw on a robe and stumbled to the door. She looked through the peephole, then opened the door on the chain. It was her neighbor from across the hall.

"I'm so sorry, Larry. I'm okay."

"Another bad dream?" he asked.

She nodded.

"I'm sorry for you. Glad you're okay," he said, and went back across the hall and closed his door.

Katie locked herself back in, then stood in front of the door and cried.

"How long, God?" she sobbed, and sank to her knees.

She stayed there until her eyes were swollen and her knees were numb, then crawled to her feet and began walking through her apartment, turning on lights as she went.

It was hours before she dozed back off, and then she woke up midmorning in a panic, afraid she had missed her interview. To her relief, she still had almost two hours to spare, so she flew out of bed and jumped into the shower.

By the time she came out, the remnants of last night's terrors had been erased from her face. A little bit of makeup would disguise the circles beneath her eyes, and she'd be good to go. After a cup of coffee and some scrambled eggs and toast, she felt better and went back to her closet to choose an outfit to wear.

Something in her gut said this interview was going to matter, that it was up to her not to shy away from the truth and to be her straightforward, amenable self. So she dressed with purpose, wearing a colorful blouse and slacks, carefully applied her makeup, and left her long hair hanging loose around her face.

Then she situated herself in the kitchen, using the table as a desk, and forgot that the little red schoolhouse clock on the wall behind her would be part of her background. She was staring at the screen, waiting for the link to pop up, and when she got the invitation she quickly clicked and joined in.

There were four smiling faces looking at her, and then a middle-aged woman with graying hair began to speak.

"Hello, Katie. Thank you for joining us. I'm Susan Wayne, the elementary principal. This is Andrew Sutton, our science teacher, and Priscilla Lewis, one of our fifth-grade teachers, and our other first-grade teacher, Marcy Kincaid. They are part of the hiring committee and we always ask them to sit in on the first meeting. Everyone, this is Katie McGrath. We've all read your application and are looking forward to visiting with you."

Katie smiled. "It's a pleasure to meet you."

Susan opened the file on her desk, then looked up. "I always like to jump right in, so the first thing I want to do is go over your stats. Your degree is in early childhood education, and you've been teaching for eight years in Albuquerque?"

"Yes, ma'am, that's correct."

"I see you've received a Teacher of the Year award from your school and are very successful at writing grants for your classroom. Tell me about that."

Katie nodded. "I grew up without parents. I was in the foster system until I aged out and graduated from high school, so I've always been a self-starter. I worked two jobs to get myself through college, and I was always looking for small scholarships or grants that I might qualify for, so I got in the habit of staying on top of what was being offered. Then after I went into the classroom, I soon learned that it wasn't all that different for teachers. Funding isn't always the best, and we are always seeking out new avenues for resources. I have what I call my own blueprint for writing grants, and I'm delighted every time I receive one."

"That's admirable and quite resourceful of you," Susan said. "How do you feel about leaving a big city for a town the size of Borden's Gap?"

"I love teaching, but I was ready for a change. I purposefully sought out smaller schools. And I have visited Tennessee before, so living where rain is a normal happening and so many things are green is exciting to me."

Susan made a couple of notes, and then they moved on. The other teachers had little to add to the conversation, but Katie knew they'd have plenty to say when she was no longer online.

Just as they were wrapping up, Susan had one more question.

"Katie, I just want to talk about one more thing."

"Sure," Katie said, waiting.

"I know the school you're leaving is Saguaro Elementary, the school that was the scene of a mass shooting back in March."

The smile froze on Katie's face. She blinked, then took a deep breath.

"Yes, that's true," she said.

Susan sighed. "I don't want to be insensitive, but you were very honest and up-front on your application, so we know what happened to you, and I want you to know you have our utmost admiration. You have lived our worst nightmare. Have you been released from doctor care?"

Katie nodded. "Yes. I am completely healed and released without any cautions. And I also make no apologies or excuses for the fact that I turned in my resignation because of the shooting." She stopped, took a deep breath, and then stared straight into their faces. "I cannot go back into that school, in the same hallways, without seeing where Coach Lincoln dropped dead beside me. Where my students and I ran for our lives. I still see the blood and the brain matter in my dreams. I feel the bullets in my back. I still hear the screams in those halls and the gunshots in my sleep.

"I went back there recently for an event and to tell my babies goodbye. I was their first-grade teacher, and they needed to see me for themselves…to know that I was alive and well. It made me physically sick to be there. But I am a teacher. I love what I do. I have survived the odds ever since I was born, and I am the captain of my own ship. I am choosing to move the location of my passion to a smaller community, but I am not weakened by my experience."

Susan Wayne was blinking back tears.

"Of course you aren't. And we are aware of how you saved the little boys."

"Alejandro and Kieran. They thought I died. I went back to school that day for them, for all my babies, so they could see for themselves that I was well," Katie said.

Susan nodded. "Of course that must have been hard for you, but again, you sacrificed for them. That is an admirable quality in anyone, but especially for teachers. I think we've covered everything we wanted to know. We are still interviewing, but we will notify each of our applicants when we have finished."

Katie sat up a little straighter. "Wherever I go from here, I am not arriving as the teacher from the shooting."

"Understood," Susan said. "We'll be in touch."

The connection ended, and Katie closed her laptop.

The interview was over.

It would be what it would be.

―――――――――

Two days later, Katie was on her way to meet Lila for dinner when her phone rang. She answered via Bluetooth.

"Hello."

"Katie, this is Susan Wayne from Borden's Gap. Can you talk?"

Katie's heart skipped a beat. "Yes, I'm driving. It's good," she said.

"I won't detain you, but I wanted to let you know that we were very impressed with you and are offering you the job."

Katie gasped. "Oh! That's wonderful! Thank you! Thank you so much. I accept!"

"Great!" Susan said. "You will receive an email with a contract to sign and all of the particulars you'll need to know, as well as a start date for your job. And since this is such a small community, we took the liberty of giving you the name of the only Realtor in town. She will have information on all of the rental properties and will be happy to help you find a residence. Congratulations. We look forward to working with you."

"Thank you so much, Mrs. Wayne. This is the best news."

"Susan, please. Mrs. Wayne is for school."

"Yes, ma'am," Katie said.

"Let me know when you get to town. We can set up a time to meet in person, and I'll give you the tour of the elementary school myself."

"I will," Katie said.

The call ended, and Katie was beaming. She laughed, and then she cried a little, and then laughed again. This was really happening. She had a new job! She was moving to Tennessee. She couldn't wait to tell Lila.

When she pulled into the parking lot at Ruth's Chris Steak House, the streetlights and night-lights throughout the parking lot were already on.

The scent of the desert mingled with the woodsmoke from the steakhouse grill as she walked across the parking lot toward the building. Sage and hickory teased her palate. And after that phone call, there was much to celebrate. She wasn't holding back on anything tonight.

Lila was waiting for her inside, and the moment Katie saw her, she started grinning.

Lila stood as Katie came toward her. "What?"

Katie threw her arms around Lila's neck.

"I got the job. I'm moving to Tennessee!"

Lila squealed, and hugged her again. "Oh my God. You are truly the unsinkable Katie McGrath! I am so proud to call you friend."

A few people waiting to be seated overheard the exchange and clapped for her joy, while others looked up from their phones, staring. Some recognized her face, while others recognized the name, and every one of them thought, *Could I have done the same? Would I have been that brave?*

Unaware that she'd been recognized, Katie was still bubbling with joy as she and Lila were finally seated. As soon as they ordered an appetizer and their drinks, Lila leaned forward and grabbed Katie's hand.

"You are my best friend, and you know it," Lila said. "I am going to miss the heck out of you, but I'm also so happy for you. You've had the year from hell, and it's about damn time some good stuff started happening for you. And…it's not like I'll never see or talk to you again. There's always FaceTime and Zoom."

Katie was listening and talking and laughing and

sharing food with Lila, but her mind was beginning to wander. A part of her was already gone.

———

So while Katie was focusing on a whole new venture, Megan's perfect world was beginning to crumble.

Before Mark, her job had often been simple pickups, gathering up the money their street pushers had made and getting it back to her father.

She'd get her oil changed and pick up an envelope full of cash.

She'd meet friends for lunch and get an envelope from a bartender at the restaurant.

She carried thousands of dollars in her purse every day. And then she got married.

Now, she was still making the rounds but had to get rid of what she picked up daily or hide it before Mark got home from work. It was becoming more and more difficult to come up with new reasons for being gone all day, every day, and he was getting suspicious.

And then Mark confronted her, and the world blew up in Megan's face.

———

It was the middle of June, and just after 4:00 p.m. when Megan pulled into the drive, and even as she was watching the garage door go up, her stomach was already knotting. Mark's car was in the garage. He was early. She had no idea how long he'd been home, but she'd been gone all day and there was over ten thousand dollars in her purse.

"Shit," she muttered, and in a panic, she pulled a plastic shopping bag out from under the seat, dumped the money in it, and jumped out and dropped the bag into the deep freeze and covered it with some packages of frozen meat, then snatched a package of frozen pork chops out and took it with her as she went inside.

Mark came strolling into the kitchen as she came in carrying the package of meat.

"Hi, darling," Megan said, and slid the pork chops on a plate and put them in the microwave for a quick defrost.

Mark stared at her, his hands in his pockets. He still hadn't said anything, but she felt the vibes of distrust as surely as if he'd already uttered the words.

She washed her hands at the sink, then turned around to give him a hug, and he stopped her.

"Where have you been all day?"

She frowned.

"What do you mean?"

"I've been home since ten this morning. You were gone then. I lay down thinking you'd be back soon and fell asleep. I woke up after lunch and you still weren't home. I sent you a text. Do you remember what you said?"

Megan's heart stopped. "I said I was going out to pick up dessert for tonight."

"Where's the dessert?" he asked.

She flushed. "They didn't have what I wanted, so I didn't get it."

"Who is he?" Mark asked. "Someone new, or someone in your circle of 'friends who lunch'?"

Megan gasped. "I'm not cheating on you."

Mark's eyes narrowed. "You are lying to me. And this isn't the first time you've said one thing and done another. I don't like being lied to."

"I am not cheating on you. I swear it," Megan said.

Mark just shook his head and walked out of the kitchen, and at that moment, Megan knew the dream was over. She couldn't protect herself and the business without Mark finding out. If he was suspicious, he might hire someone to follow her, and one thing would lead to another, and people would die.

She took the pork chops out of the microwave and put them in the refrigerator, then went upstairs, got out her suitcases, and started packing.

"What are you doing?" Mark asked.

"Leaving. I won't live with a man who doesn't trust me," she said.

Mark was shocked. He'd expected a huge fight. Not a surrender. And certainly not without an explanation.

"So, it's true, and your silence is proof of your guilt," he said. "Out of curiosity, what exactly turned you off? Were you ever turned on at all, or are you just a hunter? One of those women who lose interest once the chase is over and move on to something else?"

His words hurt, but not nearly as much as getting her throat slit by one of Craig's goons.

"Just drop it, Mark. I'm filing for divorce. You can either help me pack, or shut the hell up and get out of my way."

She expected him to leave, because she needed him to get out so she could get the drugs and the money she had stashed. She rarely delivered drugs, but this happened to be one of the times she was, and now she had no way to get to it.

"I think I'll watch," he said and stretched out on their bed and kicked back, never taking his eyes off of her for a second.

She began packing faster, filling one suitcase after another, and then she called an Uber to come get her bags. Her eyes were welling with tears as she came back up to carry the last bags down.

"I hope you were entertained," she said.

"I was waiting for regret to show. You have shown neither regret nor remorse. This day did not begin or end as I'd expected."

She paused.

"Why did you come home early, anyway?" she asked.

"My secretary had a heart attack. She died on the way to the hospital. We all went home."

Megan gasped. "Oh my God. How awful!"

Mark shrugged. "No, her death was tragic. *This* is awful."

Megan turned around and left their bedroom thinking Mark was right. This day had not begun or ended as she'd expected, either.

And so she was gone, with full intentions of coming back to get her stash after he went back to work.

━━━━━━━

For Katie, the next few days were filled with excitement and chaos. Connecting with the Realtor in Borden's Gap was imperative because she needed a place to live before she could move. She knew what she'd be making monthly, but she didn't know what the cost of living was like in smaller towns. So she took the information she'd been sent about Louise Parsons, the Realtor, then went online at Zillow to see available rental properties in Borden's Gap. The facts were a little daunting.

There was just the one apartment building, and none were available. The other rental properties were all houses. But Katie was pleasantly surprised by the rental rates. After going through what was online, she called Louise Parsons and introduced herself and quickly learned Louise had been expecting the contact.

"Hello, Katie. Susan Wayne told me that they'd hired a new teacher and given her my contact info, so congratulations on the new job."

"Thank you so much," Katie said. "And yes, I'm going to need your help. I've looked at everything that's listed on Zillow, and I've seen the interior pictures that were available on rentals, but not all rentals had available interiors to view. So I'm going to have to rely on you for information."

"Absolutely," Louis said. "But…I also have a little jewel that isn't advertised, because it's mine. It's a two-bedroom, one-bath cottage with sitting porches on front and back. Nice little backyard, and mowing comes with the rental. I'm kind of particular about who I rent to. Do you have pets?"

"No, ma'am."

"It rents for $800 a month, so if it sounds like something that might fit your needs, I'd be happy to send photos. Otherwise, if you have your mind on something else you've already seen online, I'll be happy to help you with that as well."

"No, no, I'd like to see what you have. The size and rent sound perfect."

"Give me your email. I'll send you a link. Just click on it, and then if it doesn't appeal to you, no harm, no foul. But if you want it, it's yours. I lease by the year."

"Yes, ma'am," Katie said. "Send the link, and I'll call you back within the hour."

"Will do," Louise said, and the call ended.

Katie got her laptop, pulled up her email, and waited.

When the email arrived, she quickly opened it and clicked on the link. Within moments, she knew this was it.

The little house was charming…white siding, gingerbread trim on the porches and eaves, and a bright blue door. There was an attached portico under which to park her car, and flower beds on either side of the front steps. Inside, the soft gray walls and shiny, wide-plank pine floors were perfect for the furniture she already had, and the kitchen had updated appliances, without losing any of the charm of the era in which the house had been built.

The living room had a gas fireplace, which appealed to Katie, and the master bedroom had a walk-in closet and an old-fashioned claw-foot bathtub with a separate shower and enough counter space at the sink for one person.

The extra bedroom, while small, would be perfect for her office and all the school stuff that came with being a teacher. There were a couple of photos of the back porch and the little postage-stamp yard and a white porch swing hanging from the porch rafters.

She was enchanted.

She called Louise back, and the business of long-distance leasing a house began. By the next day, Katie was approved. She had an official address and contact info to let Louise know her arrival date.

Now, she could begin the job of hiring a moving company to get her furniture to Borden's Gap, and she set a date for a week away. Then she began the notification to landlords and utility companies and filling out an online mail forwarding application.

Weeks ago, before school was out, Lila had taken it upon herself to gather up Katie's personal things from her classroom, and those boxes had been taking up space in Katie's living room against the wall, waiting to be put back to use. They were ready. Now all Katie had to do was pack up the rest of her life to go with them.

Borden's Gap, Tennessee

Sam Youngblood was getting ready to leave for the police station. He was wearing his next-to-the last clean uniform, had already buckled on his holster and weapon, and was pinning on his badge as he walked up the hall to the living room to see if Roxie was anywhere in sight.

Roxie Rogers had been the nanny for his twins, Everly and Elizabeth, almost from the day he'd brought them home from the hospital. Losing his wife the same day he'd become a father had nearly killed him. But the women of Borden's Gap had stepped up to help without being asked, and after a routine was established, Roxie was the one who stuck. From that day forward, whenever he was at work and the girls were home, she was with them.

He glanced out the window to look for her and instead saw Louise Parsons at her rental house across the street. He frowned, wondering if she'd rented it out again, and hoped that was to somebody trustworthy. With two six-year-old girls in the house, he was constantly on alert to keep their surroundings safe.

Then he heard little footsteps running up the hall and turned around just as Evie came running into the room holding her iPad.

"Daddy, I can't make this work."

He turned. The sight of the tiny blond with his wife's face never failed to make his heart tug.

He sat down on the sofa with the iPad. Evie scooted up beside him, then leaned against his arm as he took a look.

"Is it broke?" Evie asked.

"Nope. Battery needs to be recharged," he said.

"But I wanted to play with it now," she whined.

He leaned over and tweaked her nose, then kissed the top of her head.

"Then you should have thought to bring it to me last night," he said. "I'll plug it in now, and it will be ready to play with later. Meanwhile, you and Beth can go outside and play. It's too pretty to stay indoors."

"Is Miss Roxie coming?" she asked.

"Yes, ma'am. I think I hear her car in the driveway now."

Evie got up on her knees on the sofa to look out the window.

"It's her!" she cried, then jumped off the sofa and went running through the house. "Beth, Beth…the iPad is dead and Miss Roxie is here."

Sam grinned as he got up to let Roxie in.

Roxie was shaking her head when he opened the door.

"I heard all that," she muttered. "They're in fine form today."

"Dead iPads will do that to you," Sam said as he took the iPad into the kitchen and plugged it into a charger. "I've got a prisoner to transfer this morning, so I'm going to head on down to the station. There's homemade chicken noodle soup and stuff for sandwiches for lunch. Call if you need me."

"You made soup?" Roxie asked.

Sam grinned. "I have my moments." Then he turned around and called out down the hall, "Girls, I'm leaving!"

"Wait! Wait!" they shrieked as they came flying up the hall. "We have to tell you goodbye so you'll have good luck."

Sam caught them up in his arms, holding them close and kissing their noses and then their cheeks. He didn't know where the 'bad luck/good luck' thing had come from, but it bothered him that they'd gotten old enough to realize his job had a level of danger to it, and that he was the only parent they had.

"I love you both forever. Be good for Miss Roxie," he said.

"We will," they echoed, then wiggled out of his arms and ran back into their room.

"They're supposed to be making their beds," Sam said.

"I'll check on them in a bit," Roxie said. "Have a good day."

"Thanks," he said. He grabbed his Stetson from the rack by the door, settled it firmly on his head, and left the house.

Louise was still in the yard, picking up trash from the flower beds and sweeping off the front steps. When she saw him coming out of the house, she waved and then went across the road to talk to him.

"Morning, Louise," Sam said.

Louise nodded. "Good morning to you, too, Sam. I just wanted you to know that I've rented my little jewel. The school finally hired a new first-grade teacher for next year, and she leased my house."

"Oh, yeah? The girls might wind up in her class. What's she like?" he asked.

"All I know is she's from Albuquerque. She was a first-grade teacher there, and she's twenty-nine and single. Her name is Katie McGrath."

Sam frowned. "That name sounds familiar."

Louise knew why, but she wasn't talking. Susan Wayne asked her not to, and that was the end of that.

"I don't know any McGraths," Louise said. "There were some McGills who used to live down near the south fork of Erby Creek, but they moved to Mississippi a few years back."

Sam nodded. "Anyway, thanks for the heads-up. When is she coming?"

"Within the week," Louise said. "How are the girls?"

"Fine and full of energy. Kindergarten gave them a big jump in social behavior. All of a sudden they're trying to organize playdates because they want to go play with their friends from class."

Louise laughed. "That's girls for you, but knowing Roxie, she's got her finger on all that."

"Yes, ma'am, that she does," Sam said.

Louise waved and headed back across the street as Sam got in the police car and drove away, already thinking about the upcoming prisoner transfer.

Meanwhile, word was spreading in town about the new teacher having leased Louise's house. They all knew Louise never advertised it, which gave her more control over who would live there. So it stood to reason if she'd let the new teacher in the door, she must be something special. But, as was the way of small communities, opinions would be withheld until they'd seen and judged her for themselves.

———

Unaware of the swirling undercurrents of her imminent arrival in Borden's Gap, Katie was cleaning and packing daily to the point of exhaustion. The upside of falling into bed too tired to blink was that the nightmares took a back seat to her exhaustion. She was walking around boxes by her last night in Albuquerque and so tired of the mess that she couldn't wait to leave.

Katie called Lila and tried not to cry when they said their final goodbyes, because this was so what she wanted— needed. A fresh start, away from the possibilities of seeing her ex and his wife, and away from the place where she nearly died. She was going to Borden's Gap as a stranger. It was a new page in her life just waiting for the first words to appear.

She went through the apartment, making sure everything was locked, turning out the lights all the way to her bedroom. Wearily, she crawled into bed and pulled up the covers, waiting for her eyes to adjust to the shadows.

She'd never had a nightly routine of prayers. Some of her foster families had been big on church and God and praying, but the way they'd treated her had led her to believe she wasn't someone God would listen to. Then there were the other families, some of them good but frazzled by the number of kids they were keeping, while the others she'd been sent to looked fine on the outside but raised hell from morning to night.

She'd figured out at an early age that she should go along with the agenda of each family and keep her opinions to herself. Mark had been the first person in her life that she'd trusted enough to believe he would always have her back, and then he'd proved himself false, so here she was again, alone and figuring life out on her own.

Knowing the circumstances of how she'd been abandoned, it stood to reason that no one had cared. If it hadn't been for a homeless woman who'd found her in a box behind a dumpster a few hours after her birth, she would have died, so looking for the people who'd thrown her out like garbage was never going to happen.

Lying in her bed on her last night in Albuquerque, Katie wasn't thinking about offering up a prayer for safe travels. She was just packing up her memories, the same way that she'd packed up her belongings every time she went from one foster family to the next. She didn't know what Borden's Gap was about, but she'd find out when she got there, and she would make the best of it. That, she knew how to do.

The air-conditioning kicked on.

She double-checked to make sure the alarm was set on her phone and then rolled over onto her side and fell asleep.

The next time she opened her eyes, the alarm was going off. She threw back the covers, turned it off, then leaped out of bed.

It was the second day of July, the day of new beginnings.

Chapter Five

IT TOOK THE MOVERS OVER TWO HOURS TO GET KATIE'S furniture and boxes down the two flights of stairs. She didn't have a lot. Just living room furniture, which included a desk and bookshelves, plus her small table and chairs from the kitchen, her bedroom furniture, a couple of area rugs, and then the boxes.

By the time the movers were getting ready to leave, all there was left for Katie to do was verify they had the correct address in Tennessee. Before they drove away, they gave her their phone number and warned her it might take up to three days to get her stuff there.

Katie watched them leave, then ran back up to the apartment for one last walk-through. This place had been a good place. A comfortable place, until two men—one who was unfaithful, and one who was a killer—changed her life forever.

She made sure all the lights were off and the air conditioner set at the temperature the landlord requested. Then she left the keys on the kitchen counter and pulled the door shut, making sure it locked behind her.

By the time she got back to the parking lot and into her car, she'd made peace with what was happening and was ready to be on the road. She already knew she'd make better time than the moving truck and intended to get there ahead of them. She had a sleeping bag in her car in case she had to spend a night or two in her new house before furniture arrived, and the rest of what she might need was in a suitcase on the seat behind her.

She wove her way through the city as she headed for the interstate, and when she came off the on-ramp into the flow of traffic on I-40 eastbound, she cut her last tie with Albuquerque.

The air conditioner was blowing cool air in her face. She had iHeartRadio blasting from the dash and a cold drink in the console. All she had to do was stay on I-40 through New Mexico, across the Texas Panhandle into Oklahoma, then on into Arkansas and points east all the way to Tennessee. She planned to spend the night in Oklahoma or Arkansas and then arrive at her destination sometime the next day. Hopefully, her furniture wouldn't be far behind.

Hours later, she'd long since crossed the panhandle of Texas into Oklahoma, stopping only for pit stops and fuel, and was snacking on the road. The downside of sitting behind the wheel for so long was fighting the growing tension between her shoulder blades. She was wishing for a bed so she could lie flat and rest the still-healing muscles in her back.

In no time, she was racking up miles, and as the day

moved on, she began racing the sun, wanting to get to her next stop before it sank below the horizon behind her.

It was after 8:00 p.m. when she reached Fort Smith, Arkansas, and she was so tired she could barely think. She stopped at the first decent motel that she came to and checked in. After dumping her overnight bag in her room, she washed up and headed downstairs to the café just off the lobby.

A plate of catfish and hush puppies later, she went back to her room and stripped and showered. The hot water pelting on the sore muscles in her shoulders was heaven, and she stayed in the shower until the muscles finally relaxed. She got out, dried, and dressed in pajamas, then turned back the covers, and after setting an alarm, she fell into bed.

The air-conditioning was humming. The sheets were cool. Katie pulled the covers up over her shoulders, rolled over on her side, and closed her eyes.

All she wanted to do was rest, but before she knew it, she was back in the halls of Saguaro Elementary, marching her class to lunch. Even as they were approaching the place where they had heard the first shot, the muscles in her stomach were beginning to knot. She kept watching her students marching in a tight, tidy line, knowing what was about to happen but unable to warn them to hurry.

Katie moaned in her sleep and rolled over, sensing the need for imminent haste. Then the first shot rang out and she began reliving the confusion and panic and then the race against time before she was shot. She was on the floor, holding the boys and telling them she loved them when the second bullet ripped through her body. She woke up crying.

It was almost five in the morning. Her alarm wouldn't go off for another couple of hours, but sleep was over. No way did she want to go back to bed and revisit that, so she made coffee in her room and drank a cup as she dressed, then packed up.

The café downstairs opened at 5:00 a.m., and it was already half past. After making sure she had everything, Katie rolled her overnight bag downstairs to the café, ordered sausage and waffles, and then checked her email and messages while she waited for her food.

There was a "safe travels" text from Lila and an email responding to one of the applications she'd sent in, wanting to set up an interview. She answered it, telling them she'd already accepted a position. After that, she scrolled through the rest of the emails and deleted all but a couple she would respond to later.

She sent Louise Parsons a text that she would be in Borden's Gap sometime today around noon or later, and then her food came. She ate for the sustenance, anxious to get back on the road. As soon as she was finished, she checked out and was back in her car, heading for the on-ramp to I-40 eastbound. It was just after 7:00 a.m. when she reached the interstate and slipped into the traffic flow, driving straight into the rising sun.

Louise saw Katie McGrath's text after she woke up and decided it would not be amiss to have a little welcome gift for the new teacher when she arrived. So she went by the grocery store and got milk and cream, a box of doughnuts, some stuff to make sandwiches, and a six-pack of Pepsi, and then added a small vase of flowers to her purchases before heading toward the house.

Her heart lifted as she unlocked the cottage door and began carrying things in. She loved the little cottage and hoped Katie would be happy here. She set the flowers in the middle of the kitchen island, put the little bit of groceries in the refrigerator, and set out a package of paper plates and cups and a box of plastic cutlery. Then she checked to make sure the ice maker was putting out ice, set the air conditioner on 70 degrees so the house would be comfortable when Katie arrived, and walked out. Louise locked the door, then put the key under the front mat and sent Katie a text telling her where the key was so she could get in and saying they would meet another day.

Roxie was in the front yard at the Youngblood property, pulling weeds in the flower beds while the twins took turns watering the beds behind her. Louise honked and waved as she drove away. She wondered how Katie was going to fit in to Borden's Gap, then let it go. That was Katie McGrath's path to walk, and not for Louise to meddle.

———

Katie stopped for fuel at the Arkansas-Tennessee border. It was a little before noon, and it felt like forever since she'd had breakfast. So she fueled up, then went through a fast-food drive-through and got lunch to go.

She was eating a burger as she drove over the Arkansas border, and she kept right on driving when she went through Memphis on her way to Jackson, Tennessee. From there, she would take State Highway 45 south, and from that point on, the GPS in her car would do the navigating.

Borden's Gap was becoming a reality.

━━━━━━

It was just before noon at the police station. The prisoner had been transferred, and one of Sam's officers had dealt with a fender bender on Main Street while another had hauled a ten-year-old shoplifter from the local supermarket into the station.

At that point, Sam was in his office with the ten-year-old, who was bawling his head off and scared he was going to jail, but the kid's parents were there, too.

By the time Sam had all that sorted out, the shoplifter and his parents were gone. He was finishing up the report when his cell phone rang. The moment he noticed it was Roxie, his heart skipped. She never called him at work unless there were problems, so he quickly picked it up.

"Hello?"

"It's me," Roxie said, trying to talk over the crying in the background. "Beth fell outside and cut her arm on something. It looks like it's gonna need a stitch or two, and of course, Evie is crying with her in sympathy. Do I need to take them down to the ER, or do you have time?"

"I'm on the way," Sam said and headed up the hall to the

front desk to tell the clerk where he was going. "Charlie, one of the girls got hurt. I'm going home to get her. Call if you need me."

"Got it, Chief. Give her a hug from me."

Sam gave him a thumbs-up and headed down the hall and out the back door to his cruiser. It wasn't the first time he'd been to the ER with the girls and likely wouldn't be the last, but seeing them hurt made him sick to his stomach. They were his babies.

He pulled up in the drive in record time and got out on the run. He could still hear the crying as he entered the house and headed for the kitchen.

Beth was sitting on the kitchen counter near the sink, and Roxie was holding a cold compress on the cut when he walked in. When both girls saw him, they upped the volume on the tears.

Sam went straight to where Beth was sitting and patted Roxie on the back, then reached for the compress.

"Let me see," he said.

Beth screeched. "It's bleeding, Daddy!"

"I'm so sorry, baby, but I still need to see," he said, and gave her a quick kiss on the cheek. "Now take a deep breath and try not to cry for me while I look, okay?"

"Okay," she said, and ended on a shuddering sob.

Evie was still crying.

Sam looked at her. "Are you hurt, too, honey?"

She shook her head.

"Then you need to stop crying."

"Okay," she said, and turned it off so fast, the tears dangling at the ends of her eyelashes had yet to fall.

"Now," Sam said, and lifted the compress, then frowned. There was a rather sizable cut near her shoulder. "Okay, Roxie, you were right. I'm taking her to the doctor. You and Evie stay here."

"Noooo!" Beth wailed. "I don't want to go to the doctor."

"Sorry, honey," he said, and scooped her up in his arms, grabbing the compress. "Evie, I want you to help Miss Roxie clean up in here, and then both of you go out in the yard and see if you can find what Beth fell on. We don't want anything sharp lying out in our grass."

Then he headed up the hall and out the door with Beth, as Roxie and Evie began cleaning up the blood trail from the back door to the sink.

Sam buckled Beth into the passenger seat, then handed her the compress.

"Hold this tight on your arm, baby girl, and we'll have you fixed up in no time," he said, and then got in.

"Are you gonna turn on the siren?" Beth asked.

Sam grinned. "Do we need to?"

"Sirens are for 'mergencies. Am I a 'mergency?"

"Yes, you are," Sam said, then backed out of the drive, hit the siren and lights, and flew through the streets on the way to the ER.

———

It was half past three when Katie's GPS directed her to turn east off Highway 45. She was already fascinated with the forests she'd seen and the thick growths of trees. This was not the land of broad vistas of sand and cactus surrounded by distant mountains.

This was where secrets dwelled.

Hidden in green valleys.

Walled up behind dense forests and always hiding the answers just around the next curve.

She glanced at her GPS. Only eleven more miles to go.

"Please don't let me regret this," Katie said as she eyed yet another mailbox along the highway and the narrow road beyond it that led up into the trees.

She was headed east now, still driving mile after mile with the sun behind her as she slowed down for the upcoming curve. The radio station she'd been listening to was nothing but static now, but instead of searching for another station, she just turned it off.

All of a sudden, she was passing the city limits sign of Borden's Gap, which listed the population as just shy of 4,000 people. Then she topped a hill and saw the town below, nestled against the foothills and spread out across the land before her.

"There you are," Katie whispered, wondering what the future would bring to her here.

Louise had sent not only the address, but also directions on how to find it, and the starting point was the first stoplight.

Flags were flying from almost every business on Main Street, and then Katie remembered tomorrow was the Fourth of July. That meant fireworks. Her stomach was in knots as she turned left, followed the directions to go five blocks down, then took a right and drove two more blocks.

She recognized the house on sight. It was the blue door, and then the porch and flower beds, that gave it away. She sighed as she pulled up the drive and parked beneath the portico.

She was here. It wasn't home yet, but it was hers. She killed the engine and then grabbed her purse and walked up the side steps to the porch, picked up the corner of the welcome mat and claimed the key.

Moments later, she was inside.

"Hello, the house," Katie said softly, eyeing the gas fireplace that would be cozy come winter and the built-in bookshelves on either side of it.

She moved across the foyer into a small hallway, then straight into the kitchen and smiled.

White cabinets. An island with storage below and three barstools on the other side. The countertops were white quartz with a faint silver and gray veining. The appliances were stainless steel. A gas stove, dishwasher, and micro-wave. The ice-maker refrigerator was huge, with freezer drawers below. The flowers waiting for her on the island were a surprise, as was the note beneath them. She read it, then moved to the refrigerator and looked inside. The thoughtfulness of the gesture brought tears to her eyes. She was so tired. And this was so kind.

Food. Drink. Enough to tide her over for a day or so.

She sent Louise a quick text to let her know she'd arrived and to thank her for the flowers and food. Then she continued to explore the house, quickly locating the utility room where she saw more storage space and the newer-model washer and dryer that came with the house.

Her footsteps echoed as she moved toward the hall leading to the bedrooms. The first bedroom on the left would be the perfect office space. She backed out and headed for the room at the end of the hall. When she pushed the door inward, she paused on the threshold and sighed.

Pale-blue walls with white trim. Pine floors so shiny they looked wet. Huge windows with blinds open to the sunlight, and sills only inches from the floor. She walked in, checked out the walk-in closet, and then moved to the en suite bathroom with white walls, pale-blue trim, a huge claw-foot tub begging for hot water and bubbles, and a separate walk-in shower with pale-blue tiles and silver and blue tiles on the shower pan.

"Gorgeous," Katie said, then pointed at the tub. "I'll be back for you later," she said, and went to her car to bring in her suitcase and sleeping bag.

She spread the sleeping bag on the floor of her bedroom. Leaving her suitcase against the wall, she grabbed a cold can of Pepsi and went out the back door. The porch swing beckoned, so she plopped, popped the top on her can, and lifted it in a toast.

"To me and new beginnings," she said, took a quick sip, and then pushed off in the swing.

When it squeaked just slightly on the downswing, she smiled. Just like the swings out on the playgrounds. There was always one that squeaked. She felt right at home.

As she was finishing her Pepsi, she heard a string of firecrackers go off, popping in rapid succession like the shooter at the school. She broke out in a cold sweat and went back inside. It was just a holiday, and this would pass.

But without anything to do, she slipped into her sleeping bag and closed her eyes. One of her last thoughts as sleep pulled her under was wondering where her furniture was and hoping it wasn't too far behind.

———

A couple of hours later, Sam brought Beth home with the cut glued shut and bandaged, and a half gallon of ice cream for the house. She was exhausted from all the crying and the drama of getting the cut cleaned out, so he put her to bed. Roxie showed him the piece of glass they'd found out in the yard. It looked like a piece from an old Coca-Cola bottle.

"Damn it," he said. "I'll be calling the mowers on the way back to work." As soon as he got back in the cruiser, he did just that.

"Hello, this is Melvin."

"Melvin, this is Sam Youngblood. I have a question. By any chance did your crew happen to mow over a glass bottle in my yard last time they were here?"

"Yes, sir. They sure did. Dennis was on the riding mower and didn't see it until it was too late. It messed up a tire, but we got it picked up."

"Not all of it," Sam said. "Beth fell on a big piece today and has a bad cut on her shoulder. I just got back from the ER with her. Next time something like that happens, let me know immediately."

"Oh, man, I'm so sorry," Melvin said. "That just makes me sick. I'll talk to the crew for sure and make sure you're not left in the dark about anything like that again."

"Thanks, Melvin. I appreciate it," Sam said, and disconnected.

It was all he could do to focus on work for the rest of the afternoon, and as soon as the officers for the night shift came on duty, he headed home.

He noticed the car under the portico at Louise's house the moment he turned down the street. It appeared the new teacher had arrived. Without thinking, he turned up the drive at her house, got out and went to the door, rang the bell, then waited.

Then the door opened, and she was not what he expected. She was at least five foot nine, wearing jean shorts and an oversize T-shirt, and barefoot. Her eyes were dark, as were the circles beneath them. But then she almost smiled, and those dark eyes twinkled. It reminded him that he was the one who'd knocked on her door, and now it was time to speak.

"Sorry to bother you, but since we're neighbors, I wanted to welcome you to Borden's Gap. I'm Sam Youngblood. I'm also the police chief here in town, and I live across the street."

He's really tall, Katie thought, and the dark-blue uniform he was wearing made his blue eyes shine.

"I'm Katie McGrath. Nice to meet you," she said.

He looked past her shoulder to the empty house.

"Did you beat your furniture here?" he asked.

"Yes, but only for one night. I got a text about an hour ago that they'll be here before noon tomorrow."

"I have a folding cot I'd be happy to loan you," Sam said.

"I have a sleeping bag. I'll be fine, but thank you," she said.

Another string of fireworks went off like a semiautomatic strafing a yard. Katie jumped like she'd been gut-punched and then took a slow breath.

Sam hid a frown. Her face had lost all hint of color at the sound.

"Fireworks abound but they'll be over after tomorrow," he said.

"Good to know," Katie said.

Sam pulled a business card out of his pocket. "Here's my card. My cell phone and the phone to the station are both on it."

Katie's fingers were trembling as she took it out of his hand.

"Thank you again. That's very kind of you," she said.

"Yes, ma'am. Now I'd better get home so my babysitter can leave. Nice meeting you, Miss McGrath."

"Katie," she said.

He nodded, tipped the corner of his Stetson, and then jumped back in his cruiser. After backing out of her drive, he pulled up in front of his house and got out carrying an armload of uniforms.

Katie was still watching from the window when two little girls came running out of the house. One had a sizable bandage on her upper arm, but even from this distance, she could see that they were identical twins.

So, he has twins and a babysitter, which must mean his wife works, too. Katie pulled all of the shades and curtains, shutting out everything in sight, and went back to the kitchen where she'd been making herself some supper. It was comforting to know there was a policeman living across the street, she thought, and dropped his card in her purse.

———————

Once inside his house, Sam went through his normal coming-home routine. He hung up his clean uniforms, locked up his gun, and then changed into old jeans and a T-shirt before going into the kitchen.

Roxie was sitting on a barstool with a cold drink.

"How's Beth been since I brought her back?" Sam asked.

"Oh, fine until she thinks about it. I know it must hurt. And I think all of the pain meds have worn off. She's pretty cranky this evening, bless her heart."

"Yes, bless her heart is right," Sam said. "She's had a pretty rough day. Go on home, Roxie. Put your feet up and rest. You've earned it."

"I'm happier here being tired than I am at home being alone, and don't ever think otherwise," she said. "See you tomorrow, and I'll let myself out. Oh…I got chops out of the freezer this morning and put them in the fridge to thaw, if you want to cook them tonight. If not, I'll cook them for their lunch tomorrow."

"Thanks," Sam said. He was digging the chops out of the fridge as Roxie left the house.

The girls came dragging into the kitchen. From the looks of them, they were in need of a bath and an early night, and Sam felt like they looked. As soon as he got them fed, he was calling an end to this day.

"What can we do, Daddy?" Evie asked.

"Go wash your hands and you can set the table," he said.

"I don't feel like helping," Beth said.

"Then sit at the table and talk to me," Sam said. "Has your arm been hurting much?"

She nodded. "A lot."

"I'm so sorry, baby," he said. He stopped what he was doing and got her a juice box and a baby aspirin. "Here, chew this up, then wash it down with your drink. It should help with the pain."

Beth chewed the pill and swallowed, then took a sip of her drink. She watched as Sam began putting pork chops in the skillet to fry, then dumped frozen french fries on a baking sheet and put them in the oven to cook.

"Do we want corn or green beans?" he asked.

Beth looked at Evie to answer because Evie was the one who made the food decisions for them.

"We want corn tonight, Daddy!" Evie said.

"Amazing! So do I," Sam said, and then winked as he got a package out of the freezer and popped it in the microwave to cook.

Evie had just finished setting the table when Beth pointed to the fridge.

"Sissy, we need ketchup for the fries."

Evie nodded, and as she was getting the bottle out of the refrigerator, she paused and looked up at Sam.

"Daddy?"

"Hmm?"

"Can I have a juice box, too?"

"Absolutely," Sam said. "And thank you for being such a good helper and taking care of your sister while I was at work."

Evie crawled up beside Beth and patted her on the hand. "Poor sissy," she said.

Sam eyed his girls. *Poor sissy, indeed.*

He stood tending the chops until they were done, then put them directly on the plates and carried them to the table. Took the fries out of the oven and slid them on a platter; put the corn in a bowl and seasoned it with a little butter and salt before carrying it to the table, too.

He made himself a glass of iced tea and then sat down at the table with his girls and thought himself the luckiest man in the world.

"Who wants to say the blessing tonight?" he asked.

"I will," Evie said, and bowed her head. "Hi, God. It's me, Everly Ann. Thank you for our pork chops, fries, and corn, and for Daddy and Miss Roxie, and one other thing. Somebody needs to be in trouble for putting that glass in our yard. Amen."

"Amen," Sam said, and hid a grin.

Everly Youngblood might look like her mother, but she was him all over. Injustice had no place in her world, and she wasn't afraid to speak up when she witnessed it.

By the time he got their plates filled and the meat cut up, and the girls began eating, he finally tended to his own. As always, they talked about everything about the day as they ate. Sam could tell that Evie was the tiniest bit envious that Beth rode to the ER in Daddy's police car with the siren going, but she didn't seem to hold it against them. After all, Beth had a 'mergency, while she did not.

They were getting down to talking about dessert, and Sam was clearing the plates from the table when Evie offered information of her own. Something she knew that Beth didn't because she'd been asleep.

"Daddy, I saw a woman go into the empty house across the street," Evie said.

"It's not empty any longer," Sam said. "It's been rented to the new first-grade teacher. She just arrived this afternoon, and she said her furniture will be arriving tomorrow."

They both looked up, their mouths agape.

"Is she going to be our teacher?" they asked.

"I don't know. There are two first-grade classes, remember?"

"Is she nice?" Beth asked.

"She sure seemed to be," Sam said. "Who wants a cookie for dessert?"

Both of them raised their hands.

He got the cookie jar off the cabinet and carried it to the table. He watched them get a cookie apiece and then hold them together to see if they were alike in shape and size. He smiled, watching Beth maneuver Evie into them sharing a bite of each other's cookies, and thought of the woman across the street again. Now that he'd seen the teacher in person and seen the shadows in her eyes, it reminded him that he had been going to run a background check on her.

Later, after he had the girls asleep, he went into the office, sat down at his computer, pulled up a link from the precinct to run a background check, and typed in Katie McGrath, Albuquerque, New Mexico.

Chapter Six

THE MOMENT SAM SAW ARTICLES REGARDING THE school shooting in Albuquerque, his heart sank. Now he remembered where he'd heard that name. She was the teacher who was shot in the back saving two of her students. No wonder she was freaking out because of the firecrackers. The magnitude of her sacrifice left him speechless, but curiosity pushed him to delve further, and he began reading every article he could find with her name attached.

Most of them were school-related, like the story and picture of her from three years ago receiving an award for Teacher of the Year, and being lauded as a hero at the school shooting. He even found a photo and a wedding announcement dated earlier this same year, but he never found a mention of the actual wedding. *And she's here alone.* A woman with secrets. But that wasn't scandalous. He didn't know a woman without them.

After that, he dug deeper and discovered that she'd graduated from college in Chicago, then went back farther to where she'd aged out of the foster system there as well, which sent him looking for clues about why she wound up there in the first place. And then his heart broke.

Abandoned baby found in an alley.

No known family.

Two applications for adoptions that never took place.

Sam took a deep breath and logged out of all the links. He was used to background checks. It was part of his job, but this was not a perp. This was a woman who'd had not one bad hand dealt to her but one after another after another, and through no fault of her own. He felt like a Peeping Tom.

He'd always thought of his girls as deprived because they were growing up without their mother, but this had given him a whole other perspective. They had him and each other. They had two sets of grandparents, and they knew of their mother and that their daddy loved them.

He felt like crying, but pinched the bridge of his nose instead, then got a beer from the fridge and slipped out onto the back porch.

The sky was clear and star-filled. The night was still and cooling off from the warmth of the day. Someone's dog barked, and another answered in the distance as Sam took a quick sip.

Fireworks were popping off all over town. He frowned. They had a city ordinance against shooting them off in town, but it was so old that it had been ignored as far back as when he was a kid. There were a couple of army vets in town who hated fireworks and left town every Fourth of July to keep from being triggered by flashbacks, and now there was Katie McGrath in an empty house, fighting demons all alone.

She had awakened every ounce of empathy within

him. The vow he'd taken to serve and protect was in the forefront of his mind, but she hadn't asked for help. He wasn't even sure she needed it. From what he'd read, she'd done a damn good job of taking care of herself and the children in her care.

He frowned at the sound of a car speeding through the streets somewhere to the north and then heard a siren and relaxed. His men were on the job.

He took another sip, remembering the shadows in her eyes and on her face. The face of someone living with ghosts and PTSD. How could she not?

She looked so sad. He wondered how laughter would change her face, and then let it go. Unless she was in need, he did not have the right to interfere.

━━━━━

Across the street, Katie was in a similar mood. She had showered and washed her hair and was sitting out on the back porch in the dark, letting it air-dry.

Somewhere nearby she could hear the sounds of voices and caught the scent of meat on a grill and then the sound of a speeding car, followed by sirens. Dogs were barking at each other and because of the fireworks. She empathized with the frenzy with which they were barking—trying to tell their humans that it hurt. That they were scared. Trying to find a place to hide.

Someone fired off a Roman candle nearby, and when she heard the high-pitched whistle as it shot up into the sky, her skin crawled.

Don't run. Don't run. It's just fireworks.

Her hands were locked onto the arms of the old wicker chair as the Roman candle exploded into a red, white, and blue shower of sparkles. But as the sparks began to fall toward earth, they were also burning out and taking some of her anxiety with them.

Katie looked up, lulled by the beauty of the night sky. The moon was on the wane, but the stars were brilliant. She stood up and walked out into the yard, then looked up again and began looking for the North Star, then the Milky Way and the Big Dipper and the Little Dipper, remembering a foster father who'd been an astronomy enthusiast and had let all of the kids in their house look through his telescope at night. He made them call him Papa. She frowned, wondering why she remembered that now, then shrugged it off and went back inside.

She was tired, and although it wasn't late, she double-checked all of the locks, then crawled into her sleeping bag, shifted around until she found a comfortable spot, and closed her eyes.

The faint odor of pine-scented floor cleaner still lingered. Someone started up a car next door and drove away. And as time passed, the fireworks faded.

The sounds of a city were missing, but what she heard wasn't foreign. She knew what the sounds were and was comforted by the normalcy of ice being dumped from the ice maker and the faint hoot of an owl somewhere nearby.

But as she fell asleep, she drifted back into the darkness of bitter memories and dreamed until she woke up gasping for breath and confused about why there were no beds and why she was on the floor. It wasn't until she got up and began turning on lights that she remembered the journey that brought her here.

Unwilling to go back to sleep for now, she went to the kitchen, got a cold bottle of pop, sat down on one of the barstools, and took a big drink.

The liquid sliding down the back of her throat made her nose burn and her eyes water, but her focus had shifted, which was her intent. Later today, her furniture would arrive. Having the familiarity of her own things around her would be comforting and settling. And when she had that behind her, she needed to call her new principal, Susan Wayne, for a face-to-face.

New town.

New school.

New life path.

After she settled down, Katie took her pop back to her sleeping bag, got her phone, and sat cross-legged within the downy coverings and started scanning social media.

She noticed Lila was beginning to post pictures of herself with her new boyfriend on Instagram and Snapchat. Seeing her friend happy made Katie happy. However, she wasn't in the mood for the maelstrom of national news and opted not to read any of the newspapers. In this instance, ignorance was bliss. After a while, she laid her phone aside and slipped down into the sleeping bag. With every light still on in the house, she drifted back to sleep.

Sam was a light sleeper, and when he heard Beth crying in the night, he immediately got up to check on her.

"What's wrong with my baby?" he said softly as he sat down on the side of her bed and scooped her up in his lap, holding her close against him.

Tears were rolling down her face.

"My arm hurts, Daddy."

"I'm sorry," Sam said, angry all over again that his yard guys had been that careless. He needed to give her something for pain again, but she was so little he was afraid it would make her sick. Maybe if he could get her to eat something first, he could give her one more baby aspirin. "How about we have some of that ice cream we brought home?"

She leaned against his bare chest and nodded.

"Just us?" she whispered, looking at Evie who was sound asleep.

Sam nodded, then stood and carried her to the kitchen. He sat her on down in one of the chairs, then dipped ice cream for both of them.

Beth took a bite, then closed her eyes. "Mmm, good, Daddy. Thank you."

"You're welcome," Sam said, and ate with her until her bowl was empty before he got another pain pill. "Here, chew this up."

She chewed, made a face, and then took a drink of the water he offered before taking their bowls to the sink.

"Back to bed you go," Sam said. He carried her down the hall and into the girls' bedroom and put her back in bed with Evie. "Sleep tight," he whispered, as he pulled covers up over the both of them and then left the door open as he went back across the hall to his room.

It was almost 4:00 a.m. Out of habit, he moved the curtains aside in his bedroom to look out and saw the house across the street ablaze in lights. It appeared he and the girls weren't the only ones having trouble getting any rest. After a quick glance up and down the street, he went back to bed, crawled in between the covers, and closed his eyes.

He lay there, listening to make sure the girls were quiet, and then relaxed. The next thing he heard was his alarm going off. Just like every day, he showered and shaved before going to make breakfast for himself and the girls.

Today felt like a pancake morning, so he got out a griddle and a bowl and began mixing batter.

———————

Katie woke up flat on her stomach with her arms rolled under her. She'd been dreaming she was holding onto the boys, telling them she loved them, when something woke her.

She was stiff, and her eyes were burning, and all the lights were still on. She rolled over with a groan and grabbed her phone to see if she had any messages from the movers.

And she did.

They had given her a 10:00 to 11:00 a.m. time frame of when she could expect them, and it was almost nine. She leaped out of the sleeping bag and ran to the bathroom. Ten minutes later, she came out freshly showered and looking for something to put on, including shoes. No bare feet allowed when furniture is being moved.

Once she was dressed and her sleeping bag rolled up, she raced to the kitchen and made herself a glass of Pepsi. She needed caffeine and this would have to serve in lieu of the coffee she wanted. She grabbed a doughnut, silently thanking Louise Parsons all over again for the food, and then went out to the front porch and sat down on the top step with her breakfast.

A middle-aged man walked by with a little dog on a leash. He looked startled to see Katie, but when Katie waved, he nodded and smiled as he moved past.

So far, she felt good about her decision to move here, she thought, taking another bite of the doughnut. A few moments later, she noticed a robin in the grass a few yards away.

"Well, hello, sir. You are my first guest, and all I have to share is this doughnut," she said, then pulled off a piece and gave it a toss toward the bird.

It hopped over to the morsel, looked up at her, and then picked up the bit of sweet dough and flew away.

"Gotta eat and run, huh?" she said. She put the last bite in her mouth, chewed and swallowed, then chased it with Pepsi.

She was still on the porch when her phone signaled a text. It was the moving van. They were in Borden's Gap. She returned the text, telling them she was in the yard watching for them, then dropped her phone back in her pocket. She ran back into the house with her glass and set it in the sink before hurrying back out into the yard. Within minutes, she saw the big red moving van turn down the street and drive toward her.

I am sleeping in my bed tonight, she thought, and then lifted her arm and waved.

The driver began slowing down, then backed up her driveway and got out.

"Morning, Miss McGrath. I'm Evan."

"Good morning, Evan! Did everything go okay?" Katie asked.

"Smooth trip. No hitches here," he said. "Wanna give me a quick tour of the interior so I'll know where stuff goes?"

"Sure," Katie said, and walked him through the rooms, pointing out which was her bedroom and the other that would be the office.

"Looks good. We'll have your things inside in no time."

"You guys will set my bed back up, right?" Katie asked.

"Yes, ma'am," he said, and then went out to the truck.

The two other men in Evan's crew were already removing packing blankets, and while she watched, they brought what was left of Katie's life back under her roof. No two flights of stairs to maneuver. No short turns on the landings.

After they had finished unloading and setting up furniture, they left. Katie locked her front door as they were driving away and went straight to her bedroom to find the box with her bedding in it. No matter what else got done today, she was going to sleep in her bed tonight, between her own sheets.

━━━━━━

The twins were in the living room watching morning cartoons when they saw a big red truck stop in front of their house. They ran to the window long enough to see the new teacher in the yard and men carrying furniture in the house, before they turned and ran.

"Miss Roxie! Miss Roxie!" they shouted.

Roxie stepped out of Sam's bedroom into the hall.

"I'm here!"

Evie got to her first. "We saw the new teacher, and there's a big red truck in her driveway."

"Men are carrying furniture into her house," Beth added.

"Well, I'll say," Roxie said. "That's probably the moving van with her things. I'll bet she's glad they have arrived."

The girls nodded, then ran back to the window to watch. Every time Katie stepped out of the house, they commented on a different aspect of her appearance.

Beth pointed. "Evie! Look how long her hair is."

Evie nodded, then added, "She's tall."

"But not as tall as Daddy," Beth said.

Evie agreed. "No one is as tall as Daddy."

"Her kitchen table is white. Ours isn't white," Beth said.

"Her sofa is kinda black," Evie said, frowning.

"No, it's dark gray, I think," Beth said.

"I like red," Evie said. "She should have a red sofa."

Beth giggled. "We don't have a red sofa."

Evie shrugged. "I still like red ones. When I grow up, I will have a red sofa."

"Yeah, a red one," Beth said.

They watched until the big red truck drove away and they saw the teacher close the door.

"Is she going to come back out?" Evie asked.

Beth frowned. "I think she'll unpack now, like we do

when we come back from Granny and Papa's house after Christmas."

"Yeah, like that," Evie said, then nudged her sister. "Go ask Miss Roxie if you can have a juice box."

Beth frowned. "Why don't you ask?"

"Because you got hurt and she won't tell you no. Just don't forget to ask if I can have one, too."

"Okay," Beth said, and went to the laundry room. "Miss Roxie, can I please have a juice box?"

Roxie was switching laundry from the washer to the dryer and nodded absently.

"Yes, sure. Get your sister one, too, okay?"

"Yes, ma'am," Beth said, and then ran to the refrigerator, snagged a couple of the juice boxes, and went running up the hall to their bedroom. "Ta-da!" she said, as she entered carrying the juice.

Evie grinned. "See, I told you she wouldn't tell you no. Let's do this puzzle while we have our juice. It will be like snack time at school."

"Yes! Snack time," Beth echoed as her sister dumped the pieces of a puzzle out on their play table.

They sat down together and, without competition, began searching out the pieces that formed the edges like their daddy had taught them.

———

While Katie was unpacking and hanging her awards on the office wall, and Sam's girls were playing school, Sam was headed to the east side of town to mediate an argument between neighbors, and it all started over a cat named Puppy.

For months, Helen Primm's cat, Puppy, had been using Martha Desmond's flower bed for a litter box, despite Martha's constant complaints to Helen and her disgust at the odor. It finally came to a head this morning when Martha went out to plant a flat of pansies and wound up with cat shit all over her gardening gloves and the knees of her jeans. When Martha realized what it was, she screamed, stormed over to Helen's house, rang the doorbell, and then smeared the cat shit from her gloves all over Helen's front door.

Helen smelled it even as she was opening the door, and then Martha came at her, wiping her hands on the front of Helen's shirt, while still screaming in hysterics.

"Smell that?" Martha shrieked. "That's what your cat leaves in my flower bed every day. I've asked you and asked you to stop letting it out your front door, and yet you persist. I went out to plant pansies this morning, and this is what I got. Today was the last straw. I've had it with you!"

"How dare you!" Helen shouted, and drew back and slapped Martha so hard it knocked the banana clip out of her hair.

"No! How dare *you*!" With a flying tackle, Martha took Helen down on the porch.

One of their neighbors heard the screaming, came out on their porch long enough to see the two women fighting, and ran back inside and called the police, which was how Sam wound up in the middle of a cat fight—about a cat.

The moment Sam rolled up to the address, he called in his location, then got out and strode toward the porch. Neighbors from both sides of the street were in the front yard watching.

"Why have none of you tried to stop this?" Sam asked.

"I'm smart enough not to ever get in the middle of two fighting women who are covered in cat shit," one man said.

Sam paused. Looked at the brown stuff all over their faces and clothes and on the door and groaned.

"Are you serious?" he muttered.

The woman from across the street nodded. "Helen lets her cat out the front door every morning. It goes straight to Martha's flower bed and poops. Been going on for months. I guess Martha finally got enough of it."

Sam looked around, saw a garden hose coiled neatly near the front steps, and headed for it. He turned on the water at the spigot, dragged the hose up the steps, aimed the spray nozzle at the two women's faces, and let them have it.

Martha was cursing a blue streak and got a dose in her mouth and up her nose.

Helen was screaming and scratching ruts in Martha's neck with her red Hot as Hell dip nails when the water went in her ear and eye.

Both women rolled over on their backs, their hands flailing in the air as they tried to get away from the blast.

"Stop! Stop!" they screamed.

Sam shut off the spray. "Ladies—and I use that phrase lightly—this morning, you have just made asses of yourselves in front of God and everybody who cared to drive down this street."

Martha sat up, saw the crowd on Helen's front lawn, and groaned as Helen was shaking water out of her ear.

Martha's rage deflated, and she was in tears again. "Her cat poops in my flower bed. For months, I've asked her to please let it out the back door instead of the front, but she ignores me. This morning, I went to plant pansies, and the first hole I dug was nothing but fresh cat poop. It was all over my gloves and on my jeans before I knew it. So I came over to Helen's house to return her property."

"You smeared it on my door. You smeared it all over me!" Helen whined.

"You started it," Martha snapped.

"And I just ended it," Sam said. "Now. You two have a decision to make. You will stand up and apologize to each other and mean it, or I'm hauling you both to jail for disturbing the peace."

Martha rolled over onto her knees and got up, blood dripping from the scratches on her neck.

Helen thought her vision was blurred from the water in her eyes, and then realized one eye was nearly swollen shut.

They saw the disgust on Chief Youngblood's face, then looked at each other, then down at their feet.

"Sorry," they mumbled.

"Nope. I didn't get any sincerity from either of you," Sam said.

Martha frowned. "I'm sorry I lost my temper."

Helen eyed the blood on Martha's neck. "I'm so sorry I hurt you."

Then they threw their arms around each other, crying as they hugged.

Sam sighed. "That was step one. Step two has to do with a cat. Helen, you have a moral obligation to not let an animal that belongs to you be a nuisance in your neighborhood, and you know that. Do you have a litter box in your house for the cat?"

She nodded.

"So, either that cat uses the litter box, or you take it out in your backyard, wait until it's finished its business, and then bring it back in your house. Under no circumstances do you ever let it out in front again. If you do, Martha will call animal welfare. Martha, do you hear me?"

Martha nodded.

Sam turned back to Helen. "When Martha calls, the cat will get picked up and you will pay a fifty-dollar fine to get it back, or else."

Helen gasped. "Not 'or else'! You can't put my cat down for pooping."

Sam shook his head. "Oh, that's not my choice to make. It's yours. If you love your pet the way you claim, then you will do what's best for that pet. And trust me, fifty dollars per poop and landing in animal control is not your best bet."

At that point, everyone in the yard began laughing.

Sam turned around to see what was funny and saw a giant Maine Coon cat over in Martha's yard, covering up poop. Helen gasped, and then realized the door to her house was wide open, water was standing in the entryway, and her cat had just taken a dump in Martha's yard. Again.

"Oh my God," Helen groaned. "I'm sorry. I guess I

didn't shut the door when we started fussing, and Puppy got out. I'll get him. And I'll clean up what he just did. And I promise it won't happen again."

Sam pointed at them, his voice stern. "Miss Martha, you go on back home. Miss Helen, you go get your cat and the new deposit of poop, and then you bring your neighbor two fifty-pound bags of potting soil and put them by her flower bed so she can start fresh with her pansies. And don't make me have to come back here again."

"Yes, sir," they echoed.

Sam waved at the crowd. "Go home. There's nothing left to see."

The neighbors dispersed without comment.

Martha trudged back home, wrinkling her nose in disgust as she passed her flower beds, while Helen came racing along behind to reclaim her cat and its poop.

Sam headed for his car and got in. "So far, weirdest call of the year," he muttered. "And I'm going to have to put this in a report."

Chapter Seven

KATIE WAS IN HER ELEMENT. THE AREA RUG THAT WENT with her living room furniture fit perfectly, and her own things were a welcome sight in her new surroundings. She had the beginnings of an office in the spare bedroom, a small dining table and four chairs in the kitchen, and her bed was made up. Next thing on her agenda was unpacking dishes and cookware so she could feed herself.

She wasn't sure about how TV, internet, and Wi-Fi worked in Borden's Gap. A place this small and this far away from bigger cities might not have cable, and she'd seen a whole lot of houses with satellite dishes on the roofs, but Louise would know, so she gave her a call.

Louise answered on the second ring.

"Hello."

"Louise, this is Katie McGrath. My furniture is finally here, and as I'm putting things away, it dawns on me that I have no idea what my options are for hooking up my television and Wi-Fi for my office."

"Ah…of course," Louise said. "You have two options. Got a pen?"

Katie scrambled to find pen and paper, then sat down with them.

"Got it. Go ahead."

Louise gave her info for New Cingular Wireless and for satellite-dish services.

"What do you have?" Katie asked.

"Cingular Wireless," Louise said. "I needed better access because of my Realtor status and opted for that. I haven't been disappointed."

"Thank you so much," Katie said.

"You're welcome. How do you like your house?" Louise asked.

Katie sighed. "I love it. The house is amazing. My stuff fits in the rooms. Thank you for leasing it to me."

"Absolutely," Louise said. "I'm glad it's not going to sit empty. Happy unpacking, and if you need anything else, just ask."

As soon as Louise disconnected, Katie started making calls. By the time she was finished, she had appointments set up for one technician to come out and hook up her technology and another one to put a satellite dish on the roof. Then she dropped her phone in her pocket and went to the kitchen to unpack pans and dishes.

A couple of hours later, she was in her car with a list of cleaning and food supplies and off to find a supermarket. She'd googled grocery stores in Borden's Gap before she left the house and learned the closest thing to a supermarket was Welby's Grocery. The other choices were Dollar General Store and two mini-marts that sold gas and basic groceries, so the decision was easy. Welby's it was.

The culture shock of realizing she could see the beginning and end of Main Street was real. Twelve blocks from one city limit sign to the other. There were businesses all along Main, as well as several on side streets, with one stoplight in the middle of town.

This definitely wasn't going to remind her of Albuquerque, which was the whole point. And hopefully, the layout of the school was different enough and small enough that she would be able to assimilate without making an ass of herself.

Like most small towns in the South, there was an abundance of churches, as well as a barbershop and two hair salons, a funeral home, and a florist.

She passed a pharmacy, Arnold's Antiques and Gifts, a small clothing boutique, and a food truck that sold barbecue sitting in a vacant lot.

There were two signs on Main, one directing her to a small hospital-clinic east of Main and the other directing her to the high school football field.

She passed an auto parts store, a feed and seed store that took up half a block just off Main, and a plumber with a sign on the window that said ENTRANCE IN THE ALLEY.

Welby's Grocery was near the far end of Main, and when Katie pulled into the parking lot, she easily found a place to park. She was on her way toward the entrance when a dusty black pickup truck of indeterminate age came flying into the parking lot, sped past Katie, and came to a stop in one of the handicapped parking spots.

The driver, a thirtysomething man with a stubble of black whiskers, leaped out and strode into the store, almost stomping in anger.

Katie arched an eyebrow as she walked inside, pausing

to locate the shopping carts and the signs on the aisles. She was still getting her bearings when the same man came out of an aisle carrying a huge carton of beer and staring at her on the way to the checkout.

"There's a reason to be grateful I'm not married," Katie muttered. She got out her list and began pushing her cart down an aisle, away from the front of the store.

She was in the store for almost an hour before she headed up to check out, pausing momentarily at a display of paperback books and magazines. It would be a couple of days before she would have her TV hooked up, so she picked up a couple of magazines and settled on a book of romantic suspense by Dinah McCall, one of her favorite writers. Happy that she had food to cook, a new book to read, and her own bed to sleep in tonight, Katie went to check out.

She drove home with a whole new outlook on small-town living. When she pulled up into the drive, she noticed the police chief's children and their babysitter out in their front yard.

As soon as she got out, both girls turned and ran to the edge of their yard and waved. Their babysitter got up off her knees from the flower bed she'd been weeding and walked to where the girls were standing.

"Hello! Do you need a hand?" she asked, seeing all the sacks in the back of Katie's SUV.

"We can help! We can help!" the girls cried.

Katie smiled. She didn't need help, but it appeared the little girls had a need to help, which was a whole other thing and nothing she would ever want to discourage.

"Thank you. That would be great," Katie said.

Roxie smiled, grabbed each girl by the hand, and walked them across the street.

"I'm Katie," she said.

"I'm Roxie. Resident nanny-babysitter for Sam's girls. Girls, introduce yourselves."

Evie giggled. "I'm Everly, but everyone calls me Evie."

Beth blinked. "I'm Elizabeth, but everyone calls me Beth."

Katie smiled. "It is so nice to meet you all. Beth, I see a big bandage on your shoulder, so I'm going to give you the bag with bread and chips to carry because it is very lightweight. Evie, do you think you can lift this bag with cookies and spices?"

"Yep. Look how strong I am," Evie said and flexed her arm, then took the bag Katie offered.

"I cut my arm. Daddy took me to the 'mergency in his police car," Beth added.

"She got lights and sirens," Evie said wistfully.

Katie could tell Evie was sorry she missed the ride.

"Well, Beth, I'm sorry you were hurt, but it's good to know you're healing now. Here. You carry this bag. It won't hurt your arm."

Beth took it with care. She knew all about not squishing bags with bread or chips.

Roxie grabbed two handfuls of grocery bags, and Katie slipped the rest of them on her arms, and into the house they went, following Katie into the kitchen.

"Thank you all so much!" Katie said, and took the bags the girls had carried, while Roxie unloaded hers on the island.

"The girls saw the moving van this morning. I'll bet you were glad to get your things," Roxie said.

Katie nodded. "I sure was. I slept in my sleeping bag on the floor last night."

The girls' eyes widened, and then they giggled.

"What's funny?" Roxie asked.

"She slept in a bag," Evie said.

Katie was trying not to laugh. "Not like a grocery bag. Haven't you ever seen a sleeping bag before?"

"Nope," Beth said.

"Wanna see it?" Katie asked.

"Yes!" they chimed.

Katie glanced at Roxie. "Do you have time for all this?"

Roxie chuckled. "Sure do."

"Then have a seat," Katie said. "I'll be right back." She left the room in a rush and came back moments later carrying what looked like a shiny, puffy red quilt rolled up like an egg roll.

Evie gasped. "It's red! I looove red."

"Come into the living room where there's more room to unroll it," Katie said, and everyone followed her back to the front of the house. She untied the cord and unrolled the bag onto the floor, then unzipped it enough for the girls to see how it worked. "Climb in," she said, and pulled the edge back like she was turning down a bed.

Roxie was laughing as they squirreled their way into the bag, rolled over onto their backs, and pulled the top up to their chins.

"It's snuggy," Beth said.

"It's red!" Evie added.

Roxie watched the interplay between the young teacher

and Sam's girls with delight, but she was also noting the shadows beneath Katie's eyes and the hollows in her cheeks. For whatever reason, she knew Katie was grieving.

Sam had looked like this for the first two years of the girls' lives. And then one day something shifted, and he began getting better. She hoped something would shift soon for Katie. She seemed like a very nice person.

"Sam tells me you're going to be the new first-grade teacher," Roxie said.

Katie looked up, smiling.

"Yes. I'm really looking forward to teaching here."

"Is this your first teaching position?" Roxie asked.

Katie's heart skipped. "No. I taught in New Mexico for several years, but decided I wanted a change of pace and of scenery. Tennessee is beautiful. I love all the trees."

All of a sudden, Evie let out a shriek. Katie's heart stopped, but then she realized it was delight as she turned and looked. Evie had crawled all the way to the foot of the sleeping bag, and Beth's feet were on Evie's head.

Evie's voice was muffled, but not enough that they couldn't hear what she said. "Look, Miss Roxie! Beth is standing on my head!"

Katie leaned over and unzipped the bag all the way around, then yanked back the cover.

"Just like peeling a banana!" she said, and laughed at the looks of surprise on the girls' faces.

"Okay, girls. That's enough," Roxie said. "Miss Katie will be wanting to put up her groceries, and we need to finish weeding that front flower bed before your daddy comes home."

"Okay," they said, and then got out of the sleeping bag, fiddled with it until they had it zipped back up again, and got up.

"Thank you for showing us your sleeping bag," Beth said.

"Yes, thank you," Evie echoed.

"You're very welcome. It was nice to meet you. Now I know some of my neighbors."

"Neighbors! We're your neighbors!" the girls chimed.

Roxie got up, grinning wryly. "You may or may not look upon this as a plus."

"Oh, always a plus. I'm a teacher. I love the littles."

Evie paused. "Are we littles?"

"You are to me," Katie said.

Beth was dancing from one foot to the other. "I know why. 'Cause you're so tall, we look little."

Roxie just shook her head and herded them out the door and across the street.

Katie watched until they were safely across, waved at them one last time, and then headed back inside and went to work.

———

Sam came home that evening and barely got his weapons locked up and his clothes changed before he was inundated with news of their visit to Miss Katie's house.

"Daddy! We talked to the teacher. We went in her house!" Evie said.

"And she's almost as tall as you," Beth added.

"We were in the front yard weeding when she drove

up," Roxie said. "It looked like she'd bought out Welby's, so we helped her carry in the sacks."

"Nice move," Sam said. "She looks like she'd blow away in a stiff wind. I hope Borden's Gap is good to her. She needs some TLC for sure."

Roxie nodded, wondering what Sam knew about their new neighbor that she did not.

"She has a bed today, but last night she slept in a bag!" Evie said.

Sam grinned, remembering Katie saying she had a sleeping bag. "A bag? Really?"

Beth nodded. "She showed us. It was in a roll and then she unzipped it. We could both get in it. It was puffy and soft and slick like Grandma's nightgowns."

"And red!" Evie cried. "It was slick and red."

Sam blinked. All of a sudden he had an image of a tall, leggy woman with dark hair climbing out of a red nylon sleeping bag. He didn't know what to do with that, so he changed the subject.

"Roxie, tomorrow and Sunday are my days off, but you know how that can go. So if you have plans for the weekend, just let me know now. I won't have you changing your days off just because of my job. I can always find a babysitter if the need arises."

"No need," Roxie said. "I'll be in town, regardless of what I'm doing, so if an emergency comes up and you need me, just call. Otherwise, I'll see you Monday."

"Deal," Sam said. "Girls, tell Miss Roxie bye."

"Bye," they said in unison, hugged her, then took off outside, running toward their swing set.

"They're still wired from the visit with the new teacher. They played school all afternoon, and I guess now it's recess," Roxie said.

Sam laughed. "One thing's for sure: there's never a dull moment around here. Have a good weekend," he said.

"You too," Roxie said. She gathered up her things and headed home while Sam began poking through the refrigerator for the hamburger meat he'd put in there this morning to thaw.

The girls weren't fans of meat loaf, and he didn't want hamburgers, so he settled on spaghetti and started the meat to browning. He was just about to put water on to boil for the spaghetti noodles when he heard a shriek from the backyard and knew it wasn't a playful one. His first thought was one of them was hurt on yet another stray piece of glass, so he turned off the burners and ran.

━━━━━━━━

Evie and Beth were at their swing set, climbing up and sliding down, over and over. Evie was at the steps and getting ready to climb when Beth came off the slide and started running back to do it again.

Evie began climbing as Beth started up behind her. Then all of a sudden Evie yanked her hand back from the hand rail, screaming. She was so shocked by the pain that she lost her grip, and then her footing, and began falling backward.

Beth was only a couple of steps below her, and when she saw her sister starting to fall, she tightened her grip on the handrails and braced herself for the impact of Evie's body.

Sam was already out of the house and running when he saw Beth catch Evie's fall, and he lengthened his stride.

Evie was crying, and Beth was in a panic when she saw Sam.

"Daddy, help!" she cried.

Seconds later, Sam had both of them in his arms and started carrying them back to the porch.

Evie was cradling her hand against her chest and sobbing, and Beth was in a state of shock.

"She slipped, Daddy. I thought I was going to drop her," Beth said, and started to shake.

"You did good, darling. You saved Evie from falling. Did it hurt your arm?" Sam asked.

"No. I'm okay," Beth said, as he smoothed the hair away from her face.

Then he reached for Evie's hand. "What happened, baby?"

"I don't know, Daddy. I was climbing and something hurt my hand."

Sam turned her little palm up, frowning as he saw the red swelling.

"Looks like you got stung," he said. "Let's go inside so I can pull out that stinger, and then we'll put some medicine on it so it will feel better. Okay?"

"Okay," Evie said.

Sam picked her up and carried her inside, with Beth trailing along beside them. They went straight to his bathroom, and this time it was Beth consoling Evie.

"Daddy will fix it, Sissy," she said, patting Evie's knee.

"Do I hafta go to the ER?" Evie asked.

"No. I can fix this," Sam said, and winked as he got
out tweezers and quickly pulled out the stinger, then got
a bottle of witch hazel from the medicine cabinet and
poured it in her hand.

The astringent immediately began working. The burning subsided, and when the pain lessened, Evie declared
herself healed.

"I feel better, Daddy, and I'm starved. What are we
having for supper?"

Sam sighed. These two were going to scare him into an
early grave.

"Spaghetti," he said.

"Yay! How long 'til we eat?" Beth asked.

"Give me about fifteen minutes. You two wash up here
and then go play in your room until I call."

He left them splashing water and pumping liquid soap
and told himself it didn't matter. A messy bathroom was
nothing as long as they were okay.

A short while later, he drained the excess liquid from
the cooked spaghetti noodles, then filled three plates,
added sauce, and carried the plates to the table.

"Girls! Supper is ready!" he yelled, then grinned when
he heard them thundering up the hall. To be so little, they
could make an amazing amount of noise.

Sam got an earful of everything to do with Katie
McGrath as they ate, and his curiosity grew. The new
woman across the street had made an impact on the girls.
If she wound up being their teacher, he might be hearing
a lot more about Miss Katie with the red bed and the long
dark hair.

Mark Roman was in his house, trying to pick up the pieces of his life. He'd hired a lawyer, changed the locks on his door, and had been working from home for days. He didn't have a secretary, although the company was interviewing, and he could work from home as easily as going to an office.

But Mark staying home was screwing up Megan's plans. There was so much riding on her being able to get back in the house that even her father was getting antsy, and he wasn't easily rattled.

Nobody wanted to make Craig Buttoni mad.

Katie spent the next two days at home unpacking and acclimating herself to the amenities and locations. It wasn't until Sunday evening when she saw Sam and the girls leaving the house that it dawned on her that no woman had appeared at the house as their mother. She saw him buckling the girls up in the back seat, then laughing at something they'd said, and was coming to the conclusion that Sam Youngblood might be a single parent. She wondered why, but had no one to ask, so she went to bed with her new Dinah McCall book and fell asleep reading. Going to sleep with the romantic suspense story in her head seemed to offset the nightmares, at least for the time being.

Katie was already awake the next morning and getting ready for the technician to show up to get her hooked up to technology, and the satellite dish installed this afternoon, when she glanced out the window and saw Roxie arriving at the Youngblood residence and going inside.

Katie smiled at the thought of being greeted by the twins and their squeals, imagining it was not unlike the way she was greeted each morning at school. Then she sighed and went to back to the kitchen to refill her coffee cup and pop a frozen waffle in the toaster. She ate it like buttered toast, finished off her coffee, and was waiting for a text from the technician when Lila called.

"Good morning!" Katie said as she put her cup in the sink.

"Hi, Katie! It is so good to hear your voice. I'm not gonna lie. I sure do miss you. Did your furniture arrive okay?"

"I miss you too, and yes, everything arrived without damage. I spent the weekend unpacking, so I'm pretty much settled."

"Send me pictures of your house. You know I'm jealous. I hate apartment living," Lila said.

"Are you and the hunky neighbor still a thing?" Katie asked.

Lila sighed. "Yes. Jack is amazing."

"Awesome," Katie said. "I'm happy for you, my friend. Send me pictures."

Lila laughed. "Deal. Oh, have you met your principal yet?"

"No, but I'm doing that tomorrow. I'm counting on seeing my room, getting a key, and finding out how many kids I'll have, so I can start planning."

"You sound excited," Lila said.

"I am, and a little anxious, too," Katie said. "But I'm

counting on new faces and a new location to make the transition easier."

"Do they know…about the shooting, I mean," Lila asked.

"Yes. I was up-front with everyone I interviewed with, but I told them I wasn't coming as the teacher who got shot. I'm just the new teacher, and they understood where I was coming from. It remains to be seen if they kept it to themselves."

"Well, hell, Katie. You didn't rob a bank. You have nothing to be ashamed of. It won't be the end of the world if they do find out," Lila said.

Katie laughed. "True, and I'll keep that in mind."

"I have other news," Lila said.

"Like what?" Katie asked.

"Guess who's getting divorced?"

"I have no idea," Katie said.

"Mark."

The hair suddenly crawled on the back of Katie's neck. "You're kidding me!"

"No, I'm not, and she filed. They didn't last six months. Karma, if you ask me. I'm telling you this because I have a feeling he's going to reach out to you, and I don't want you blindsided."

Katie snorted. "I would never answer a phone call or text from him. He no longer exists in my world. And for the love of God, don't tell him where I am. No one knows but you… and maybe some at the administration level in Albuquerque, if my principal here called to verify my application."

"Girl, you know I'm not talking to that ass. Your location is safe with me."

"Thanks," Katie said, and then her doorbell rang. "Hey, someone is at the door. Hopefully it's the guy who's going to hook up my internet. Love you. Talk to you later."

"Love you," Lila said, and disconnected.

Katie ran to the door, saw the van and the logo, and opened the door.

"Yay!" she said.

The man grinned. "Thank you, ma'am. It's nice to be appreciated. I'm Paul, your technician."

"Come in," Katie said. "I'll show you the locations and what I need, and then I'll leave you to work your magic."

"Yes, ma'am," Paul said.

Every day, Katie was faced with the difference between conveniences in a big city and what it took in the more rural parts of America to get the same services, and today was another instance.

A little over two hours later, Paul the technician was gone, and Katie had internet and Wi-Fi. It was time to get back on her laptop and catch up on email and final bills waiting to be paid, and by the time the sun went down, she had a new satellite dish on the roof and a working TV. All was right with her world.

———

As Lila and Katie were talking about Mark, he was on his way back to work. The company had finally hired a secretary, but he was dreading the dance of breaking in a new employee.

And there was another aspect of his job that had become

apparent while he was home. He worked for his father-in-law. And the boss's daughter had just dumped his ass and was divorcing him. His job was as tenuous as his future.

He was just pulling into the parking garage when he got a text from Megan. They'd parted on such angry terms that he couldn't imagine she had anything left to say and thought about not responding. Then she sent a second text, and he pulled them up and read them.

> Mark. My key won't work and I need in the house. I forgot something.

He rolled his eyes, and then glanced down at the second text.

> Please.

> Your key doesn't work because I changed the locks. Whatever you forgot, go buy another one.

When she didn't respond, he wondered what was so important that she was willing to contact him again to get it back. She'd been so secretive about everything, and then the way she'd just quit without so much as a fight? It made him wonder. Maybe he'd give the house a second look when he got home.

But the moment he got up to his office, the secretary sitting outside his office looked up and, without introducing herself, delivered a message.

"Mr. Roman? Mr. Lanier would like to speak with you in his office."

Mark felt sick. Kind of like he'd felt right before he'd called Katie the day of the wedding. *This is it. I'm about to get fired.* He turned around and walked down the hall to his father-in-law's office and went in.

An hour later, he walked out with his ears still ringing and a neat little settlement package buying him out of his contract, knowing full well the old bastard expected Megan to get it back in alimony. And with best wishes in his new life.

As soon as he got in the car, Mark called his lawyer and told him what had happened and was reassured again that without a prenuptial agreement and with less than six months of marriage to a wealthy woman, it did not constitute alimony of any kind. And then, while he was riding a wave of relief, he impulsively called Katie.

He didn't know why, other than he wanted to hear her voice.

It did not surprise him that she wouldn't answer, so he drove to her apartment complex, but then when he parked, he didn't see her car. Still intent on making contact, he went up to her apartment to leave her a note, and walked up on a couple moving in.

Holy shit! She moved out?

Suddenly, he realized he'd just lost his last connection to her. If she wasn't answering calls, and he didn't know where she lived now, he'd actually really "lost" her. He turned around and went back to his car and headed home, but the closer he got, the deeper the pain in his chest became.

It hurt to breathe. He thought he might be having a heart attack. What if he died? He didn't want to die. Then he wondered if this was how Katie had felt when he'd betrayed her. What the hell had he been thinking?

He sighed. He knew what he'd been thinking about.

Money.

Power.

Prestige.

That's what he'd been thinking.

Fuck. Fuck. Fuck.

"I am a worthless son of a bitch," Mark said.

By the time he pulled into the garage, he was crying.

Then he remembered Lila. She'd know where Katie was! He scanned through his contacts and found her number. When he called, Lila answered so fast it startled him to the point of being speechless.

"What?" she said.

"Uh, this is—"

"I know who it is. Caller ID, dumbass. What do you want?"

"Uh, Katie moved and—"

"She didn't just move. She's gone. Between you and the nut who shot her, she never wants to see Albuquerque again. I'm not about to tell you where she is, and if you go looking for her, I will find you and remove your balls with a garlic press. Do you understand me?"

Horror rolled through Mark in waves. He knew Lila well enough to believe she meant every word of what she'd said. He'd lost a good woman to a bad one, and he'd betrayed her to do it. He couldn't take that back. He was as sorry as he could be, but not sorry enough to part with his balls. He hung up without saying another word and went into the house.

He hadn't just lost a wife; the job she'd come with was gone, too.

House of cards.

All fall down.

Chapter Eight

MARK MOPED THROUGH THE EVENING AND ORDERED in his dinner. As he was waiting for it to arrive, he remembered Megan's claim she'd left something behind, so he got up and went upstairs to their bedroom to see if he could find it.

Her clothes were gone, of course. He'd watched her packing them. And she'd taken all of her jewelry with her as well. He checked her side of the vanity in the bathroom, then the little end table on her side of the bed. Nothing was there but an old charger cord to a phone she no longer owned.

The drawers in her dresser were empty, too, but he looked anyway, and then, as he went to push a bottom drawer shut, it stuck. So he pulled it out, straightened it, and went to push it shut again, and again it stuck about halfway in.

Frowning, he pulled the drawer out again, but this time lifted it off the track and pulled it all the way out to see if a piece of her lingerie might have fallen out and was keeping the drawer from shutting. But when he stood the drawer up against the wall with the bottom facing forward, he froze, unable to believe what he was seeing.

A pouch full of tiny little bags of white powder barely

larger than postage stamps was taped to the bottom of the drawer. His skin crawled. That couldn't be... She would never...

He yanked out another drawer and turned it over and found another pouch. Then he pulled out the other four drawers and turned them over and nearly lost his mind.

Hundred-dollar bills sealed up within resealable bags.

He peeled the money off the drawers and counted over thirty thousand dollars in one-hundred-dollar bills. He had no idea what was in the bags, but he knew it had to be some kind of drugs. His big decision now was what the hell to do with it.

When his doorbell rang, his heart nearly stopped. He grabbed his phone to check the camera on his Ring doorbell and saw the delivery guy from DoorDash.

Dinner was served.

He flew down the stairs to retrieve the delivery and hurried back up, frantically locking the door behind him before carrying the food into the kitchen. He was so rattled that he couldn't even remember what he'd ordered and felt the pressure of what was upstairs weighing heavier and heavier on his conscience.

Then, in one of his rare moments of doing the right thing, Mark Roman called the cops on his wife. He didn't care what kind of trouble she was in. All he knew was that he wanted no part of it.

Thirty minutes later, his house was crawling with cops. They were taking the house apart, looking to see if there was more than what he'd found, while a detective from Narcotics was taking his statement.

Mark couldn't quit shaking.

The only positive thing about the whole fiasco was that the cops actually believed him innocent of abetting. It was obvious from the level of shock he was in that he had not been involved, and the text on his phone from his wife, wanting back in the house after she had filed for divorce and moved out, only bolstered his alibi of how he'd found what she'd hidden and his innocence in what she'd been doing.

They didn't find any other drugs, but they did find another stash of money totaling a little over twenty thousand dollars in a Walmart sack hidden in the deep freeze in the garage beneath a ham and a box of steaks.

Megan Roman was going down. She just didn't know it yet.

As the police were leaving, the detective from Narcotics paused, then turned around and gave Mark a stern look.

"Don't call and tell her we're coming, or we'll be coming back for you."

Mark just shuddered, then shook his head. "All I'll be doing tonight is putting my house back together and trying not to puke from the shock of it."

The cop nodded, then went out the door.

Mark locked it behind him, set the security alarm, and then went back to the kitchen. His dinner was cold, and he still hadn't looked in the sack to see what it was, so he shoved it in the fridge, then got out a beer and took it with him to the bedroom.

He took a drink before remaking his bed. Then he headed for the closet to hang up everything that had been tossed, and after that, he put the bathroom back together before he quit. The rest of the mess would be waiting for him tomorrow. And he had to call his divorce lawyer again to let him know about this, as well.

He might still be going to court, but it wouldn't just be divorce court. And it would be his testimony and what the cops recovered that would send his wife to prison.

———

Megan was pissed. She'd waited all this time for Mark to go back to work, only to find out he'd changed the locks. She'd panicked and sent him a text, which went nowhere. Then she got a call from Walt, her father, telling her he'd just fired Mark, which meant he'd be home again.

"Fine, but you just made this mess worse," she muttered.

"No, ma'am. You, darling daughter, are the one who made the mess. Now clean it up," Walt said.

Megan knew he was right and quickly made other arrangements. She knew a guy who could get her into the house the next time Mark left. Then she could get in, get her stuff, and get out without him ever being the wiser.

When her father came home that evening, he knocked on her bedroom door.

"Come in!" Megan called.

Walt opened the door without stepping over the threshold and gave her a look.

Megan rolled her eyes at him. "I'm working on it. I have someone staked out on the house, and the next time he leaves, I'm there."

He nodded. "See you at dinner," he said, and shut the door behind him as he left.

She sighed. Sitting down to dinner with her father and then having an early night sounded like a splendid idea, and she had about an hour to get ready.

It was nearing seven o'clock when Megan left her room. She was coming down the stairs feeling good about herself, wearing a favorite pair of slacks and a red and black silk blouse, when the doorbell rang.

Carmen, their maid, came through the hall to answer, nodding at Megan as she passed, and then opened the door to two detectives flashing badges as they identified themselves, with at least three uniformed officers behind them.

Megan saw them at the same time they saw her, and when they pushed past Carmen and headed toward her waving an arrest warrant, she almost fainted. She thought about running. And she thought about the gun in her purse upstairs. But there was that detective already coming up the stairs after her, so she stayed put.

"Megan Elaine Roman, we have a warrant for your arrest!" he said.

Megan heard him begin informing her of her rights and felt the handcuffs going around her wrists, but none of it felt real.

Carmen was screaming when Walt came out of his study. He saw strangers in the hall surrounding his daughter and began shouting at the staff.

"Call the police! Call the police!"

And then an officer shouted back, "Sir! We are the police! Stand down."

Walt Lanier was in a panic. What the hell just happened?

"What's going on?" he cried, and began walking toward them.

"For starters, your daughter is under arrest for possession and intent to distribute," a detective said.

Walt's disbelief was real, not because of what they'd said, but in disbelief that they knew.

"Megan! What's going on?" he asked.

She was pale and shaking, and in utter shock that this had happened. Mark wouldn't have found anything or turned her in. And her mind was racing about who would have given her up.

"I don't know, Daddy! I truly don't know! Call our lawyer," she cried.

Walt nodded, but his head was spinning. The only upside right now was that they'd come for Megan and not him.

At that point, Megan clammed up and let her father do all the talking. She didn't know how this had happened, but she knew that when Craig Buttoni found out she'd been arrested—and he would find out—her life wouldn't be worth a damn.

———————

Because Katie knew she was going to her new school tomorrow, she dreamed about the old one all night.

She ran throughout the dream, dodging bullets, getting shot, and then the dream would go back to the beginning and start over.

Sometimes she was carrying students.

Sometimes they were all running in front or behind her.

Sometimes Coach Lincoln was beside her and then she was stepping in his blood.

She wanted to wake up, but her sleep was stuck in rewind.

She'd run past windows with her students in her arms, but she could never find a door to get them out of the hall.

And just when she thought she had them all together, she'd realize two were missing, and they were all off and running again, trying to find who was lost, while bullets flew past their heads.

She ran and ran until the alarm went off. She woke up, bathed in sweat and with tears on her face.

"Son of a bitch!" Katie moaned as she slapped a hand on the buzzer to shut it off, then threw back the covers and got up.

She looked at herself in the bathroom mirror, half expecting to see herself covered in blood, but all she saw were the tangles in her hair and the shadows beneath her eyes.

"Damn, girl. You look like a hooker who just pulled an all-nighter," she said, then jabbed the mirror and made a face at herself and turned on the shower.

As soon as she was dressed, she went to the kitchen to make breakfast.

"Nobody should go to school without breakfast. Not even teachers," she said as she carried her plate to the table, then sat down and ate.

Just for something to do, she checked messages on her phone as she was eating—and nearly choked on a bite when she realized she'd missed a call from Mark. She shuddered. Lila had been right. He had tried to contact her.

She took another bite and then proceeded to block that number. She'd already deleted him from her contacts and couldn't imagine what he was thinking. He had to be the most obtuse person walking the face of the earth.

Later, she gathered up her phone and purse and headed out the door.

Roxie's car was in the drive across the street, and Katie could hear squeals and laughter coming from behind the house. She guessed the twins were playing in their backyard.

For a moment, she thought of their father and how difficult it must be to be the chief of police and a single father to two children. Every day, he had to juggle serious responsibilities at work and at home, and hope they didn't overlap. She gave him high marks for perseverance.

Then she glanced at the time and got in her car and drove away.

She knew where the school was. She'd driven past it a couple of times when she was running errands to remind herself how to get to it, but she still drove there with a knot in her stomach. She was about to walk into a school with the expectation of holding her emotions as carefully as she was expected to hold the position for which she'd been hired.

It scared the shit out of her.

She was so focused on not losing control that she almost missed her turn. When she arrived, she parked in the employee parking lot and got out.

The school looked like most every other school she'd ever seen, but smaller. A long, rectangular building with lots of windows and a sidewalk that led from the curb at the street to a set of steps leading into the entrance.

There was a flagpole out front, with a flag flapping in the breeze. The grounds were green and recently mowed, with huge shade trees lining both sides of the sidewalk—a most picturesque approach to education.

Katie's stomach was in knots as she entered the building, but then she paused and took a breath. She could have been blind and still recognized it as a school. It smelled just like all school buildings. Old walls. The scents of industrial-strength cleaners and generations of sweaty little bodies having run up and down these halls.

But she also imagined she could feel the energy of educators, persevering regardless of their situations, teaching with what they had, doing without what they needed, still doing a good job, and still helping little people grow.

There were goose bumps on her arms as she approached the office directly in front of her, and then she opened the door and went inside.

The secretary's desk was empty, but Katie had already been told to bypass it and go straight to the office behind it. The door was open, and she called out.

"Katie McGrath approaching!"

Susan Wayne appeared in the doorway, smiling.

"Welcome! Come in my office," she said.

Katie eyed the principal as she sat down, thinking Susan was shorter than she had imagined, but her voice was soft, her eyes were kind, and she had an infectious smile. Katie felt welcome and comfortable.

"Welcome to Borden's Gap Elementary. Have you settled in at your residence?" Susan asked.

"Yes. Thank you for giving me Louise's contact information. She made finding a house easy," Katie said.

Susan smiled. "Excellent. Now, before I give you the grand tour, I want you to know that I will go out of my way to make this transition easier for you, because you're worth it. And I don't say that lightly. So if there's something here that is triggering to you, I will remove it. Okay?"

"I don't expect special treatment," Katie whispered.

"Doesn't matter. You deserve it, so there's that."

Katie blinked as the first tears welled and rolled down her cheeks. She swallowed, then nodded.

"Thank you."

"Anytime," Susan said, then opened her desk drawer, pulled out some keys, and stood. "Let's go for a walk. It's just you and me, so if something freaks you out, say so."

Katie felt like someone had just wrapped her up in a great big hug. It was okay if she got rattled. It was going to be okay if she froze. It was going to be okay because Susan Wayne had her back. She took a deep breath, then exhaled as the emotional target fell off her back.

They walked from one end of the building to the other without issue, even though she kept fighting the urge to look over her shoulder as they went. Halfway down the hall, she realized there was a whole other wing not visible from the street.

Susan pointed to it as they passed. "We serve kindergarten through sixth grade here. There is a gymnasium that also serves as an auditorium when the need arises.

The youngest students' classrooms are closest to the cafeteria. We have staggered dining times, with the earliest beginning at 11:00 a.m., which will include kindergarten and first and second grades."

"The blessing of smaller schools. No long walks to the cafeteria," Katie said. "That's wonderful."

"Was that an issue?" Susan asked as they continued walking.

Katie looked down a moment before she answered. "We were not in our classroom when the shooting started. We were in the hall on our way to the cafeteria with no immediate place to shelter."

Susan shuddered. "Every teacher's nightmare," and then she pointed. "Your classroom is coming up on the right. And the doors to the cafeteria are right in front of us." She pulled out her keys and unlocked the door. Her eyes were twinkling as she stepped aside. "I can't carry you across the threshold, but I want you to go in first, with the intention of claiming the space as your own."

"Thank you," Katie said, then opened the door, stepped in, and began turning on lights.

There was a wall of windows in front of her with all the shades drawn. A set of cabinets and a small sink were along the wall to her right, and a large storage closet stood at the end of the room with deep shelves on three sides.

There were cubbies for each student and pegs on the wall for them to hang coats. It didn't have the same white walls and tile floors as her other classroom and was definitely an older building, but in a weird way, it felt cozier.

"I like this," Katie said.

Susan beamed. "Good. We try to keep surroundings simple but comfortable for the little ones." Then she began filling Katie in on all of the technology she would have in her room. "They furnish each first grade with four computers. You will be given a school laptop, along with keys to the building and to your room. You will be free to come work on setting up your room and the bulletin board outside your door any time after the first of August, and we'll be bringing the tables and chairs for centers back into the room next week."

Katie was already getting ideas and becoming excited about the prospect of being back in school.

"Do you know how many students I will have?" Katie asked.

"No more than twenty, and likely less," Susan said. "You're free to set up your centers however you wish. The first-grade curriculum is the same for both first grades, but you already know that. The other first-grade teacher, Marcy Kincaid, who you met during our Zoom meeting, will be your teammate. You two will coordinate curriculum. I'm assuming you are familiar with this teaching format?"

"Yes. There were four classes of each grade level where I taught before."

"Then you're downsizing, while will be an adjustment," Susan said, smiling.

"Maybe, but a welcome one," Katie said.

They proceeded into the cafeteria, but just as Susan was showing Katie the exits from cafeteria to playground, there was a loud boom above their heads and then the sound of running feet.

Katie gasped, jumped, and then broke out in a cold sweat.

Susan immediately grasped her arm, talking quickly to alleviate Katie's panic.

"Oh no! I forgot to tell you there is a crew on the roof. We had a leak last time it rained, and they're applying a fresh layer of tar. I'm so sorry. Are you okay?"

Katie's heart was pounding. "Yes. It just startled me."

"Don't apologize," Susan said. "It scared me, too. Now, let's head back up to my office and I'll get your supplies for you."

A short while later, Katie left the building carrying a tote bag with the school logo on it. It had her school laptop and a folder with more info in it. It was another thing grounding her to this place. As she reached her car, she looked back at the school and saw the roofing crew.

"Nearly died of a heart attack before I even got started," she muttered.

She drove home long enough to drop off the laptop and tote bag, and then drove back uptown to the pharmacy.

She was getting out of the car when her cell rang.

"Hello?"

"Katie, it's Louise. I forgot to mention that yard mowing comes with the rent, so you don't worry about that. The man who mows my yard will mow yours as well. You don't have to be home. Just know it's being taken care of."

"Oh, that's wonderful," Katie said. "Thank you."

―――――

Sam was in the first aid aisle with a shopping basket over his arm, gathering up items for the jailhouse, when he saw

Katie walk in. She paused in the doorway, scanning the signs over the little aisles to figure out where she needed to go, and then headed for skin care. He was on the far side of the pharmacy where he knew she couldn't see him, and he debated whether he should go speak to her. But when she tucked her hair behind her ear, giving him a clear view of her profile, he decided to stand his ground and enjoy the view instead.

As she began moving down the aisle, he moved with her, gathering up more first-aid items. When she meandered toward a shelf of bath products, he stopped, wondering if she'd go for shower gel or bubble bath.

She put a bottle of bubble bath in her basket, and his gut knotted, imagining her climbing out of a tub with tiny clusters of bubbles still stuck to her skin. And then the moment he thought it, he chided himself.

Dang it, Youngblood. What the hell's wrong with you?

That was an image he did not need to live with, so he immediately looked away. He checked his list against what he had in the basket, then went back up the aisle, replacing the items he didn't need, and headed for the register to check out. And then he heard footsteps behind him, caught a whiff of lilac, and wondered if that was her.

He got all the way to the register before he turned around. She was smiling at him, but those shadows in her eyes were still there.

"Hello, Katie. You look really pretty today."

"Thank you. I toured the school today, so I wanted to look my best. And I met my principal. It's been a good day."

Then the clerk interrupted.

"Hey, Chief. Do we bill the PD for this stuff?"

"Yes. It's for the jail," Sam said, and then turned back to Katie while the clerk rang up the items, but she'd run back to pick up something she'd forgotten.

Accepting that he'd missed his chance, he grabbed the sack with his purchases and was on his way out as she came hurrying back up front.

He turned and waved.

She smiled, waved back, and then slid her basket onto the counter as he went out the door.

Sam sighed. *Dammit.* Then he got in the cruiser and drove back to the station.

———

Katie watched through the plate-glass windows as he walked toward the cruiser, measuring the width of his shoulders and his long legs as he got in and drove away. He looked like a man fully capable of handling the aspects of his job. She wouldn't let herself think of him beyond the fact that he was a neighbor and the chief of police. She didn't want to be attracted to anyone. Or want anyone attracted to her. Right now, Katie was all about self-preservation.

———

Craig Buttoni was at the Las Vegas airport, about to get on a plane to Chicago, when he got a text from Walt Lanier.

> FYI. Megan was arrested. It was not circum-
> stantial. I just bonded her out. She's been
> living with me, so I'll likely be next. But she's
> going to need a top-notch lawyer, and that's
> on you. I'm already gone.

Craig grunted like he'd been punched in the gut.
Lawyer? Like hell.

He stepped out of line and headed for a secluded corner of the boarding area and made a call. It rang twice, and then a man answered.

"Cleaning Service."

"We have an emergency at the Walter Lanier residence in Albuquerque. Contact Megan Roman regarding cleanup."

"Understood," the man said, and disconnected.

Craig dropped his phone back in his pocket and headed for the ticket agent at the check-in desk. He got in line, but it was all going too slow for his comfort, and he kept shifting his carry-on from one shoulder to the other. His palms were itching. And at any moment, he expected someone to come up behind him, tap him on the shoulder, and arrest him in the middle of the airport.

And then finally the person in front of him was gone and he stepped up to the desk.

"Ma'am, I just got a message that will require me to change my plans. I will not be boarding the plane to Chicago after all. I need to be on the next flight to London. Can you help me?"

Megan went to jail, thinking it was the most mortifying time of her life, and she was right. The holding cell was like something out of a dystopian nightmare. A single toilet against a grimy wall. Old mattresses without bedclothes on the cot frames.

And she wasn't alone. She took one look at the two other women in the cell with her, and when they nudged each other and then started catcalling and making snarky comments, she knew she was out of her league.

A lanky, too-thin woman with big boobs, a pockmarked face, and a leather miniskirt with a matching leather bustier cackled out a laugh and pointed at Megan.

"Damn, Leezy… Look what we got here. Hey, bitch, is that blouse real silk? I always wanted a real silk blouse."

Megan's gut knotted. She was scared half out of her mind, but she couldn't let them know it. Either she got her point across now, or she was toast. It took everything she had to walk toward them, but she needed to get in their faces. And once she had their attention, her eyes narrowed, and her voice went soft and emotionless as she looked from one to the other.

"You! The toothless wonder. And you! The dominatrix with the stick-on nails. I'm already pissed, and you do not want me shifting into full-blown rage, because the medicine I take to keep from slitting people's throats is still in my purse…at home. So don't think for a fucking minute that the two of you have any leverage over me. Don't look at me again. Don't talk to me. And whatever the hell you do, don't touch me. Because I will willingly die before I quit trying to kill you. Understood?"

They nodded, wide-eyed and silent.

Megan looked them up and down, and then turned her back on the both of them and went back to her cot, sat down with her back against the wall, and pulled her legs up into a lotus position and closed her eyes.

The women wouldn't look at each other, and they wouldn't look at her again. The toothless wonder lay down on her cot with her back to the wall, afraid to close her eyes, and the dominatrix needed to pee, but the toilet was too close to that crazy bitch's bed, so she sat down on the side of her cot and held it.

———————

Hours later, the two hookers made bail and were gone. Megan spent the night in the holding cell alone. She was arraigned before noon the next day, and the family lawyer bonded her out of jail, then called an Uber for her and sent her on her way. But when Megan arrived home without keys, she had to ring the doorbell.

Carmen answered. "Miss Megan! Welcome home!" Carmen said, and quickly stepped aside.

"Thank you," Megan said. "Where's Daddy? I need to talk to him."

Carmen ducked her head. "We don't know. He left with suitcases last night. He did not tell us where he was going."

Megan ran upstairs to grab her cell phone and called his number, but it went to voicemail. Then she called his office. His secretary answered.

"Lanier and Associates, CPA."

"Barbie, this is Megan. I need to speak to Dad."

"I'm sorry, Megan. He's not here. There was a message on my phone when I got to work this morning to refer his clients to the other CPAs until further notice."

"Did he say where he was going?" Megan asked.

"No, ma'am."

"Okay, thanks. I'm sure there's just been a miscommunication between us. He's probably somewhere on a plane, assuming I know where he is."

She hung up, absolutely certain that was not the case. He'd gotten her out of jail, but he'd abandoned her to save himself, which meant there was now no one standing between her and Buttoni.

The panic she felt was evident in her voice when she called their lawyer, Keith Voight. The moment he answered, she dumped her reality into his lap.

"Keith! My dad is gone, which means he knows the authorities will eventually link him to what they have on me. And when our boss finds out I was arrested, my life won't be worth shit. He doesn't leave people behind who could bring him down. Can you reach out to the feds? See if I have anything worth bargaining for?"

"I'll see what I can do," Keith said. "Just stay calm and stay put. I'll get back to you."

"Easy for you to say," Megan said, and then got on the house phone.

Carmen answered.

"Yes, Miss Megan?"

"This is to inform you and the rest of the staff that I am not seeing visitors, so do not let anyone in the house. Do you understand? No one."

"Yes, ma'am," Carmen said, but she was shocked.

They were still reeling from Megan's arrest and finding out she'd been involved in drug trafficking. Then when Walt disappeared last night carrying a butt-load of suitcases without explanation, they were leery of even being here.

Carmen gathered the rest of the staff to inform them of the new orders and then bravely spoke up about their own well-being.

"I tell you, I am scared. First the cops stormed the place. Then Mr. Walt left without telling us where he was going or if he'd be back. Now the boss lady is out of jail, and giving us orders not to let anyone in the house? So who is she afraid of? Not the cops. It has to be the people she and Mr. Walt worked for. I'm not going to be collateral damage when they come after her. I quit."

Then she took off her apron and headed for her room. Within thirty minutes, she was packed and gone.

The gardener didn't live on the premises, but he agreed with Carmen. He abandoned the job he'd been working at outside and got in his truck and drove away, prompting the two women from the cleaning service to do the same.

The house was empty now but for Megan, who was curled up on her bed, two sleeping pills to the good, and drooling on her pillow.

═══════════

Buttoni's hit man was staked out on-site at Walt Lanier's property. He'd seen his target get out of an Uber and go into the house, so he settled in to wait for the landscaper and the cleaning company to leave the premises before making his move.

Then all of a sudden, staff began coming out of the house and piling into their vehicles in haste. He didn't know what had taken place inside, but watching them leaving the property was like seeing rats abandoning a sinking ship.

From all appearances, his target was alone in the house, or enough so that it made no difference, and he was not a man for wasting time. Whatever video they would get of him would never give him away. His disguises and stolen vehicles were part of his wardrobe, and he did not leave DNA behind.

He drove onto the premises in a delivery van he'd hot-wired from a bakery company, then went around back as if he was dropping off deliveries. He was already wearing a wig, a fake mustache, and sunglasses, and once he put on a pair of surgical gloves and a cap, his own mother wouldn't have known him. He got out of the van, grabbed a couple of bags of bakery goods from the back of the van, and headed for the service entrance.

He tried the doorknob, expecting it to be locked, and when it wasn't, he grinned. Whatever had prompted the rats to abandon ship, they forgot to lock up behind them. He walked inside, set the sacks on the counter, and pulled his handgun from the inside of his jacket, testing to make sure the silencer was secure on the barrel before he started through the house.

He quickly cleared all of the rooms on the first floor and then headed upstairs. He knew Megan Roman was still here somewhere because he'd watched her go in and she was not with any of the others who'd come out.

He found her in a lavender and pink bedroom, lying curled up on her side on a canopy bed with her back to the door, sound asleep.

He walked all the way to her bedside, looked carefully to make sure she was his target, then picked up a loose pillow near her feet, laid it lightly over her head, shoved the barrel into the pillow, and pulled the trigger.

She jerked.

It was the only reaction to her exit out of this world.

He lifted the pillow to make sure she was done, laid it back on her head, and walked out.

———————

Unaware of the spreading carnage from turning in his wife, Mark was at home, depressed, despondent, and sending out résumés. He'd already accepted his fault in all this. He was a shallow excuse for a man, and his comeuppance was both shameful and painful.

Megan Lanier's pursuit had stoked his ego beyond anything he'd ever experienced. She was the wild hair he should have gotten out of his system during his college years, but had not.

He felt like such a patsy. He'd done the books for the company. But looking back, they were the set of books the IRS saw. He was so drawn into the lifestyle of wealth and privilege that he never thought about how Walt Lanier managed this exorbitant lifestyle. But after what Mark had found out about Megan, it was all making sense now.

He wondered if they'd laughed about him. The socially

inept accountant who'd walked away from the woman he loved because she was a simple schoolteacher. Because of being the asshole he was, he had weighed being married to a woman who'd been a throwaway kid and didn't even know her bloodline against the cachet of a socialite who happened to be his boss's daughter. He'd chosen the rich one, thinking that would elevate him socially and financially, until karma came knocking.

A part of him wished he was a kid again, still living on the family farm in Kansas. He'd hated that life, but it sounded like paradise now.

He fell asleep on the living room sofa, woke up some time in the middle of the night and took himself off to bed, then woke up again the next morning as the garbage truck was going by and cursed.

He'd forgotten to put out the trash.

———

Keith Voight was beginning to worry. He'd been trying to call Megan Roman all morning, but she'd never picked up. She'd been in such a panic for help last night, and now she wasn't answering her phone.

It didn't make sense.

Finally, he called the police and requested a welfare check on her at the Lanier property. He told them about her recent arrest on drug charges, that she had just bonded out, and that the last conversation he'd had with her she'd seemed afraid for her safety.

Two officers, Officer Taylor and Officer Sutter, were

sent out to the property. Sutter rang the front doorbell, but no one came to the door.

"A place this size is gonna have staff," Sutter said. "Taylor, go around back and see if anyone answers at the service entrance."

Taylor nodded and quickly circled the house.

A couple of minutes later, he opened the front door and started talking.

"The back door was unlocked. Her car is in the garage, but no one seems to be on the property."

At that point, Sutter walked inside, and together they began going through the house, calling out "Albuquerque PD" over and over.

But no one answered.

They cleared the downstairs before heading up and almost immediately found the body.

"Is that her?" Taylor asked.

Sutter pulled up the mug shots from Megan Roman's arrest.

"Yep, that's her. Call Homicide. Tell them we need detectives and the crime lab out here ASAP, then get the scene secured. This looks like a hit. I'll stay with the body."

And that's how Keith Voight found out his client was dead and her father was gone.

With Walt Lanier missing, the police only had one family member to notify, and that was Mark Roman. Even though divorce papers had been filed, Mark was still Megan's legal next of kin.

Chapter Nine

MARK WAS NUKING A CHICKEN POT PIE WHEN HIS CELL phone rang. He picked it up from the kitchen counter, saw caller ID, and frowned.

"Hello, this is Mark."

"Mr. Roman, this is Detective Clyburn, Homicide. I am sorry to inform you that your wife was found deceased in her family home this morning. There was no one else on the property."

"Oh my God! What happened?" Mark asked.

"She was in bed. She'd been shot once in the back of the head."

Mark was crying and didn't know it. "It's all because of the drugs and money, isn't it? Someone was afraid she'd talk. Wait! Where's Walt? Where's her father? Was he killed, too?"

"We don't know where he is. He isn't answering his phone. There was no staff on the premises. We are trying to locate and interview people who worked there, but for now that's all we know. We understand you two were in the middle of a divorce, but technically, you're still married, which makes you the next of kin. Her body has been taken to the morgue for autopsy. You'll be notified when it's being released for burial."

Mark wiped away tears, and cleared his throat.

"I have to ask. Was Walt in the business with Megan?"

"We're still gathering evidence," Clyburn said.

"He was, wasn't he? Oh my God. This is a nightmare that won't end," Mark mumbled.

"I'm sorry for your loss," Clyburn said. "We'll be in touch."

Long after Clyburn had disconnected, Mark was still holding his phone and staring off into space. It was the *ding* from the microwave, signaling his pot pie was done, that brought him back to focus.

He put the pie on a plate and set it aside. Eating was the last thing on his mind. So Walt was in the wind, which meant the company would be floundering without the boss. Why did he feel like he'd just escaped a bullet by getting fired—with pay—before everything fell in?

And there was still that phone call to make to his lawyer because he wasn't getting a divorce from Megan after all. Just paying for the funeral to bury her.

———

Megan Roman's murder made the local and national news. Having a well-known Albuquerque socialite arrested for drug trafficking was scandalous. Finding out she was murdered the same day she was released on bail was a shocking but obvious message. She'd known too much to stay alive.

———

Walt Lanier was at a hotel bar in Mexico, nursing a drink and waiting for his food to arrive, when the story came on the TV. He understood Spanish well enough to know that his daughter was dead. She'd been murdered in her bed.

For a few moments, he thought he was going to pass out. Buttoni hadn't called a lawyer. He'd called a hit man.

Walt forgot about the food, ordered a bottle of tequila, and took it to his room. The ocean view from there was picture perfect... Blue skies. Bluer water. White sands. But he didn't see it.

Everywhere he looked, he saw Megan. As a baby, being placed in his arms. As a child, running to him and laughing. As a teenager, growing into the selfish, demanding woman he'd taught her to be.

He sat down on the side of the bed with the bottle in his hands, then closed his eyes and saw the look on her face when the police took her out of the house. It was the same look she'd always given him, expecting him to fix what was broken.

He looked out at the ocean. Tears were running down his face. There was a part of him wishing he'd stayed with her. He would have died with her. Instead, he'd fed her to their respective shark and saved himself.

But the longer he sat, the more certain he was that he wasn't safe from Buttoni, either. He'd just prolonged his demise. Megan was gone, but he was still connected to her, which meant the cops would be after him, which meant he was a threat. He was a loose end, and it was only a matter of time before Buttoni tied it up.

Despair washed through him like a hurricane through an open window. He opened the tequila, took a big swing from the bottle, then got a glass from a tray off the minibar and got shit-faced drunk.

Craig Buttoni was on a plane over the ocean when the news broke on TV, so he was unaware that his request had been fulfilled. But when he landed in London, the first message he received was: "Cleanup successful."

He smiled. *As expected.* Then he grabbed a cab to his hotel.

As soon as he'd checked in, he paid the cleaner via bank transfer and went to bed. He never could sleep on planes. He was exhausted from the flight, and he had another plane to catch tomorrow evening.

He'd always meant to go to Monaco, and the farther away he was from New Mexico right now, the better off he would be.

The old-world charm and the casinos of Monte Carlo beckoned.

Now that Katie had the school visit behind her and her things unpacked, she was at loose ends about what to do with herself. The next day she walked out to the mailbox at the curb to see if her mail had caught up with her yet, but it had not. She paused a moment, looking up and then down the street, and for the first time really looked at the beautiful trees in the neighborhood.

The weather was warm. The sky was a picturesque conglomeration of blue sky and white puffy clouds, and she had an urge to go for a walk. The only thing stopping her was her reticence to step out into unfamiliar territory, and she needed to get over that. She went back inside to get her phone, changed into her running shoes, then grabbed a bottle of water and her sunglasses and locked the door behind her as she left.

Without thinking, she turned left, taking the route she drove to get to Main, and set off with an easy stride. Throughout her adult life, she'd been faithful about staying fit, and it was all because of a scare on campus while she was still in college. While walking home one night after work, she was accosted near her campus apartment but managed to escape without coming to actual harm. After that, she enrolled in a martial arts class and wound up with a black belt. She'd never had to use the skills, but after moving to New Mexico, she'd stayed in practice at her local gym. There was no gym in Borden's Gap, but there were still plenty of places to walk, and today was her maiden voyage afoot.

The sun was warm, but it felt good, so she lengthened her stride and kept moving past the houses, admiring the lush growth of everything blooming and everything green.

A teenage boy was mowing a yard at a house across the street, and when he saw the pretty stranger, he stopped and stared until Katie waved.

Startled to have been caught gawking, he managed an embarrassed grin and went back to his mowing.

An elderly woman sitting in a chair on her front porch was reading so intently that she didn't see Katie as she passed by, but the man coming down the street in a blue pickup truck not only saw her but rolled down the window and whistled at her as he drove past.

A little startled by his unabashed flirting, Katie kept her gaze on the sidewalk and kept moving.

She was almost at Main Street when she saw that same old dirty pickup truck and the same man driving that she'd seen at Welby's Grocery when she first arrived. He glanced at her as he passed and then looked away.

Katie shuddered, then took a big drink and kept walking, refusing to let anyone mess up her good day. Even one of the local creeps.

She paused to admire a grand old house surrounded by an overgrowth of shrubbery and thought she saw movement on the porch.

All of a sudden, a little Yorkie darted into view and then scampered down the steps and started a kind of running bounce toward the street.

She heard a woman's faint cry of dismay, then saw the owner, an elderly woman with a crown of white hair, coming down the steps far slower than her puppy. Without hesitating, Katie bolted across the street to try to catch the dog before it got away.

"Rhett! Rhett Butler…you come back here right now!" the old woman shouted.

Katie was loping toward Rhett the Yorkie, trying not to laugh at the name.

The Yorkie spied her and took a right, bouncing like a rabbit as it changed directions.

"Oh no!" the old woman cried, and then clapped her hands. "Rhett! Come here to Mama! Come here right now!"

Rhett was either deaf or not interested in the invitation

and kept running up the street. But those tiny legs were no match for Katie's long ones. She not only outran him, but got in front of him and scooped him up before he had time to change directions again.

The moment she picked him up, he licked her nose.

Katie laughed. "Oh my lord. You *are* something of a lover, aren't you? But kisses will get you nowhere with me. You scared your mama, you little imp."

Rhett had nothing to add and happily let her carry him home, panting like he'd just run a mile.

Katie met up with the old woman at the end of her drive and handed him over.

The woman hugged the little Yorkie to her.

"Bad boy, Rhett. Bad boy. Running from Mama like that."

Rhett licked her nose. He had his moves down pat.

Then the woman looked up at Katie and sighed.

"Sugar, I don't know who you are, but thank you for catching my baby. He's such a bad boy, and I'm getting too old to walk him like I used to. Oh…and excuse my manners. I'm Delilah Cash, and this is Rhett Butler."

Katie smiled. "So nice to meet you, Delilah. I'm Katie McGrath. And Rhett and I have already met and traded kisses," she said.

"I don't believe I know you," Delilah said. "Are you visiting here? Maybe I know your people."

The simple Southern way of connecting felt charming to Katie, even though she had no people.

"I just moved here. I'll be teaching first grade when the school year begins."

Delilah smiled again. "Oh! You rented Louise's cottage

with the blue door. She keeps that for special people, so you must be special. Welcome to Borden's Gap."

"Thank you," Katie said.

Rhett yapped, and they both laughed.

"He was welcoming you, too," Delilah said. "I'm sure glad you were out walking or he'd still be running. My granddaughter used to walk Rhett for me, but she's gone away to college now."

"I'll be walking most every day that the weather allows until I start work," Katie said. "I'd be more than happy to swing by here and take your lover boy for a little trot around the block."

"Really?" Delilah said. "That would be so thoughtful of you. He's ten years old, so a walk around the block is more than enough. He usually gets carried the last block home."

"I can do that," Katie said.

"I'd pay you," Delilah offered.

"No, ma'am. It would be my pleasure. I don't have a man in my life, and who wouldn't want Rhett Butler."

Delilah clapped her hands. "This is just wonderful. Do you want to start tomorrow, or—"

"How about right now? I can walk him a couple of blocks, then head back this way."

"What about the dog poop?"

Katie threw back her head and laughed. "I teach first-graders. I've had throw-up in my lap, in my shoes, and down the back of my shirt while I was sitting down. Picking up a little dog poop in a plastic bag is nothing. Let's go get Rhett's leash and a pooper bag, and you get yourself something cold to drink and wait on the porch for us to come back. Okay?"

"You are so precious," Delilah said. "I don't know how to thank you," she added as they started toward the house.

"I don't need thanks. This will be a delight, and it will give you time to find someone permanent to walk him."

"Perfect," Delilah said, and once they reached the house, she handed Rhett back to Katie. "Give me a couple of minutes."

"Don't rush. We'll just be here standing in the shade having ourselves a drink," Katie said. And as soon as the old woman went inside, Katie poured a little of her water into an indentation in the sidewalk, and Rhett promptly lapped it up. "More?" she asked, and poured a little more.

The little Yorkie lapped that up, too, and then waited for Katie to pick him up again.

Delilah returned. They clipped the leash on Rhett, and Katie stuffed the pooper bag into her back pocket.

The moment Katie clipped the leash onto Rhett's collar, he turned his head, picked up the leash in his mouth, and waited for her to start walking.

"Oh, I forgot to mention, Rhett likes to be in charge of his leash. He takes himself for walks. All you have to do is hang on," Delilah said.

Katie was in love. "This is the best day I've had in a very long time. Thank you, Delilah. We'll see you soon."

Delilah waved them off, then climbed the steps back up to her verandah and sat down. So now she'd met the new teacher. She was one up on all of her friends and couldn't wait to tell them what a sweetheart Katie was.

Sam was on his way to the house to drop off lunch and groceries for Roxie and the girls when he saw Katie walking toward him on the opposite side of the street. He recognized Rhett Butler immediately because at one time or another, all of the officers in town had been put on alert that the little Yorkie was on the run. Rhett Butler had more BOLOs on him than a hardened criminal.

Sam slowed a bit just so he could look at Katie longer. Like Rhett, she walked with a bounce in her step and her chin up. Even though she was wearing sunglasses, he couldn't help but notice how happy she appeared, and when she suddenly saw him driving toward her, she waved and smiled.

Sam's heart skipped a beat as he gave her a thumbs-up.

After he'd driven past, he wished he'd stopped long enough to say hello. When he'd dropped off the groceries, he retraced his path, but she was gone. As he drove back to the station, he couldn't help but wonder how she and Delilah Cash had come to meet. It must have been a momentous occasion for Delilah to let Katie walk her precious Yorkie.

Less than an hour after he got back to the station, a dangerous situation arose. The Tennessee Highway Patrol was in pursuit of Leif Munson, an inmate who had escaped from the jail in Nashville. It was reported that he'd hotwired a car and made it out of the city, then robbed and beat up an elderly couple in Jackson before stealing a hunting rifle and their car.

Borden's Gap had been given a heads-up because the inmate had grown up in the hills east of town and was suspected to be heading that way.

The moment Sam found out, he headed straight to dispatch.

"Frank, dispatch all available officers to the west edge of town, ASAP. I want roadblocks set up on the far side of the city limit signs. This is the BOLO I received. Give them a heads-up on the car, but do not read out the driver's name on the radio because everyone in town who has a scanner would hear it."

"Will do, Chief, but why not?" Frank asked.

"Because the escapee grew up in the area. I'll be on scene," Sam said, and took off out the back.

Frank's eyes widened, but he never said another word and began dispatching officers and relaying orders.

Everything but the immediate need to stop a felon went out of Sam's mind. They couldn't let him get past the roadblock and go flying through town, putting everyone in danger.

He called Roxie on the way and told her to stay inside with the girls until she heard from him, then ran hot out of town with lights flashing and his siren screaming, with other patrol cars converging behind him, heading west out of town.

Within minutes of their arrival, Sam and his officers had their patrol cars parked at angles blocking the highway and portable barriers and stop strips in place.

Their radios were crackling with updates, and they had advised the highway patrol of the evasive tactics they had in place. They were each standing behind an open door on their patrol cars, weapons drawn, braced for whatever was coming at them.

They'd cut the sirens, but the lights were flashing. The sun was at their backs, which meant it would be in the escaped prisoner's eyes. Every man standing knew Leif Munson, and this situation had just put them on opposite sides of the law.

Sam glanced at his officers. "Everybody okay?"

"I'm good," Carl said.

"We've got this," Ben echoed.

Sweat was running out from under their hats, running into their eyes and down the backs of their necks, as they stood braced and waiting.

Then they began to hear the sound of an engine coming so fast that it sounded like a whine, and within the whine, the bleating sounds of the sirens of the highway patrol still in pursuit.

"They're coming!" Sam said, and in that moment, he thought of nothing but getting this right so they could all go home tonight.

All of a sudden, sirens were coming up behind them, too. Three other highway patrol cars coming in from the west to back up the roadblock.

"Hell yes," he muttered as the patrol cars came to a sliding halt behind them and officers jumped out and took a stance behind the doors of their vehicles with weapons drawn.

And then a car came over the hill so fast it was little more than a gray blur, and Carl let out a soft groan.

"Oh hell, Chief. He ain't gonna stop."

"Yes, he is. We're going to stop him," Sam said.

The car kept coming closer and closer, and Sam tensed. His gut told him Munson was ready to die and didn't care who he took with him.

Son of a bitch.

When Munson hit the stop strips, all four tires blew. The car slid sideways, then began to roll before finally coming to a halt, upside down. Before officers could grab their fire extinguishers, the gas tank exploded and the car burst in flames.

Sam radioed the station to dispatch fire and EMS, while every cop there was running toward the wreck with their fire extinguishers. He grabbed his and followed, but it was too late to save the driver. The car was fully engulfed.

━━━━━━━

Those with scanners knew something big was going down, and the news had spread like wildfire throughout the town. When they heard the explosion, people who were inclined to pray were already down on their knees.

Roxie had the television turned up extra loud and had given the girls a bowl of popcorn and juice boxes as they were watching cartoons.

They were used to sirens. That just meant Daddy was working. But when the explosion happened, Evie looked up.

"Miss Roxie, what was that sound?"

Roxie shrugged. "I don't know. We'll have to ask Daddy when he comes home."

Satisfied with the answer, the girls went back to cartoons.

But Roxie was still worried. When there was trouble, Sam always let her know he was okay when it was over, and she'd heard nothing.

Katie was on her way back to Delilah's house within thirty minutes, carrying Rhett the last block. The Yorkie showed his appreciation with constant chin and nose licks, and by the time Katie handed him and the sack of poop back to Delilah, she'd fallen hard.

"Thank you so much," Delilah said as she dropped the sack in her garbage and took Rhett by his leash.

"It was my pleasure," Katie said. "Around the same time tomorrow?"

"Yes, please," Delilah said.

"Oh…do you have a cell phone?" Katie asked.

"No. I still have my landline."

"If you'll give me your number, I'll call you when I get home and you can write down my number. That way if something happens to change your routine, all you have to do is call and let me know."

"Oh, good idea," Delilah said, and recited the numbers while Katie entered them into her contacts.

"Got it," Katie said. "I'll call you after I get home." Then she scratched Rhett's little head. "Bye, buddy. I'll see you tomorrow," she said.

Rhett yapped.

Katie laughed.

"I think you have made a friend. He's telling you goodbye," Delilah said.

"I made two friends today. You and Rhett," Katie said, then walked down the steps and back to the street and headed home.

She was hot and hungry and thinking about what to eat for lunch when she began hearing sirens. She thought of Sam. What was it like for people married to cops? She was about to set herself up to worry when her cell phone rang.

When she saw it was Lila, that distracted her.

"Hello, my friend!"

"Hey, Katie. Do you have a few minutes?" Lila asked.

"I do. I've been out for a walk and am on my way home. What's up?"

"Watch your national news tonight. Mark and Megan made the news and not in a good way."

Katie stopped in the middle of the sidewalk.

"What happened?"

Lila began reciting the sequence of events of Mark finding drugs and money and turning Megan in, then her getting bonded out of jail and going home to find out her father was missing.

Katie was horrified. "Oh my God! I can't wrap my head around this. I met Walt Lanier several times during the three years Mark and I were together. I can't believe he was mixed up in drug trafficking. I never liked Megan the few times I saw her, but I'm blown away by the extent of criminal activities they were in. Is Mark implicated?"

"The authorities say he is not. It appears when he found the evidence, he called the police. He was going to be a witness in Megan's trial, but that's no longer happening," Lila said.

"Why?" Katie asked.

"Because after Megan bonded out of jail, she went

home and went to bed, and sometime afterward, she was murdered in her bed. They're calling it a hit and looking for her father."

Katie gasped. "Murdered? No! He wouldn't kill her. He must be dead, too."

"He left the night before she came home…like he knew something was going to happen."

Katie started walking again, talking as she went.

"This is shocking and horrible, and I can't believe I know someone who's mixed up in this mess. I miss you, but right now the last place I would want to be is in Albuquerque, facing the media as the woman Mark jilted to marry a criminal who just got whacked."

"Oh wow. I never thought of how this might fall back on you in any way."

"Well, the criminal part would not, but you know the media these days and how they like to report all the dirt before they bother with the truth."

"I'm sorry. I hated to call you with this, but I didn't want you to be blindsided by it when you heard it on the news, because it's gone national."

"No, I appreciate you letting me know. Are you and Mr. Right still okay?"

"We're great," Lila said. "However, knowing what a scuz Mark Roman turned out to be after seeming so perfect has made me leery of men in general, and Mr. Right knows it. And now this. My head is spinning. Instead of divorcing Megan, he's going to have to bury her. He's legally her next of kin."

"Sorry she was murdered. Sorry Mark is in such a mess, but he chose that woman and all that came with her."

"I agree. We'll talk again soon, and hopefully with a better subject," Lila said. "Love you."

"Love you, too," Katie said, and increased her stride. Now she just wanted back in her house to regroup.

None of this had anything to do with her, but it still felt like someone had pinned that target on her back again. As she was walking, she remembered to call Delilah to give her cell number.

Delilah answered, then grabbed a pen and paper.

"Okay, Katie. I'm ready."

Katie gave out her number, listening as Delilah read it back.

"Yes, that's correct," she said, and then heard Delilah sigh, most likely with relief.

"Thank you so much for doing this," Delilah said.

"It is my pleasure," Katie said, and kept walking, but all she could think about was Mark, and drug trafficking, and now a murder.

Dammit. She wanted to forget Mark Roman had ever existed.

She was going up the driveway to her house when she heard more sirens and realized they were coming from out of town and passing through. Now she was beginning to get worried all over again as she let herself in.

Being the newcomer in town meant she had no one to call for info, so she went to wash up and then headed to the kitchen to make herself a sandwich.

A few minutes later, she was sitting at the kitchen table, reading her Dinah McCall book as she ate, when she heard what sounded like an explosion. Was it gunfire?

All of a sudden, the kitchen faded from view and she

was back in the hall in Saguaro Elementary, waiting for a bullet in the back. She jumped up and ran, looking for her students until she reached the end of the hall and then realized where she was at.

Her heart was pounding and the shooting had stopped. Was that just her imagination, or had she heard real gunshots? And if they were real, what had happened? Was there danger anywhere nearby?

She stood for a few moments, staring blindly up the hall, waiting, but nothing happened. All was quiet again.

Slowly, she made her way to the living room and then cautiously moved a curtain aside just enough to look out.

The middle-aged man was walking his dog past her house again, and the sprinkler was on in a yard two houses down from where Sam lived.

Everyone was going about their business, except for her. She was standing in her living room, debating whether she was losing her mind. Now she was stressed all over again about going into a classroom. She couldn't come undone in front of a room full of children.

She walked back through the house in a daze, saw her food still on the table and dumped the sandwich in the trash, then sat down at the table and burst into tears.

Chapter Ten

THE HIGHWAY PATROL HAD TAKEN CONTROL OF THE scene. The chase was theirs. The dead man was theirs to deal with. And as soon as Sam and his men removed the stop strips and their barricades, they headed back to town.

Once Sam was back at the station, he sent Roxie a text to let her know he was okay. He knew she would be worried, and he also knew that when he'd brought groceries home at noon, Roxie hadn't been well. He had given the girls orders to be quiet. But he also knew that if Roxie wasn't on patrol, they'd get into some kind of trouble. It was just the age and the nature of his little beasts. Then he settled into writing up the report and as soon as he was finished took off early and went home.

It wasn't until he saw Katie's car parked at her house that it occurred to him all the noise and sirens might have upset her, but he was more concerned about Roxie, and hurried inside.

He found Evie and Beth hovering where Roxie was resting. He could tell they were both bothered that she wasn't well.

"Daddy, Daddy, Miss Roxie isn't moving!" Evie cried.

"Not moving," Beth echoed.

"Quiet down, girls. Miss Roxie is just trying to rest. Go play." Then he knelt down beside the sofa where Roxie was lying. "I'm so sorry. If it hadn't been for all the hoorah earlier, I would have just taken off today," Sam said.

Roxie shook her head. "I would have had this headache wherever I was. The girls didn't make anything worse. Are you okay?" she asked.

Sam nodded. "It was a mess. It got ugly. But it belongs to the highway patrol."

"All I care about is knowing you guys are okay," Roxie said. "Help me up."

Sam stood, then pulled her up to a sitting position.

"We are just fine. Go home, lady."

After Roxie left, the girls reappeared, hovering around Sam as he was making supper.

Evie was setting the table, and Beth was adding the salt and pepper shakers and paper napkins. As they worked, Sam could hear them whispering to each other in undertones. He kept catching bits of the conversation, most of which consisted of who was going to ask Daddy.

Finally, he turned around and fixed them both with a look. "Ask Daddy what?"

They looked startled, then Beth poked Evie, and she blurted out what they'd been bothered about.

"Daddy, is Miss Roxie old enough to die?"

"What on earth made you ask about that?" Sam asked.

Evie shrugged. "She was lying down a lot today. We were scared she would die, and we don't know how to drive a car to go get you."

Sam sighed, turned off the fire beneath the goulash he was making, and sat down at the table.

"Come sit on my lap," he said, and they both crawled up. "Okay, here's the deal. Age isn't always what makes people die. Diseases and accidents can also cause that. Yes, Miss Roxie didn't feel well today, but this isn't the first time, and it won't be the last. Sometimes she has migraines, which are bad headaches, and when she gets one of those, lying down and being quiet helps them go away."

Beth listened, but she wasn't satisfied. "Don't you think we should learn how to drive, just in case?"

Sam frowned. "Not until you're old enough. It's the law, and I represent the law, so no, ma'am. And we aren't discussing driving lessons in this house again until you're teenagers. Got it?"

"Got it," Evie said. "But just in case, what do we do if she dies on us?"

Sam wanted to laugh, but they were serious.

"You already know what to do. You pick up the phone and call for help. Now tell me the number you call."

"911," Evie shouted.

"911," Beth echoed. "We dial 911 if she dies on us."

Sam hugged them to him. "Yes, that's what you do if she dies. Now. Are you two getting hungry?"

"Starving!" Evie said.

"Starving," Beth echoed.

"Then go wash up. When you come back, supper will be ready," he said.

They slid off his lap and left the room running.

Sam sat for a moment, his head spinning and his heart

in a bit of a bind. They were growing up so fast. One day they'd be asking questions he couldn't answer. Stuff a mother would have been teaching them, and stuff a mother would need to tell them. God. Why did life have to be so beautiful and so sad at the same time?

———————————

Katie's supper was baked lasagna from the freezer section at Welby's Grocery. The house smelled good, and since she'd thrown away her lunch at noon, she was beginning to feel hungry. The shock of her flashback was lessening, and she had quit stewing about what Lila told her. She gave herself a lecture on not owning other people's troubles and took the lasagna out of the oven.

But when the national news came on TV, she was eating her supper sitting on the couch and waiting to see if they mentioned Megan Roman's murder. What she hadn't expected was to see footage of Mark coming out of the police station with his head down, sunglasses on, and dodging the media hammering him with questions.

She sat there a minute, wondering if she was about to feel sorry for him, and then thought… *Nope. I had to face a church full of people and tell them you dumped my ass. You're fine. You're coming across here as the "good guy" who turned in his own wife just to do the right thing.*

She took another bite of lasagna, listened to the updates on the case from the news anchor, and then changed the channel and finished eating.

It was nearing sundown when she went out on her back

porch with a piece of pecan pie from the bakery section at Welby's and ate it sitting in the porch swing.

The day was cooling off a bit, and there were storm clouds on the horizon. Earlier, the weatherman had predicted the possibility of rain, so Katie eyed the clouds as they continued to build into massive thunderheads. Off in the distance, she could hear the beginnings of a rumble. Even though it was a long distance away yet, the sound gave her goose bumps.

When she was little, she had been afraid of thunder, and when a storm would come up full of lightning and thunder, she would hide under her bed. Then one of the boys in her foster family told her that sound in the sky was just potatoes rolling around in the tater wagon. She believed that for enough years to get her over the fear. The boy, who was already sick, later died of leukemia, but his kindness had not been forgotten.

She sat outside until the sun went down and the wind began to rise. Then she went back inside, put the rest of the dirty dishes into the dishwasher, and started it up.

All she wanted to do was run a tub full of hot water and soak until her skin puckered, then crawl in bed, and read some more of her new Dinah McCall. The book was a thriller with a psychic and missing people, set on an old Southern plantation. The romance was hard to get through right now, because love was so far off her radar, but as with all things, this too would pass. The rest of it rocked, and she couldn't wait to see what came next.

So she locked up the house, set the thermostat as she turned off lights in the front of the house, and headed back to her room. Her comfy bed and the old claw-foot bathtub were calling her name, and Dinah's story was waiting.

————————

Across the street, Sam Youngblood had seen the same newscast about the murder of a young socialite in Albuquerque and her involvement in drug trafficking. As they began unweaving the tangled story for their listeners, Sam keyed in on the name of the husband who'd turned her in and then saw the clip of Mark Roman coming out of the police precinct and frowned. That name rang a bell. He'd read that name recently, but where?

He kept thinking about it as he was getting the girls into bed, and listening to their prayers for Miss Roxie not to die, and hoping to God the girls didn't bug Roxie about her impending demise tomorrow.

Later, he went into the office and sat down at the computer to pay a couple of bills. That's when he remembered where he'd seen that name.

At this computer. The night he'd done a background search on Katie McGrath. If he wasn't mistaken, that was the name of the man in her wedding announcement. And there had been a photo. Now he wanted to see it again. It probably wasn't the same man, but he knew he wouldn't rest until he investigated further.

So he typed in the names "Mark Roman" and "Katie McGrath" and "wedding in Albuquerque" and up popped the same news item he'd seen before, with a picture of the couple.

It *was* the same man.

He dug deeper and typed "Mark Roman and Megan Lanier wedding" and found an announcement about an elopement to Las Vegas, but he was stunned by the date.

The son of a bitch married another woman the day before he was supposed to marry Katie. He jilted a schoolteacher for a drug-pushing socialite. I wonder what he thinks about his choice now?

The more he learned about Katie McGrath, the more his intentions grew to do his part to make sure she felt safe and wanted here.

<hr>

Katie had fallen asleep with the book in her lap and all of the lights still on. For once, she wasn't having nightmares and was blissfully sleeping when lightning and thunder announced the storm's arrival.

She jumped, felt the book sliding off her lap, and immediately grabbed at it as she opened her eyes, then groaned when she saw the time. It was just after 2:00 a.m.

The storm sounded bad. Strong winds. Rain hammering against the windows and the roof. Other than her bathtub, she didn't have a tornado shelter, so she quickly turned on the TV to check weather reports. After a quick search of channels, she found a local station with a weather alert on a continuous scroll at the bottom of the screen.

Strong winds, thunder and lightning, and a good soaking. No chance of tornadoes or hail. That'll work. Katie got up, leaving the lights of her bedroom to walk through the darkened house, lit only by the intermittent flashes of lightning.

The whole noise of the storm and the psychedelic flashes of light coming through shades and curtains gave her an eerie feeling. She hadn't lived here long enough to know what would hold together in a storm and what might leak, but a quick check of the house would answer all those questions soon enough.

She opened the door leading out to the back porch, only to be met with a blast of wind and rain.

"Yikes," she cried. She slammed the door shut and locked it and went to the front door, then out onto that porch.

Sheltered from the wind and rain, Katie sat down in the chair next to the door and clasped her hands in her lap. The rain was at downpour status, forming a gray curtain between her and the streetlights. Water was pouring off the roof into the gutters and gushing through the downspouts, and the longer she sat watching it, the more mesmerizing the rain became.

The urge to step off the porch out into the deluge was strong, making her wonder if it could wash away her past, leaving her clean and new, like being baptized. But the intermittent lightning within the storm took away that choice.

And then through the rain she saw the lights in Sam Youngblood's house suddenly come on and imagined Sam hurrying to his girls to calm their fears.

He was an interesting man. She'd guess he was in his midthirties, and the phrase "tall, dark, and handsome" could have been coined for him.

Square jaw. Roman nose.

Chiseled features.

Sea-blue eyes.

A man's man.

Police chief.

Raising two little girls on his own.

One might say he was remarkable.

And so she sat watching as the lights finally went back out across the street. Knowing children as well as she did, she guessed that whatever had happened had been dealt with. In a flight of fantasy, she wondered if Sam Youngblood made house calls to end adult nightmares. What she wouldn't give to be rid of them.

She had no idea that Sam had paused on his way through the house to look out his front windows. At first all he saw was the rain, and then in a flash of lightning, he caught a glimpse of someone sitting in a chair on Katie's porch.

It was her!

His girls weren't the only ones disturbed by the storm. He hated the thought of her over there alone, living with the memories of demons that had passed through her life, and without thinking he opened the front door and walked out into the storm. The porch did not shelter him from the blast of wind and rain, but he wanted her to know he saw her. He wanted her to know she was not weathering a storm alone.

A gust of wind whipped around the corner of the house, making Katie shiver. Her feet were cold, and her summer pajamas weren't nearly warm enough for this. It was time to go back inside.

And then in a flash of lightning, she saw Sam, chest bare to the storm and his pajama bottoms plastered to him like skin. She didn't know whether to acknowledge his presence or just sit, but she no longer felt so alone.

And then he lifted a hand, and before she thought, she waved back.

He stood a moment longer and then went back into his house, leaving her all too aware of her surroundings. The storm had given her a false sense of safety within the darkness, until his sudden presence was a reminder of her vulnerability. With the energy of the storm around and within her, she went back into the house, her hands trembling as she locked the door.

No way was she going to sleep now. Not with the sight of Sam's rain-soaked body still fresh in her mind, so she went to the kitchen, turning on lights to guide her way.

It occurred to her, as she sat having milk and cookies, that her food choices often matched the food choices of the children she taught. She was a child at heart, still looking for a family to love her.

Sam woke up before the alarm went off and lay within the silence of the house, thinking about the woman across the street. Maybe because he knew so much of her past, there was a part of him that felt led to protect her future. He knew the highlights of who she was, but he didn't know the things that mattered, like what made her laugh. What she liked to eat. Her favorite color. What music she liked. And what she liked to do for fun.

And the moment all this went through his mind, he panicked. He had his hands full being a cop and raising kids. He didn't have a spare second of his life to devote to even considering a relationship. What was even scarier was that she was the first woman since Shelly died who'd made him want one.

Even though he knew the loneliness of being left behind.

Even if she was so achingly lovely.

Even if she lived across the street.

He scrubbed his hands across his face, then threw back the covers and got up. Life was already pulling at his conscience, reminding him to get himself ready so he could feed his babies, get something ready for their lunch, and hope to God he got them through one more day without issues.

He heard them stirring as he was buttoning up the shirt on his uniform, so he went across the hall to get them focused before they started bouncing on the bed.

"Good morning, my sweet girls," Sam said as he sat down on the mattress.

"Daddy!" they said in unison, and crawled out from under the covers and into his lap.

He pulled them close, feeling the warmth of them in his arms as they wound up for the day. Within minutes, they were talking in rapid-fire bursts of questions and information, ending with "What's for breakfast?"

"It's a surprise," Sam said. "Get dressed and make your bed, then come find out."

"We love surprises," Beth said as they both bailed out of his lap.

"And I love you," Sam said, but they were already digging through their dressers for clothes, which was his signal to go make a little magic in the kitchen. It was going to involve a microwave and precooked food, but he felt no guilt. He was a cop, not a chef.

By the time the girls came flying into the kitchen, he had created his own version of Happy Meal breakfasts. Sausage and egg on an English muffin, with little hash-brown nuggets and vanilla pudding cups. The icing on the cake was the "prizes," because there was always a prize in a Happy Meal.

Being the father of little girls meant keeping a stash of all things girlie. So he'd pulled out kits of stick-ons for their fingernails and laid a little kit beside each of their plates.

The girls stopped at the table, eyeing the daddy version of an Egg McMuffin, their own little hash browns, orange juice, and a prize.

"Happy Meals! We have Happy Meals! Yay!" Evie cried.

"Yay!" Beth echoed.

"Dig in, but no playing with your prizes until you've eaten," Sam said.

"Promise!" they chimed, and climbed up in their chairs.

"Where's yours, Daddy?" Evie asked.

"I ate mine while I was making yours. I have to leave as soon as Miss Roxie gets here. Busy day for Daddy."

"Poor Daddy," Beth said, and before he could stop her, she'd opened her prize, peeled a rainbow star off the sheet of stick-ons, and stuck it on his thumbnail. "You deserve a prize, too."

Sam felt the badge on his shirt and then rubbed the star on his thumbnail and felt like he'd won the lottery.

"I already won the prize when God gave me you and Evie, but thank you."

"The guys at the station are gonna be jealous, aren't they?" Evie said.

Sam grinned. "Oh yeah…big time."

Then the doorbell rang. Sam loped through the house and opened the door.

"Morning, Roxie."

"Morning, Sam," she said, then came in and shut the door behind her.

"How did you fare through the storm?" he asked.

"I slept through it," Roxie said.

He arched an eyebrow. "Lucky you. We did not."

She grinned and then walked into the kitchen.

"Miss Roxie! Miss Roxie! Daddy made us Happy Meals for breakfast," Evie said.

"And we have prizes but we can't play with them until we clean our plates," Beth added.

"Good move, Daddy. Have a good day," Roxie said.

"Yes, ma'am." He gave each girl a kiss on the top of her head, then gave them a starry thumbs-up, and left the house.

He couldn't help but glance across the street as he was walking to his cruiser, and then glanced down at the sticker on his thumb and got in and drove away.

Katie woke abruptly, glanced at the clock, and then relaxed. Still plenty of time before she went to Delilah Cash's house to take the Yorkie for a walk. It felt good to have a purpose until her classes began, and the luxury of not living by an alarm did not go unappreciated.

After a leisurely breakfast of fruit and cereal, she put on her oldest pair of jeans and a tank top, and decided to dig out the little backpack she used to wear to go hiking. She dropped in her house keys and wallet, added a couple of bottles of water, a small plastic dish, and some wet wipes, then grabbed her sunglasses as she left the house.

She paused a moment, eyeing the puddles left over from last night's rain and feeling the unexpected heaviness of humidity in the air, then slipped her arms through the straps of the backpack and took off down the street.

She'd been walking for almost an hour when she finally headed toward Delilah's. There were shade trees along almost every residential street in town, but after last night's rain, the heat of the day was turning Borden's Gap into a sauna. The humidity of rural Tennessee was a one-eighty from the dry heat of New Mexico. Sweat was running down the middle of her back and between her breasts as she walked up the steps at Delilah's house and rang the doorbell.

When she heard an abrupt burst of yapping, she grinned.

Rhett was announcing her arrival.

Delilah came to the door, smiling. "He's ready!" she said. "Are you ready for Rhett?"

Katie laughed. "Yes, ma'am," she said. She poked the poop bag Delilah gave her into her hip pocket and took the leash attached to the Yorkie's collar. And like yesterday, the little dog had the leash in his mouth.

Katie reached down and gave him a quick pat.

"Are you ready, buddy?"

Rhett Butler bounced down the steps like a little rabbit, leading himself and Katie off on their walk.

Katie waved at Delilah, and they were gone.

And like before, their parade did not go unnoticed.

Today, Beau Newton had parked his landscape truck and trailer along the curb of the grand blue house at the end of the block where Delilah lived. It belonged to George and Flo Welby, the owners of Welby's Grocery.

Beau was down on his knees pulling weeds out of Flo's flower bed when he saw the pair coming up the street. He knew who the woman was. He'd seen her around town, and he knew whose dog she was walking. Rhett Butler's reputation for prowess had long since preceded him. Rhett was the only dog in town who chose to participate in controlling his own leash.

Intrigued, Beau wanted an excuse to talk to her, so he jumped up and hurried toward his truck, grabbed a little hand-size hoe out of the toolbox, and then casually turned around just as the duo approached.

"Morning, ma'am. I'm Beau Newton. I own Newton Landscaping." He pointed at his truck as if to prove the validity of his statement. "I see you and Rhett are having yourselves a fine walk."

"Nice to meet you, Beau. I'm Katie McGrath."

"You're the new teacher, right?"

Katie nodded, but Rhett was already tugging on the leash.

"As you can see, Rhett's not through with his walk, and it's getting hot, so we need to be on our way. Nice to meet you," she said, and resumed her walk.

Feeling empowered that she'd stopped to talk, Beau jumped in with both feet.

"Uh, say…Miss Katie, I would love to take you out for coffee some morning."

"That's real sweet of you," Katie said. "But dating is not on my agenda right now."

Beau was disappointed, but he didn't let it show. "Yes, ma'am. Anyway, it was nice to meet you. See you around town."

Katie breathed a sigh of relief and kept walking. After sniffing multiple trees and flowering bushes and hedges along the ensuing two blocks, the little Yorkie found a satisfactory place to poop, then waited patiently while Katie recovered it.

As she was tying up the bag, she laughed at the expression on his face.

"You think you really did something, right?"

He yapped.

She was still grinning as she dropped the bag in a public garbage bin on the street. A few yards down, Katie stopped and sat down on a public bench, pulled Rhett up in her lap, and poured some water in a little plastic bowl. She set the bowl down beside her, and watched in quiet delight as Rhett Butler abandoned her lap for a drink.

"Are you through?" she asked, when he finally looked up at her, water dripping from the little chin whiskers around his mouth.

Rhett yapped.

"Excellent," Katie said. She emptied what was left in the bowl and put it back in her backpack, then put Rhett back down.

But instead of picking up his leash, Rhett looked up at her and yapped again.

Katie slipped the backpack on and scooped him up in her arms.

"So that's the end of the walk, is it? Now you're just along for the ride."

Rhett licked her chin.

She kissed the top of his little head, then wrapped the leash around her arm, settled him against her breasts, and headed to Delilah's.

The older woman was sitting outside on the verandah when Katie came up the steps.

The Yorkie saw her and yapped excitedly, wiggling to be put down.

"Yes, there's Mama," Katie said, handing over the leash. "He did his business. He had a drink, and we're home. See you tomorrow?"

"Yes, and thank you," Delilah said. She was kissing and cuddling her fur baby under her chin as she went inside.

It was almost noon by the time Katie headed home, and now that she didn't have the little dog on board, she was about to kick into a jog when she heard a car coming up behind her.

She realized it was a police car when it passed her, and then a few yards ahead of her, the brake lights came on and it stopped. As she came abreast of it, Sam Youngblood got out.

"Hey, neighbor. I'm on my way home. Want a ride?"

She hesitated, but only for a moment. She was hot. She was tired. And there was no earthly reason to refuse.

"I won't say no, but I'm a hot, sweaty mess."

Sam grinned and opened the passenger door.

"Well, hop on in, sweaty mess."

Katie laughed as she slid into the passenger seat and closed the door.

He paused a moment, his hand on the trunk of his car, thinking *Now I know her laugh.* Then he circled the car and got in.

"Thank you again," Katie said.

He nodded. "You're welcome."

She glanced at him, at his silhouette, then the badge, and the gun on his hip.

"Do you go home every day for lunch?"

"When I can, or when Roxie needs something for the girls."

The mention of his daughters and their nanny felt like a safe subject of conversation.

"Roxie is really nice. She and the girls helped me carry groceries into the house right after my move."

"They told me," Sam said. "Evie was quite taken with your red bed."

Katie blinked. "I don't have a red… Oh! The sleeping bag!"

"Yes. The red bed. Red is Evie's favorite color," he added.

"Ah. That explains her fascination with it. They're delightful, but you know that, don't you?"

Sam beamed. "I know they make my chaotic life all worth it."

"Be proud of what you are achieving," Katie said. "After all my years of teaching, I can attest to what a big difference it makes, being able to keep your children at home rather than have to leave them at daycare while you work. It's not always so for parents, and you are really lucky to have someone like Roxie willing to come to your house for them."

"She was just one of the women of Borden's Gap who were here waiting for me when I brought the girls home from the hospital. I don't know what I would have done without them, but Roxie is the one who stayed."

Katie's heart stopped. "Uh…"

Sam suddenly realized she didn't know why there was no mother in the picture.

"I'm sorry. I just assumed Roxie might have mentioned it. Shelly…my wife…died the day the girls were born. Brain aneurysm."

Katie's eyes welled. "Oh my God. I cannot imagine… I'm so sorry. I didn't mean to bring up—"

Without thinking, Sam laid a hand on her arm.

"No, it's not like that at all!" Sam said. "The first two years nearly killed me, but the girls were my saving grace. Still are my saving grace. There are many levels of loss. Once you get past the mind-numbing grief, you find new ways to cope. And new ways to be happy in the world."

"Are you happy now?" Katie asked.

He grinned. "Mostly." And then his eyes narrowed. "Are you happy, Katie McGrath?"

She looked out the window at the passing houses and then back at him. He arched an eyebrow. Waiting.

She managed a crooked grin, echoing his response.

"Mostly."

Sam nodded. "Understood."

Katie glanced at him again. "Can I ask you something?"

"Sure."

"I heard what sounded like a lot of gunfire yesterday. Was it gunfire or an explosion?"

"It was an explosion," Sam said. "We had a roadblock set up outside of town to aid the highway patrol in their pursuit of an escapee."

Katie thought about him in the line of fire. His job involved risk and danger, even in a small town.

"Was that what I heard?"

Sam sighed. "Yes."

"Did you stop him?"

"We had to. He wouldn't stop on his own. He hit the stop strips, and the car rolled and burst into flames. He'd already beaten up an elderly couple and stolen their car and a gun. He was a very dangerous man. I guess he decided he'd rather die than go back to jail."

She nodded. "Thank you."

He looked a little surprised. "For what?"

"For putting yourself in danger to keep us safe."

"Oh. Well, it's part of the job," Sam said.

"I know. Police saved me once. I just don't take that lightly."

Sam waited for her to tell him about the shooting, but when she didn't, he guessed it was nothing she wanted known here, and he was good with that.

"Well, I'm real glad they did," Sam said, and then pulled up into her driveway. "Delivered safe and sound, ma'am. You have a nice day."

"Not ma'am. Katie. And I'm glad they did, too," Katie said. "Thank you for the ride."

Then she got out carrying her backpack, and as she started up the steps realized she was smelling freshly cut grass and noticed the yard had been mowed. Louise Parsons was as good as her word.

Sam waited until her front door closed before he backed up and pulled into his drive. He sat a moment, gathering himself and switching from Sam the man to Sam the daddy before he got out. Then he grabbed a sack from the back seat and headed into the house.

Chapter Eleven

WALT LANIER HADN'T BEEN SOBER SINCE THE NIGHT HE found out Megan was dead. Every time the alcohol began to wear off, he would remember. And then the burden of abandoning his daughter would lay so heavy on his heart that he wanted to die. If only he could go back—back before he met Craig Buttoni and lost so much money to him in a poker game that he was going to have to sell his home to pay it back.

If only he'd known this was how Buttoni operated. How he pulled so-called respectable people into his web, using them for drop-offs and deliveries. Using them until they were so involved that it wouldn't have mattered if they'd finally paid off their gambling debts to him, because he had them up to their eyeballs in trafficking drugs.

If only he hadn't involved his own daughter, but he had. If only he hadn't called Buttoni for help, but he had.

He wanted to die, but was too big a coward to off himself.

He was not, however, too big a coward to off Buttoni. All he had to do was find him.

But first, he had to get stone-cold sober and then start putting out feelers to find out where Buttoni had gone.

Buttoni was in Monte Carlo on a hot streak, winning money hand over fist and making a name for himself in Europe comparable to the reputation he held in the States. One day ran into the next, and then the next. He kept his finger on the pulse of his network back home, but he was also creating new contacts in Monaco that would expand his side business throughout Europe.

He liked Monte Carlo. He spoke enough Italian to be comfortable there. The weather was glorious. His accommodations were spectacular. He was in his element in the casino and so far from home that he believed he was safe, which made him careless.

He quit paying attention to the strangers around him and took it as his due that all they wanted of him was for his luck to rub off on them.

It had taken Walt Lanier a good deal of money to find Craig, but he'd known who to bribe to get what he wanted. It had taken even more to get a new identity and papers to go with it before he left Mexico.

He'd been in Monte Carlo for a couple of days now, watching Buttoni coming and going in the hotel, watching him disappear into private rooms for the big games.

Watching him spending with random abandon.

Watching for a break in the routine.

Watching for the moment to make his move.

Waiting for him to let down his guard.

Walt wanted his face to be the last thing Buttoni saw before he died.

———

Craig Buttoni was tired but elated. He'd been at the poker table for almost twenty-two hours straight before the game came to an end as he took the final pot.

He walked out of the private game room with his head up, strutting through the casino with a small entourage accompanying him. His winnings were banked, and after smugly being lauded and congratulated by men who dealt daily with far wealthier men than he would ever be, he bypassed the need for food and headed to his suite.

He got on the elevator, yawning as he pressed the button for his floor. The doors were just beginning to close when another man jumped into the car, mumbling an apology in an accent Craig did not recognize. Craig watched him press a button for a floor two levels above his and thought nothing more of it.

He yawned again and rubbed his eyes with the heels of his hands. When he opened them, the man was in front of him with a knife at Craig's throat.

"I don't have any money on me!" Craig gasped.

"I don't want your money, you son of a bitch. You had my baby killed, and I'm going to watch you die."

Craig's eyes widened in disbelief.

"Lanier?"

"In the flesh," Walt said, and slashed Craig's throat so fast Craig choked on the words coming up his throat.

He grabbed his throat with both hands and slid down the back of the car. His hands fell limply into his lap as his chin dropped onto his chest.

Walt dropped the knife near the body, pushed the button for the next floor and got off. Then he pressed the Up arrow. The elevator doors closed, and Walt headed for the stairwell.

He ran up to his floor and then hurried to his room.

Within seconds, he had stripped out of the clothes he'd been wearing, removed a fake mustache and makeup that had given his skin a darker appearance, put on workman's clothes, added a little French beret, then packed a bag with two changes of clothes and his money and credentials. Keeping his head down, he went back to the stairwell and strolled out of the casino. He was already blocks away among the tourists when he heard the first sounds of sirens.

They'd found the body.

And they'd be looking at security footage.

And they'd see the man come out of the elevator, follow him through the footage to the stairwell, and then up several floors to get in his room.

They'd get DNA, but Walt Lanier was not in the system in the States. He'd never served in the military. He'd never even had a speeding ticket. And the images on the security footage looked nothing like the man he was. The man who was on his way to the airport.

He'd never been to England, but his papers listed him as a citizen of Great Britain. All of the money he had stashed in a bank in the Caymans could easily be transferred. He felt no satisfaction at what he'd done, other than he had avenged his daughter. But in the end, his guilt at ever putting her in that position was forever on his shoulders.

He was so lost in retrospection that he didn't realize the lights had changed, and when he stepped off the curb, he walked straight into the path of an oncoming delivery truck.

A woman screamed, and then kept screaming.

It was the last earthly sound he heard. Karma had delivered him from his misery, and the false identity he carried would soon be revealed.

It would take longer for them to match the DNA taken from Craig Buttoni's body to the body of the man lying in their morgue, but when they did, that led authorities back to New Mexico, Buttoni's principal residence, and in doing so explained the mystery of Walt Lanier's disappearance.

For the Albuquerque police, there was only one reason Walt Lanier would go halfway around the world to kill a man from his own hometown: to avenge the murder of his daughter. It was circumstantial and supposition, and they needed proof of a connection between Megan Roman and Craig Buttoni for the scenario they'd laid out.

And then they subpoenaed Buttoni's phone records, got a search warrant for his estate, and opened his safe. That's when the last piece of the puzzle fell into place.

Mark Roman was in shock.

The police notified him that they'd located Walt Lanier

but he was dead, and that he'd died in Monte Carlo, Monaco, while masquerading as someone else, false papers and all. Mark couldn't begin to imagine why he'd been there, other than hiding from whoever had murdered Megan.

Then the police asked him what he knew about Craig Buttoni, and all Mark could say was "Who's he?"

He'd never heard the name or had any notion of Buttoni's relation to the Lanier family. But that wasn't all. He'd received a letter from the law firm representing the Lanier estate, only to learn that while he had been fired from the family company, he was still the official son-in-law of record. And with Walt's demise, Mark was all that was left of the Lanier family.

The irony of his disastrous choice in picking a wife kept pulling him back into a family that had rejected him. Because Lanier was one of Buttoni's many traffickers, his home and business property became part of the property seizure happening within Buttoni's estate. But not the life insurance or the trust fund Megan had inherited from her mother, which according to their wills, would now go to Mark. Their involvement in Buttoni's world was all over the news. Mark couldn't go out in public without being accosted by the media and was screening his calls to weed out requests for interviews.

He tried to call Katie again and again, although he didn't know why. Maybe it was because she was his last connection to decency.

Not only were his calls not going through, but he never got a voicemail to leave a message.

She'd blocked him.

More than two weeks had passed since Katie started walking Rhett Butler. And in that time, she guessed she'd met every single man in Borden's Gap, as well as those willing to philander.

Some of them had used subtle approaches and some blatant, but the messages in all of them were clear. They wanted to take Katie out.

But for every invitation she received, the man got a turn-down that was as polite as any they'd ever received. Katie McGrath was such a charmer that they couldn't bring themselves to feel like they'd failed in anything but being exactly what she deserved.

Katie was patient and, after the first couple of times, began to realize how rare a new face was in a small town, and how being new and single immediately put her on the market.

They talked to her in Welby's Grocery. They hit on her when she was gassing up her car. They politely stalked her as she walked Rhett and when she was picking up take-out. She even got hit on at the barbecue food truck three times, all while she was standing in line.

But the only man who piqued her interest lived across the street from her. He was exceedingly friendly and polite, but did not cross the line into getting personal, so she took it as another rejection of who she was and let it go.

Time had flown by since Katie's arrival in Borden's Gap. She was due to report to work come next Monday, and she was itching to get to her classroom and start setting it up.

Delilah already had another dog-walker lined up beginning Sunday, but Katie was going to miss taking Rhett for his walks and receiving his little puppy kisses.

When Friday evening rolled around, Katie was outside in her freshly mowed yard, pulling weeds from the flower beds, when she heard Sam's cruiser coming up the street. She rocked back on her heels to watch, and when he flashed his lights at her, she grinned and waved.

And then to her surprise, when he got out, he didn't go into his house. He crossed the street instead and walked into her yard.

Katie stood, then held up her hands. "I'm innocent, I swear."

Sam chuckled. "That's what they all say. Anyway...I come in peace, and with an offer to come eat with us tonight. I've been promising the girls we'd grill hot dogs for days, and they want you to come be our guest. They're learning to set the table, and they've done it in front of Roxie so many times she is no longer impressed. They need a new audience, and I'd love to eat a meal with an adult, so there's that."

Katie burst into laughter. The invitation was so ingenuous and sincere that she couldn't say no.

"I would be honored," Katie said. "I love hot dogs from the grill. Should I bring anything?"

"Nope. I've got food covered. Give me a few minutes to get changed and in gear, and then come on over... Oh...

and thank you for not being insulted by the last-minute invitation, but I've been afraid to ask."

Katie frowned. "Why?"

Sam shrugged. "Because I know every single man in town has been dogging your trail for weeks, and I didn't want you to think I was just one of the pack."

She blinked.

"You knew all that was going on?"

He grinned. "I'm the police chief…in a really small town. There isn't much I don't know about here. I also know that all the young, single ladies see you as a threat to their chances of landing any one of Borden's Gap's finest."

"Oh, for the love of God," Katie muttered. "If they only knew—" Then she caught herself. "Never mind. But if you hear any of them commenting again, you might throw in the fact that I'm not on the make. I'm not on the market. And I don't want any part of their fine chances."

Now Sam was laughing. "Yes, ma'am. I will surely do that. In the meantime, go wash the dirt off yourself and come on over. Just ring the doorbell. The girls are also practicing social manners on how to greet guests."

"I can't wait," Katie said, and realized she meant it.

Sam looked at her for a few seconds, then smiled.

"Me either," he said, and then loped across the street.

Katie watched him go, reeling from the unexpected invitation. Then it dawned on her she needed to clean up and change, too, so she hurried inside.

This was momentous for Katie. She wasn't calling it a date. But it was an event in which she was going to spend time looking at Sam Youngblood in close proximity.

This was momentous for Sam. He wasn't calling it a date. But it was time he was going to spend with a woman who intrigued and delighted him. She was the first woman who'd been invited to his house since he lost Shelly, and the girls were all on board, which made it even better. With them at the table, there were never awkward silences at a meal. Just the occasional awkward question he had to ignore or redirect.

The twins met him at the door.

"Is she coming, Daddy? Is the teacher coming to eat hot dogs with us?"

"As luck would have it, yes, she is," Sam said.

Roxie met him at the door with her purse over her shoulder.

"I have a late hair appointment, so I gotta run. Have a good evening. You deserve it."

"It's not a date," Sam said.

"Doesn't matter what you call it," Roxie said. "Just have fun."

Sam grinned. "Yes, ma'am," and then pointed at the girls. "Go wash up. Miss Katie will be over here soon."

"May we answer the door, please?" Evie asked.

"Yes, the door," Beth echoed.

"Yes, but with clean hands and faces," Sam said.

They took off running and shrieking down the hall, with Sam right behind them. They ran into their room, racing to get to the sink, as he went the opposite direction into his bedroom. He quickly locked up his weapon, then changed in record time and went out back to heat up the grill.

It felt good to be happy. It felt even better to be excited about who was coming to dinner.

———

Katie jumped into the shower to freshen up before changing into turquoise capri pants and a white knit top with turquoise stripes. After slipping into a pair of sandals, she paused in front of the mirror.

Except for moisturizer, she wasn't wearing makeup, and her face was pink from working out in the yard. Added to that were the strands of hair that had come down around her face from the ponytail she'd put it in earlier.

"I can't believe he even offered the invitation with me looking like this," she mumbled, and pulled out the elastic band, brushed her hair out, and left it loose.

With eyebrows naturally arching like wings and lashes as dark as her eyes, she opted for lip gloss only and went to get her phone and house keys.

Walking out of the house was like opening a door into a new dimension. Life had rejected her so many times that her trust had turned to rust. Thank God the offer had been hot dogs, or she would not have had the guts to walk across the street.

Her heart was pounding as she went up the steps and rang the doorbell. But her nervousness disappeared when she heard little girl squeals and running footsteps.

"I'll get it! I'll get it!" they shouted.

And then the door opened, and they were both hanging onto the knob, water droplets still visible on the fronts of their clothes, wearing smiles brighter than the polish on their toenails.

"Hello, girls," Katie said.

"Hello, Miss Katie," Beth said.

"Please come in," Evie added.

Katie stepped over the threshold and shut the door behind her, and as she did, the twins both turned around and ran toward the kitchen, shouting, "Daddy, she's here!" and left her standing.

Suddenly Sam appeared with a pair of tongs in one hand and a kitchen towel in the other. He was grinning.

"Well, at least they got you inside before they abandoned you. Feel free to approach," he said, then waved the tongs. "Follow me."

Katie's laugh welled up behind him as he went back into the kitchen, and all he could think was how pretty she was, and that she was in his house.

The scent of hot dogs on the grill made Katie's mouth water.

"Everything smells so good," Katie said, and then looked at the girls standing sentinel at the table. "Oh my! How pretty this table looks."

"We did it!" the girls said.

Katie clapped her hands. "Way to go! Everything is exactly where it's supposed to be, even the napkins. I am so impressed!"

They beamed, then high-fived each other.

"You get to sit here," Evie said, patting the back of a chair.

"Daddy sits at the other end because it's the rule. Beth and I have to look at each other when we eat and remind each other not to talk with our mouths full."

Katie nodded, listening to them rattle. She'd learned a long time ago that the easiest way to communicate with children was let them do the talking and comment only when necessary. And this was one of those times.

And then Sam interrupted both of them.

"Thank you, girls. Now Katie is going to come outside with me while I finish grilling. You can come with us, or you can go play until I call you."

"We'll come with you," Evie said.

"With you," Beth echoed.

"There are cold drinks in the refrigerator," Sam said. "Would someone grab a Pepsi for me, and help yourself," he said, and hurried out to the grill.

Smoke billowed as he opened the lid.

The girls were at the fridge.

"Miss Katie, what do you want to drink?" Beth asked.

"I'll take a Pepsi, too," she said.

Evie grabbed one for Katie, and then handed her another one. "This one is for Daddy."

"Got it," Katie said, and walked out behind the girls, who were carrying their juice boxes.

She sidled up close to Sam to hand him his drink, and when he turned around to take it, they almost bumped heads.

"Sorry. I'm as bad as the girls. No filter. No sense of personal space," he said.

"No harm done," Katie said, and settled into a folding chair near where he was standing.

Sam unscrewed the lid on the pop, took a quick drink, set it aside, and pointed his tongs at Katie.

"How do you like your dogs? Faint grill marks? Definite grill marks? Or black on at least one side?"

"Um, black on one side, for sure," she said.

Sam smiled. "You just keep getting better and better," he said, and then was so shocked that he'd said that out loud that he turned around and began turning over the wieners as if his life depended on it.

"Daddy, we don't want any black," Evie said.

"No black dogs," Beth added.

"I'm on it," he said, and pulled a couple of wieners away from direct heat.

The girls moved to where Katie was sitting and began eyeing everything about her.

"I like your pants," Evie said.

"You have pretty knees," Beth added.

"And your shirt matches, doesn't it?" Evie asked.

"Do you polish your toes?" Beth asked.

Katie leaned forward, her elbows on her knees, and their conversation began.

"Thank you for the compliments, girls."

"What are compaments?" Evie asked.

"Yeah, that," Beth echoed.

"It's when you say something nice to someone. Like when I said what a good job you two did setting the table? That was a compliment."

"I knew that," Evie said.

"I knew it, too," Beth echoed.

Katie grinned, then glanced up at Sam and caught him

watching them. And then Evie was in Katie's personal space, leaning against one side of her chair and Beth was leaning on the other. They were so close, she could see her reflection in their eyes. They were so endearing, it was all she could do not to reach down and hug the both of them.

Then they spoke in unison.

"Miss Katie, can you tell us apart?"

Katie had already nailed their differences the day she met them. Evie was the boss, and Beth was the one who gave in. Evie had a tiny mole on the right side of her mouth. Beth had one on the left side.

"I sure can." She pointed her finger. "You're Evie, and you're Beth!"

They giggled. "Daddy! She did it! Nobody ever gets it right!"

Sam was staring. "I see that, and I am properly impressed."

Katie shrugged. "You can't fool a teacher. They see all, know all."

The girls' eyes widened. "Really?"

"Pretty much," Katie said.

Sam saw the rapt expressions on his daughters' faces and then had to look away for fear Katie might see the same look on his face.

He took the last of the wieners off the grill and turned off the gas.

"Okay, everybody. I think we're ready to eat," he said. "Grab your drinks and let's get inside out of this heat."

The girls flew back into the house and were sitting in their chairs waiting when Sam put the platter down on the table. Then he pulled out Katie's chair.

"Thank you," Katie said, and scooted into her seat.

Both girls looked at each other and giggled, then caught Sam's look and sucked it up.

"Katie, please help yourself while I fix the girls' hot dogs."

"We can do it, Daddy," Beth said.

"Last time I let you 'do it,' I was the one wearing ketchup. So I'll be doing it for you tonight. You can get your own chips."

Katie put a blackened dog on her bun, shot it with mustard, then licked a speck of mustard off her thumb before adding pickle relish. But all the while she was putting her hot dog together, she was super aware of Sam.

Sitting at the table with him was like the day she'd ridden in the police cruiser with him. Then, she'd thought it was the gun and the badge that had given him presence, but now she was feeling it again, and he had neither. He was calm, patient but firm, and the girls didn't argue with him. She was impressed.

"Don't wait on us," Sam said. "Dig in."

Katie took a bite. "Mmm, oh my gosh…so good."

Sam was more pleased than he had a right to be. It was just a hot dog, but Katie was treating it like fine dining.

"Okay, baby girls, remember the rules. Hot dogs on the plates. In your mouths. Not on your clothes."

The girls giggled.

"Daddy made a rap," Evie said.

"That's 'cause Daddy can't sing," Sam said. "Now calm down and eat. Dessert is a surprise."

"We love surprises!" they said.

Katie smiled. "I love surprises, too."

Sam shook his head. "Even if it's on the same cooking level as hot dogs?"

"Most especially if it's on a level with hot dogs," Katie said.

Sam sighed. "Then all I have to say is you are so in the right place."

Katie gave him a thumbs-up because there was no way she could voice what she was feeling.

As the meal progressed, the girls were full of questions, but they'd obviously been warned not to be nosy because instead of asking Katie outright, they would turn and first ask Sam if they could ask Katie. And the longer it went on, the more comical it became.

Evie waved a potato chip to get Sam's attention and then poked it in her mouth, chewing and talking at the same time.

"Daddy, came we ask Miss Katie about her brothers and sisters?"

"Don't talk with your mouth full!" Beth cried.

Sam flinched, but before he could respond, Katie answered.

"I don't have any brothers or sisters," she said. "Are you girls getting excited about school starting?"

They nodded, then Beth held up her hand for permission to speak.

"Daddy, can we ask her if she's going to be our teacher?"

Katie just smiled at Sam and shook her head as if to say *I've got this.*

"I don't know who will be in my class," Katie said. "And I'm not the one who will choose. They'll be assigned to me."

"We can't read so much," Evie said.

"Yeah, not much," Beth added.

"You're not supposed to know all that before you start a new grade. That's what you'll learn during the next school year. Every year, you learn new things, right?"

They nodded and were about to nail her again when Sam ended what was becoming an interrogation.

"Who's ready for dessert?" he asked.

All three females raised their hands.

Sam grinned, and when he got up, Katie got up, too, and began clearing the dirty plates from the table.

"You don't have to do that," Sam said.

"I'm not doing it because I have to," Katie said.

Sam didn't say anything more, but it felt good to have a partner in the kitchen. By the time he had ice cream sundaes made, the table was cleared.

The girls clapped when they saw their desserts. Vanilla ice cream with chocolate syrup and sprinkles.

"We love sprinkles," they echoed.

"Who doesn't love sprinkles?" Katie said, and dug a bite out of the top of the sundae and popped it in her mouth. "Yum."

The girls took bites and swallowed. "Yum," they repeated, and then for the first time, they were silent.

Sam winked at Katie. "I think the cold has frozen the words on their tongues."

"No, my words aren't frozen," Evie said. "Just my tongue."

Sam sighed. He'd spoken too soon.

Katie stifled a laugh.

As soon as dessert was over, Sam sent the girls to their room to play. The ensuing silence was welcome, but for Sam, a little scary. He almost wished he didn't know anything about Katie. It would have been easier to make small talk. And there wasn't much left to talk about, since his daughters had pretty much covered what was left.

But Katie came to his rescue and started asking questions about him while he was loading the dessert dishes into the dishwasher.

"Did you grow up here?" Katie asked.

"I grew up just outside of Nashville. My parents still live there. Where did you grow up?" he asked.

"In the Chicago area. I was a foster kid. I got moved around a lot."

Sam looked at her. "It must have been rough."

"Mostly," she said, and then shrugged. "What made you want to go into law enforcement?"

"My dad was a cop with Nashville PD. He retired right before the girls were born. I just followed in his footsteps."

"It takes a special kind of person to do the job you do. I'm sure the girls are proud of you."

"They just love me. I represent safety and order and love in their life. They aren't all that tuned into what I do, except for the lights and siren on the cruiser."

Katie laughed.

"That's perfect." And then she added, "Tonight was perfect, too. I didn't know how much I needed this. It's been a while since I've had normal in my life. Thank you for inviting me."

"It was absolutely my pleasure," Sam said. "And I was serious about eating with adults. I don't do a lot of that, and you are a charming dinner companion…and a trouper. I wasn't expecting the girls to interrogate you."

"That's pretty normal for that age. What's unusual about your girls is that they make their feelings and needs known without worrying if they're going to be in trouble. Whatever you're doing with them, you're doing it right."

Sam sighed. "Thank you. I needed to hear that."

"And…I think I've taken up enough of your evening. Thank you so much for the meal, the conversation, and the pleasure of the company," Katie said.

Sam hated to see her leave, but he didn't want to spook her, either.

"It was selfishly and totally my pleasure," Sam said.

They were caught in the moment between what to say next when there was a crash down the hall, followed by one mutual shout.

"We're okay!"

"Shit," Sam said.

Katie grinned. "Hope it's nothing you have to mop up. I'll let myself out."

Sam shoved a hand through his hair in frustration. "Turn on the porch light after you're inside so I'll know you're okay."

"Deal," she said, and headed toward the front door as Sam took off down the hall.

She was smiling as she stepped out into the nightlife of Borden's Gap.

One dog barking. Somebody's baby crying. A porch full of people down the block talking and laughing.

She took a deep breath and left Sam's yard, crossed the street into her own, and when she'd unlocked her door and went inside, she turned on the porch light. It was a small thing, but it mattered to her that someone cared enough to want to know she was safe.

Chapter Twelve

It wasn't late, and Katie was too wired to sleep, so she got into her pajamas, made herself a glass of iced tea, and went to the living room to watch TV. Her cell phone rang as she was searching for something to watch, and when she saw it was Lila, she answered.

"Hello from the piney woods of Tennessee."

Lila laughed. "You're sounding awfully happy. Is there something you'd like to tell me?"

"No. Just ate supper with new friends. How are you and Jack doing?"

And that's all it took to redirect Lila's conversation. She was raving on and on about him and what they'd been doing, and how fast summer had gone, and she couldn't believe it was time to start school all over again, when Katie finally got a word in.

"I start to work this Monday. I've seen my room. I can't wait to begin setting it up. I am so grateful that you packed up my room at Saguaro or I'd be starting over."

"That's what friends are for," Lila said. "Have you been keeping up with the latest on Mark and the murder?"

Katie frowned. "You mean there's more?"

"Oh, girl!" Lila said. "The authorities finally located

Walt Lanier. In Monte Carlo. He was killed in a traffic acci-
dent, but with fake identification. They found out who he
really was because his DNA matched DNA they found on
a big-shot gambler named Craig Buttoni who was murdered in the elevator at a casino. And during the investigation into the murder, that led them here to Albuquerque
and Buttoni's connection to the Laniers."

Katie gasped. "Wait! What are you saying? That they
think Walt killed the man?"

"Uh...they know he did from the security footage."

"I am beyond floored," Katie muttered. "None of this
makes sense."

"Don't lose me here. I'm still unwinding the tale.
Buttoni has a permanent residence in Albuquerque. They
subpoenaed his phone records and matched texts from it
to Megan's phone. Then they found a second set of books
at the Lanier residence belonging to Walt and learned he
was one of Buttoni's major drug distributors in the area.
They also discovered that Buttoni originally held a huge
gambling note on Walt Lanier, and they are guessing that's
how Walt was pulled into trafficking for Buttoni."

"So this Craig Buttoni trafficked drugs, and Walt and
Megan worked for him?"

"They were but two of many."

"But who killed Megan, and why? Was that why
Walt killed this Buttoni? Because he blamed him for his
daughter's murder?"

"They aren't saying, but gossip around town is that when
Mark and Megan began having trouble and she filed for
divorce, it was because Mark thought she was cheating on

him. And Megan was afraid that he'd hire a PI to trail her and she'd get caught making her drops. So she just decided to leave him and save herself from discovery. Only Mark found a stash she left behind in their house and turned her in. And that is how Humpty Dumpty came tumbling down."

Katie was horrified. "This is so ugly to hear. And unbelievable. And Mark, the dumbass, was right in the middle of it and never knew."

"Well, the dumbass is about to come out of this smelling like a rose. The hero husband who turned in his dirty wife is still her next of kin. And now Walt's dead, too, and Megan was his only next of kin...and Mark is the only person legally connected to the Laniers. It appears he's about to inherit Megan's trust fund and Walt's CPA company...the one Mark got fired from after Megan filed for divorce."

"You couldn't make this up," Katie muttered.

"I always hate to keep bringing him up because I'm afraid it will make you sad all over again," Lila said.

Katie snorted. "Sad? What's sad is that I ever fell in love with someone this shallow. What about him did I miss... you know? Anyway, I have recently met my own Rhett Butler. I've been going on walks with him every day for the past few weeks. I get kisses. I get to pick up his poop. I get—"

Lila gasped. "What the hell, Katie?"

Katie laughed out loud. "My Rhett is a teeny Yorkie. I've been dog-walking for the dearest woman here in town, but this weekend will be my last days, and then I'll go to work."

"Okay! You got me!" Lila said. "I had visions of that old *Deliverance* movie in my head, and you had been bewitched by backwoodsmen and moonshiners."

"No, but there is this really sweet single father who lives across the street from me. He has twin daughters who will be in first grade this year, so they may or may not wind up in my room."

Lila frowned. "We're teachers. We've seen every family mess and the children caught up in them. What's his name? Why is he a single father? Is the mother in the background raining hell down on his life? What does he do?"

"His name is Sam Youngblood. His wife died giving birth. He's the chief of police in Borden's Gap. I am seriously safe in every respect, except from myself. I don't want to get attached. I don't want to fall in love again for fear I'll be dumped."

"Shut up! Does he like you?"

Katie sighed. "I think so. They're the 'friends' I just ate supper with tonight."

"How old are the girls?"

"Six, and he's done an amazing job raising them. They're funny, smart, precocious because…twins…and they grilled me like a burger tonight."

Lila laughed. "Then, sister, I only have one piece of advice: enjoy the ride for as far as it goes. No what-ifs. No maybes. Just today. Every day."

"Yes, I know you're right," Katie said. "But I so do not want to get my heart broken again."

"Maybe he feels the same way," Lila said. "Maybe this Sam fellow is afraid of loss just like you're afraid of rejection."

Katie blinked.

"I never thought of it like that."

"That's why you have me," Lila said. "I love you. Call

me. Don't make me always be the one calling you. It makes me feel like a stalker."

Katie burst out laughing. "Okay. I'm sorry. I'll call you Monday evening after my first day at work."

"Deal," Lila said, then giggled and disconnected.

Katie was staggered by the news that the man Mark had worked for all those years had been a pusher for some local drug kingpin. She didn't feel sorry for Mark. She didn't feel anything. He was where he was because of decisions he'd made, and he was none of her concern.

───────

It was the middle of the night, but Sam had just taken a load of sheets and clothes from the washer and put them into the dryer.

The noise they'd heard as Katie was leaving was the girls upending Fishy and his fishbowl in the middle of their bed, and tipping over the table it had been sitting on in the process.

Sam had rescued the fish and the bowl, then had to strip their bed down to the plastic mattress pad, grateful he still had it in place. But everything, including the girls and the bedclothes, was soaked.

The girls were okay until they saw the look on Daddy's face. That's when they burst into tears. It had taken hours to put their room back together and settle their world back on its axis. But the crash had been traumatic for all concerned. Fishy was still alive, but Sam was dreading tomorrow for fear he'd wake up with Fishy belly-up in his fishbowl.

So Sam was in bed, watching TV with the sound turned down and waiting for the clothes to dry. And in spite of all that drama, he couldn't quit thinking about Katie McGrath. He'd had the best time with her that he'd had in years. The girls were curious about her but definitely accepting of her presence, only he was scared.

He'd never loved anyone in his whole life but Shelly. But he also knew she would be the first one to tell him it was time to let her go.

The thought made his heart hurt.

But Katie made him ache in a way he thought he'd never feel again. He knew way too much about her life—about her past. And getting jilted only months ago? What if he fell for her and she wasn't over Mark Roman? What if Roman's betrayal had done such a number on her that it was unlikely she would trust again?

He didn't want to fall for her, then lose her.

But he couldn't help thinking...hoping...that maybe she was afraid, too. Afraid of yet another rejection in her life.

So it came down to Sam.

Did he want to take a chance on her, if she was willing to take a chance on him?

He took a deep breath, then sighed. His chest ached, and there was a knot in his stomach. He had this innate need to protect, and if ever there was a woman who needed to know she was safe—that she was loved—it was Katie.

He turned off the lamp beside his bed, turned off the TV, and slid down into his bed.

To hell with wrinkled clothes.

He was too tired to care about them.

All he wanted to do was sleep.

Mark Roman was going home—to Kansas. His family knew everything. He'd talked to them for hours. And after all was said and done, instead of blaming or judging, they just told him to come home. It was all he needed to hear. They'd given him permission to fail.

The house he'd shared with Megan had been stained by lies, drugs, and death. He'd already contacted a Realtor to put it on the market. He didn't want to live there anymore and was spending his nights in a downtown hotel.

His lawyer was running interference for him with the legalities that had arisen after Megan's and Walt's demise. Everyone was lauding him as a hero for doing the right thing, but in his mind, he'd caused Megan's death. Even though none of it would have happened had they not been involved in illegal activities, his spirit was yoked by guilt.

And if that wasn't bad enough, learning he was inheriting anything from the Laniers felt like blood money, and he wanted no part of it.

He drank himself to sleep every night, with the nightmare running in a loop in his head.

If he hadn't turned Megan in, she would still be alive.

And if Megan was still alive, Walt wouldn't have run away and wound up dead.

And if neither of those things had happened, then Mark would never have known Craig Buttoni existed.

But he had, and they did. And his sense of decency had brought down the house.

He wanted out of Albuquerque. Where people didn't associate him with any of it. He didn't want to be a hero. He didn't want any aspect of earned money from drugs, and when he sold his house, it would release him from the last thing tying him to this city.

He poured another shot of whiskey into his glass and tossed it back like medicine, then followed the burn all the way to his belly. He was wondering where the hell his food was, because if room service didn't get here soon, he'd be too damn drunk to eat it.

Then just as he thought it, there was a knock at his door. He looked through the peephole. It was the server from room service.

"About damn time," he muttered, and opened the door to let the man in, added a tip as he signed the ticket.

When the server began to remove the covers, Mark waved him off.

"I'll do that," he said, and turned the dead bolt after the server left.

Journalists had been trying to get to him for a story since the whole nightmare began, even going to the extreme of pretending to be hotel employees just to get into his room. Now he was more cautious about who came and went.

But this was his last night in the hotel. Tomorrow he had to go back to his house and have movers pack up his personal belongings. After that, he was going home to Kansas. Back to the family farm.

Maybe getting dirt under his nails and on his clothes again would help him forget the dirt on his soul.

―――――――

Katie woke up early to make blueberry muffins. She wanted to take some to Delilah when she went to walk Rhett Butler. The old woman had become dear to her, and she was going to miss seeing her every day.

She was stirring up the batter and had it ready but for the blueberries draining in a bowl, when there was a knock at the door. She was barefoot, wearing an old-fashioned bib apron over her pajamas, with her sleep-tangled hair clipped up high on her head. And while she was debating about answering the door looking as she did, whoever it was knocked again. At that point, she ran to answer.

To her horror, it was Sam.

He looked at her and grinned.

She sighed. "Well, all the magic just rubbed off the mirror, didn't it?"

He shook his head. "You look adorable."

"I'm baking blueberry muffins. Please, come in. Is everything okay?"

"I won't come in. I shouldn't have come without calling. But I need to ask you something and tell you something."

"Okay, ask away."

Sam's future hinged on her answers, but she was so sexy standing there that it was hard to focus.

"You need to know I was afraid to come over here. I still am. But the chance that you might not turn me down is worth the fear." Then he took a deep breath. "You are the first woman I've wanted to get to know since…since Shelly died. But I sense you have reservations about men in general, and I don't want to push where I'm not welcome."

"Oh, Sam, I—"

He held up his hand. "Let me finish before you say what you have to say."

She nodded.

Sam took another breath. "I want to know if you would be interested in us seeing each other."

"Is it my time to speak now?" Katie asked.

Sam tensed. "Yes."

"Then my answer is yes. I am interested. I have issues, but not with men in general. Just one in particular. And I'm not pining away. I would not throw water on him if he was on fire. But he broke my trust in a very big way, and I guess I'm kind of like you…afraid to let anyone climb over the wall again."

"I'm not into breaking down walls. I prefer waiting for someone to just open a door and invite me in."

Katie's heart skipped. "Well, the door is already open. And this is your official invitation. You are welcome in my home, Sam Youngblood."

Sam exhaled. "Thank you, Katie."

"So, are you coming in?"

"I don't feel like pushing my luck. I think I'll just let this settle right here," Sam said. "You're baking muffins and the girls are playing, and I don't leave them alone for long."

"Oh…today's your day off, right?"

"Yes. So if you get lonesome, we're across the street raising hell."

Katie laughed. "What was the crash about last night?"

"They dry-landed Fishy," Sam said.

"What?"

"They 'accidentally' dropped the fishbowl with their goldfish onto the bed, and turned the table over that it was on, although… (A.) They weren't supposed to be moving the fishbowl. (B.) Fishy told them he didn't like being in the moonlight. And (C.) You're too damn cute for words, and you have made my day. I want to ask you out, but it all hinges on finding a babysitter."

"Consider the invitation received and accepted right now. But I don't want to be the woman who suddenly takes away the girls' daddy time. Maybe we could keep it simple at first. Stay close to home and take them with us?"

Sam was surprised. "Are you serious?"

"Sure. You can't just shift loyalty to accommodate me. They're your babies. They're always going to have to come first."

Sam's eyes were shining with unshed tears.

"God, Katie…you are so dang near perfect, I can't stand it."

Katie tucked a lock of her hair behind her ear. "Nearly perfect? It's my hair, isn't it? Or was it my bare feet?"

Sam stepped across the threshold, cupped her face, and kissed her square on the mouth.

"Perfect," he said softly, rubbed his thumb across her lower lip, and left her standing there.

Katie shivered. *You, sir, are a thief in hiding. I think you are planning to steal my heart.*

Then she remembered the muffins, hurried back to the kitchen to finish the batter, and couldn't think of what she was doing before she stopped.

"Oh yes…the blueberries," she said, and folded them into the batter.

Her lips were tingling as she put the muffins in to bake. She was still thinking about the way his mouth felt on hers.

She was riding a high that this was happening, and so afraid of the fall if it ended. But she was taking Lila's advice. Ride the ride. Take the risks. Love while you can. Heartbreak won't kill you.

While the muffins were baking, Katie went to get dressed. She had things she wanted to do before work began Monday, so after she walked Rhett Butler, she was going downtown. There was a small clothing boutique she'd been wanting to check out, and she had an appointment at the beauty shop to get her hair trimmed.

A short while later, she and the muffins were on their way to Delilah's.

She pulled all the way up in the drive and went to the front door with the muffins and rang the doorbell.

Rhett was barking as Delilah opened the door, but when she saw how Katie was dressed, she was confused.

"You look too pretty to go dog walking," she said.

Katie smiled. "As soon as Rhett and I do our thing, I'm going to get a haircut. And I brought you some blueberry muffins."

Delilah beamed. "I love blueberry muffins. Thank you."

"Awesome. Trade you," Katie said, then handed the

box to Delilah and picked up Rhett's leash. "Hi, baby. Are you ready to go?" she asked as she clipped on his leash.

Rhett chomped the leash and led Katie down the steps.

"See you later," Katie said, and down the drive they went—Katie in her black slacks and a red-and-silver-striped blouse, the little Yorkie in his blinged-out collar. Neither of them aware they were the subject of conversation between three women in a car a couple of blocks behind them.

———

"See, there she is, just like I said."

Betty Looper pointed and then tapped the brakes on her baby-blue Dodge Dart so they could observe Katie unseen.

Kay Ritter was in the back seat, peering between her two best friends occupying the front seat, and leaned forward for a better view.

"She's so thin. I wonder if she diets. I'll hate her for sure if she's naturally thin."

Charlene Smith poked Betty on the arm. "Go around the block the other way so we can see her face as we pass."

"She's about to turn right," Betty said.

"How do you know that?" Charlene asked.

"Because I've been watching her for days. She walks Delilah's dog around the block, moving at a slow pace until it poops, then she picks up the poop in one of those little bags, and usually winds up carrying the dog the rest of the way home," Betty said.

"I wonder why Delilah's granddaughter's not doing this anymore," Kay said.

Betty snorted. "Oh, girl! You don't pay attention to anything. She graduated last year. She's about to finish her first year of college. Delilah's been walking Rhett, and you know how tottery she is these days."

"Well then, I thought this woman was hired to be a teacher. So who's gonna walk Rhett Butler when she's in school?" Charlene asked.

"Oh, for the love of God!" Betty said. "We came to scope out the competition, and here you are worrying about walking a dog."

Charlene glared at Betty.

Kay leaned over the seat again. "I still want to see her face. It would ease my jealous soul if she was homely."

Betty shook her head. "She's not homely. She's real pretty. And they say she's real nice, too."

"Shit," Kay said. "Now I'm gonna feel guilty for being jealous. I need to add myself to my good-night prayers."

Then they all burst out laughing as Betty stepped on the gas, turned the corner, and began gaining on Katie.

Just as they were about to pass her, Rhett Butler wandered off into the grass and squatted, and when he did, Katie turned her back to the street and walked with him—thereby nullifying the scouting expedition they'd been on.

"Shoot fire!" Charlene whined.

Betty shrugged. "You're just gonna have to take my word for it. And we've all got to remember...from what I've heard, she hasn't accepted one single invitation from any of the guys. So it's not like we're out of the running."

"We're out of the running because we've already dated

every damn one of them at one time or another," Kay muttered. "Let's face it. We all grew up together. There's nothing new to know. Not for us about them. Not for them about us. It's not her fault they are enchanted...so to speak."

"We could always sign up for one of those online things where single people meet other single people," Charlene said.

"And then you get catfished," Betty said.

"What's catfished?" Kay asked.

And they drove off to lunch, while Charlene and Betty explained the finer points of being tricked and scammed.

Unaware of the drama she was creating, Katie and Rhett Butler were already on their way back. And as usual, Rhett's last half of the walk was in Katie's arms.

When they reached the house, Delilah was sitting on the porch, visiting with a young man. They were deep in conversation as Katie came up the steps, but the moment the young man saw her, he stood.

Katie smiled at him, then gave the little Yorkie a kiss and a hug.

"I'm gonna miss you, sweetie. You be good for Miss Delilah," she said, and then put Rhett in Delilah's lap.

"Thank you, Katie dear. You have been a lifesaver. My new walker begins tomorrow." And then she realized her nephew was impatiently waiting for an introduction. "I'm sorry, Katie. Where are my manners. This is my greatnephew, Walker Cash. He's my oldest brother's grandson. Walker, this is Katie McGrath. She's a new teacher at our elementary school."

Katie saw a glimmer of expectation in Walker's eyes, and she was about to put out the fire before it had a chance to burn.

Walker beamed. "It's a pleasure, Miss McGrath. Aunt Dee speaks highly of you."

Katie smiled politely and then winked at Delilah. "I think a lot of her, too. It's nice meeting you, Walker. Miss Delilah, I've got to run, or I'll be late for my appointment. You and Rhett take care."

Then she flew down the steps, jumped in her car, and drove away without looking back, and went straight to Coiffures and Colors by Maxine.

The hair salon was nestled in between the Dollar General and a barbershop. Katie eyed the cars in the parking lot at Dollar General and then parked at the curb in front of the shop and hurried inside.

A bell rang at the back of the salon as she opened the door. There were four chairs in the salon, and patrons in three of them, all in various stages of getting styled. And at the moment all three stylists and their customers were staring at Katie, when a middle-aged woman with pink hair came out of a doorway in the back, saw Katie, and headed toward her.

"Hello! Are you Katie?" she asked.

Katie nodded.

"Well, then come on back and we'll get you started. I'm Maxine, and it's real nice to meet you."

For Katie, it was like standing on the shores of Lake Michigan and watching the ice break. The stylists all began smiling at her, and their clients gave her a little wave from beneath their capes as she followed Maxine to her station.

"You're the new teacher in town, right?" Maxine asked as she ran her fingers through Katie's hair.

"Yes, I am," Katie said.

"You have great hair," Maxine said. "What are we doing with it?"

"I want the ends trimmed, and then my hair washed and styled," Katie said.

"We can do that," Maxine said. "Let's get you to the shampoo station."

And for the next hour, Katie was in the hands of a master.

She got her hair washed and then taken back to the styling chair where Maxine began massaging her head and neck. When she finally stopped and began combing her out, Katie was completely relaxed.

"How much off the ends?" Maxine asked.

"No more than an inch," Katie said.

Maxine nodded, but her eyes were narrowing. "You know, you'd look real good with some highlights."

"I'm a bit of a traditionalist," Katie said. "Just a trim."

Maxine nodded again, then began sectioning off Katie's hair, and the trim began.

An hour after Katie had walked in, she left with her hair in a soft, swingy style.

And although she'd only gone in for a haircut, she was leaving the beginnings of her reputation behind her. The new teacher was pretty and nice, and she laughed at people's jokes and left Maxine a nice tip.

In a small town like Borden's Gap, that was gold.

Chapter Thirteen

KATIE GOT IN THE CAR AND THEN HEADED BACK UP
Main. In Albuquerque, there would have been countless
places in which to shop for gifts. In Borden's Gap, there
was one.

Arnold's Antiques and Gifts. Heavy on the antiques.
Easy on the gifts.

Katie wasn't letting the displays in the window deter
her joy in exploring her new surroundings. She was hopeful that the majority of her shopping experiences while
living in Borden's Gap did not include long drives to
Jackson or online at Amazon.com.

Still feeling fresh and sporty from her trip to the hair
salon, she walked into Arnold's with a bounce in her step
and was immediately overwhelmed in the very best way.

The interior was laid out in vignettes. The gift-shop por-
tion of Arnold's was all up front. But the deeper a shopper
moved into the store, the more entrenched they became
in antiques. One whole display counter held antique jewelry. Another area was devoted to paintings and old frames
and all manner of decor. And in the very back, the apparent
quality of antique furniture was on a level with what Katie
had been accustomed to seeing in Chicago.

She was still taking it all in when a tiny little man with a shock of snow-white hair approached.

"Morning, miss. Are you looking for something in particular, or do you just want to feast your eyes?"

Katie looked down at the smile on his face and was enchanted, both by the way he'd phrased his question and his elfin appearance.

"I'm looking for a gift for two little girls, but at the moment, I am somewhat spellbound by the surrounding magic."

The old man clapped his hands together. "You're feeling the ages," he said. "Only a true sensitive would recognize the power. I'm Billy Arnold, the owner, but I've been called Bitty all my life…for obvious reasons."

Katie held out her hand. "I'm Katie McGrath, a new resident to Borden's Gap. I'm pleased to meet you, and if you don't mind, I'll call you Billy. Your mama must have loved the name or she wouldn't have given it to you."

In that moment, and for only the second time in his life, Billy Arnold fell a little bit in love.

"I would be honored, Miss McGrath."

She held up a finger, unaware she'd shifted into teacher mode. "Katie…please, and I love antiques, so I'd like to look around a bit. Out of curiosity, how did you get started in collecting?"

Billy smiled. "Oh, that's easy. As I was losing three generations of my family, I kept inheriting their treasures. At first, I couldn't bear to part with any of it because it reminded me of them, but when I became the last of our Arnold lineage, I finally realized their things were not keeping me company. Just crowding me out of my own home."

"You have a most unique, descriptive voice. You should have been a writer," Katie said.

Billy beamed. "Why, thank you. How about you? What sparked your interest in antiques? Do you have some from your family as well?"

Katie shook her head. "I don't have family. I was abandoned as a baby and never adopted. The only past I have is my own. But I grew up in Chicago and saw some amazing antiques there. I guess that's where my love of grand design, dark wood, and art carved within the surfaces began."

Billy Arnold took a deep breath. She'd stolen his heart with a smile and a laugh, and now she was breaking it. He could not fathom a life without family.

"Well now…I've taken up far too much of your time. Wander to your heart's content, and if you have a question, just call out. The sound carries in here, and my hearing is still quite good. In fact, I've accidentally overheard the most amazing bits of gossip from some of my customers, so if you get a phone call, you have been warned."

Katie burst out laughing, then gave him a thumbs-up as she began winding her way through the aisles, unaware Billy Arnold was doing a little shopping of his own.

She spent the better part of an hour prowling, then searching through the gift shop before she found two perfect little gifts for two perfect little girls and carried them to the register to pay.

"I'll take these," Katie said, as she laid down two little-girls' headbands—one red, one blue—both covered with rhinestones.

"Good choices," Billy said, and rang them up, then

bagged them separately. "Little ones do like to open their own gifts, right?"

"Yes, they do, Billy, and thank you for letting me wander about in here. It was such a pleasure to meet you."

"The pleasure was mine," he said, and then took an object from beneath the counter and set it before her. "I would be honored if you would accept this little gift from me to you. The figurine sitting at her dresser reminded me a bit of you. While it is within a globe, it is not a snow globe. It is a music box. If you wind it up, it plays 'Clair de Lune,' which is one of my favorite music-box tunes. I don't know who it belonged to, and you don't know who you belonged to, and it's quite charming, as are you. I wanted you to have your own antique. I have cleared it and blessed it, so there are no lingering entities attached...but who knows? It may be the trigger to an antiques addiction of your own."

Katie's eyes welled. Tears rolled before she could stop them, and then she couldn't get her emotions under control.

"I don't know... Nobody ever... Oh my God...thank you. You have no idea how treasured this will be."

Billy wrapped the music box in layer after layer of tissue, then boxed it up and slipped it into a gift bag.

"Your joy is my joy," Billy said. "Enjoy. And if the music box quits playing, bring it in. I know how to fix them."

"Yes...oh my...thank you," Katie said, blinking back tears.

She carried the bag clutched to her breasts as if it was a newborn as she left the store. Billy Arnold hadn't just given her a gift. He had acknowledged her existence.

Katie's real identity was a mystery, as was the original owner of this music box. They'd both been lost by fate and time until Billy had become their intermediary. Billy had cared enough to give Katie her own antique, and the music box was no longer lost. She felt grounded by another woman's history—a woman she would never know.

She drove away, still blinking back tears. She was too full…spilling over from the love she'd been given. She'd been acknowledged. She felt seen.

She drove until she found an empty parking lot, then pulled in and parked before she realized it was a church. She sat for a few minutes, trying to pull herself together and wondering at the irony of ending up here at this moment.

Katie'd quit talking to God years ago because she didn't think He was listening. She would pray for a family. She'd pray to be removed from one bad foster home to another. She'd prayed to be rescued…somehow…in any way He saw fit. But it never happened. And the broken child she was believed God could neither see nor hear her because she did not matter.

Now, when the most wonderful thing had just happened to her, she found herself here. She laughed, but in it were the sounds of anger and disbelief.

"What am I supposed to do here?" she cried. "Bow down at Your feet when You left mine bare? Join a church and listen to a man I don't know start telling me how I'm supposed to live? If You've been following the shit show that has been my life, what about it do You expect me to thank You for?"

She closed her eyes and leaned back against the seat, choking on sobs, and then all of a sudden there was a knock at her window. She opened her eyes and groaned.

It was Sam.

She swiped at the tears on her face and then rolled down the window.

"What's wrong?" Sam asked.

Katie shook her head. "Nothing you can fix."

"Try me," Sam said.

She sighed. "I'm not dying. I have no physical pain. I just… I just… I guess the dam broke."

"May I get in?"

She shrugged.

Sam didn't give her a chance to change her mind. He got into the passenger seat and then closed the door. The cool air inside was a far cry from the heat outside, but he could feel her rage as if she were on fire.

Then, instead of grilling her, he just held out his hand.

Katie shuddered, knowing if she took it, he would never let her go. And in that moment, as crazy as she felt, it was his steadfastness that pulled her in.

She reached out. His fingers curled around her hand, and then he gave it a quick squeeze.

"Trouble shared is trouble bared. And when secrets are no longer hidden, their power is gone."

"Oh, Sam…you have no idea what you're asking," Katie muttered.

"I ask nothing of you. But I'll give anything to you that you need."

"Why?" Katie asked.

"Because you're worth it."

The words hung between them like a white flag in a war zone.

What was it Lila said? Something about taking the ride, regardless of how the journey ended?

"You should never have knocked on my window," she said.

Sam still held her hand without force, but refusing to let her go. She was going to have to be the one to pull way.

"I already knocked on your door. I already let you under my skin. Trust me, girl."

Unconsciously, Katie tightened her grip. "I don't know who I am. I don't know where I came from. I was abandoned in an alley in Chicago as a newborn. A homeless person found me, and the police picked me up and took me to a hospital. I have lived in so many different foster homes, I lost count. Sometimes they were good to me. Most times they were not. I was to be adopted twice, and both times the people backed out. I never knew why. I grew up unloved. Unwanted. I aged out of the foster system and worked two jobs to put myself through college. I wanted to be someone. I needed to be someone special for others. So I became a teacher…and I was loved. And I began to love myself."

Sam pulled a handful of tissues from the box in the seat beside him and handed them to her. She wiped her eyes and her nose. She wouldn't look at him. She just kept talking.

"And that's when I met Mark Roman. A nice young CPA who charmed me and swept me off my feet. Three years later, we're getting married. I'm at the chapel, in my wedding dress, ready to walk down the aisle, and I get a phone call. He's in Las Vegas with his new bride…who just happens to be his boss's daughter. He left me to face the guests…to tell them I'd been jilted, and to take their gifts with them when they left. I don't know why I didn't see it coming. I've never been good enough to choose."

Sam's heart was breaking. He already knew all this, but hearing the pain in her voice was his undoing.

"Well, he's the original dumbass," Sam said. "But never mind my opinion. Just get it all said because once it's out, it never has to be spoken of again."

Katie sighed. *If only.*

"Anyway, I went back to work a week later with my tail between my legs, bearing the pity of my coworkers and wallowing in the shared anger of the people I considered friends. The blessing was that my students were oblivious. Miss Katie was back, and their world settled onto its axis. Less than two months later, we had a school shooting where I worked. Saguaro Elementary in Albuquerque. I was shot twice in the back and was the only staff member to survive out of the five who were shot. But I kept my kids safe, and I healed. Sort of. I could not go back in that school without getting sick.

"I have PTSD. Anything that sounds like gunshots throws me back into the moment when I'm running with my students, trying to get them out of the hall before the shooter catches up with us. I have nightmares almost every night. I am so broken, I'm not worth keeping. I didn't tell you the truth about myself because I wanted to forget it. But that's lying to you and to myself."

Sam lifted her hand and kissed the back of her knuckles. "I'm not scared of you. But I am pretty scared of losing you before I can even call you mine."

"Oh, Sam," Katie said.

He shook his head. "Don't 'oh, Sam' me. What happened today, Katie?"

"I went into Arnold's Antiques and Gift shop to buy the girls a little gift apiece. All I have to say is, Billy Arnold is magic. He charmed me and we got to talking, and, well…he pulled me into history I don't have a claim to and then gave me a piece of it. A beautiful music box. It's antique and probably worth a fortune, but he gave it to me because he didn't know who it used to belong to, and since I didn't know who I belonged to, either, he thought it should belong to me. And it shattered me, but in the very best way, and that's why I was crying. And so I pulled into this parking lot, not realizing it belongs to a church, and I quit talking to God years ago because no matter what I prayed about, I felt ignored. I was absolutely certain I didn't matter. A part of me still believes that."

Sam wanted her in his arms, but there was the console between them, and seeing as how he was the chief of police and had an image to maintain, for both their sakes he couldn't bring himself to make out with the new teacher in the church parking lot.

"Look at me, Katie."

"I can't," she said.

"Yes, you can. Look at me," he said, and tugged her hand.

She sighed and then turned her head. He had tears in his eyes.

"I'm looking," she said.

"Then listen to me, too. You think God doesn't know you exist, and yet you lived through that school massacre. You think God abandoned you, but that wasn't God.

That was the woman who gave birth to you. She's the one who failed you. Not God. He kept you alive through a lot of hell, didn't He? He helped you grow into a survivor... didn't He? He has to wait for you to see yourself, before you can see Him.

"I have wondered for six long years why God took Shelly away from me and my girls. And you arrive, not just in town but across the street from where we live. Maybe God meant for us to meet? And whatever we make of it is up to us? Life is full of mysteries and secrets. And I'm a cop. I'm good at solving mysteries and getting to the bottom of secrets. Not one damn thing you've told me changes my opinion of you, other than maybe to admire you more. If this doesn't work between us...it won't be because I quit. That will have to come from you. Understand?"

"Understood," Katie said.

Sam's two-way crackled. The dispatcher was paging him.

"Well, hell. Duty calls. Are you going to be okay?"

"Yes."

"Don't forget...you are my hero," Sam said.

Katie sighed. "You're in danger of earning your own medal. Maybe I need to go back to Arnold's and get one more blingy headband for you."

Sam grinned. "Maybe a bottle of nail polish instead. I won't let the girls paint my fingernails, but I will let them paint my toes."

Katie burst out laughing.

Sam's radio crackled again. "I've gotta go. Just remember you are one kick-ass woman, and I am proud of you."

Then he got out of the car answering the dispatch,

jumped into the patrol car, and took off out of the parking lot, burning rubber.

Katie wiped her face, then glanced up at the church and sighed.

"Okay…maybe I wasn't seeing the whole picture," she said. "I'll give You and me some more thought."

Then she blew her nose, fixed her makeup, and was starting to go home, when something within her said *No more hiding*. And so she turned uptown.

There were three places to eat in town, and she hadn't eaten all day. Not even one of her own blueberry muffins. Maybe it was time to debut her presence somewhere besides Welby's Grocery and the hair salon.

She'd already been to the barbecue food truck, but she wanted to eat out somewhere—in public. She was missing Lila. Lila would have been up to try anything.

Hillbilly Pizza was coming up on the left, but she wasn't in the mood for pizza, so she drove on up the street and pulled into the parking lot at Ronda's Café. She checked her makeup one last time to make sure her crying spell wasn't written all over her face, and then got out and walked inside.

There was a sign that said HANG ON A MINUTE.

Katie took it to mean "Wait to be seated," and grinned. Moments later, a woman came hurrying into the lobby.

"Hi, hon! Table for one?"

"Yes," Katie said, but as the hostess was walking her through the dining room, someone shouted out Katie's name.

She paused, looked around, and saw Louise Parsons smiling and waving.

"Are you alone?" Louise asked.

Katie nodded.

"Come eat with us!" Louise said, and pointed to an empty chair.

The hostess paused. "Y'all wanna sit with them?"

"Yes, please," Katie said, and then followed the hostess to Louise's table where she laid a menu at the vacant seat.

"Your waitress will be with you shortly. Enjoy," she said.

Katie sat, smiling at the three women at the table.

Louise reached over and patted Katie's arm.

"Hey, girl! Good to see you. These two are my bowling buddies, Rita and Shirl. Girls, this is Katie, the new first-grade teacher."

"Nice to meet you," they said. "Do you bowl?"

"Barely," Katie said, which brought a huge round of laughter.

She grinned. Apparently they weren't going to hold it against her. And then a waitress appeared to take her drink order, which was the signal for Katie to read the menu and find something to eat.

Later, after food came and they were eating, Rita took advantage of a pause in the conversation.

"Hey, Katie. Do you know who your students are going to be?" she asked.

"Not yet," Katie said. "I'll get a class list soon."

"Well, I have a grandson who's going into first grade, so you might have him and you might not. His name is Donny Tiller. He's a little chatterbox but really sweet. He's my youngest daughter's boy."

"I'll be looking for the name," Katie said, and was reaching for her drink when a loud crash rolled through the dining room. In the following moments when conversation stopped, she was holding onto the seat of her chair to keep from bolting.

Louise saw the wild look in Katie's eyes and realized what was happening. Without calling attention to Katie's panic, she calmly reached beneath the table and put her hand on Katie's arm.

"Someone's pay is going to get docked for that," Louise said.

Shirl rolled her eyes, and Rita laughed.

"'Bout scared the pee out of me," Rita said, which made Shirl laugh.

And then the diners picked up their conversations as if the crash had never occurred, and slowly, Katie's heart kicked back into a normal rhythm. As Louise turned loose of Katie's arm, Katie leaned back in the chair, giving Louise a grateful glance.

Louise winked and then spotted a scattering of crumbs on her blouse and looked up at the girls.

"When was one of you gonna tell me these crumbs were on my shirt? It looks like I've been puttin' out bird feed, for pity's sake."

They laughed again, and then ate their way through dessert before parting ways.

Louise walked out with Katie.

"You doin' okay?" she asked.

Katie shrugged. "I think so, and then stuff like that happens. My reactions are all over the place."

"My daddy was in Vietnam. It's going to take time, but you will get better. He did."

"Thank you for that," Katie said.

"Sure thing. And anytime you want someone to go to lunch with…or supper with, give me a call. I hate to cook, so I'm always ready to go out."

"Will do," Katie said. "Thanks again. Your friends are really nice, and so are you."

"Any time," Louise said, then she went one way and Katie the other to get to their cars.

Katie went home, carried her gifts into the house, unwrapped the music box, and then took it to her bedroom and set it on the dresser. She stared into the globe until her eyes were burning with unshed tears, then wound up the music box and set it back down.

Her eyes were still burning as she changed into an old T-shirt and a pair of shorts. She'd cried so much today that she'd given herself a headache, so she took something for the pain and stretched out on the bed.

Just to rest.

Just until the pain meds kicked in.

And fell asleep with the lilting notes of "Clair de Lune" spinning in her head.

———

Sam's day calmed down after answering the call that had taken him away from Katie.

Family feuds were pretty common in the South, and Borden's Gap was no exception. And if it wasn't old enemies fussing, it was just as likely to be two drunks, or two neighbors, trying to make new enemies of each other.

By the time he headed home, he was tired to the bone of people who couldn't get along, and Katie was on his mind. He'd left her so abruptly, he was concerned, and when he saw her car under the carport at her house, he turned into her drive instead of his own. It wouldn't take long to check on her, and he needed to know she was okay.

He hurried up the steps and rang the doorbell.

———

Katie was taking a load of clothes out of the dryer when she heard the doorbell, so she dumped everything in a basket and went to answer.

It was Sam. The moment she saw him standing in her doorway, she felt the world settle beneath her feet.

"Come in," she said.

He stepped inside. "Something smells good."

"A chicken pot pie or laundry. Take your pick," she said.

Sam cupped the side of her face.

"I pick you. And I stopped to see if you're okay. I hated to leave you when I did."

"I'm okay… In fact, I'm good. I wound up having lunch with Louise and her two bowling buddies, Rita and Shirl. It was a good time. And speaking of a good time, when would be a good time for me to give the girls their gifts? I don't want to mess up something you have planned, but I wanted to give them thank-you gifts for being such good hostesses."

"Anytime is good," he said.

"Then as soon as I take the pot pie out of the oven, I'll

bring them, okay? And just so you know…I forgot your nail polish."

He grinned. "Good. Then I'll see you soon?"

She nodded, and before she knew it, he was hugging her.

"That was for me," he said when he let her go. "I felt like I abandoned you in a time of need."

Katie was still reeling from the feel of him. "If that hug was for you, then where's mine?" she asked.

Sam reached for her again, but this time pulled her closer and held her longer, slightly rocking her where she stood before he turned her loose.

Katie sighed as he stepped away. "You give the best hugs. I'll take that any day, with thanks."

He grinned. "It's good to know I haven't lost my touch," he said. "I'll see you soon." And then he was out the door.

As she shut the door behind him, she remembered her laundry and the pot pie and hurried back to check on it. The pie was a perfect golden brown. So she set it aside to cool and went to tend to her laundry.

It took a few minutes to hang the clothes, and then she put on a pair of sneakers, grabbed the gift bags and a little box with some of her blueberry muffins, and headed out the door, noting Roxie's car was gone as she walked across the street, then rang the doorbell.

Sam had obviously given the girls permission to answer again because Katie heard them coming at a lope, shouting "I'll get it! I'll get it!" all the way to the door.

And then it swung inward. The girls were standing there, grinning at her in silence.

"Hi, girls," Katie said. "May I come in?"

"Yes!" they echoed. This time, they didn't run off and leave her because they were too interested in the two small gift bags she was carrying.

Sam appeared in the hallway, then motioned toward the living room.

"Girls. Show Miss Katie to the sofa."

Evie turned and pointed. "There it is!" and then grabbed Katie by the hand and walked her to it.

"Thank you," Katie said, and then sat. "Beth. Evie. I brought each of you a little thank-you gift for being such great hostesses the other night."

The girls were dancing from one foot to the other, so excited they couldn't stand still.

"We like surprises," Evie said.

"Yes, we do," Beth added.

Katie peeked into the bags to make sure she was giving the right headband to each girl, and then handed them over.

"Evie, this one is for you, and Beth, this one is yours. I hope you like them."

They took the bags, dropped to the floor with them, and then dug through the tissue paper to pull their gifts out.

Evie's eyes widened, and then she gasped and squealed. "It's a red headband with jewels! Like a princess!"

Beth pulled hers out and waved it over her head. "Look, Daddy. My headband is blue with jewels. I will be a princess, too!"

"Thank you, Miss Katie!" they cried, and launched themselves at her, hugged her madly, then shoved the headbands on their heads like the old pros they were and bolted out of the room to find a mirror.

Sam was still grinning.

"Good choices, Miss Katie. You rock," he said.

"So it would appear," Katie said.

"Since you forgot my nail polish, will you at least stay and visit with me long enough so I don't feel left out?" Sam asked.

"I brought blueberry muffins instead," she said.

"All the better," Sam said, and pulled her up into his arms and hugged her. "What's your poison?" he asked as he opened the refrigerator door.

"I'll take a Pepsi," she said, and set the box of muffins on the table.

"Coming up," he said, as he unscrewed the lid and then set the drink on the table in front of her. "So, where did you eat lunch?"

"At Ronda's Café," Katie said.

"Ah…gossip central. So, tell me what's going on in Borden's Gap."

"Since I don't know the people they were talking about, I'm not sure what's new and what's not, but I don't think Rita likes her son-in-law, and Louise just sold the old Butterfield house to someone's son who just got married. And Shirl is on the hunt for husband number three."

Sam waved a wooden spoon in her direction.

"For someone who doesn't know the area, you got a lot of useful info. You'd make a good witness," Sam said.

Katie thought of Mark and the mess he was in. "I try not to get involved in anything that might send me to the witness stand."

Sam laughed it off, but he knew immediately what she

was referring to. However, she had not shared any of that with him, and unless she did, he knew nothing.

The girls came running into the kitchen to show off their headbands and insisted Sam take pictures.

"Send them to Granny and Papa!" Beth said.

"And Gram and Grandy," Evie added.

"Those are my parents and Shelly's parents," Sam said as he wiped his hands and picked up his phone.

Katie watched the twins posing and noticed that in most of the pictures they were either hugging each other, had their arms around each other's waists, or had their heads together. It was such a visual image of how connected identical twins could be.

"Okay, girls, I have the pictures, and if you want any supper, then you need to go find something to play or it's not going to get cooked."

"We're starving!" Evie cried.

"Starving!" Beth echoed.

Katie grinned. "So am I…and mine's already done. I'm leaving, too, so Daddy can get busy. The girls can walk me to the door and you just keep cooking, 'cause they're starving."

Sam rolled his eyes. He hated to see her leave, but he had no good reason to keep her beyond just wanting to be in her presence.

"Come back anytime!" he yelled as she was walking out the door, and then she was gone.

Chapter Fourteen

Mark Roman had forgotten how flat Kansas was, but there was something about the prairie that called to him, and now he was back and only a half a mile from home, wondering if he would be able to hear it again.

His parents knew he was coming. It was almost suppertime. He knew his mom would have made something special, even though she shouldn't have. It had been so long since he'd been home that he didn't deserve special.

As he turned off the highway and started up the long blacktop road to the farmhouse sitting in the middle of hundreds of acres of waving wheat, he shuddered.

His dad would be awkward.

His mother would cry.

And his room would be a time capsule of who he'd been, which was better than a visual of who he was now.

As he drove toward the house, the wheat growing along the edges of the road was waving as if in welcome, but when he glanced in the rearview mirror, it appeared as if the road was disappearing behind him. Closing him in.

He'd escaped from here once.

It wouldn't happen again.

And then he was pulling up to the house and parking

beneath the wide three-car portico. As he got out, he heard a cry of welcome and turned around.

His mother was running toward him, her arms out-stretched, with such a look of joy upon her face. And he was in shock.

When had she grown old?

His dad came down the steps behind her, slower, less certain of how to receive the prodigal son.

Mark's eyes welled. He started walking toward them, and then caught his mother up in his arms and held her.

"I'm sorry, I'm sorry," he kept saying over and over.

And then his dad was there, holding the both of them.

"Welcome home, Son," he said. "Welcome home."

Mark had left to make his fortune and come home with the scars of what he'd done to himself.

He would never get over it.

He would never forget.

But here was where he'd learned right from wrong, and here was where he needed to be to reset his moral compass.

———

Monday came in a flash of light as the first rays of sun appeared, still hidden behind the looming hills and the treetops of the Tennessee pines.

Katie had alternated between nightmares and dreams. She was awake before her alarm went off and dressed before dawn. It was a workday at school. There was a meeting in the cafeteria with coffee and doughnuts as an added incentive to show up on time, and then everyone was off to work in their rooms.

Katie was fully prepared to be the new kid in school. She was a pro after all her years of being moved from foster family to foster family. It was nerve-racking and a little exciting to have a whole new set of students again.

So when the time arrived to set off, she was anxious to get there and excited at the thought of a new year in a new location.

She walked out of the house to get in her car and found a huge handmade sign in her yard.

HAPPY FIRST DAY OF SCHOOL, MISS KATIE!

She took out her phone and quickly snapped a picture, then looked across the street and saw two little faces peering out the window, with Sam standing over them, waving.

"Oh my God! Thank you! Thank you!" Katie shouted, then put both hands over her heart to indicate she loved it and blew all of them kisses as she got in her car and drove away.

She was still smiling when she parked in the school parking lot and walked into the building. According to the letter, all of the teachers were to meet in the cafeteria. Even though she remembered where it was, she could have found it blindfolded by following the aroma of fresh coffee and the chatter of voices. She was so focused on getting to the meeting that the long hallway and empty classrooms never registered.

She walked into the cafeteria, looked around for an empty chair, and left her things before heading to the buffet of coffee and doughnuts.

Susan Wayne had been watching for Katie, and when she saw her at the buffet table, she hurried over.

"Good morning, Katie! Are you ready for this year?"

"I am," Katie said, and then pulled her cell phone out of her pocket and pulled up the picture she'd just taken. "Look what was on my front yard when I came out this morning."

Susan laughed. "That's awesome! Who do you think did that?"

"Oh, I know who did it. Sam Youngblood's little girls, with some help from Daddy."

"So, you've met the chief?" Susan asked.

"I live across the street from him," Katie said.

Two teachers at the buffet looked up at Katie and groaned.

"Hi, I'm Justine. You said you live across the street from Sam?"

"Lucky you," another teacher said, then smiled at Katie. "I'm Wynona, by the way."

"I'm Katie, and it was none of my doing. I just leased a house long distance from Louise Parsons, packed up my stuff, and headed east," Katie said, and then changed the subject. "The doughnuts look so good, and I skipped breakfast for them."

"Get a couple," Susan said. "There's going to be plenty."

"I won't say no," Katie said. She piled up a little paper plate with two big glazed doughnuts and carried them and her coffee back to her seat.

Wynona sidled up to Justine and lowered her voice. "Just look at those long legs and slim hips. Some people have all the luck."

Susan frowned. "Looks do not signify luck. I think you'll come to learn that she's a most remarkable woman, and I expect every one of my teachers to be professional and kind to the newcomer among us."

Justine flushed, and Wynona was immediately apologetic.

"I didn't mean anything by it. I just—"

"Let's take our seats so we can get started on time," Susan said, and the day began.

By the time the meeting was over, they'd all identified themselves and what they taught, and then headed to their rooms.

Marcy Kincaid, the other first grade teacher, ran to catch up.

"Hi, Katie. I'm Marcy, your teammate."

Katie had already spotted her across the room. It was the bright-red hair.

"Great to meet you in person," Katie said. "Let's do this."

They chatted the rest of the way down the hall and then went their separate ways when they entered their own rooms.

The building was already coming alive. Voices echoed in the halls, and doors were banging. But Katie's room was different enough from what she'd had that it wasn't an immediate trigger. The furniture had been moved into the classrooms, and her desk and chair were shoved up against a wall. The basics were there. It was now up to her to bring it to life.

And so it began.

Day after day, one little thing after another was added. A braided oval rug for story time. A banner with all of the letters of the alphabet. Another banner with numbers from one to twenty. Bringing her collection of storybooks from home and filing them in a shelf in her reading center. Working on her bulletin board out in the hall beside her door.

And nearly every night, she spent a little time at Sam's house, or he and the girls spent a little time with her. It wasn't enough time to suit Sam, but he wasn't going to ruin what was happening between them by pushing her into a commitment she was afraid of.

And Katie wasn't just falling for Sam anymore. Evie and Beth were working their own magic on her—to the point that she began imagining herself in their lives on a permanent basis, and how that would be.

Then every day, she'd go back to school and add more to her classroom. Things that were both sensory and visual, and setting up the computer area, and then six child-size chairs for every tiny round table, until it was only two days before actual classes began.

Katie had the list of students who would be in her class, and as fate would have it, Beth and Evie were on the list, as was Donny Tiller, who was Rita the bowling buddy's grandson.

Eighteen students in all.

And tonight was Back to School Night.

Time for the parents to bring their children to school to find out who their teacher would be for the year and where their classroom was located.

The fact that she and Sam were seeing each other had played heavily into her concern about the girls being in her class. But after talking to Sam, and then Sam talking to the principal, they all decided to leave the last as it was. The girls were already used to minding Katie, and she wasn't the kind to play favorites. Sam knew she was going to be their teacher, but the girls did not.

He would bring them to see their room, and their

cubby where their things would go, and the hooks where they would hang their backpacks and coats, and he, along with all the other parents, would get their own set of rules and a chance to meet the teacher.

Katie had been teaching long enough to expect at least one set of parents who demanded more of the school and expected less of their child. They would argue the child's failures and expect instant gratification for their child, whether they deserved it or not.

She had on a new pair of purple slacks and a lavender long-sleeved blouse. She'd clipped her hair back away from her face, leaving the length of it hanging well below her shoulders. The lanyard around her neck identified her as Miss Katie, First Grade.

She was in her room and ready when the first wave of parents and students began.

———

At the beginning of entering pre-K, then kindergarten, Sam had informed the principal and teachers that his girls were never to be separated in different classes, that they functioned and listened and learned far better together than when they were apart. And since learning was the objective, that was his decision. So now the girls' initial anxiety of being in different classes was no longer an issue.

Getting out of baby school, which was what the twins called their previous years, was a milestone. They were beside themselves with excitement at going into first grade. They wanted to hurry and get to school to see how many of their friends from last year would be in their class.

They'd dressed themselves in shorts sets and were wearing their "Miss Katie" headbands. Their toenails were painted and poking out from their little sandals, and they were sitting in the living room, shouting down the hall at Sam.

"Daddy! Are you ready yet?" Evie yelled.

"We're ready," Beth shouted. "We're ready to go."

"Coming!" Sam said as he gave himself one last look in the bathroom mirror, then grabbed his wallet off the dresser, made sure the toes of his boots were shiny, palmed the key to his patrol car, and headed up the hall.

The girls bolted for the door and were already on the porch by the time he grabbed his Stetson. He settled it on his head, then led them to the car, buckled both of them up in the back seat, and headed to school.

"Are you excited?" Sam asked.

"Yes! We get to see our friends and find out who our teacher will be," Beth said.

"I want Miss Katie to be our teacher," Evie said.

"Yes, Miss Katie," Beth echoed.

"I don't have anything to do with that, but it will either be Miss Marcy or Miss Katie, and whoever it is, you will be happy and not make a fuss. Do you understand?"

They nodded. "Yes, Daddy. We promise we won't have ourselves a hissy fit," Evie said.

"No fits," Beth added.

Sam hid a grin. "Excellent choices," he said.

They held hands as he drove, and when he finally got

to the school and got them out, they each grabbed hold of Sam's hands.

"I guess I'm too big to carry?" Evie whispered.

Beth looked worried. "I guess I am, too?"

"We're holding hands. That's better," Sam said, and led them into the building.

The principal was standing at the doorway, greeting each family as they arrived and exclaiming how tall the children had grown over the summer.

When she saw Sam walking in with his girls, she sighed. There was something so endearing about that big man. Him, and all of the authority he represented in Borden's Gap, being led by the two tiny beings at his side was a sight to behold.

"Good evening, Chief," Susan said. "Good evening, Beth. Good evening, Evie."

"You got us backward!" Evie said. "She's Beth. I'm Evie," and then they giggled.

Susan sighed. "My apologies, but you two are such peas in a pod."

"Miss Katie can tell us apart easy," Evie said.

"Every time," Beth added.

Sam grinned. "She did. Right from the start."

Susan laughed. "She's a fine woman with a multitude of skills. You all enjoy your evening and go find your room."

Now that they were inside the building, the girls got braver, remembering the layout as they moved farther down the hall.

"We went that way last year," Evie said.

"But first grade is this way," Beth said, and began skipping along beside Sam until they reached the first-grade rooms. There was a list of names on the bulletin boards just outside of each door.

"Find our names, Daddy! Find our names!" Beth said.

"You know your name. Look for it," Sam said.

And as luck would have it, they read the list on Katie's door first.

"Here they are!" Beth said. "Our names are here!"

"Then go through that doorway and you will see your teacher," Sam said.

They got as far as the threshold, saw Katie up talking to other parents, and turned to Sam and whispered.

"Miss Katie! We get Miss Katie!" they said.

"Wow. And so you do. Let's go say hello."

Sam had expected squeals of delight, but they seemed subdued.

"What's wrong?" he asked.

"We have to mind Teacher," Evie whispered.

"Yes, mind her," Beth added.

"Do you even know what that means?" Sam asked.

They looked at each other.

"Do what she says?" they echoed.

"Right. Just like you have to mind me."

"We never had to mind Miss Katie before."

"Well, you wanted her for a teacher, and you got lucky. If you don't want to be here, I can go ask the principal to move you to the other class."

"No! We'll stay here. We're just being silly gooses."

Sam chuckled. "Where did you hear that?"

"That's what Roxie calls us when we eat with our fingers instead of our forks."

"Then don't be silly gooses," Sam said.

They giggled, and then made a beeline for Katie.

———

Katie saw them coming and grinned. "Surprise," she said.

"We're silly gooses," Evie said.

Katie looked up at Sam, waiting for an explanation.

"It's a long story," Sam said. "Your room looks amazing. I wish I'd had a first-grade teacher like this."

One of the other fathers was standing nearby and poked Sam on the shoulder.

"That's what I said."

"Oh, hey, Palmer. How's it going?"

"Stu's repeating first grade," he muttered.

"Good move," Sam said. "Kids don't mature at the same rate. Now's the time to let him catch up, instead of falling farther behind."

Then they both turned and looked at Katie, moving about the room with a half-dozen children already following behind her like a broody hen with new chicks.

"She sure seems nice," Palmer said.

"She's in her element, isn't she? And she's pretty," Sam added.

Palmer grinned. "Well, since my wife is standing right there I wasn't gonna say it, but I won't call you a liar, either."

"She's my neighbor," Sam added.

Palmer sighed and stuck his hands in his pockets.

"Right over there is one of our neighbors, and I'd damn sure trade you."

Sam followed Palmer's line of sight, wondering who he was referring to, and then saw Justin Tiller and his family and frowned.

Justin Tiller was a regular in the drunk tank and trouble waiting to happen.

"I'd better go catch up with the girls," Sam said.

———————

Katie had zoned out of any fear of panic. She was in her element with the parents and children, answering questions and explaining a little of what the first few weeks of first grade would be like. Then she met Miranda and Jeff Dooley and their son, Thor, and quickly realized they were going to be this year's pains in the ass.

Miranda's hair was dyed jet black and curled high up on her head. She had diamonds in her ears, diamonds on her hands, and the tightest jeans Katie had ever seen a woman wear. Jeff Dooley's blond hair was buzzed on the sides and long in the back—a mullet worthy of a second look, for sure. He kept patting his wife's butt as if it was his pacifier. Their son, Thor, was wearing Levis, a leather vest, and cowboy boots, and sporting a mullet like his daddy.

Jeff Dooley had already taken a snipe at Katie's height.

"Boy howdy, lady. You didn't know when to stop growin', did you?" he drawled.

Before Katie could respond, Miranda gave her the once-over and then pointed to the cubbies.

"I want Thor's cubby to be one of the middle ones. So he won't have to reach up so far."

"They're in alphabetical order," Katie said, "and none of them are out of a first-grade reach. Here, let me show you." She pointed at the cubbies. "Thor, can you show me your name on your cubby?"

The little boy grinned. "I can read and write my name good!" he said. He swaggered over to the wall, slid his little hand right in the one with his name, and patted the name tag. "This says Thor, and this here little hole is where I put my stuff. Right?"

Katie beamed. "You are so right!" she said. "Good job."

And then she heard her name being called and turned to see Beth and Evie coming toward her.

"Them are my girlfriends," Thor said.

"Both of them?" Katie asked.

Thor shrugged. "I can't tell 'em apart, so I just call 'em twins."

"I understand your confusion," Katie said, then shook hands with both parents. "It's so nice to meet you. I look forward to a great learning experience for all of us this year, and Thor, I'll see you in the classroom."

At that point, Evie and Beth came to a sliding halt before her with their hands clasped beneath their chins in pure delight.

"Guess what, Miss Katie?" Evie said.

"Yes, guess!" Beth echoed.

"I can't imagine," Katie said.

"We're in your class!" they shrieked, and then bounced...once...from the excitement of it all.

"I know! It was a surprise to me, too," Katie said, then saw Sam coming toward her from across the room and sighed.

He made her stomach flutter, and that was a fact.

"Are those computers for us to use?" Beth asked.

"Yes, but we'll all have to take turns, because there are only four and there will be eighteen students in this class."

Then Katie felt a pat on her arm and looked down. It was Donny Tiller, Rita's grandson. And to her dismay, his father was the angry man in the old black truck who she'd seen when she first moved to town.

"Miss Katie, that won't come out even," Donny said.

Katie frowned. "What won't come out even?"

"The kids. At the computer," he said.

Katie's heart skipped. "How do you know that?"

He shrugged. "I just do."

Katie was dumbfounded. "Can you tell me how you figured that out?"

The little boy stood there a moment, frowning, trying to figure out a way to show what he already knew in his head, and all he could say was "Because we don't have enough kids in our class to make it even."

Katie was excited, but the teacher in her was in awe.

"Can you show me what you mean?" she asked.

He nodded. "Can I use the dry-erase board?"

Katie ran to get a marker. By now, Donny's parents had come to see what was going on, and when Katie and Donny went to the dry-erase board, a number of other parents, including Sam, followed them, curious about what was going on.

Katie handed Donny the marker.

"You said eighteen kids, right, Miss Katie?"

She nodded.

Donny gripped the marker, then began counting aloud, "One…two…three…four…," making a black mark for each number and keeping them side by side across the board, all the way down to the last ones, "sixteen…seventeen…eighteen." Then he pointed at the marks. "That's how many kids will be using four computers. So only four kids at a time can play, right?"

"Right," Katie said, wishing Susan was here to witness this, wishing Marcy could see this, because she knew what was coming.

"So," Donny said as he went back to the first of the line of marks and counted down four, then drew a circle around them. Then he counted down four more and circled them, and then again, and then again, until he had four circles on the board encompassing sixteen black marks, with two lone marks left out of the circles. "See… it can't come out even. There will always be only two kids playing by themselves at the end…unless two kids move away, or two new kids come to school, and then it would be even again."

Parents were staring.

Sam whistled beneath his breath.

"You are absolutely right!" Katie said, and put her hand on Donny's back. "Good job, Donny. Good! Job!"

He beamed.

Katie noticed Justin and Frieda Tiller were silent, and Justin looked angry.

"Mr. and Mrs. Tiller, I hope you know that what your son just exhibited is a grasp of math far beyond his age group. I have never had a student like him before."

They looked at Donny as if they'd never seen him before, and then Justin appeared to be embarrassed.

Donny Tiller was just a six-year-old kid, a little rumpled from head to toe, sadly in need of a haircut, and missing two buttons on his shirt.

But he was more...so much more than he appeared.

All of a sudden, Justin Tiller turned his back on all of them and started issuing orders.

"Frieda! Get the kids and hurry up. We're done here and I got places to be," he said, then stalked out of the room.

Frieda ducked her head, muttered "Nice to meet you," and grabbed Donny's hand. "Come on, Son. We gotta go find Connor and Lee. Daddy's ready to go."

Their exit broke up the crowd, and parents began going to retrieve their children. Some would be going on to different rooms with older children, while others were going home.

Sam put a hand on Katie's shoulder. She turned, saw the look of concern in his eyes, and then looked around for Beth and Evie. They were sitting on the oval rug in the reading center with some of their friends, chattering and playing.

"It's good to see you," Katie said.

"Are you okay?" Sam asked.

Katie managed a wry smile. "Lord, yes. Hateful people don't scare me. It's the quiet ones you have to watch out for."

"Like Justin Tiller?"

She nodded.

Sam lowered his voice.

"Go do your thing, honey, and don't worry about him. People who cause trouble in this town are my problem, not yours. Understand?"

"Yes, and thank you," Katie said, and then put on her teacher face and her teacher smile and went to mingle.

After the evening was winding down, Katie sent a text to Marcy and Susan, asking them to come to her room when they got a chance.

Marcy was right across the room and showed up first.

"How did your evening go?" she asked. "Did everything go off okay?"

"It was fine," Katie said.

"So, what's up?" Marcy asked.

"I kinda want to wait until Susan gets here so I don't have to tell it twice."

"Oh…I saw her coming down the hall. She should be here… Oh…there she is now," Marcy said.

"Is everything okay?" Susan asked.

"I want to show you something," Katie said, and walked them over to the dry-erase board. "This all began because the kids found out they were going to get to use computers. Then questions arose about there being only four of them. So as I was in the middle of explaining how only four students at a time would be using them, and that there were eighteen children in our class so we'd have to take turns, Donny Tiller walked up beside me, patted me on the arm, and quietly blew my mind."

"What do you mean?" Susan asked.

"He said, 'Miss Katie, that won't come out even.' I asked him what he meant, and he just repeated, 'That won't come out even,' and then it hit me. Long story short, I asked him to show me what he meant, and he did this. He made eighteen marks. Then counted off four, and then four more, and again and again, until there were only two left. Then he said, 'See. It won't come out even.'"

Marcy was staring in disbelief, but Susan wasn't surprised.

"His pre-K teacher mentioned early on that Donnie had an unusual grasp of grouping blocks and counting. His kindergarten teacher said he was good at math, but you know how it goes. We don't test kids for those kinds of concepts that young. But this? Wow! Being able to calculate something like that in his head and then be able to lay it out so simply is amazing. But I sense a hesitation," Susan said. "What else happened?"

"I don't think his father was happy with me, or with Donny. He seemed angry, then ordered his wife to get their children and left the building."

Susan sighed. "Justin Tiller has issues."

Marcy rolled her eyes. "That's a nice way of saying he's feral, mean, shiftless, drinks like a fish, and can't hold a job."

Katie frowned. "I've had plenty of parents like him over the years. They don't scare me. But what does scare me is a child being born with such a gift and then never having a chance to let it grow or use it."

"We'll see about getting him tested," Susan said. "He may excel in other aspects as well. And don't worry about

Justin Tiller. He has to come through me to get to any of my teachers. So…good job, everyone. Let's go home."

Marcy gave Katie a quick hug. "Before we go, I noticed you got Thor Dooley. He's a sweetheart, but his parents are a mess. They are also considered part of the high society side of Borden's Gap."

Katie grinned. "What does Jeff Dooley do for a living?"

"He plays random backup in bands in Nashville for any country singer in need of someone who can play guitar."

"Nashville? That's quite a drive from here. Why don't they live in Nashville?"

"Because Miranda wouldn't be noticed in Nashville, but in Borden's Gap, she's a big deal. For her, it's all about 'Do I want to be a little fish in a big pond, or a big fish in a little pond?' She chose the puddle in which to reign."

Katie laughed. "That analogy should be a bumper sticker. 'I choose the puddle in which to reign.'"

They were still laughing as they locked up their rooms and walked out together into the warm summer night.

Chapter Fifteen

KATIE WENT HOME SATISFIED WITH HER FIRST PUBLIC event. There had been a few moments during the evening when she'd hear a childish squeal or hear a door bang and feel a surge of anxiety. But there were so many people around her to pull her out of it that her anxiety never bloomed into full-blown panic.

She was getting out of the shower when she got a text. She dried and hurried into her pajamas, then went to see who it was from.

It was Sam.

> You were a huge hit! People were talking about you and it was all good. I am guessing there were moments when it was stressful for you, but it never showed. Proud of you, honey. Sleep in tomorrow, and if you're not doing anything, I want to take all my girls out to eat at noon, and that includes you. Around eleven thirty?

Katie quickly responded.

> Invitation accepted and thank you.

Then she laid her phone aside and hugged herself. For the first time in months, she was feeling joy again. Sam was going out of his way to let her know she mattered to him, and still giving her space. Just thinking about him made her ache, but it was all too new and too soon. So she crawled into bed, wishing she had another Dinah McCall book to read, then turned on the TV instead.

———

Justin Tiller was on a rampage. He'd done nothing but curse and shout since they'd come back from school and was downing beers as fast as he could swallow them.

The boys were in the kitchen, eating snacks and playing games on their iPads, while Frieda was folding a load of towels on top of the dryer.

Justin slugged down the last swallow of beer and got up to get another, but when he opened the refrigerator and realized he'd just finished the last one, he threw the empty beer can against the wall and shouted.

"Dammit all to hell!"

The boys grabbed their iPads and made a run for their rooms as Frieda appeared in the doorway.

"Justin! What's wrong with you? The boys were playing," she said.

"And now they're not!" he shouted. He fumbled in his pocket for the car keys, and started out the door.

Frieda's heart skipped a beat. "Where are you going?"

"To get beer. We're out."

"There were eight in the fridge when we came home.

If you've already downed that many, you're too drunk to drive," she cried, and tried to take the keys out of his hands.

"Get your hands off me!" he shouted, and then doubled up his fist and hit her on the jaw. She fell backwards and didn't get up.

Justin toed the bottom of her foot with his shoe.

"Get up, dammit!"

She didn't move.

Frowning, he staggered to the sink, ran water in one of the pans in the drainer, and then threw it in her face.

She moaned.

Satisfied that she was still alive, he threw the pan in the sink and left the house.

As soon as he was gone, the kids came running into the kitchen, saw their mother on the floor, and began drying her off and helping her up. It was standard operating procedure at their house.

Justin got all the way to a convenience store to get his beer, then had his credit card rejected. He stared at the six-pack on the counter, and then at the clerk, his eyes narrowing.

But the clerk knew Justin all too well.

"Don't do it," the clerk warned. "You take it without paying for it, and I'm calling the cops."

"Fuck you," Justin muttered. He staggered back to his car, managed to get home, then missed the carport, stopped the car halfway into the front yard, and passed out in the grass.

———

The next morning, Frieda woke up to a swollen jaw and a black eye and was on her way to the kitchen to get some ice when she saw Justin's truck sideways in the drive.

"Oh my God," she muttered, then looked out the window and saw him passed out in the yard.

She was way past being embarrassed by anything he did, so she thought about leaving him there. But she needed to move his old truck so she could get her own car out of the driveway and get to work.

She went outside to look for the keys. They weren't in the truck, so they had to be on him, but she couldn't roll him over.

"You are such a piece of shit," she muttered, and then saw the garden hose strung out in the grass, turned on the water and then dragged the hose across the yard and turned the full blast of the water on the side of his face.

He woke up spitting and cursing, then rolled over onto his back and saw Frieda and the hose.

"What the hell do you think you're doing?" he shouted.

"The same thing you did to me last night," she screamed. "Give me your keys. I need to move your stupid truck out of the yard so I can get out of the drive and go to work. Someone in this family has to earn a living."

"Go to hell," he mumbled.

"I live in hell...with you. Give me your keys, or I swear to God I will ram my car into that piece of shit until it's out of my way."

Then she hit him in the face with the water again.

Justin fumbled in his pockets, threw the keys at her, and then rolled over onto his belly in the standing water, and groaned.

As she started up his truck, it did pass through his mind that she just might run over him for the hell of it, and then he lay there anyway. But she only moved the truck into its parking place, left the keys in the ignition, and then went back in the house.

The boys were all huddled together in Donny's bedroom, wide-eyed and awaiting instructions.

"Your daddy passed out in the yard last night. Now, he's lying in water, but you leave him alone. If he even pretends to raise a hand to you, call Grandma. She'll come get you kids and deal with him. Otherwise, you have your chores. Help each other and you'll help me, okay?"

They nodded.

Frieda hugged them. "I love you so much, and I'm so sorry we're in this mess. I'm going to get enough money saved up to get us out of here. I promise."

"We're okay, Mama," Connor said. "He yells at us, but he wouldn't dare hit us."

"Why are you so sure?" Frieda asked.

"'Cause Grandma told him if he did, she'd kill him… and he believed her."

Frieda blinked, tried to grin, and then winced and grabbed her jaw.

"Gotta go now or I'll be late. Always call if you need to."

And then she was gone.

———

Katie's nightmares took her through a wedding that never happened and the school massacre again. She woke up bathed in sweat, her heart pounding, and was in a mood until she remembered she was having lunch with Sam and the girls. She didn't know where they were going, and she didn't really care. Just being with them was the gift.

She glanced at the clock, then checked her phone. There was a message from Sam.

It's Hillbilly Pizza. There is no dress code.

She burst out laughing, and then threw back the covers and headed for the shower.

After she had her hair dry and was dressed for the date, she took her coffee and a muffin to the back porch. The food settled her stomach, and the peace and beauty of this little town nestled among the surrounding hills took away the lingering memories of last night's pitiful excuse for a good night's rest.

———————

Sam's morning was anything but peaceful.

The house cleaners had arrived, so to keep the girls out from underfoot, he found a Disney movie for them to watch in their room and then started a load of laundry.

In the middle of switching loads, he got a call from the station. Just seeing that number pop up made him groan. This wasn't just his day off. It was to be a day with Katie. If this turned into a big mess, he was not going to be inclined toward leniency.

"This is Sam."

"Chief, this is Carl. Jeff Dooley just reported a robbery. Ben and me were dispatched to the scene, but Jeff is insisting you need to be in attendance."

Sam frowned. "Was anyone hurt?"

"No, sir."

"What all did they take?"

"He's not sure, but he saw someone on their Ring doorbell sneaking away in the night with something in their arms."

"Did their security alarm go off?"

"No, sir."

Sam sighed. "So then where did the thief enter the house?"

"Uh…well, the back door was unlocked, but Miranda admitted she forgot to lock it last night, so…"

"So the security alarm didn't go off. Nothing is missing. And all they have is someone walking away from their house in the night?"

"Yes, sir," Carl said.

"Can you send me the video from their Ring doorbell?" Sam said.

"Yes, sir, but what do I tell Jeff?"

"Not a damn thing. He's not in charge of policing this town, I am. And two perfectly capable officers were sent to investigate what appears to be a wild-goose chase. I want to look at the video. And in the meantime, go see if some of their neighbors caught anything on their security."

"Yes, sir," Carl said, and disconnected.

"Have mercy," Sam muttered, and then took off to his office to check his email for the video.

The video arrived in an email. He clicked on the message, opened the attachment, and then sat there watching a shadowy figure walking away from the Dooleys' front door. It did appear the person was carrying something, but it was hard to say what…and Sam wasn't even sure if it was a man or a woman.

He played it over and over, trying to spot something in the shadows, or a car waiting for the person down the street. But there were only two streetlights in the cul-de-sac, and vision was poor. He began watching the video from frame to frame, and when he did, he spotted something he hadn't noticed before because it immediately blended into the shadows in the following frames.

He grabbed his phone and called Carl.

When Carl answered, he sounded breathless.

"Hello?"

"Carl, where are you with the neighbors' security cameras?" Sam asked.

"We've been all over the neighborhood. Either they weren't aimed in the right direction, or they aren't working, or they don't have one."

"Well, unless Jeff has discovered property that's missing, I think there is no robbery. In a couple of frames, and assuming it's a man, I see what looks like a dog's tail hanging out from under his arms. I'll bet you both a Coke that somebody let their dog out to pee, it didn't come back, and the owner went looking for it. He either found it in Jeff's yard or on the porch, and simply picked it up and took it home. Ask Jeff if he has a neighbor with a wandering dog, then ask around the neighborhood. It has to be someone nearby because there was no strange car parked at the curb. The guy was afoot."

"Ooh, good call, Chief. I'll let you know what we find out."

"No problem," Sam said, and went to check on the girls.

When he walked into their room, they were on their bed watching the movie, leaning against each other and holding hands. He paused a second, thinking how unique twins were. Linked at all times. Finishing each other's sentences. And if his two slowed down or were sitting side by side, they were always holding hands. Like they weren't fully turned on without the link. He couldn't imagine what growing up and growing apart was going to be like for them, but it was inevitable that change would come.

Then the girls looked up and saw him.

"Daddy! Is it time to go to pizza yet?"

"Not yet," Sam said. "I was just checking on you."

"We're fine," Evie said. "We're staying out of the cleaning ladies' hair."

"Out of their hair," Beth echoed.

"Thank you," Sam said, and gave them a thumbs-up as he walked out.

The cleaning ladies met him in the hall with a handful of candy wrappers.

Sam sighed. "Where did you find them this time?"

"They were poked up in the vacuum cleaner. I assume they thought they'd just get sucked up into the hose and in the bag and no one would be the wiser...but they kind of plugged it up instead. They're getting better at hiding places, though," one of the cleaners said, and giggled.

Sam frowned, then backtracked to their room and hit Mute on their movie.

"Daddy! Why did you do that?" Evie cried.

"Yes, why?" Beth said, her eyes welling.

Sam opened his fist and let the candy wrappers fall out on the bed in front of them.

Their eyes widened as evidence of their thievery was revealed. They looked up at Sam, then at each other, and waited.

Sam was not happy. This had been an ongoing issue for months, but after the big speech he'd given them, he believed they'd moved past it.

"I thought we talked about this. You both promised me to quit snitching candy without asking. Now this! What do you have to say for yourselves?"

"We haven't snitched since we promised," Evie said.

"Not since we promised," Beth said.

"Then how do you explain all this…poked up into the vacuum cleaner?"

"We didn't hide wrappers in the vacuum, Daddy. And those are old wrappers," Evie said.

Beth nodded and even picked up a little wrapper.

"See, Daddy! This is Valentine candy."

Sam knew them. They might sneak candy, but they'd never lie.

"Then how do you explain that the vacuum worked all this time until today?"

"We didn't hide any up a vacuum. We hid it under your bed."

Sam blinked. "My bed?"

They nodded. "We didn't think you would look there."

"I'll be right back," Sam said, and went to look for the cleaning ladies. They were in the living room, getting ready to dust the woodwork. "Uh…ladies, by any chance did you just vacuum under my bed before the vacuum suddenly quit?"

They nodded.

He sighed, then shoved his hand through his hair in frustration.

"False alarm. This was not a new theft. This was Valentine candy wrappers that the girls hid beneath my bed. You just vacuumed up the evidence of an old crime. Before we had the talk where they promised not to snitch candy anymore. I am a cop, and I cannot stay ahead of my own children," he muttered.

Their laughter followed him down the hall and back to the twins' room. There was absolutely no reason to beat a dead horse, so he gathered up the candy wrappers, unmuted their movie, and left the room.

He went back to doing laundry and was folding a load of towels in his bedroom when his cell phone rang. It was Carl.

"Hello," Sam said.

"You called it," Carl said. "Once I asked Jeff Dooley if he had a neighbor with a wandering dog, he turned about two shades of red and said yes. Then we went back and looked at the video again and we saw the tail you mentioned, and that pretty much ended his fit. He went down the street to talk to his neighbor. And it was him, carrying his dog home. So all is well. Good eye, Chief."

"Okay then. Just write up the report when you get a chance, and thanks for keeping me in the loop," Sam said, and hung up.

It was almost time to go get Katie. Knowing he was going

to spend at least the next couple of hours with her made this the best day he could remember in a long, long time.

———

Katie had just finished a Zoom meeting with their principal and the teachers at the elementary building. Susan had given them feedback about Back to School Night, and to Katie's relief, being the new teacher had not garnered any negative comments. So she was riding a high as she went into the living room and saw Sam loading the girls up in the car. Instead of making him drive over to pick her up, she just grabbed her purse and ran out of the house and across the street.

The girls saw her coming and started pointing.

"Daddy! Daddy! There comes Miss Katie."

He looked up, and the sight of her coming toward him was like sunlight on his face. She brightened everything around her and didn't even know it.

"Hey. I was going to pick you up," Sam said.

Katie shook her head. "I'm too far out of your way. The least I can do is meet you."

Sam grinned and then went back to buckling the girls in.

"Not too tight?" he asked, as he pulled the shoulder strap across Beth's chest.

"Just right, Daddy," she said, and reached for Evie's hand.

Sam saw it. They were linked up, which meant they were ready to go. He turned around and opened the door for Katie.

"Thank you," she said, leaving a faint aroma of her shampoo with him as she passed by.

She smells like summer, Sam thought. Flowers and strawberries and heat.

He waited until she was seated, then circled the car to get in. Moments later, they were backing out of the driveway and heading uptown.

Sam knew the girls were talking to each other about Katie and wondered if she could hear them. When she looked over at him, her eyes twinkling, he knew she had.

Sam shook his head, speaking softly.

"You have to accept your uniqueness within our little nest. Except for Roxie, who's always been a fixture in their lives, you are the first female to have penetrated our fortress, which makes you the current topic of conversation today."

"No complaints. I feel blessed to have been allowed in," Katie said.

Sam reached across the console and gave her hand a quick squeeze, and when her fingers curled around his, his heart skipped a beat. If this was what Beth and Evie felt like holding hands, then he got it. Everybody needed somebody to belong to. He could only hope that Katie was feeling the same way.

Within minutes, they turned off Main and pulled into the parking lot.

"Looks like we weren't the only ones intent on pizza today," Sam said.

The parking lot was nearly full. He found a place to park and they headed inside. It had not occurred to him what a statement they were making by going to eat pizza, but they had just announced to Borden's Gap that Sam Youngblood was seeing the new teacher.

The sight of them walking in with the girls hand in hand, and Sam's hand on her back, was way too familial to suit the single females. As for the guys who'd been hitting on her for weeks, it all became painfully clear. It wasn't that she didn't like them. She just liked Sam better.

Sam nodded at families as they were taken to their seats, and Katie noticed a few familiar faces from her Back to School Night.

The kids noticed their new teacher and started calling out to her.

"Hi, Miss Katie!"

"Look, Mama! It's Miss Katie!"

Katie smiled and waved and kept walking.

As soon as they were seated, with menus, the twins piped up.

"Daddy! You know our pizza's name. You order for us!" Evie said.

"Order for us," Beth echoed.

"You got it," Sam said.

"I'll have some of whatever you're eating…as long as there are no anchovies on it," Katie said.

The girls' chatter ceased.

"What are ant choies?" Evie asked.

Beth stuck out her tongue and pretended to gag. "We don't eat ants either, Miss Katie."

"Don't look at me," Sam added. "I don't eat ant choies, either."

"Then it's all good," Katie said.

When Sam threw back his head and laughed, every diner in the room turned to look, all coming to the same conclusion.

Sam was stuck on the teacher. It was a revelation they never thought they'd see.

And then their waitress arrived to take their orders, and Katie realized it was Frieda Tiller, with a bruise on her jaw and an eye turning black.

"Hello, Chief. Hello, Miss Katie. Are you ready to order?"

Sam looked up, saw her face, and frowned.

Frieda sighed. "I'm all right, Chief." She glanced at the twins and then shrugged. "I fell."

"With help," Sam muttered, and then let it go. Frieda had the police department on speed dial. If she wanted help, she knew how to get it.

Frieda took their drink orders, and then their pizza order, and left.

A server came by a few minutes later with drinks and breadsticks, and their meal began.

When the large pepperoni pizza was delivered to their table, the girls clapped their hands. It looked and smelled so good that Katie had to resist the urge to clap, too. Instead, she watched Sam deftly dealing with cutting a big slice in half, then putting a half on each girl's plate.

Evie frowned. "You gave away half of my slice."

"No. I gave away half of Beth's slice," Sam said.

Beth smiled. "It's okay, Evie. We share."

Evie looked at their plates.

"Next time, we share my slice," she said.

Sam nodded. "Right." Then he glanced at Katie. "Do you want to share?"

Katie saw the look in his eyes and felt like he'd just hugged her.

"I love sharing," she said.

Sam put a huge slice on his plate, cut it in two pieces, and slid one half on Katie's plate.

"Thank you," Katie said. "Next time, we share my slice."

Sam winked, and then reached for red pepper flakes.

Frieda came back every few minutes and had something kind to say to the girls as she refilled their drinks.

Katie was getting full, and the girls had already quit eating and were talking to one of their school friends who was sitting at the neighboring table. Sam had just swallowed his last bite when he saw Justin Tiller walk in, then stop just inside the door.

Justin waved away the hostess and pointed at his wife.

Sam's instinct for trouble began to amp up as he watched the hostess deliver a message to Frieda. He watched Frieda look at Justin and then turn her back on him and keep working. The hostess went back and said something to Justin that obviously made him furious. And after what Justin had done to his wife last night, he knew it wasn't over.

Katie saw Sam go still, and then looked over her shoulder and saw Justin Tiller standing in the doorway. When she turned back around, Sam caught her gaze, glanced at the girls, then shook his head.

Katie got the message and patted Beth's arm to get her attention.

"Girls, Daddy's getting ready to pay. But I want to go to the bathroom and wash the pizza off my hands before we go. Can you both show me the way?"

"Yes, Miss Katie! We know where it is," Evie said.

"We know," Beth added, and when Katie got up, they each took her by the hand and led her through the dining area.

When his girls were out of sight, Sam breathed a sigh of relief. Justin Tiller was shifting from one foot to the other like a junkie in need of a fix, and then he shouted at his wife from across the room.

"Frieda! I need to talk to you!"

Frieda filled the glasses at one of her tables and then turned to go back into the kitchen, and that's when Justin lost it.

He pushed his way past the hostess, knocking her down. Then he pushed past a busboy carrying a tray of dirty dishes and sent them flying to the floor. The crash ended the diners' conversation, as the whole room went still.

And then all of a sudden, Sam was in front of Justin Tiller. He grabbed Tiller by the arm, twisting it behind his back, then turned him around and walked him toward the exit, with Justin cursing a blue streak all the way out the door.

With Tiller's arm still in a twist, Sam shoved him face-down on the hood of the nearest car and called the station.

"Lucas, this is Sam. Dispatch an officer to the Hillbilly Pizza parking lot ASAP. No need for sirens."

"Yes, sir," the dispatcher said as Sam slipped his phone back in his pocket.

Tiller was furious. "Damn it, Chief. I got a right to talk to my wife if I want to."

"From the looks of her face, you already said enough to her last night," Sam said.

"That's none of your business," Tiller shouted, and then winced when Sam pushed Tiller's arm a little higher up his back.

"But what you just did inside the pizza place is my business. You were disturbing the peace. You assaulted an employee. You caused property damage. And you frightened diners."

"But—"

"Stop talking," Sam said, and shoved the side of Tiller's face against the hood of the car.

Within a couple of minutes, a patrol car pulled up and Ben got out.

Sam yanked Tiller upright.

"Cuff him and book him for assault, property damage, and disturbing the peace inside the Hillbilly Pizza."

"Yes, Chief," Ben said, and as soon as he had Tiller cuffed, he put him in the patrol car and took him off to jail.

Sam walked back inside just as Katie and the girls came out of the hall from the guest bathrooms.

The hostess was back on the job. The staff was cleaning up the tray of broken dishes. But Frieda was ashen and visibly shaken, while still serving tables.

Sam caught Frieda's eye and gave her a thumbs-up.

She mouthed a quick thank-you and went back to pick up an order.

Sam felt bad for her and left a generous tip along with money for their tab.

"We're ready to go," Katie said.

Sam smiled, realizing Katie was wearing Evie's red headband.

"Nice hairdo," he said.

"We're sharing, Daddy," Evie said.

"Nobody's sharing mine," Beth said.

Sam didn't blink an eye. He'd just kicked ass in the Hillbilly Pizza. Surely he could wear a headband without having his manhood questioned.

"You can share it with me," Sam said.

Beth gasped. "You'll wear my headband, Daddy?"

Sam leaned over. "Put it on me, sugar. I feel like sparklin' today."

She giggled, took off her headband, and carefully slid it into place on Sam's head.

The room erupted into laughter. It was the perfect antidote for the bad taste Justin Tiller had left in this room.

"Are we going home now?" Beth asked.

"Lord, I hope so," Sam said, then winked at Katie. "But we match."

Katie nodded and grabbed Evie's hand as Sam walked out with Beth.

She'd heard enough while they were in the bathroom to know there was a ruckus happening, and delaying their exit from the bathroom had been imperative, which was how trying on headbands became a thing.

But now, seeing how easily Sam had solved Beth's feeling of being left out was the best. She'd never known a man this charming, who was this secure in his own sense of self. When they got into the car and headed home, Katie glanced at him, sitting behind the wheel, glittering like a Christmas ornament, and sighed.

Sam caught her staring.

"Just so you know...you're quite beautiful, Miss Katie."

Katie shivered inside. "So are you, sir. Inside and out."

Chapter Sixteen

SAM PULLED UP INTO KATIE'S DRIVE.

"Thank you all for inviting me to pizza," Katie said, and she pulled off the red headband and handed it to Evie.

"You're welcome, Miss Katie. We like sharing with you," Beth said.

Sam took off the blue headband and handed it to Beth.

"You girls stay put. I'm going to walk Miss Katie to the door, and then we'll go home."

"Okay, Daddy," they said, and began putting their headbands back on as Sam and Katie got out.

Sam slipped a hand beneath her elbow as they went up the steps.

"Thank you for getting the girls out of the line of fire," he said.

"Of course," Katie said. "It's weird… I think I was expecting a small town to be low key. Not necessarily crimeless, but nothing scary. Only I'm realizing that wherever people abide, there will always be the good ones and the bad ones."

"That's for sure," Sam said. "It's just a little easier to figure out the good from the bad in small towns. It's hard to hide your truth when you're acting like an ass every other day of your life."

Katie unlocked the door and walked in, then turned to thank him, but Sam was right behind her.

Without saying a word, he slipped a hand beneath her hair and cupped her neck, then leaned closer—so close he could feel the warmth of her breath.

Katie sighed, slid her arms around his neck, and ever so slowly, leaned into his kiss.

Lips met with intention, sent blood pressure rising, and turned on a longing Sam had never expected to feel again.

For Katie, the kiss was hope she thought she'd lost.

Sam slowly pulled back, his gaze searching her face to see if he'd overstepped.

Her eyes were at half-mast and his thumb was on the pulse in her neck.

He sighed. She was fine. Just fine.

"God, Katie…you're making me feel things I thought I'd buried with my wife. I'm not asking for miracles here… but I have officially tossed my hat into the ring with you, and now you know it."

Katie put her hand in the middle of his chest, feeling the steady thump of his heartbeat. "If you can take comfort in the fact that I have turned everyone else away but you, and you can give me the space to get past the nightmares that haunt me, then I am with you all the way. I'm still not sure what's going to happen at school with me and the PTSD."

"No pressure, love. Just an admission of intent," he said, and then headed back to the car.

Katie closed the door behind him, then kicked off her shoes and padded through the house, thinking how special Sam was, and how easy it would be to get hooked into believing his family could be hers, too.

But being out in public was exhausting. She spent so much time trying to control her anxiety, and she had a headache. So she crawled onto the bed, pulled a blanket over her feet and legs, and rolled over, remembering all the other times when she'd believed the people who swore they wanted her and instead had walked away. Sam felt trustworthy, but Katie didn't trust her own judgment anymore.

She exhaled slowly as she closed her eyes.

She could hear life going on outside, but her house was quiet and a place of safety and comfort, and so she slept.

———

Mark Roman stood at the window of his upstairs bedroom, watching it rain. It was actually more of a downpour. No wind. No thunder and lightning to speak of. Just a curtain of rain between the house and the barn.

He and his dad, Joe, had done the morning chores before the rain came and were just finishing their noon meal when the sky unloaded.

Joe looked up from the table and frowned.

"Well, that changes this afternoon's plans."

His mom, Laura, reached over and patted her husband's hand.

"You work too hard all the time. This is just God giving you an excuse to rest."

Mark watched the gentleness with which they spoke to

each other and couldn't help but compare it to how he and Megan had communicated.

Instinctively, he had known this was the way marriage was supposed to be. He'd witnessed their kindness to each other every day of his childhood and never realized that it didn't just come because they were married. It was there because they chose to treat each other exactly how they wanted to be treated.

They were actually living the Golden Rule.

Mark stood and began clearing the table.

"Mom, why don't you and Dad go put your feet up. We're all going to have a slow afternoon. Let me clean up the kitchen."

"Thank you, Son. That would be wonderful," Laura said, and as she got up to leave, Mark could see she was favoring her right leg again.

Mark watched the two of them leaving the room together and looked away.

After he was finished, he slipped up to his bedroom, and now here he was, watching it rain. Maybe after the storm passed he'd check email. His house still hadn't sold, and the lawyers were still bugging him about how to disburse the Lanier fortune. He didn't know what to do with it, either, but he knew he didn't want it.

—————

Katie spent all day Sunday going over the week of lesson plans, making sure she had everything ready in her room that she was going to need, and then in the evening she called Lila.

"Hey, bestie! What's happening in your world?" Lila said.

Katie curled her feet up beneath her and settled in on the sofa for a visit. "Tomorrow is our first day of school."

"Oh wow! You are starting earlier than we are."

"I know, but I'm ready. I have eighteen students so far, and I also have my neighbor's twin daughters in my class."

"Your neighbor, the police chief?" Lila asked.

"Yes, ma'am," Katie said.

"So, how's that going?" Lila asked.

"You mean with Sam? He's fine. A really sweet man and I like spending time with him and his girls."

"Yikes. Are the girls always along?"

"Yes, because I suggested it. His job is demanding. They have a nanny all through the week. They should not be expected to have to share their daddy time with a girl-friend. Besides, if I was a six-year-old girl with no mother, I wouldn't like that girlfriend if she took my daddy away from me. So…it takes pressure and guilt off of Sam. The girls are great fun, and they like me."

"That's actually a great diagnosis of the situation, my friend. Does Sam like you, too?" Lila asked.

Katie sighed. "Yes."

Lila persisted. "Do you like Sam?"

"Yes. A lot. But I'm having nightmares almost every night, and sometimes a sound will trigger a PTSD epi-sode, so I'm not making any permanent plans until I trust myself again."

"Oh, honey. I'm so sorry," Lila said.

"Yeah, so am I," Katie said. "And here I thought getting jilted was the worst thing that could happen to me."

"I think that the worst of that will fade in time," Lila said. "And it's not even been six months since the shooting."

Katie groaned. "I know, but it feels like I don't know who I am anymore. I don't trust me not to freak out. And I don't see the police chief marrying a crazy woman he can't trust with his children."

"Well, that sucks, and I'm not going to accept that, and neither should you. Just assume you *will* be better. Not if…but when. Okay?"

"I hear you, but it's easier said than done," Katie said. "And that's enough about me. Any Jack and Lila updates?"

Lila laughed. "I'm at the 'I don't kiss and tell' stage."

Katie giggled. "That's a first."

"Okay, fine. So I'm a blabbermouth. But I'll keep the details to myself," Lila said. "On another front, gossip is that Mark Roman has refused everything to do with the Lanier inheritance. His house is up for sale, and he's gone. I heard he went back home to Kansas."

Katie felt nothing. At least one good thing had happened with her move. She never had to see his face again.

"I'm sure his parents are happy," Katie said.

"Oh…hey…Jack is here. We're going out to dinner. Love you. Gotta go."

"Love you, too. Have fun," Katie said, and heard the line go dead in her ear.

She sat for a few moments, watching the lights going out in the house across the street. Sam was putting his babies to bed. Tomorrow was their first day of a new school year, too.

She thought of the children and families she'd already

met and wondered about the few who hadn't gone to Back to School Night, but it didn't matter. Water always found its own level, and so would school life.

She was tired and decided to go to bed, but not before she double-checked her rolling cart to make sure everything she planned to take tomorrow was packed. The first thing she noticed was that the school laptop wasn't there, and then she remembered it was still on the kitchen table. She grabbed it and tucked it in beneath a stack of files, added the bag of candy she had for the grab bag, and tossed in a couple of extra boxes of tissues for snotty noses.

Now there was nothing to do but set her alarm and go to bed. She had clothes picked out. Comfortable shoes chosen for the day, and the school ID lanyard in her purse.

Katie McGrath was ready for school.

———————

Sam had Beth and Evie tucked in bed, storybook read, last trips to the bathroom made, and last drinks of water, and last hugs and kisses.

The night-light was on in their bathroom, and they were lying on their sides facing each other, eyes closed, holding hands, when Sam eased up from the side of their bed and left the room.

Some days he wanted to slow time down, and other days it was a joy to watch them maturing and exploring the world into which they'd been born. He did every-thing he knew how to enrich their lives, while keeping them safe. But he also knew that the older they became, the more leeway they would have to be given. Spending nights with their girlfriends. Going on school trips. Challenging his authority. That was what he dreaded most—when they were becoming young women, because those were the times when a wrong decision made by a teenager could be fatal.

However, tonight he was just grateful that the only thing they were facing tomorrow was beginning first grade, and knowing Katie McGrath was going to be their teacher was comforting. They already knew and liked her, and Sam couldn't lie: he was falling for Katie, too.

He began going through the house, locking up for the night, and glanced across the street at her house. There was a faint glow through the blinds. She was either watching TV in the dark or was already getting ready for bed.

Tomorrow, she was going back into an environment that had nearly killed her. He knew she was anxious, but he'd watched her during Back to School night. She was a natural with children and had an easy manner with parents. He wanted so much for her to find happiness again—and he wanted it to be with them.

But they all had to come to an understanding. So while Katie was teaching his children, it would be his job to prove to her that he was a man she could trust. He wished he could go knock on her door and kiss her good night, but there were the girls to consider.

So he sent her a text instead.

Thinking of you. Wishing you were here so I could hug you good night. Tomorrow is the beginning of a whole new facet of your life, and I'm so glad you chose Borden's Gap to make it happen. Have the best day ever.—Sam

He hit Send, then finished locking up and headed for bed.

———————

Katie was getting ready to get in bed when she heard her phone signal a text. When she saw it was from Sam, she opened the message and read it. Her eyes welled as she crawled into bed, then sat and read it again before responding.

I feel the hug in my heart. Thank you. I'm a little anxious, but also so looking forward to getting back in the classroom. It's such a huge part of who I am, crazy days or not... I need to make it work.—Katie

———————

After all of the embarrassment at her job site, Frieda Tiller had a peaceful weekend. Once Justin was hauled off to jail, Frieda called her mother, told her what happened, and Rita went to get the kids and kept them until Frieda got off work.

Saturday night came, and Justin never came home, so Frieda assumed he was still in jail. She took her kids to her mother's on Sunday on her way to work and then again picked them up on her way home.

The boys were excited for their first day of school tomorrow, and Monday was Frieda's day off. They had their school supplies inside their new backpacks, and thanks to their grandma Rita, they had new sneakers for school.

Every time Frieda's phone rang, she was afraid it would be Justin wanting to be bailed out, but he never called. She guessed it was because he knew she didn't get paid until tomorrow. But what he didn't know was that she wasn't using their rent money to bail his sorry ass out of jail again. She didn't care where he was, as long as he wasn't under her roof.

She locked up for the night, then checked on the boys one last time before she went to her room, and then a short time later turned out the lights and went to bed.

Tomorrow would be a busy day getting Connor, Lee, and Donny up and dressed. She so wanted this school year to be good for all of them.

———————

Justin Tiller cursed the cell he was in. The mattress on the cot was lumpy and worn, and the single cover he had sure didn't smell like Frieda's laundry soap.

He was sober now and had been most of the weekend. When he was sober, he was painfully aware of his egregious errors. He'd actually punched his own wife in the face—again. He'd knocked her out. He was an ass.

But he'd been thrown in jail for public drunkenness

and disturbing the peace so many times that he'd ruined his chances of ever getting work in Borden's Gap again. And he was also coming to realize that if he didn't change his ways, there was a really big chance that Frieda would divorce him. He was being arraigned in the morning. Bail would be set, but he didn't know who to call to get him out. He'd punched that last ticket when he'd knocked Frieda out.

———

The glow from streetlights filtered through the blinds in Katie's bedroom, leaving slices of light along the wall.

The shower had a slow drip.

And the ice maker in the kitchen had just dumped a tray of cubes into the bin, but Katie never saw or heard any of it. Her body was in bed in Tennessee, but her spirit was back in New Mexico, still trying to outrun a killer.

Gunshots!
One scream, then the sounds of running feet.
More shots…one after the other. Methodical. Purposeful.
Run, children, run!
Heart pounding.
Blood all over Alejandro's face.
Miss Katie! Miss Katie! I fell.
Run, Kieran! Run, baby, run!
Gunshots behind us.
Shoulder burning. Oh God, oh God, we're going to die.
Don't talk. Don't move. I love you.

Katie woke up with a gasp, her face covered in tears, her heart pounding as the nightmare ended. The nightmare always ended in the same place because she'd lost consciousness then, and there was nowhere else to go.

She glanced at her clock. It was just after 5:00 a.m.

Damn fine way to begin a school year…with a memento of how the last one ended…in a blaze of gunfire and death.

She threw back the covers and got up, angry that this kept happening when she was asleep and defenseless. She shouted at the world because she needed to hear the sound of a human voice, even if it was just her own.

"Damn it! Whatever bad juju keeps throwing this at me will change nothing because I didn't die! I don't break! I don't quit! Now bug off! I have work to do!"

After venting, she stomped off to the shower, and by the time she came out, she'd calmed down. She needed coffee and something in her belly to settle it. This was not her first rodeo. She'd been teaching for years. This was just a new location to do what she did best.

When she finally left the house, she was primed for the day in navy-blue slacks and a red, white, and blue blouse with short, fluttery sleeves. She had red ladybug earrings in her ears and a butterfly clip in her hair to coordinate with the bulletin board she'd created outside her room.

Katie had always dressed for the students. Even if it felt like a costume, they were always enchanted with the efforts she took to keep school fun. She'd learned early on that if children didn't like coming to school, they weren't going to absorb what was being taught.

She glanced across the street as she was loading her

things in the trunk. Lights were on. She could just imagine the ongoing chaos in the house, with Sam trying to get two little girls fed, dressed, and their hair done before taking them to school. Roxie's car wasn't there, and then it dawned on her that it wouldn't be while they were in school.

Katie knew she would see the girls later, so she got in the car and headed to work. The trip there was short, but there were already cars in faculty parking when she arrived.

Everything seemed to slide in place as she got out to unload her things. This was school.

She was a teacher.

She knew what to do here, and no ghosts from the past could change what had become inherent to her. She entered the building, pulling her cart behind her, and saw Susan standing near the door. Her eyes almost disappeared as she smiled.

"Good morning, Katie. Are you ready for this?" Susan asked.

Katie smiled. "Yes, ma'am."

"Have a good day. Shout out if you need anything."

"Thanks," Katie said, and headed for her room.

As she started down the hall, she could see her bulletin board in the distance. When she got to her room, she paused outside the door, eyeing it to make sure everything was still in place. She'd come up yesterday for final touches and was pleased by how it had turned out.

The display was supposed to represent a green garden plot, with a gate ajar. On the crossbar above the gate were the words MISS KATIE'S GARDEN.

Beyond the gate were what looked like little brown rows of dirt that had been turned for planting. Popsicle sticks were poking up from within the rows, with what looked like an empty seed packet on each stick to mark what had been planted beneath.

Each seed packet bore the name of a student that was being planted in first grade. There was a single gummy worm in its own little plastic bag on the dirt just below every stick, and when noon came, they were to get the worm out of the garden as they went to lunch, so it wouldn't eat the newly planted seeds.

There were butterflies in the air above the garden and ladybugs on the sticks and crawling on the dirt. She had put a little gopher sticking its head up from a gopher hole and a rabbit at the far end of the garden, as if waiting for the garden to grow. It looked like a place full of fun and hope and possibilities, which was what beginnings were about.

Delighted with the message it sent, Katie quickly unlocked her door and began putting up what she'd brought from home. With her ID lanyard around her neck and her cell phone on vibrate, she walked out into the hall to wait on students.

Marcy was finishing up in her room, saw Katie come out into the hall, and gave her a thumbs-up.

"I love your bulletin board! What a darling idea!"

"Wait until you see how it grows," Katie said.

"Perfect for first grade… 'Mary, Mary, quite contrary, how does your garden grow?'" Marcy said.

Katie giggled. "'With silver bells and cockleshells, and pretty maids all in a row.'"

Marcy nodded. "Yes! My granny used to recite that nursery rhyme to me. It's very old-fashioned, but I love it. I never really got the meaning, but I did love the idea of silver bells and cockleshells, and I fancied myself a pretty maid when she said it to me."

"You are very blessed to have had family like that," Katie said.

"I know, and I have cousins all over the place," Marcy said, then pointed. "There comes Mr. John. Probably collecting for the pool."

Katie turned. She didn't know what the pool was about, but she'd already met the janitor weeks ago. He was a short, sixtysomething man with bow legs and gray hair that stood up like the crest on a woodpecker. And as always, in denim overalls and a plaid short-sleeve shirt. He was coming up the hall carrying a clipboard.

"Mornin', ladies. Y'all want in on the Puke Pool?"

Katie blinked. "Uh…what on earth is the puke pool?"

John looked at Marcy and winked.

"You mean you ain't told her about the pool yet?"

Marcy shrugged. "Not exactly. You tell her."

John nodded, and then focused on Katie. "What you do is put a dollar in the pot, then pick a day, a time, and a teacher who you think will have the first kid to puke in the new school year. The one who gets the teacher and the closest time right gets the jackpot money to use in her room."

Katie laughed. "Are you serious?"

John nodded. "Yes, ma'am, I sure am. So are you in or not?"

"I'm in," Marcy said, and ran to get a dollar.

"I guess I'm in, too," Katie said, and did the same.

Marcy paid up, then chose a second-grade teacher and three days away at 12:30 p.m.

Katie chose the pre-K teacher at 9:00 a.m. today, then gave John her dollar.

John saw her pick and chuckled. "You ain't got much faith in four-year-olds, do you?"

"I've taught pre-K. There are always one or two who will be so upset to be away from Mama that they'll either throw up, wet their pants, cry all day, or a combination of all three."

"You ain't wrong about that," John said, and wandered off, still running down teachers to finish out the pool before the last bell rang.

Katie was still talking to Marcy when they began seeing students in the halls, and when Katie recognized some of hers, she waved.

As she greeted every student, they in turn saw the additions to the bulletin board and started pointing and talking.

"Miss Katie. I see my name in the garden!"

" I know! I planted you there," she said.

"Is that a gummy worm?" a little boy asked.

Katie nodded. "Yes. And it might eat up my garden. So when noon comes, I'll need all of you to pick your worm out of the garden and take it with you to lunch. Instead of that worm eating our garden, you can eat the worm!"

That seemed to be the funniest thing to all of them. Their laughter filled her up.

And then she saw Evie and Beth coming down the hall hand in hand with their backpacks bobbing. They began waving when they saw her.

"Good morning, Miss Katie," they said, and then both of them saw the candy worms all over the garden.

"There are worms in the garden!" Evie cried.

"Worms!" Beth echoed.

Katie nodded. "Yes, and when we go to lunch, you'll have to get the one by your name to keep it from eating up the garden."

"Yay!" Beth said. "I love gummies."

"We love gummies," Evie said, confirming her sister's statement, and then they went into the room.

One of the last students to arrive was Donny Tiller, and he was running.

He got to the doorway just as the last bell rang.

Katie gave him a quick pat on the back.

"Good morning, Donny. Happy first day of school."

He was a little breathless but beaming as he slipped into the room.

Katie walked in behind him, counting heads as she went, and the morning began.

━━━━━━

As soon as Sam dropped the girls off at school, he reminded them that Roxie would be picking them up and taking them home, and then waited until he saw them running inside before he drove away.

He had a stop to make before he headed to the station and went straight to the florist. It had been years since he'd bought anyone flowers, but he wanted Katie to know he was thinking of her.

He pulled up to the curb in front of Billie's Blooms just as she was turning the CLOSED sign to OPEN. When Billie Woods saw the chief getting out to come inside, she held the door for him.

"Good morning, Chief."

"I know it's early. Are you open for business?" Sam asked.

"Absolutely," Billie said. "Come on in."

Sam was assailed by the aromas of floral foam, eucalyptus, and flowers as he entered the shop.

"Do you want to browse, or do you know what you want?" Billie asked.

"I know. I want a large bouquet of mixed flowers…the more pastel colors you can put in it, the better."

Billie was at the register now, writing up the work order. "Okay. Do you want us to deliver, or are you picking it up?"

"Deliver, please. I've got to get to work," Sam said.

"Who do you want it sent to?"

"Katie McGrath, at the elementary school. She's the new first-grade teacher."

Billie's eyes widened. She quit writing and looked up.

"What do you want to put on the card?"

"I'll write my own," Sam said, then chose a card and envelope from the rack and began writing. When he was finished, he put it in the envelope and sealed it. "Here you go," he said.

"Right," Billie said, and paper-clipped the envelope to the work order. "Did you have a price in mind?"

"No. Just make it pretty and feminine…and get it to her this morning as soon as possible, and bill me for whatever it costs."

"Yes, sir," Billie said. "I'll get right on it."

"Thanks," Sam said, and left the shop.

Billie was on the phone to Louise Parsons before he backed away from the curb, and the moment Louise answered, she started talking.

"Hey, girl, it's me, Billie. You will *not* believe who was just in here ordering flowers before I barely got the shop open."

"You woke me up, so it better be good," Louise mumbled.

"Sam Youngblood just ordered a big bouquet of cut flowers delivered to the new first-grade teacher. He signed the card himself and sealed it up so I couldn't see it. He's sweet on the teacher!"

Louise chuckled. "Well, what do you know... My instinct to rent my little jewel to the new teacher is turning out to be more than a good thing for me. I'm thrilled. I hope it lasts. Sam deserves happiness, and so does Katie McGrath."

"Oh yeah? So what do you know about her?" Billie asked.

"Enough," Louise said. "But she's one in a million, for sure."

"Okay... Well, I gotta get busy on that bouquet. Chief wants it delivered this morning. That man don't mess around. Sorry I woke you," Billie said.

"That's okay. This is the kind of news worth waking up for," Louise said, and hung up.

Billie pinned back her curls, put on a work apron over her jeans and shirt, and headed for the cooler to get the flowers. Her husband, Hershel, drove the delivery van so she sent him a text not to dawdle over morning coffee. They had an important delivery to make.

Today was about the students learning rules of the room, and for Katie to see how far along they were educationally.

She was delighted to see they could all write their names and count aloud to ten. However, a couple had problems writing the numbers, which told her they'd memorized the order without knowing which number went with the amount it represented.

Then they all had a turn sitting in front of the computer, turning it on, finding how to click on a link, and how to mute it.

And then she went through the rules about talking in class, using their inside voices, and then reminded them to get their school supplies out of their backpacks and put them in their cubbies.

That took them through midmorning, and Katie wanted them to refocus and knew just how to do it.

"Okay, boys and girls, if you will please choose a seat at the big round tables, we're going to have snack time."

One little boy's hand shot up in the air. "Miss Katie! I don't have a snack."

A couple more kids echoed the same complaint.

"It's okay. I brought enough snacks for the first week of school because it's hard to get everything organized. I have been assured there are no food allergies in our class, so if you brought a snack, go get it before you sit down. If you did not, just sit down and hold up your hand and I'll bring it to you."

Evie and Beth jumped up to go get their snacks out of their backpacks.

"We have chips and hummus dip, Miss Katie," Evie said.

"We like it," Beth added.

"A good, healthy snack," Katie said.

"Daddy says we have to eat it because we threw a hissy fit in Welby's to get it," Beth said.

Katie grinned. "Have you had it before?"

They nodded.

"And did you like it?" she asked.

"It's okay. It tastes like pudding without the sugar," Evie said.

"Without the sugar," Beth added. "Next time, we're not having hissy fits."

It was all Katie could do not to laugh. "Good choices," she said.

Then she went about the room, passing out snacks for those who didn't have any, and Donny Tiller was one of them.

"My mama gets paid today," he whispered. "I'll have a snack tomorrow."

"That's okay, Donny. I have a snack for you today," she said.

Thor Dooley had a beef jerky stick and a juice box, but couldn't get the wrapping off the jerky.

"Miss Katie, I need help," he said, waving the stick of jerky in the air.

Katie moved across the room to where Thor was sitting.

"I can't get the wrapper off," he said.

"I can help," Katie said, and quickly peeled it down like a banana, leaving wrapper on the bottom half to keep the snack from being messy, then handed it to him. "Here you go."

Thor took a big bite and started chewing and talking at the same time.

"My daddy eats steaks. This here is like a little rolled-up piece of steak."

"Need any help with your juice box?" Katie asked.

He nodded. "I'm tough like Daddy, but I'm not so strong yet. But I will be. I'm a-learnin' how to be a man."

"I think you're just right," Katie said as she opened his juice box and poked in the straw, wondering what the hell else they were drilling into this little boy's head in an effort to "make a man" out of him.

Katie straightened up and glanced around the room, making sure everyone had a snack and a drink, and then noticed one little girl sitting quietly to herself. Her name was Ariana Phillips, but she wouldn't answer to anything but Ree. She had a little plastic bag with Goldfish crackers in front of her she had yet to open.

Katie moved over to where she was sitting.

"Ree, do you need help opening your snack bag?"

"No, ma'am," she whispered.

"Are you just not hungry?" Katie asked.

Still whispering, she leaned close to Katie. "I can't eat them."

Katie frowned. "Why not?"

Ree whispered in Katie's ear.

"They have faces. I can't eat something that's looking at me."

Katie opened the bag and took out one goldfish. Sure enough, the crackers were smiling.

"What if you turn them around and just eat the tails and leave the heads in the sack? Want to try that?" Katie asked.

Ree's eyes widened. "I don't know. Maybe."

"I'll open the sack and you get one and try it," Katie said.

"But what will I do with the heads?" Ree asked.

"You can toss them out in the grass at home to feed the birds," Katie said.

Ree was frowning when she pulled a goldfish out of her snack bag, then turned it around between her tiny fingers and bit it in half, laid the head on the table, and chewed.

"Okay?" Katie asked.

Ree nodded and pulled another cracker out, bit off the tail and began making a pile of the goldfish heads.

"Good job," Katie said, and walked away, leaving Ree to behead the rest of her snacks.

This behavior bothered Katie. Ree was one of the students who hadn't come to Back to School night, so she knew nothing about her family.

Chapter Seventeen

THE KIDS WERE CLEANING UP THEIR TABLES AND TOSS-
ing trash in the trash can when there was a knock at Katie's
door, and then the school secretary opened it and walked
in, carrying the most gorgeous bouquet of flowers Katie
had ever seen—a plethora of pale pinks, lush lilac, sunshine yellows, deep mauve, and light-blue flowers among
tendrils of dark-green ivy.

"A delivery for you, Miss Katie," the secretary said,
and handed the bouquet to Katie. "Somebody sure thinks
you're special," she added, and then left the room.

Katie carried the vase to her desk. Her hands were
shaking as she took out the card, although she knew in her
heart who they were from before she read it.

*Beautiful flowers for a beautiful lady. Have the best
day ever.*

Sam

She grabbed her phone before she thought and sent
a reply.

Sam. Oh my God. Thank you.

Then she remembered she wasn't supposed to use her phone for personal reasons during school hours and put it back in her desk.

Her class crowded around her table, all wanting to be a part of the unexpected arrival, and with the bouquet came the questions.

"Who are they from?"

"Who sent you flowers?"

"Is it your birthday?"

"Did you win a prize, Miss Katie?"

"My mother is 'llergic to flowers."

"My daddy buys my mama flowers when he messes up."

The twins eyed the flowers, pointing without touching, trying to sniff the blooms to see what they smelled like.

"They're so pretty, Miss Katie," Beth said.

"They are, aren't they?" Katie said. "Now, boys and girls, did you clean up where you had your snack?"

"Yes, Miss Katie," they said.

"Okay, then everyone get out a pencil and paper and take a seat. I'm going to write three words on the whiteboard, and I want you to write the same words on your paper."

The scramble began to get paper and pencils, and they were finally settled, except for a little boy named Freddie.

"Miss Katie, I ain't got no paper or pencil."

"Not 'ain't,' Freddie. I *do not* have any paper or pencil."

"Then ain't neither one of us got any," Freddie said.

Katie stifled a laugh. "Never mind for now. I'll get some for you," she said, and tore a sheet of lined paper from a tablet on her desk, took a pencil from the pencil holder, and laid both in front of him. "Here you go, Freddie."

Then Katie moved to the overhead projector aimed at the whiteboard and turned it on. Lines appeared on the whiteboard, like the lines on tablet paper. "Now everyone watch how I write the words."

She began with the word *my* and showed them how to move the pencil up and down on the paper without picking it up to make an M and how to make a Y by making two marks.

Then she wrote the second word: *name.*

Then the third word: *is.*

Then she wrote the whole thing in a sentence. "*My name is…*" to show them how connecting words can make a sentence. And at the end, they were to write their own names.

"Now you can begin and if you need help, please hold up your hand."

Eighteen little heads bent to their papers.

Eighteen little hands gripped their pencils.

Donny Tiller wrote the whole sentence in a few seconds, then held up his hand.

"Yes?" Katie asked.

"I finished. Do I bring it to your desk?"

"Yes. You can put it in the basket," Katie said, pointing at a wire basket on the corner.

She saw the neat writing, that he'd stayed within the lines, and that he'd capitalized the first word in the sentence. And he'd done it all in such a short space of time that she was guessing his reading ability was likely as good as his math and spelling. "If you've finished, you can pick out a book from the library to look at until it's time to go to lunch."

Only Donny didn't pick out a book to look at. He picked out a book to read, and Katie made a mental note to remind Susan again to get this child on a testing list.

One by one, the children turned in their papers.

Beth and Evie's looked identical except for their names...like one of them had written both papers, right down to the way they dotted the *i*.

Thor Dooley drew a guitar on the bottom of his paper, still wanting to be like Daddy.

Freddie's paper was illegible, and he drew a stick figure of a man with a club in his hand.

Ree's writing was so small Katie could barely see it. She didn't know anything about her family, but something was amiss. The child was afraid of faces on crackers and doing her best to stay invisible—both symptoms of something bigger being wrong in the little girl's world.

"Now that everyone is finished, I want to remind you about talking when you're supposed to be listening. Evie...are you talking or listening?"

Evie blushed. "I'm talking, Miss Katie."

"Can you please wait to talk until I'm finished?"

Evie nodded.

"Thank you," Katie said. "I don't like loud voices or loud noises, so it's nicer when I don't have to talk loudly to be heard."

No sooner had she said that than there was a loud boom and the sounds of crashing metal outside their window.

"What was that?" Freddie asked.

"Sounded like war," Thor added.

"Somebody wrecked," a little girl added.

Katie was shaky as she walked to the window and looked out. The trash truck was driving away. She breathed a sigh of relief.

"Nope! Nothing bad. Nothing dangerous. Just the trash truck emptying the dumpster. Now! Where was I?" she said.

Evie held up her hand. "Telling me not to talk!"

Beth nodded. "Not to talk."

Katie wanted to laugh—both from the relief of identifying a normal sound and the innocence of children who had yet to learn the art of the lie.

She looked at her bouquet again, tenderly touching the petals of a pink rose as tension eased within her. *Thank you, Sam…for the reminder that there is beauty in the world.*

"Class, we still have some time before lunch, and this is the first day of school, so let's have some share time. Today, let's share our favorite game. What is your favorite thing to play? Who wants to go first?"

Hands went up. Katie scanned the room. "Freddie, what is your favorite game to play?"

He looked surprised that teacher had called his name, and then he grinned.

"Me and my brothers like to ride our bikes out in the woods behind our house. Daddy cleared us a real dirt-bike trail. I like that best."

"That sounds like fun," Katie said, then pointed to Ree. "Ree, what is your favorite game to play?"

Ree looked up.

Katie saw the wide-eyed look of horror on her face that attention had been called to her.

"It's okay. You don't have to share if you don't want to," Katie said.

"I have Barbie dolls. I play dolls," she said.

"We play dolls!" Evie cried.

"Yes, Barbie dolls," Beth added.

And so it went until the last child had spoken. At that point, Katie began organizing them to head to the cafeteria.

"Boys and girls, it's time to line up for lunch. If you brought your lunch from home, go get it now and then get in line. If you're eating lunchroom food, start lining up. Donny, would you please be the leader today, and then I'll choose a new leader every day. Just remember, in Miss Katie's room, you earn the right to be a leader by being kind and following rules."

One little girl held up her hand.

"Do we get to do special stuff for making the best grades?" she asked.

Katie shook her head firmly. "No. Doing your best every day is your job. That's why you're here. Now everybody line up behind Donny today, and as we go out, show me your name in Miss Katie's Garden and get that worm before he eats up the seeds."

Giggles erupted.

Katie opened the door and then stopped at the bulletin board and began taking down the worms for the kids who couldn't reach.

"Remember, don't eat them now. Lunch first. Worms for dessert."

Her class trooped to the right and straight into the cafeteria chanting, "Worms for dessert."

Katie didn't have cafeteria duty, so after she got all of her class settled with their food and opened milk cartons and juice boxes, she got a tray from the lunch line and sat down at the teachers table a few feet away.

The moment Marcy joined her, the first thing she asked was "Who sent you flowers? They're gorgeous!"

"A friend," Katie said.

Marcy poked her on the arm. "Does that friend have a name?"

"Sam," Katie said, and popped a french fry in her mouth.

Two other teachers' heads came up. Now there were three eyeing the blush on her face.

Marcy gasped. "Sam, as in Youngblood…our police chief?"

"He's my neighbor," Katie said.

"Well, damn," one of the teachers said, and then two others shushed her. "No cursing," they whispered, and then grinned at Katie.

Katie grinned back and just kept eating her meal, knowing that it could come to an end at any moment, and for a multitude of reasons.

———

Sam was in his office finishing up a report when his cell signaled a text. When he saw it was from Katie, he smiled, then opened it.

The brief message said it all.

If only he could follow up tonight with some Katie alone time, but it wasn't meant to be. Tonight, the girls would be full of news about their first day at school, and he needed...wanted...to be on hand to receive it. Still, it felt good knowing he was filling up Katie's life with joy and beauty, and she was filling up his life with what felt like the beginnings of love.

He hit Save, then Print, and was turning around to grab the paper feeding out of his printer when he heard Lucas dispatching an officer to the scene of a domestic quarrel. He grabbed his phone and headed up front.

"Lucas! Where's the domestic disturbance?"

"The Raymond Phillips residence on Duck Street."

"Who called it in?" Sam asked.

"Cheryl Phillips called it in on her husband. She was screaming and crying. I dispatched Ben. Carl's down at the courthouse with Justin Tiller, who's being arraigned this morning."

"Ben is going to need backup. I'm heading there now," Sam said, and left the lobby on the run.

He was in the patrol car, running hot with lights and sirens, when he heard Ben's voice frantically requesting backup, and dispatch telling Ben backup was en route. Sam accelerated. He didn't know what was happening, but he did not want this call to end with someone dying.

He slid to a halt at the residence with his lights still flashing, and heard shouting and screaming even as he was getting out. He took his service revolver out of the holster, entering the house just as Raymond pulled a gun on Ben.

Sam shouted, "Phillips! Don't do it!"

Raymond jerked at the sound of another voice, saw Sam and the gun aimed at his chest, and froze.

"Drop it!" Sam shouted. "Do it now!"

Ben was breathing heavily, blood dripping from a cut above his eye, but Sam's arrival was a lifesaver. He pulled his revolver and aimed at Raymond.

Raymond's face and chest were on fire from the deep gouges Cheryl had put in his flesh. He was bleeding profusely and hurting like hell as he considered his options. Now there were two cops, both with guns aimed straight at his heart. His wife, Cheryl, was lying on the floor, moaning. For two cents he'd just shoot her and take his chances on getting life in prison. But he also knew his life wouldn't be worth shit once the inmates found out why he was there.

Death by cop seemed like the answer. He took a deep breath; his finger twitched as he swung toward Sam with his weapon aimed, but Sam was faster. All of a sudden Raymond's knee exploded beneath him. He fell backward, screaming. The gun fell from his hand, and Ben ran to retrieve it as Sam radioed dispatch for two ambulances.

Raymond was screaming and cursing as Sam cuffed him, leaving Ben on guard as he went to check on Cheryl.

She was lying on her side, moaning.

"Mrs. Phillips, it's Chief Youngblood. I'm going to roll you over onto your back so I can check for injuries. Can you tell me what happened?"

Cheryl moaned again as Sam moved her, and then she slowly opened her eyes.

"When I found them, I went crazy. I tried to kill him with

my bare hands. He hit me in the stomach so hard…over and over. My ribs… It hurts to breathe. Did you kill him?"

"No, ma'am. But he's wounded."

Cheryl moaned. "You should have killed him. He killed us. Call my mother. Call Pansy Fields. Tell her…" Cheryl choked, gasping for air. "Tell her… Get Ree. At school. Keep her until I come get her."

They could hear the ambulances approaching, their sirens louder now than Raymond's shrieks, and Sam still didn't know what happened.

"Found what, Cheryl? What did you find?"

She moaned, clutching her stomach. "What he was doing to our baby. Pictures…all over our bed. I want him dead."

Ben looked at Sam, then shook his head.

Sam's stomach turned. "Do you know what she's talking about?"

"Yes, sir," Ben said, and there were tears in his eyes.

"Jesus," Sam muttered.

And then the ambulances pulled up to the residence.

"Let them know it's safe to enter," Sam said, and Ben turned on his heel and hurried out.

Seconds later, EMTs flooded the room, with Sam's other officer, Carl, behind them.

"What can I do, Chief?" Carl asked.

"Make sure Ben gets first aid, then rope off the area… We have a crime scene."

Cheryl was crying now. "Call my mother," she said. "Call Pansy."

Sam ran back to where they were working on her. "I will, I promise," he said, then tapped one EMT on the shoulder. "Make sure they keep these two separated in the ER, as in not even close. Not being able to see or hear each other. Understand?"

"Yes, Chief," he said.

Moments later, they had Cheryl on a gurney and were rolling it out of the house and into an ambulance, while the other team was still working to establish an IV in Raymond's arm and get a tourniquet on his leg.

One medic had Ben out on the porch, cleaning up the cut over his eye, and patching it up until he could get to the ER.

They finally hauled Raymond out on the other gurney, still screaming and cursing at Sam for not killing him. Sam started through the house, looking for the master bedroom. In the small, two-bedroom house, it wasn't hard to find, nor was the evidence.

Polaroids…lying all over the bed…and a laptop open with a screen filled with pictures…of a little girl…and her daddy.

Sam saw them, but he didn't touch. Couldn't touch. They were an abomination beyond anything he'd ever seen. And he knew who she was…little Ree…the same age as his babies. Whatever God had intended for her, Raymond Phillips had destroyed from the evil within him.

Sam grabbed his phone and called the office of the FBI in Memphis, Tennessee. Child pornography was a federal offense. Raymond Phillips was never going to see the light of day again as a free man. And then Sam called the station.

"Dispatch, this is Lucas."

"Lucas, this is Sam. I need you to get the phone number for Pansy Fields, call her, and then patch me through."

"Yes, sir," Lucas said, and hung up.

While Sam was waiting for Lucas to call and the federal agents to arrive out of Knoxville he sent Roxie a text.

> I will likely be late coming home. Yes, there was a shooting, but my men and I are fine. Food in the fridge.

He hit Send and soon received a thumbs-up emoji, then sighed. God bless Roxie. And then he thought of Katie... and his girls...and the sirens, and sent one more text.

> I know you heard sirens. Tell the girls Daddy is fine and that he'll see them later. And I need to see you, too, before I sleep. It's been a hard day.

A few minutes later, he got the call from Lucas.

"This is Sam."

"Pansy Fields is on hold. I'm patching you through," Lucas said.

Sam waited, heard the click, and then spoke.

"Mrs. Fields, this is Chief Youngblood."

"Oh my God! What's wrong?" Pansy asked.

"There was an incident at your daughter's home. She was injured and asked us to notify you and ask you to please pick Ree up from school and keep her at your house until she can come get her."

Pansy gasped. "Oh Lord, Lord. What happened to her? Where's Raymond? Was he injured, too?"

Sam cleared his throat. "Your daughter will probably want to fill you in with all the details, but you need to know that she discovered Raymond has been sexually molesting your granddaughter."

Pansy moaned.

"God, oh God, oh God. I never saw… She never said… Oh, my poor little Ree. I'm gonna be sick," she said.

Sam heard the phone hit the floor and then the sound of running feet. He closed his eyes and waited.

A couple of minutes later, she was back.

"I'm sorry, Chief. This has broken my heart. I am so sad for my little grandbaby and for my daughter that I don't know what to say. Is Cheryl hurt bad?"

"I can't say for certain, but it appeared she might have some broken ribs. I can't speak for the possibility of internal injuries, but I think your daughter lit into Raymond with the intention of killing him with her bare hands, which is how she got hurt. He looks like a bobcat got hold of him. But she did manage to call the police, which is what saved her life. When we arrived, he pulled a gun on us and took a shot in the knee. He'll need surgery to repair it, and then he'll be going to jail and facing federal charges. But I need to know if you will be able to pick up your granddaughter from school?"

"Yes, yes, of course. In the meantime, I'm going to the hospital to check on Cheryl."

"Yes, ma'am," Sam said. "I'm sorry. So sorry."

"So am I," Pansy said, and hung up.

———

Being the small town that it was, nestled in the Tennessee hills, Borden's Gap was a place where sounds carried—even echoed. So when all of the sirens began sounding, everybody in town heard them, as did everyone in the schools.

It was an unsettling thing for all the children to hear, not knowing what had happened, and all were wondering if their loved ones were safe.

Katie was in her chair in the reading center with her toes at the edge of the red-and-blue braided rug. The whole class was sitting on the rug in front of her, their attention fixated on her face and the emotion in her voice. She was reading *If You Give A Mouse A Cookie*, and every time she turned a page, she showed the children the pictures before she continued. They were as quiet right now as they'd been all day, exhausted from the whole school experience.

Donny had fallen asleep, curled up against the wall, and Beth was lying with her head in Evie's lap, still holding hands.

Several of the kids were lying down, but still awake and listening. Ree was sitting on the rug at the far end of the oval, curled up with her knees beneath her chin and staring off into space somewhere behind Katie's left ear.

Story time was Katie's favorite thing, and she liked to do it toward the end of the day, when the kids were tired and already losing focus on learning. They needed these moments to recharge, and story time was the perfect way to do it.

Katie had just turned the page when they began hearing sirens, and the moment she heard them, her stomach was in knots. She knew whatever was happening, Sam was involved. And from the looks on Beth and Evie's faces, so did they.

Katie kept on reading, adding more emotion and making funny faces, and when the sirens stopped, she and the children relaxed.

And then they heard a whole new set of sirens, and Katie took a deep breath. Ambulance and police sirens did not sound alike, and if she wasn't mistaken, those were ambulances. More than one.

Beth sat up and reached for Evie's hand. Unlike the other children in the class, they had a daddy who was always involved with those sounds, and they were worried all over again.

Katie paused in the story and leaned forward.

"Whatever is happening, all of you are safe right here in our room. So let's finish the story and then I have a little treat for everyone."

The idea of a treat was interesting, and the children calmed again, but even as Katie was finishing the story, sirens fired up again. By now, she was sick to her stomach and trying not to let it show.

As soon as she was finished reading, she shut the book and put it aside. She knew Evie and Beth were bordering on panic, so she called them up and put them to work.

"Everyone go get back in your seats. Beth and Evie, I need helpers. Will you please come to my desk?"

The twins bounced as they jumped up and then

hurried across the room. Katie got a grocery bag out of the storage closet and set it on the floor beside her desk. Then she got a package of napkins from the bottom drawer of her desk and handed them to Evie.

"Evie, would you please put a napkin at everyone's place? I know you know how to do this because you set the table at your home."

"Yes, ma'am," she said, and started at the nearest table.

"And Beth, I'm going to need you to put one of these little snacks on top of each napkin. I'll carry the bag, and you get them out for me."

"Yes, ma'am," Beth said, and marched along beside Katie as they went from chair to chair, giving each student a snack-size bag of pretzels.

Then they served themselves and sat down, and the chatter began.

"Remember to use your inside voices," Katie said.

They giggled, and nodded, and tore into the bags.

Katie returned the extras to her storage closet and went back to her desk with a bag of pretzels for herself. She tore into the bag and popped a crunchy little twist in her mouth, letting the salt melt on her tongue before she chewed.

The kids had calmed. The scary time had passed, and then she got another text. *To hell with rules*, Katie thought, and grabbed the phone. She'd hoped it was from Sam, and it was. The message was a huge relief, and at the same time, she guessed something bad had happened. Just not to him.

She got up and walked over to where the girls were

sitting and squatted down beside them long enough to deliver a message.

"Girls, your daddy wants you to know he's fine, and he'll see you later."

Their relief was visible.

"Yay," Evie said.

"Yes, yay," Beth echoed.

Katie stood, touched the backs of their heads, and then walked around the room, talking to the kids, making sure they all had a measure of her attention.

"I like these," Thor said.

"I do, too," Katie said, and winked, and then moved toward Ree, who was carefully looking over every pretzel before putting it in her mouth. The little girl wouldn't look up, and Katie wasn't about to force her to interact, but as a teacher, she felt warning bells going off.

"When you finish, you know where to put your trash," Katie said, and one by one, the children finished and cleaned up behind themselves.

When the bell rang to go home, Katie had already sorted her bus riders, car riders, and the ones who walked home into three different groups before they filed out of their room and down the hall. Doors were banging. Kids were running, and someone shouted, "No running in the hall!" Katie broke out in a cold sweat and kept walking, making sure with every step that her kids were still with her.

As soon as they were out the door, she herded her separate groups to the designated on-duty teachers getting children in the right transportation groups and headed home, because once school was out, lingering on the school grounds was not allowed.

Katie saw Roxie in the line for car riders and watched as she picked up Sam's girls. She saw Justin Dooley drive up in a shiny black truck to get his son, Thor, and saw Frieda Tiller picking up her three boys. Donny ran headlong into his mama's arms, talking with great animation as she loaded them all into her car.

And in the middle of the chaos, Ree Phillips began moving herself into a panic when she didn't see her mother's car. The teacher on car duty was trying to calm Ree down when Katie saw Ree in hysterics and hurried over.

"What's wrong, sugar?" Katie said.

"Mama's not here. I can't go home without Mama," she cried.

Katie knelt down beside her and pulled her close.

"You aren't going to be left alone. I'm right here with you until your mother arrives, okay?"

Still sobbing, Ree nodded and leaned into Katie's arms.

Then all of a sudden, a light-blue car pulled up, and the driver was honking. The door opened, and an older woman came flying out of her car, calling Ree by name.

"I'm here, ReeRee. Granny's here!" she cried, and then swept Ree up into her arms. Ree tucked her face against her grandmother's neck and held on for dear life. Pansy looked straight at Katie. "I'm Ree's grandmother, Pansy Fields. I am allowed to pick Ree up when the need arises. Cheryl, Ree's mother, is in the hospital. I'm sorry I was late. I got here as quick as I could. Cheryl is going to be fine, but she's there for a couple of days."

Ree started sobbing. "I want my mama."

Pansy rocked Ree in her arms.

"You're coming home with me, darlin'. And you'll be staying with me until Mama can go home. And don't worry about anything. Not anymore. Do you understand? We know what's been happening. You're safe, baby, you're safe now."

And then she carried Ree away, leaving the teachers in shock.

"What was all that about?" Susan asked.

"I don't know," Katie said. "The parents weren't at Back to School night, so I never met them, and this is Ree's first day with me." And then she lowered her voice. "All I know is she wouldn't eat the Goldfish crackers that were sent for her snack because they were smiling and she couldn't look at their faces, and then the paper she turned in to me was almost impossible to read because the writing was so tiny. It's like she doesn't want to be seen. She was trying to be invisible. I had already made a note on my daily log to talk to you about her," Katie said.

They all looked at each other, none of them voicing what was going through their heads, but they didn't have to. Teachers saw the best of parents and the worst of parents, and they knew the signs of what was happening in the homes from the ways their students acted out.

Immediately, Katie thought of the sirens and couldn't imagine what might have happened to put Cheryl Phillips in the hospital.

Finally, all the students were gone and the teachers had gone back inside to finish up in their rooms so they could go home to get ready for another day.

Katie gathered up her things, piled them all into her little rolling cart, then glanced at her beautiful bouquet before turning out the lights. She was leaving it here because this was where she would see and enjoy it the most. And it was something to look forward to seeing when she came back tomorrow.

She left the door open, knowing Mr. John would be in there shortly sweeping up and emptying trash cans, then headed for an exit.

As she walked, the sounds of her footsteps echoed in the nearly empty building, but she didn't feel any threat here. She didn't feel unsafe here. And she kept thinking to herself *I did it. I did it. One whole day without losing my shit is what I call a good day.*

Chapter Eighteen

KATIE THOUGHT ABOUT REE PHILLIPS AS SHE SWUNG by Welby's Grocery. It was already obvious that she was going to need a stash of snack foods for the ones who had nothing at home. She made herself a mental note to send an email to remind parents about sending something for their child to have at snack time.

She was going up and down the aisles, unaware that Betty, Kay, and Charlene, the same three women who'd followed her in the car when she was walking Rhett Butler, were now one aisle over, heads together, whispering in their own little frantic shorthand.

"The new teacher's in the next aisle!" Charlene hissed, pointing behind her.

Betty's head came up. "Be right back!" she said, then headed for the end of the aisle and took a left, disappearing from view.

Kay rolled her eyes. "Doesn't matter. He sent her flowers today."

Charlene gasped. "Sam did that?"

Kay nodded. "Billie told me."

Charlene sighed, then dug a stick of gum out of her purse, peeled off the wrapper, and popped the gum in her mouth. "Well, damn."

Meanwhile, Betty had made her way up the aisle to where the new teacher was standing and stopped, pretending to peruse the stock on the shelf. But when the teacher saw her and smiled, Betty lost her cool.

"Oh! Hi! You're the new teacher."

Katie laughed. "I know. My name is Katie."

"Uh…Betty. Oh. I don't mean you're Betty. I'm Betty. Betty Looper. Like Cooper, but with an L. Nice to meet you," she said, and made a U-turn with her shopping cart and left the aisle, cursing herself for ever opening her mouth.

Kay and Charlene were staring at Betty as if they'd never seen her before. Then they lowered their voices back down to a hiss and began whispering to each other again.

"We heard you," Kay whispered.

"Idiot," Charlene said, and rolled her eyes.

Betty nodded. "I know. She's nice and pretty."

"Sam sent her flowers," Kay said.

Betty's shoulders dropped. "We struck out again, didn't we?"

Charlene shrugged. "No. We were just looking in the wrong direction. I don't want to raise someone else's kids anyway. I'm going home, too."

Accepting their fate as still single, the trio turned their shopping carts around and headed to the front of the store to check out.

Unaware that her presence in Borden's Gap had destroyed three women's daydreams of Sam Youngblood, Katie finished her shopping and headed home. As she drove, Ree Phillips popped back up in her thoughts.

Something was wrong in that house, but Katie was hopeful there was a resolution taking place.

Sam's cruiser was not at the house, but Roxie's car was.

As Katie got out, she heard the girls' laughter coming from their backyard and thought how vastly different people's lives could be. She wondered if Ree ever laughed. Her instincts said no. Her instincts also told her to get her groceries put up before the butter began to melt. So she unloaded her school stuff and then her groceries and took them inside.

———————

Justin Tiller finally used his phone call and called Frieda before he went to court, but she didn't answer, which was all the answer he was going to get.

After that, he was cuffed and hauled off to court where he was arraigned, pled guilty, and was sentenced to thirty days in jail. The way he looked at it, he would have three squares and thirty days away from three noisy kids and a bitching wife before he had to go home and face the consequences.

Frieda heard the news from a friend who'd been in the courtroom to contest a traffic ticket and breathed a huge sigh of relief. A whole month of peace and quiet in their house equaled thirty days to get enough money together to file for a protective order and a divorce.

In the middle of a life full of lemons, life had just handed her enough sugar to make lemonade.

———————

The residents of Borden's Gap knew something bad had gone down at the Phillips house. They'd seen Cheryl taken away in an ambulance, and then Raymond emerged surrounded by cops and cuffed to the gurney he was on, shrieking in pain. A short while later, crime scene tape went up, and Chief Youngblood was still on scene.

Three special agents arrived from the FBI office in Memphis about two hours after Sam's call. They introduced themselves, and Sam led them through the house, explaining what had happened from the call into the station to now.

"Did the suspect say anything, or admit to anything?" one of the agents asked.

"Other than screaming and cursing and being pissed that I didn't kill him, he said nothing to me," Sam said. "I haven't touched a thing in here, but my officer, Ben Adams, was the first officer on the scene. He's at the ER getting patched up. You can get his statement later."

They nodded, then turned back to the bed. "Our crime scene team will be here shortly. We'll be gathering evidence, and from the photos, it appears the molestations took place mostly in her bedroom, so we'll be taking DNA samples from the little girl's bedroom, too."

Sam wiped a hand over his eyes and then looked away.

"Tough to see, I know," the agent said.

Sam shook his head. "I have twin girls. They're the same age as this child. I can't wrap my head around a son of a bitch this sick, or how this little girl will ever recover from something like this."

They all nodded in agreement.

"Thank you for calling us, Chief. We'll be taking over from here. We'd like copies of your report and your officer's report sent to us at the Bureau. Here's my card with contact info. Where is Raymond Phillips now?"

"Likely in surgery. I shot him in the knee before I knew about this. I'm glad I didn't know until the altercation was over. I might have been tempted to aim higher."

"Will you notify the family that they can't come back in here yet? We'll be collecting evidence up into the night after the crime scene team arrives."

"His wife, Cheryl, is in the hospital, too. I'm guessing broken ribs and maybe internal injuries for her, but she literally dug holes in him with her nails after she found this. He'll wear those scars for life."

"What about the little girl?" the agent asked.

"Her grandmother, Pansy Fields, has her. She lives here in town. We won't see her scars, but they'll be there. Nobody 'gets over' this kind of hell. And on another note, if you have need of anything, call the station. We'll be happy to assist."

The agents nodded.

Sam walked out of the house into the sunshine and felt like he'd just crawled up from the pits of hell. He was sick at heart on a level unlike anything he'd ever known. But he still had reports to write and people to call, so he headed back to the station.

The sun was going down by the time Sam left the station. He couldn't wait to get home and hug his babies. Then he turned the corner on his street and saw Roxie's car and knew they were safe. He saw Katie's car and felt a wave of longing wash through him. He needed to see Katie before he could face his daughters. Monsters were in this little town and because they'd been in hiding, a child had come to harm on his watch.

He pulled up into her driveway and got out. He was on his way up the steps when the door suddenly swung open and Katie was standing on the threshold. He walked in without a word, kicked the door shut behind him, then wrapped his arms around her.

Katie knew the moment she saw Sam getting out of the car that the day had been bad. Even though it was dusk, she could see the weariness on his face. The despair within him was evident when she opened the door. Something bad had happened today.

Sam inhaled the sweetness of her, from the scent of her shower gel to the softness of her skin, and when she wrapped her arms around his waist, they were the glue he needed to keep from coming undone.

"I can't stay long," he finally said.

"Come sit," she said, and led him to the sofa.

Sam clutched her hand all the way and didn't let go, even after they were sitting down.

"We arrested a man today for molesting his daughter. His wife found pictures. So many pictures. She tried to kill him with her bare hands."

"Oh my God," Katie whispered.

"When she called the police, he began hitting her in

the stomach. I think broken ribs. Hopefully no internal injuries. He pulled a gun on me and one of my officers. He wanted us to kill him. I shot him in the knee instead."

Katie clutched Sam's hand tighter.

"I can't get the pictures out of my head. She's just a little girl…like mine."

"It was Ree Phillips, wasn't it?" Katie said.

Sam blinked, a little startled, and then he remembered Pansy had to get Ree at school. She must have said something.

He nodded. "So it's all over town already?"

"I don't know about that. But Ree is in my class. Today was the first day I'd met her, and from the start I knew something was wrong with her. And then when her grandmother came to get her after school, it was what she said, what she alluded to… I knew then my instincts were right."

Sam frowned. "What do you mean?"

"Keep in mind, I've been teaching for years. Teachers see all kinds of broken children, and I always see the little ones. They're still too young to lie…and too innocent to know they're being victimized."

And then she began relating all of the incidents with Ree today, from not wanting to eat anything with a face, to not interacting with children, and how tiny she wrote… like she was trying not to be seen.

Sam was surprised. "I see what you mean about knowing something was wrong. Do kids like that ever recover?"

"I did," Katie said, and Sam broke.

His eyes welled. "Jesus, Katie… Jesus."

She sighed. "The upside was that it wasn't my father. I didn't love him, then have that trust broken. I didn't even know his name when it happened. But I was eight and I told, and I don't know what happened after that because Social Services just moved me to another area of the city. Ree will need counseling and treatment…probably for a long, long time. She needs to go straight to counseling. School is not the place for her right now. The stress on her of being around people was obvious today.

"And everyone in town will soon know why the man was arrested, and then there will be the people who will remember this, and they won't want their daughters playing with her, and she'll be ostracized because they'll be afraid of Ree…because she knows things they don't want their babies knowing, and no matter how old Ree gets, and how successful her ability to move forward, they won't let her forget. My heart is broken for her and her mother… and her grandmother. They'll blame themselves now and never look at her the same way again."

Sam swiped his hands across his face.

"It's hard being a cop and accepting there will always be people you can't save."

"No, you're looking at this all wrong," Katie said. "You already saved them. Today. Just like you saved Frieda Tiller when you hauled Justin off to jail. Just like you do every day, in ways you never see. Your mere presence in Borden's Gap is a deterrent, Sam. You're not God. You're just a very good man with a very big heart, doing the best that you know how to do, and that's all anyone can ask. You're saving me and you don't even know it."

Sam looked at her then, at the steady gaze she held on his face.

"You are a sleeper, aren't you, Katie? You look all fragile and womanly, and your gentle manner belies the warrior within. I hope someday you realize how much you've come to mean to me, because I want you in my life. Thank you. I needed this. I needed you. And you came through for me like the champ you are. And now I need to get home so Roxie can leave. And I need to hug my babies and pray to God to keep them safe when I'm not there."

"Well, you already have Roxie in your corner. And I'm their teacher, so while they're at school, they are under my wing. I think you're already covering all bases."

Sam stood and then pulled her up into his arms and kissed her...hard and fast, then sighed when he let her go.

"Thank you, Katie."

"You're welcome...and just so you know...what you've said to me goes no farther than this room. Whatever secrets are told in this town won't come from me."

He nodded.

She knew he was overwhelmed, but she had faith in Sam Youngblood that he would always do the right thing.

━━━━━━━

Frieda Tiller picked up her paycheck and paid bills, bought groceries, then went home and cleaned and did laundry all day. The house was spotless by the time she went to pick up the boys at school. When she saw Donny running toward her with a big smile on his face, she laughed. There were so few times in their family when true joy abounded. And knowing now what a brilliant mind he had gave her purpose. She needed to make certain that all her boys had a safe and healthy environment in which to grow up, so that they could be all they were meant to be.

They were all three talking at the same time, their voices rising in their need to be heard, when Frieda stopped on Main for a red light.

"Hey, guys, I have something to tell you," she said.

"What is it, Mama?" Donny asked.

"Your daddy is in jail. He was sentenced to thirty days for disturbing the peace and destruction of property."

"Okay," they echoed. "What's for supper?"

And Frieda sighed. *Okay, girl. There's your sign. Get out while the getting's good.*

———————

Cheryl Phillips couldn't quit crying. She was as broken as her ribs.

After so many tries to have a baby, and so many miscarriages, she and Raymond finally got pregnant. Their joy had been boundless. He was a hands-on father from the start, and she'd been fooled by his utter devotion to their daughter, to the point that she'd never seen him through her daughter's eyes.

Ree had been a happy baby. A playful baby, until somewhere around three years old when she began to change.

Cheryl hadn't understood Ree's withdrawal as anything but being shy. And when Ree clung to her to the point of desperation, she just hugged her and called her a mama's girl. She had failed her child.

Cheryl didn't even know where to start for them to begin to heal, but she knew small-town life. People there would never let this die. She didn't know where they were going to go or what they would do, but when she got out of the hospital, she and Ree were moving.

She wouldn't take her back to that house of horrors.

Ree needed counseling and new surroundings, and that didn't just mean a move across town.

Pansy Fields was hysterical and trying not to show it. She couldn't look at Ree without wanting to scream, and kept patting her and talking quietly as they drove home.

"Why is Mama in the hospital?" Ree asked.

Pansy took a deep breath. At that moment, she wouldn't have lied to that child to save her soul.

"Your daddy hurt her. He's in jail."

Ree's eyes grew so big and opened so wide Pansy was suddenly afraid that she'd told a baby things she didn't need to hear, and then she remembered what this baby had already endured and decided the baby would be relieved to know the monster couldn't get to her anymore.

Only Ree started shaking. "I didn't tell! I didn't tell!" she wailed.

Pansy frowned. "Tell what, baby?"

"Daddy said if I told, he would kill Mama and he would kill you. I didn't tell about the games."

"Jesus wept!" Pansy shrieked. "He said that to you?"

Ree nodded, still crying.

Pansy pulled over at a curb and grabbed Ree by the hand.

"Look at me, sugar! You're safe now! He can't ever hurt you again! Do you understand that? He's going to prison for what he did to you. They will lock him up behind bars. He is going to live the rest of his life there, where he can't hurt anyone else for as long as he lives. And your mama is going to get well and come get you at my house, and you're going to be fine. Granny and Mama will see to that. Now, when we get to my house, we're going to have a good supper, and you can sleep with me every night if you want to."

"Am I going back to school?" Ree asked.

"Not yet. We have things to do," Pansy said. "Is that okay?"

Ree nodded. "I don't want Goldfish crackers."

Pansy didn't know what the hell that meant, but she was fine with the request.

"Me either," Pansy said. "Now, Granny loves you, and we're going to find a way to take away your sad, okay?"

The little girl nodded.

Pansy handed her a tissue. "Here, baby. Wipe your eyes. We're going to get ice cream before we go home. What kind do you like best?"

Ree's eyes lit up. "I like chocolate, Granny. Can I have chocolate in a cup?"

"You can have anything you want," Pansy said, and drove away from the curb.

———

Raymond Phillips came out of surgery with titanium rods and screws in his knee. He had stitches on his face, and his chest and arms were bandaged from the gouges Cheryl had dug out of his flesh.

Even through the veil of drugs, and handcuffed to the hospital bed with a guard outside his door, he was in misery. He'd always known there were dangers in playing the games, but he'd never expected the situation to unwind as it had. If that damn cop had just shot him dead, then this would all be over.

But Sam had crippled him instead, and the doctors had put him back together. Now he would die in a federal prison, and it wouldn't be pretty and it wouldn't be swift, like a bullet. Of that he was certain.

———

Roxie was waiting for Sam when he walked in the door. She wasn't a touchy-feely kind of woman, but at that moment, she'd never wanted to hug a man as much as she did him.

"Roxie, thank-you is never enough," Sam said.

"Hey. We've been doing this too long to get all apologetic and squishy. You're the chief of police, not an insurance salesman, and the closest thing I'll ever have to a son. You're welcome. Now. There is a meat loaf in the warming oven, buttered corn on the stove, and potatoes baking. They should be done in about fifteen minutes."

Sam hugged her. "That's for the meat loaf. I hope to God I never have another day like this in my life."

Roxie frowned. "My phone has blown up with town gossip, but I'm assuming a lot of it was exaggerated."

Sam just shook his head. "We had a monster in Borden's Gap, and that is not an exaggeration."

Roxie's eyes widened, but before she could say more, the girls came running.

"Daddy! Daddy! We had the funnest day!"

"I'm going home now," Roxie said. "Girls, I'll pick you up again after school, okay?"

"Okay," they echoed and waved as she left, and then they were chattering, unloading a play-by-play of their day.

"Wait!" Sam said. "Let Daddy get out of his work stuff and then we'll all go to the kitchen."

"To the kitchen," Beth said, and then skipped off to their room, with Evie right behind her.

Sam's feet were dragging as he walked into his room and began shedding the armor of being a cop. Gun locked up. Uniform dumped with the others to go to the cleaners, and then a shower. He had to. He couldn't touch his girls until he washed off where he'd been.

A short while later, he left his room, barefoot and wearing old jeans and a T-shirt, then went into their bedroom where they were playing and sat down on the bed.

They dropped their Barbie dolls and piled into his lap, one on each knee as he pulled them close against him.

"Do you know how much Daddy loves you?" he asked.

"This much?" Beth asked, holding her arms out wide.

Then Evie grabbed onto one of Beth's hands and spread her arms, too.

"No, Daddy loves us this much, because there are two of us."

"Yes, two," Beth said.

Sam pulled them so close against him that they started wiggling.

"You're squishing us!" Evie squealed, giggling uncontrollably.

"Squishing!" Beth said, giggling too.

"I'm hungry. Let's go set the table and finish supper," Sam said.

"I'm starving," Evie said.

"Me, too," Beth said, and they both slid out of Sam's lap and made a run for the door.

He got up and followed. They were just the medicine he needed.

The baked potatoes were done, so there was nothing to do but make plates for everyone, then sit down. He already knew it was salt and butter only on the girls' potatoes, and ketchup for the meat loaf because it was not their favorite. The corn had to go in the middle of the plate, like a mountain. Repetition was a good thing when you were trying to find true center, and finally Sam's world reached just that.

The twins talked about Miss Katie this and Miss Katie that, all the way through supper. They talked about sitting on the red-and-blue rug in the reading center when Miss Katie read them a book, and that Freddie fell asleep, and they wrote their numbers to ten and said their ABCs.

"We ate worms!" Evie said, and then dissolved into hysterics.

Sam frowned. "Worms?"

Beth giggled. "Yes. Gummy worms out of Miss Katie's garden by the door."

Sam had a vague memory of seeing the bulletin board, and the story began to make sense.

"What did your worms taste like?" he asked.

"Mine was yellow and squishy. It tasted like lemon," Beth said.

"Mine was red and squishy. It tasted like cherry," Evie said.

"Wow. You two sure are lucky. I never had a teacher who let me eat worms, or read me stories on a big red-and-blue rug."

They beamed. "We're lucky," they said.

"Do you know what that means?" Sam asked.

They immediately shook their heads no.

"It means you got good stuff without asking for it. That you have a really nice teacher who does things for you because she wants to."

"We love Miss Katie," Beth said softly.

Evie nodded. "Yes, we love Miss Katie so much. Even when she asked me to listen and not talk."

"And use our inside voices!" Beth added.

Sam grinned. "I may have to take a page out of Miss Katie's book."

They immediately frowned at him. "No, Daddy. You're not allowed to take pages out of books, remember?"

Sam laughed. "You're so right. My bad."

They giggled. "Daddy's bad," they said, and at that point, Sam knew he'd lost control of the conversation.

By the time bedtime rolled around, the girls were so tired he could barely keep them awake long enough to get their baths and help them into their nightgowns.

When he turned down their bed, they crawled into it without talking, lay down facing each other, clasped hands, and closed their eyes.

"Do you want to hear a story tonight?" Sam asked.

"My ears can't hear anymore today," Evie mumbled.

"Anymore," Beth said.

"Sweet dreams," Sam said, and sat until he knew they were out before he left the room.

Long after they'd been in bed, Sam was still up. He couldn't bring himself to close his eyes for fear he'd see the horror in those photos again. Finally, he got a beer from the fridge and slipped out the back door and eased down onto the steps and took a drink.

The cold, yeasty brew felt like silk as it slid down his throat. He took another couple of sips and then kicked back, listening to the night song of Borden's Gap.

He could hear music from two different directions, so he wasn't the only one suffering a sleepless night.

Someone's dog began to bark, and another howled back in answer. He heard a man yell at the howler, and then a door slamming. Silence followed.

The sound of traffic was always present, because their Main Street was also an old state highway, but the traffic was much less at night.

He thought of Ben and the stitches he wound up with over his eye.

He thought of Cheryl Phillips and how valiantly she had tried to slay her dragon, and of Pansy and little Ree.

And then finally, he let himself go there and pictured Raymond Phillips handcuffed to his hospital bed, and a rage rose within him.

He hoped the pain Raymond was in would last for the rest of his miserable life. He hoped that knee would ache when it rained, and when it got cold, and when he walked, and when he tried to find an easy spot in bed to ease the pain. He wanted that man in utter misery until he took his last breath on earth, and it would still not be the justice his daughter deserved.

Then Sam finished off his beer and went inside.

After one last peek in on his babies, he crawled up onto his bed, still in his jeans and T-shirt, and closed his eyes.

And fell asleep.

Chapter Nineteen

The principal met Katie as she was coming in the door the next morning.

"Ree Phillips has been withdrawn from school."

Katie's shoulders slumped. "Okay, but I'm not surprised. I'll clean out her cubby."

"Wait," Susan said.

Katie paused and turned. "Yes, ma'am?"

"You have a gift. You saw the genius in one student and danger signs in another, and both on the first days you met them. I feel very fortunate that you accepted this job. I just wanted you to know you are appreciated."

"Thank you," Katie said. "I feel very fortunate that you offered it. And today is a whole new day."

And it was.

The class was so new, and Ree had been so quiet, that the children never noticed she was gone. Each day after that for the entire week was busy, and hectic, and fruitful in one way or another, and each evening, Katie went home feeling satisfied.

Teachers' meeting was on Wednesday after school, so Katie was delayed in leaving. Once the meeting ended, she raced back to her room to get her things. She was getting ready to leave when she saw a little blue blinged-out headband on the floor beneath one of the chairs. She knew immediately it was Beth's and picked it up and took it with her. She had a couple of stops to make before she headed home, and by the time she pulled into her driveway, Sam was home and Roxie was gone.

She unloaded her school stuff, then grabbed Beth's headband and walked across the street and rang the bell. Even before the door opened, she could hear crying. Then Sam was standing in the doorway with a harried expression on his face, and the wailing was even louder.

Katie held up the headband.

Sam rolled his eyes, pulled her into the house, and hugged her.

"You are a freaking saint," he muttered. "This has been nonstop since I came home. Come with me." He grabbed her hand and led her to the girls' bedroom.

Evie was sitting on the bed with her arm around Beth, crying right along with her, because that's how they rolled.

Katie walked in with Sam, then sat down on the bed beside the girls and put the headband in Beth's lap.

Beth squealed in the middle of a sob and immediately slid the headband on her head.

"I found it under a chair near the reading center," Katie said.

Tears were running and snot poured, but Beth was smiling through it all.

"Thank you, Miss Katie. I thought it was lost," Beth said.

Katie grabbed a handful of tissues, scooted Beth onto her lap, and began wiping up Beth's face, then wrapped her arms around her and gave her a big hug.

"I'm sorry you were so sad, but it's all better now, right?"

Beth nodded and leaned against Katie's shoulder as she looked up at Sam.

"Daddy, I'm not sad anymore," she said.

Not wanting to be left out, Evie scooted close to Katie.

Without thinking, Katie pulled her close, too.

"Did you girls tell Daddy about what we did in science today?" Katie asked.

"Science? Is that the bean?" Evie asked.

Katie nodded.

And all at once, Sam was inundated with the story.

"We had a cup. And we had dirt. And we had a bean," Beth said.

"Then we put the bean on the dirt and pushed it down," Evie added.

"And what else?" Katie asked.

They frowned, thinking, and then Evie shouted.

"We gave it a drink!"

Sam laughed. He was relieved the crying was over and moved by the sight of his daughters in Katie's lap.

"Okay," Katie said. "I have to go home and get stuff ready for tomorrow, and I know you two and Daddy have supper to make. I'll see you tomorrow," she said, then gave the girls a last hug.

Sam walked her to the door, then cupped her face and kissed her.

"Every day you dig yourself a little deeper into my heart," he said.

"You are an irresistible man, Sam Youngblood, but be patient with me. Like those beans, taking root takes time," Katie said, and went home.

The next day after work, Katie brought her bouquet home, put it on the kitchen table, and started digging through the pantry. She'd been wanting chocolate cake for days and couldn't stand it anymore. After changing and making herself something cold to drink, she turned on the oven and began getting out what she needed to make cupcakes.

Soon she had the batter mixed up, and she was putting the paper liners in her cupcake pans when her phone rang. When she saw it was Sam, she quickly wiped her hands and answered.

"Hello."

"Katie, it's me. I am in a bind. Roxie left early for a dentist appointment and I just got called back in. There's a wreck, and both drivers are fighting in the street. Can the girls come stay with you for a bit until I get this sorted out?"

"Absolutely," Katie said. "Head them this way and I'll go out to meet them."

"Thank you so much," Sam said, and hung up.

Katie ran out of the house and was already crossing the street when the girls came out of the house with Sam between them.

"I owe you," Sam said as he passed the girls over to Katie.

Katie took each girl by a hand. "Who wants to help me make cupcakes?"

"Me! Me!" they said.

"Then let's go to my house, because that's where the good stuff is happening!"

"You rock. Save one for me," Sam said. He jumped in

the patrol car and took off up the street with lights flashing as Katie led the girls into her house.

"I smell chocolate!" Beth said.

"That's because I'm making chocolate cupcakes," Katie said. "Are your hands clean?"

They held them up. "Daddy washed our faces and hands before we came over."

"Awesome, but you need to be a little bit taller. How about you sit up here and you can put the papers in the cupcake pans?" Then she lifted them up onto the barstools, pushed the pans toward them, and began separating the cupcake papers from the stack.

All of a sudden, the giggling stopped and the girls got serious. Beth chose only the blue and yellow papers, and Evie chose only the pinks and whites.

"Perfect," Katie said as they worked, and when they had finished, she began dipping batter into each paper.

As soon as the tins were full, she slid them into the oven to bake, set the timer, and then saw the girls eyeing the batter bowl and grinned.

"I think we need a little taste of what's left on the bowl, don't you?"

They nodded, watching as she pulled three teaspoons from her cutlery drawer. She handed one to each of them and kept one for herself.

"Does Daddy let you lick the bowl when he bakes sweets?" she asked.

"Daddy doesn't do this," they said. "We buy them at the bakery."

"Well, this is how you lick the bowl," she said as she

ran her spoon along the inside of the bowl and got a little bit of batter and popped it in her mouth. "Try not to get batter on your clothes," she added.

They nodded. With the bowl between them now, they scraped and licked and scraped and licked until there was nothing left but a smear of brown in the bottom.

"That was good, Miss Katie. When the cupcakes are done, can we have one of those, too?" Evie asked.

"Absolutely," Katie said. "But right now, let me get the sticky off your hands and faces."

While they were stirring up sweetness in the kitchen, Sam and Carl had the two drivers separated and sitting yards apart on the curb, while their argument was still ongoing, and there were witnesses galore.

Lucas, the dispatcher, had given a heads-up to both officers due to come on duty for night patrol that their presence was needed at the scene. So while help was on the way, Sam was guarding the two drivers, and Carl was directing traffic around the wreck and waiting for the tow trucks.

"Now," Sam said, eyeing the two combatants. "I'm going to ask each of you the same question, but I only want one answer at a time, so while Lenny is talking, Bobby shuts up. Got that?"

They nodded.

"Lenny, have you been drinking?" he asked.

"No, sir," Lenny said.

"Bobby, have you been drinking?"

"I had a beer about three hours ago, Chief, and that's all, I swear it."

"Are both of you willing to take a Breathalyzer test?"

They nodded, and so he proceeded to administer the test, which they both passed.

"Okay. Neither one of you is drunk, so what caused this wreck?"

Lenny pointed. "He swerved into my lane, and I didn't have anywhere to go to miss him."

"No. He swerved into me!" Bobby shouted.

Then Delilah Cash, who was standing nearby with Rhett Butler in her arms, raised a hand and called out to Sam.

"Chief Youngblood!"

He looked up and paused. "Yes, ma'am?"

"They were both looking down at their phones. I saw them. They drove right into each other like they were playing bumper cars. And they were going too fast on Main Street," she added.

Sam looked around. "Can anybody else verify Miss Delilah's statement?" Hands came up. "I'll be needing your names," he said. "See me when this is over." Then he looked down at the men. "Anybody here wanna call Miss Delilah a liar?"

Delilah Cash was a treasure in Borden's Gap, and nobody would have even dreamed of disputing her word.

Lenny dropped his head. "No, sir," he said.

"Me either," Bobby said, and covered his face.

"So, if you both knew you were at fault, then what the hell made you think it was a good idea to get out of a wreck and start fighting?" Sam asked.

They shrugged.

"Well, you're both getting ticketed for speeding, and for causing a wreck, and for disturbing the peace, and for creating a hazard on a main thoroughfare. And the EMTs are on the scene, so both of you get checked out right now."

"Can I get my wallet and phone out of my car first?" Lenny asked.

Sam nodded. "You can both remove your personal effects, but neither vehicle is drivable, so your insurance adjusters will be viewing the cars at impound."

The men groaned in unison.

"You're both lucky you weren't going any faster. People die texting and driving…every day."

Sam got the names of the other witnesses, then wrote up tickets for Lenny and Bobby and handed them over. He waited, watching to make sure they were still civil to each other as they dragged themselves over to their cars. Within moments, they were on their phones again, but this time calling someone to come get them.

The two night-duty officers arrived to assist Carl with diverting traffic as the tow trucks arrived.

Once Sam was satisfied his men had everything under control, he walked over to where Delilah was standing.

"Thank you, Miss Delilah."

"You're welcome," she said. "I'll be on my way now. Rhett Butler and I were just out for a stroll and we're tired."

"I can give you both a ride home, if you'd like," Sam said.

Delilah sighed and hugged her little Yorkie close. "Yes, I think I've used up all my pep for the day."

Sam told his men he was leaving, then escorted his witness and her canine companion to his patrol car and drove away. In less than five minutes, he was in Delilah's driveway and helping her out of the car.

"Thank you again, and give Katie my love," Delilah said.

"You're most welcome, and I will be happy to do that."

Then the Yorkie yapped at Sam.

He grinned and gave the little fuzzball a scratch on the head.

"You're welcome, too."

He waited until they were safely inside the house before driving back to get the girls, hoping he got some cupcakes and a kiss along with them.

━━━━━━

The cupcakes had long since come out of the oven and were on cooling racks. Katie had icing stirred up in a bowl, two big empty baking sheets, and two little bowls of sprinkles, one on each sheet.

"Okay... Are we ready to do this?" she asked.

"Yes! We're ready!" the twins shrieked.

"Remember...I'll put frosting on them, and then you will take turns putting sprinkles. The baking sheets are your work area, just like at school."

They nodded, their little eyes shining with delight as Katie scooped up a dollop of icing with a small offset spatula and swirled it onto a cakelet, then set it on Beth's baking sheet, and quickly iced one for Evie.

"Not too many sprinkles," Katie said. "Just enough to be pretty. And when you've sprinkled enough, just push your cupcake to the side and you'll be ready for the next, okay?"

They nodded, totally intent on their tasks.

Katie pretended she didn't see the icing getting on little

fingers, or the sprinkles sticking, or the licking off of sprinkles as they stuck. Like the girls, she was in her element. So she dipped and swirled, and they sprinkled and licked. They were in the middle of the process when the doorbell rang.

Katie guessed it was Sam and ran to answer.

"We're a mess," she said. "Enter at your own risk." She ran back to the kitchen before disaster could strike.

Sam followed the sound of his babies' laughter and the delectable aroma of warm chocolate all the way to the kitchen and saw the girls with little chocolate smears on their chins, and multicolored sprinkles stuck to their fingers, and a stray one here and there stuck to their lips, and laughed.

"You have been having way more fun than I did," he said, and then gave Katie a quick kiss on the cheek. "That's from Miss Delilah and Rhett Butler. They send their love."

Katie was startled that he'd kissed her in front of the girls, but they thought it was hysterical and had their heads together, giggling.

Then Sam leaned down and kissed Beth on the cheek, and then Evie on the cheek, then licked his lips.

"Um, chocolate and sprinkle kisses. This is my lucky day."

"We know lucky!" Evie said.

Beth nodded. "When you get something good without asking for it."

Sam looked at Katie. "It was a lesson that came with a Daddy speech."

"Sounds like a good one," she said. "And we're almost finished. The girls have not eaten any cupcakes yet, but we did lick the batter bowl."

"It was so good, Daddy," Evie said.

"Good," Beth said. "But we didn't save you any."

"Oh, that's okay, baby. I'd rather have one of those," he said, pointing to the cupcakes.

"Oh…you have to save me from my sweet tooth. You two are getting more than one apiece," Katie said.

"Yay!" the girls said.

"Yay!" Sam echoed.

Katie laughed. "Youngbloods rule! Now let's get these last three iced and sprinkled and we'll be done!"

Sam watched it happening—the magic between his daughters and his girl. Still yearning for her, still wanting so much more.

And then they were finished. Katie eyed the messes on their hands and faces and pointed down the hall.

"Girls, why don't you go show Daddy where the bathroom is so he can wash all the sticky off of you while I box up some cupcakes for you to take home."

"We know, Daddy! Help us down, please!" Beth said.

As soon as their feet hit the floor, they were off.

"There are clean washcloths and hand towels in the cupboard below the sink," Katie said.

"Thanks," Sam said, and ran to catch up.

All the while Katie was packing up cupcakes, she could hear the laughter and the squeals, and the occasional complaint of "Daddy, you're wiping my face too hard," and always, the calm, steady tone in Sam's voice.

She shivered, longing to feel Sam's hands on her body, and knew it was just a matter of time.

A few minutes later, the trio came back.

"I have your cupcakes all ready for you to take home," Katie said.

Evie threw her arms around Katie's legs and hugged her.

"Thank you, Miss Katie. This has been the best day ever!" she said.

Beth stepped into the gap and hugged both Evie and Katie.

"Ever," she echoed. "And when we do it again, it will be the next best day!"

Katie knelt down to return the hugs. "Making cupcakes together was the most fun ever!"

The girls giggled, then danced their way to the door with Sam behind them, carrying the box of little cakes.

"Where's my hug?" he said.

"Waiting for the right time and place," Katie answered.

The girls were dancing around Sam's feet as she opened the door.

"Understood," he said. "Thank you again for the rescue...and for the cupcakes."

"Always," Katie said, and then they were gone.

━━━━━━━━━

Friday evening, Katie was out in the front yard with a garden hose, watering the flower beds, when a car pulled up in Sam's drive. An older man and woman emerged and went up the steps and rang the doorbell. The front door swung inward. She saw Sam smiling and hugging them both as they entered. Guessing they were family, she went back to watering.

But a few minutes later, the couple came out with the

twins at their side. Sam was right behind them carrying two little suitcases, and that's when she realized the girls were leaving with them.

She watched Sam buckling them in, then kissing them goodbye, and then he stood in the yard waving until the car disappeared.

Then he looked at her across the street and started walking.

Katie's heart was hammering as he stopped before her.

"Grandparents," he said.

Katie swallowed past the knot in her throat. "They'll have so much fun."

He pointed at the hose and the growing water puddle in which she was standing.

"Your shoes are getting wet."

Katie jumped, and then ran to the faucet and turned it off. Sam followed her.

"Katie, I want—"

"Yes," she said.

One corner of his mouth lifted just a little. "I haven't asked you anything yet."

She shook her head. "I don't care what it is. The answer is yes."

He took a step closer. "Even if it's making love to you?"

"Yes."

He reached for her hand "Even if it's staying with me all night?"

"Even if," Katie said.

"Your place or mine?" he asked.

Katie's eyes narrowed. "Yours. Just in case you get called out."

Sam sighed. "There you go again...being all perfect and stuff."

Katie brushed her hand across his arm and then pointed at her house.

"I'm...uh...gonna go shower and pack a toothbrush and stuff."

"Take your time," Sam said. "We've got all night."

Katie wanted this, and at the same time she was afraid to believe it was happening. She flashed back on the church, and being jilted at the altar, and told herself Sam wasn't that kind of man.

"I called the grandparents. I got tired of watching your lights go out every night without me," he said.

"Lord," Katie said. "If it wasn't for every person on the block watching us right now, I'd hug your neck."

"Don't let that stop you," he said.

"Go," Katie said. "Before you get us both in trouble. I won't be long."

"The door will be unlocked," Sam said. "Lock it behind you when you come in. You'll know where to find me." Then he jogged back to his house and went inside.

Katie rolled up the garden hose as if she had nothing better to do and then calmly walked back into her house. But the minute she shut the door, she was running, stripping off her clothes as she went. Her hands were trembling by the time she finally stepped beneath the spray. She was already doubting the wisdom of telling Sam she'd stay the night, for fear she'd wake up screaming, but if this was going to work, he either accepted her reality or he didn't. And that's what scared her most—that he would not.

She showered quickly, then dried and headed for her closet. She wanted the easiest thing to put on and take off and chose a loose, over-the-head minidress and sandals. She grabbed a new toothbrush and her hairbrush and dropped them into a little toiletry bag along with her house keys, then went through the house locking up and pulled the door shut behind her as she left.

Crossing the street was an out-of-body experience. She was aware of what was behind her, but ahead of her was the great unknown. Making this commitment was a risk, but she'd been taking them all her life. And Sam was a man worth the risk.

Then she was on his porch and walking into the house. The moment she locked the door behind her, her own free will had sealed her fate.

She stood for a few moments, listening. She thought she heard water running and started walking down the hall. Sam's bedroom door was open but the lights were out. She paused on the threshold.

"Sam?"

The bathroom door swung open, silhouetting Sam against the backlight, and then he came out with a towel around his waist, his hair still damp from a shower, leaving the rest of a very long, tall body beautifully bare.

The man was ripped, and there was no other way to say it. Hard-as-rock abs. Definition in muscles without an ounce of fat on him, and legs that went on forever.

Katie froze.

Lord have mercy. What a beautiful man.

Then he started toward her, and she didn't wait for him to

undress her. She pulled her dress over her head and dropped it, letting it pool at her feet, leaving her nude but for a black bra and panties accentuating soft curves and long legs.

Sam grunted like he'd been punched and then dropped the towel.

An instant rush of lust rolled through Katie that nearly sent her to her knees. She tried to unfasten her bra, but her hands were shaking.

Then Sam was in front of her. His arms encircled her as he unhooked the bra and let it fall. As he pulled her close, he suddenly realized he was feeling scars of the gunshot wounds—proof that the woman he loved had sacrificed her body, willing to give her life for children in her care.

It shattered him all over again.

He began kissing her as he backed her toward his bed, and when she felt the mattress at the back of her legs, she fell backward onto the bed.

Sam's gaze was still locked onto her face as he removed the wisp of black silk from around her hips.

Katie reached for him as he stretched out beside her, and with near clinical precision drove her out of her mind. Not once but twice in succession, and as she was still coming undone, he slid between her legs and started over.

It was the beginning of what would become the most memorable night of Katie's life, and the realization that what she'd known before hadn't been making love, but just sex.

All this—with Sam—was love at its finest, giving more than taking.

A choked scream from the shock of a mind-numbing climax.

Laughing as she realized it was happening yet again.

And crying from the joy of knowing what she had to give was exactly what Sam Youngblood needed to feel whole again.

They finally fell asleep in each other's arms, too satiated to dream of anything but each other.

———

Sam felt Katie in his arms as he was waking up and sighed. *Thank you, God, last night wasn't a dream.*

Her long, dark hair was lying across his pillow, her cheek resting against his shoulder, and then there was the softness of her breasts pressed close against his body.

Last night had been a revelation. This woman made love as fiercely as she fought to live. He was never going to be the same. He wanted her for all time. In his bed. In his life. In his children's lives. He wanted to fill her up with everything she'd missed, so that she would never doubt again that she wasn't enough.

He felt her stirring and waited for her eyes to open. He wanted to see her waking up in his arms.

———

Katie felt body heat and the weight of an arm around her shoulders and remembered.

Sam!

She opened her eyes and saw him looking at her, and mumbled, "I just spent the night with Superman."

Sam chuckled. "Superman?" He was already hard and

aching for her all over again. "Okay then…are you ready to take flight?"

"I was born ready for you," she whispered, and rolled over on her back as he slid between her legs.

"Then hang on, baby. I'm taking you up, up, and away." And he did.

———

They missed breakfast, but by the time they finally got out of bed and showered, they were starving.

Katie picked up the dress she'd left on the floor last night and frowned.

"I need to change clothes before I go out in public. This looks like I slept in it."

"I could assure them you slept in nothing," Sam said.

Katie laughed. "And that would make being the first-grade teacher all the more interesting. Give me ten minutes and pick me up in the driveway."

Sam swept her up in his arms and nuzzled the spot on her neck that made her moan.

"When you're ready, I'll give you the rest of my life."

"Don't say that until you've witnessed the PTSD. Don't chain yourself to a woman who sleeps with demons she still can't shake."

Sam just shook his head. "I've wrestled my own demons over the years. Been so mad at God I wouldn't talk to Him. And so sad I didn't think I would survive. And then I leveled out and didn't know what I was missing until you. Now go get dressed. I'm hungry."

She grabbed her keys and the little bag with her things and took off out the door.

Sam moved to the window, watching her running, her long hair flying out behind her and those gorgeous legs moving in perfect harmony with her body, and remembered her running on the sidewalks of Borden's Gap, never dreaming she would be running right into his heart.

Katie hurried, changing into jeans and a blouse, then added sandals. She was running when she came out her door and jumped into the car with Sam. He backed up and then drove out of their neighborhood toward Main, then up to Ronda's Café.

They walked into a crowded dining room, and became the center of the diners' attention. Most of the town knew the chief had sent the new teacher flowers. And now here they were together, and without the twins.

"Hey, Sam. Where are the bosses?" an old man asked, referring to the twins.

"With grandparents, and likely ruling the roost," Sam said.

Katie laughed along with everyone else as they were seated. A few minutes later, they had food ordered and were sipping cold sweet tea when Sam's phone signaled a text. He glanced down.

"It's from the girls. Their grandparents sent a video," he said, and then scooted closer to Katie so she could watch, too, and hit Play.

Almost immediately, two identical little faces were on the screen, talking at the same time.

"Look, Daddy. My tooth fell out," Evie said.

"My tooth fell out! We blooded all over," Beth said.

Then they both smiled, showing him the spaces where the teeth used to be.

"Gran saved our teeth. We have to put them under our pillow at home," Evie said.

"'Cause the tooth fairy doesn't know where Granny and Papa live," Beth added.

"See you tomorrow! We are having so much fun!"

Katie saw the look on Sam's face and then patted his arm.

"Are you sad you missed that?" she asked.

"God no! Most especially when they blooded," Sam muttered. "I know I'm supposed to be all tough and stuff, but raising girls is hard."

Katie laughed. "It doesn't matter what sex. Raising kids is hard. I don't have any, but every year I get about twenty or so new ones who belong to other people. So in the years that I've been teaching, that's about a hundred and sixty kids, give or take, and not a one of them was alike."

Their food arrived, and Sam pocketed his phone and picked up a fork.

"To us," he said.

"I'll eat to that, and yum…breakfast for lunch. Whose good idea was that?" Katie said as she took a bite of biscuits and sausage gravy.

"I believe that was yours," Sam said, and dug into his bacon, eggs, and pancakes.

They were getting up to leave when Katie's phone signaled a text. She glanced at it, noticed it was from Lila, and then let it go for later. Whatever it was, she didn't want to know. Today was too perfect to be reminded of anything from her past. As they made their way through the dining room, everyone watched them walking away, trying to guess by the fact that Sam's hand was at the middle of her back if that meant she was officially his girl.

"The food was delicious," Katie said as they got in the car.

"The rest of it was like walking a gauntlet, wasn't it?" Sam said, and then reached for her hand. "I don't want to do anything but spend the day with you, but I know you probably have things you need to do for school."

Katie nodded. "Yes, I have to do lesson plans for next week, but I'll make time."

He gave her hand a quick squeeze. "Good. There's something I want to show you. It's here in town."

"Okay," Katie said, and buckled up, ready for her next adventure with Sam.

They drove a ways down Main, then turned left, which was in the opposite direction from where they lived, and soon Sam was driving slowly through the streets, pointing out houses as they went.

"This is the oldest part of Borden's Gap. The original town site. Some of these houses have been here since before the Civil War. They aren't as grand as the old plantation houses on the rivers, but they're amazing."

Katie leaned forward in the seat. "They're kind of like Delilah Cash's house! Look at them! Two stories. Wraparound porches and porticos. Oh look! That one even has a little carriage house at the back of the grounds!"

Sam kept driving and pointing out facets of each property that caught her eye. But as he turned down Rawls Street, he suddenly pulled over at the curb and parked.

"See that one?" he said, pointing to a two-story house with a green roof and white columns spanning the width of a deep wraparound porch. The latticed walls of a portico were dripping in purple wisteria. The grass needed mowing. The windows were dark, and the house was obviously vacant.

"It's beautiful," Katie said. "Or at least it could be. It looks sad. How long has it been empty?"

Sam frowned, thinking. "This time? Almost five years. The owner is in a nursing home in Jackson. From the first time I saw it, I wanted to live in it. Weird, huh?"

"No. Not weird at all," she said. "I call that soul memory."

Sam blinked, shifting focus from the house to her.

"What?"

"Soul memory," she repeated. "When your soul remembers something from another life and gives you the longing without you knowing the reason why."

Sam's eyes widened. Suddenly his eyes were filled with tears.

"That's beautiful, Katie."

She leaned across the console and kissed him.

"So are you," she said softly. "And don't give up the dream. If it's meant to be, maybe one day you will."

"Would you live in it with me...if it was meant to be?" he asked.

"I would be honored…if it was meant to be."

Sam sighed. "I love you, Katie. So much."

When she started to respond, he put a finger across her lips.

"No. You don't have to say anything. I just want you to know and remember that, for the times when you feel overwhelmed, and when you decide trusting me not to hurt you is a possibility."

Then he put the car in gear and drove her home. When he pulled up in the drive, he leaned across the console and kissed her.

"If I leave you alone for the rest of the day so you can work, will you spend the night with me again?" he asked.

"I would love to," she said.

"Awesome. Come over when you're ready and I'll grill steaks."

"It's a date," Katie said, and then blew him a kiss. "Don't get out. I'll see myself to the door."

He waited until she was inside before he backed up into his own drive, then got out. His house was so quiet that at first he didn't know what to do, and then he remembered. Laundry. Grocery shopping. Uniforms to the cleaner. Bills to pay. He turned back into Sam the father and got busy again.

Katie was in the same frame of mind as she went into her office. She glanced at the awards hanging on the wall, ran her fingers over the name and Saguaro Elementary, and then sat down to read Lila's text.

Only it wasn't a text. It was a photo of Lila pointing to an engagement ring on her finger, and then a second photo of her and Jack together.

"Oh wow," Katie said, and then quickly replied.

> Congratulations! I am so happy for the both
> of you.

Lila sent back a meme of fireworks exploding, which made Katie smile.

After that, she started her laundry, then began changing sheets on her bed and making a grocery list before settling down to begin some lesson plans, getting ready to be Miss Katie again.

Chapter Twenty

KATIE CROSSED THE STREET TO SAM'S JUST BEFORE 6:00 p.m. and rang the doorbell, then heard him yell "It's open."

She walked in, locking it behind her, and followed the sound of music and the aroma of potatoes baking and something marinating.

Sam met her in the hall, wrapped her up in his arms, and swooped. Mouth to lips. Heart to heart. Holding her close. Then when a slow, sad song filled the room around them, Sam whispered in her ear.

"Beautiful lady, may I have this dance?"

"Yes, and please," Katie said, and leaned into his body as he waltzed her around the table and then around the room and out into the hall—laughing when he dipped her so low she felt her hair brush the floor, then spinning her around and around beneath the light fixture until Katie was seeing stars.

The song was over, but Sam was just getting started.

"Witch," he whispered as he brushed his mouth across her lips. "My woman…my lover…my heart. Tell me how you like your steak."

Katie threw her arms around his neck. "Medium well, please and thank you."

"And how do you like your loving?" he asked.

"As long as it's with you, I'll take it any way I can get it."

Sam grinned. "I'm all yours, please and thank you."

———

The steaks got cooked. They ate as if they were starving, and they were—but not for food. They were starved for companionship. For the intimacy that comes from having a partner. For the joy of belonging, and knowing they were loved.

Long after the dishes were done and the kitchen abandoned for the bedroom, the quiet joy of being together was still celebrated. They fell asleep before they meant to, safe in the comfort of each other's arms.

And then Sam's phone rang. He reached for it even before his eyes were open, his voice husky from sleep.

"This is Sam."

"Chief, this is Riley."

Sam straight up in bed. When the night dispatcher called, it was always an emergency.

He was already turning on a lamp and reaching for his clothes when Katie woke and realized what was going on.

Sam put the call on speaker.

"What's up?" he asked, and began putting on his pants.

"Break-in in progress. Mother and two kids locked themselves in a bathroom and called 911."

Sam was dressed now, all but his boots, and had retrieved his weapon.

"Who's there?" he asked.

"Delroy and Mike."

"Send me the address. I'm leaving now," Sam said as he stomped on his boots.

"Yes, sir," Riley said, and disconnected.

Sam turned. Katie was rattled and he knew it.

"This is cop life, darlin'. I love you. Stay in bed. I'll be back before you know it."

And then he was gone.

Katie got up and ran fast enough to see his taillights disappearing down the street, then didn't know what to do. She turned on the porch light for him, then was too worried to sleep, so she grabbed her phone, wrapped herself up in a sheet, and went out on his back porch to listen, knowing if there was gunfire or ambulance sirens she would hear them.

But the longer she sat, the sleepier she became. All was quiet, and she finally convinced herself that whatever had happened had been dealt with, without gunfire, and went back to bed.

She lay there in the dark, listening for the sound of his car in the drive or his key in the lock. Listening for the sound of his footsteps coming up the hall. She closed her eyes. Just to rest them. And fell back into the nightmare that haunted her life.

Running.

Children screaming.

Gunshots.

Losing Alejandro and Kieran.

Alejandro covered in blood.

Running again. Shots closer.

Staggering from the first gunshot.

Pushing the boys down beneath her.
Don't talk. Don't move. I love you.

———————

Sam arrived on scene wearing a bulletproof vest. He turned out his lights on the last half of the block and immediately radioed the station.

"This is Sam. I'm on scene. Officers nowhere in sight," he said.

"They just went inside," Riley said.

"No visible lights," Sam replied.

"They know you're coming, Chief. They'll be watching for you."

"Going in," Sam said.

He quietly approached the house with his weapon drawn, then slipped inside. Night-lights all along the hallway furnished enough luminosity for him to see. Within seconds, one of his men stepped out of the shadows and signaled to him that there was only one perp. Sam could hear him moving around in the back of the house and nodded.

All of a sudden, they heard what sounded like someone kicking on a door, and a woman screaming and children crying, and realized the perp had discovered the residents' hiding place.

Sam gave his officers the signal. Their movement muffled by the ongoing chaos in the back bedroom, they came out of the shadows and stormed down the hall and into the bedroom, flooding the room with lights.

Startled, the armed perp spun, saw three cops with their guns pointed at him, and froze.

"Drop your weapon! Drop your weapon!" Sam shouted, and when the perp glanced toward the windows, Mike shifted his position, blocking that exit.

The man cursed and dropped the gun.

Delroy kicked it out of the way and took a step closer, backing into Sam who was moving forward now, continuing to shout at the perp to get down on the floor. When the man was too slow in obeying, they took him down and cuffed him.

Sam retrieved the weapon as Mike and Delroy walked him out to a patrol car, then Mike took him to jail, leaving Delroy and Sam on the scene.

As soon as the house was clear, Sam knocked on the bathroom door.

"This is Chief Youngblood. You can come out now. The intruder is in custody."

The door opened slowly, and a young woman emerged, carrying a toddler on her hip and with a boy of about eight holding her hand. Sam knew her from her job as a teller at the bank.

"You're Alicia, right?" Sam said.

She nodded. "I thought he was going to kill us," she said, still shaking and crying.

"Is there someone you want to call?" Sam asked.

"My husband, Charlie. He went night fishing with his dad and brother."

Sam took the toddler out of her arms.

"Call Charlie, and then let's go to the living room where you and the kids can sit. We can take your statement there."

So while Alicia's story unfolded, her husband, Charlie, was in an all-out panic, climbing out of a boat and jumping in his truck, leaving his dad and brother behind, while a drifter named Truman was getting booked into jail.

It was a good three hours before Sam finished up his report at the station and headed home. He was tired and worried about what Katie would think of all this, but then he turned the corner at his street and saw the porch light.

Suddenly, there was a lump in his throat.

Shelly used to leave the light on for him at night, and no one had ever done it since. He'd never thought of it. It was just call Roxie and run.

He pulled up into the drive, his feet dragging as he went up the steps and unlocked the door. The house was quiet. He didn't want to wake Katie, so he took off his boots at the door and washed up in the kitchen before returning to his bedroom, expecting to see her peacefully asleep.

Instead, he walked in to find her moaning in her sleep, her hands clenching and unclenching as her feet moved beneath the covers. And then it hit him. She was dreaming about the attack!

He put his weapon in the lockbox, eased down on the side of the bed and stretched out beside her, then started talking in a calm and steady voice.

"Katie, honey…wake up. You're not in school. All of your children are safe. There is no shooter. Wake up, darlin'. It's me, Sam. I'm here, and I love you."

Katie moaned, then sighed as she turned toward the sound of his voice.

He slid his arm beneath her shoulders and pulled her

to him. The thrashing subsided, the moaning stopped, and she was no longer crying.

"That's my girl," he said softly, then wrapped his arms around her and closed his eyes.

———————

Katie woke in Sam's arms. He was still asleep, still in the clothes he'd left the house wearing, and still in one piece. She'd been baptized in the fire of cop life, and all she could think was she was in love with a man who risked his life every day for others, just like the police who took down the shooter in Saguaro Elementary.

Sam stirred, opened his eyes, and saw Katie looking at him.

"Hey...how's my baby this morning?" he asked.

The softness in his voice was Katie's undoing.

"So in love with you," she said.

Sam stilled, and then a slow smile spread across his face.

"Does that mean I have passed the Katie test?"

"It means you have broken down my last wall. I give up. I give it all to you. It will be up to you if you can deal with my ghosts."

"I dealt with them just fine last night, and I'll deal again and again until they're gone."

Katie blinked. "Last night? What do you mean? What did I do?"

"Nothing worse than having a bad dream. We snuggled. It went away."

"Oh my God," Katie said, and started crying.

"Hey, hey, hey…nothing to cry about," Sam said. "I've been chasing away the boogeyman for years. I got your back, Katie girl."

She rolled over on top of him and buried her face against his neck. Crying for the broken child she'd been. For the wounded soul she was. Betting her life that this was the man who would never let her down.

Conviction washed through Sam in waves. The certainty that she would stay the course was now embedded in his heart. He had nothing more to prove. She'd given him everything when she'd given him her trust.

―――――

The girls came home by midafternoon, sporting gaps in their big grins. Their grandparents handed over the prize teeth and offered many thanks for letting them have the kids for the weekend, said their goodbyes, and drove away.

The girls ran straight to their room, just like they always did when they'd been gone. Like they needed to reestablish their ownership in the place, while Sam took their bags to the laundry and dumped their clothes in the washer.

He already missed Katie in his space, but making it permanent was only a matter of time.

The girls came bouncing back through the house, still trying to settle, and looking to see if there was anything new in the way of snacks that had been added to the pantry.

"Daddy! We want to show Miss Katie our teeth!" Evie said.

Sam chuckled. "You mean you want her to see you lost one?"

"No! We want to show her our teeth. Can we? Please?" Beth said.

Sam wasn't sure about carrying two tiny teeth across the street to show off and started trying to dissuade them.

"I don't know. What if she's busy?" Sam asked.

Evie shrugged. "You could call and ask."

"You could," Beth added.

Sam knew when he was beaten, so he took out his phone and made the call.

———

Katie was in her office working on lesson plans when her phone rang. When she saw the caller ID, she smiled and answered.

"Hello."

"Hi, Katie. It's me, Sam. The girls are home, and they want to know if we can come over long enough for them to show you their teeth. Literally…show you the teeth that fell out."

Katie burst out laughing.

"Of course! I can't wait!" she said.

"You rock," Sam said. "We'll be over in a few."

As soon as he hung up, Katie jumped up from the desk, ran to the closet where she kept school supplies, and began rummaging through a box beneath one of the shelves.

"I know I have some," she kept muttering, and then she saw the plastic bag she'd been looking for, removed two items from it, and put them in her pocket just as her doorbell rang and she ran to answer. The moment she opened the door, the girls shouted out in unison.

"We're baaack!"

Sam grinned. "Kinda reminds you of Jack Nicholson, doesn't it?"

Katie laughed. "Come in. Come in. I can't wait to see!" she said, and led them to the living room sofa.

Sam sat down in a chair, handed each little girl their tooth that their grandmother had wrapped in aluminum foil, and then sat back to watch the unveiling.

"Me first!" Evie cried, and pulled back the foil one fold at a time, like she was in surgery about to remove a kidney. She revealed her tooth, then opened her mouth and pointed to the gap. "It used to be right there before it fell out!"

"Amazing!" Katie said.

"Now me," Beth said, and unwrapped her tooth in the same methodical way, revealing an identical tooth, then opened her mouth. "My tooth was here. It fell out in my mouth and I spit it out."

Katie was trying not to laugh. "Good thing you didn't swallow it," she said.

Beth nodded. "No tooth fairy for me."

Sam chuckled. He could just hear her grandpa's voice, telling her that very same thing.

"Well, I have something for you," Katie said. "I always have these in my class for the times when one of my students loses a tooth at school." She pulled out two pink fairy tooth keepers that were attached to long plastic cording. She opened the drawer on her coffee table, grabbed a black marker, and put a B on one tooth keeper and an E on the other one. "Now, who's name starts with B?" she asked.

"Mine, mine!" Beth said.

"Then Miss Beth's tooth goes in this one," she said. She dropped the tooth in and closed the top, and put the keeper around Beth's neck.

"My name starts with E," Evie said.

"Exactly! So we need to put Miss Evie's tooth in this one," Katie said. She dropped in the tooth, closed the top, and put the keeper around Evie's neck, then put her arms around both of them. "Okay...here's the deal. These aren't necklaces to wear. These are for the tooth fairy, so when you get home, take them off and give them to Daddy, and he'll help you put them under your pillow tonight. Okay?"

"Yes, Miss Katie! Thank you!" they cried, and crawled into her lap and put their arms around her neck and hugged her.

Katie kissed each little cheek before she let them go, and caught Sam watching her.

Love you, he mouthed.

"Ditto," she said, and then Sam stood.

"Okay, you two, time to go. Miss Katie has work to do, and so do we."

They slid out of Katie's lap and raced toward the door, but Sam walked to her instead and hugged her.

"I didn't want to be left out," he said, and kissed her on the cheek, then hurried to catch up.

Katie watched them until Sam herded the girls inside and closed the door. Then she went back to work in a house that was suddenly too quiet.

As soon as Sam got the girls inside, they removed their necklaces and handed them to him.

"For the tooth fairy," they said.

"I won't forget," Sam said. After they ran off to play, he took the keepers to his dresser, then finished emptying the girls' little suitcases. Back to business as usual.

And that night when they went to bed, they put the little pink necklaces beneath their pillows. Sam waited until they fell asleep, then took the necklaces and left a dollar bill apiece beneath the pillows. Now all he had to do was hide the tooth keepers for the next ten years to make sure the tooth fairy's cover wasn't blown.

Sam went to bed, marking off yet another milestone in their lives, and was awakened the next morning by their screams. He'd forgotten about the tooth fairy and flew out of bed, but then he saw them dancing around the room waving their money like pom-poms and shoved his hands through his hair in relief.

"Look, Daddy, look! The tooth fairy came!" Evie said.

"And we didn't even know it!" Beth added.

"Wow!" Sam said. "I wonder if she left money for me?"

They giggled. "No, Daddy. You have to give her a tooth to get money."

"No way! I'm not giving up my teeth!" Sam said, and put a hand over his mouth. "Now, put your dollars in your dresser drawer, get dressed, and I'll go make breakfast."

"Don't make it hard to chew," Evie said. "I'm missing a tooth now."

"Missing a tooth," Beth said.

Sam left the room laughing.

———

Mark took his parents to church in Caldwell, their home-town, and then treated them to dinner at the Red Barn after-ward. His mother, Laura, was excited not to have to cook and clean up, and his dad, Joe, was proud to have his son back on the farm, and showing him off to all their friends.

It was a good day.

They didn't know that Mark's purpose was twofold. It was the first time he'd set foot in a church since he'd left the farm, and he'd just finished the legal disbursements of all the property he'd inherited. The last tie to his past had been cut, and that felt like a rebirth. What better way to be reborn than in the church where he'd grown up, and with the people who loved him most.

And he had made a silent vow during the sermon that from this day forward, he would never look back again.

The next few weeks in Borden's Gap passed without inci-dent. Katie heard through the school grapevine that when Cheryl Phillips got out of the hospital, she went straight to her mother's house to stay. They also heard that Ree was going to counseling one day a week in Jackson, and Cheryl was just waiting for their house to sell so they could move.

Then Sam came home from work one day with fire in his eyes.

"Raymond Phillips pled guilty and accepted sentencing from a judge. He's finishing recovery in a prison hospital. He's gonna die in there."

"Then he's where he belongs," Katie said.

"No. He belongs six feet under, but that's going to take some time," Sam said.

In some people's minds, justice had been served and everything would work itself out. Others attributed Ree's rescue to fate, or to God's intervention, but Katie kept thinking about Cheryl Phillips trying to demolish the man who'd molested her baby. Cheryl had wanted him gone from the face of the earth. She was the one who ended her husband's reign of terror.

Cheryl was the kind of mother Katie had needed as a child—the kind she had longed for. Katie had never wanted to be a princess. Or dreamed pretty dreams. All she'd wanted was to be rescued, like Cheryl rescued Ree, and she quietly celebrated that woman's existence.

As time passed, Katie's days were spent with children, and her evenings with Sam and the girls. Sometimes at his house. Sometimes at hers. For the first time in her life, she felt completely fulfilled.

———————

Then Justin Tiller was released from jail and brought a sense of anxiety back into his family. Frieda had gotten a protective order against him, but she didn't have enough money to file for divorce. So on the day Justin was released from jail, the process server was waiting for him.

Justin was descending the steps of the county jail when he saw a man standing on the street nearby. He thought nothing of it until the man approached him with a smile.

"Are you Justin Tiller?" he asked.

Justin nodded.

"Mr. Tiller, I'm Stanley Warner," he said, and extended his hand as if they were going to shake hands.

Without thinking, Justin reached out, and when he did, the man slapped a writ in Justin's hand.

"Mr. Tiller, you have just been served," he said, and turned around and hurried off, leaving Justin in shock.

He unfolded the writ, his face turning red with rage as he read.

"A protective order? Frieda got a protective order against me? The bitch, the bitch!"

And then it hit him. He had nowhere to go. He couldn't go home because he wasn't allowed to be around them. And if he did, he'd wind up right back in jail. Jackson was a long way from Borden's Gap. Walking would take hours. But even if he chose to go back, where would he stay when he got there?

He needed a job. His reputation in Borden's Gap had not preceded him here. Maybe he could find something, so he started walking, thinking—it would have to be something in construction. He was a pretty good brick mason, and he could lay tile and roof houses. He'd get a job, make good money, and get his family back. He wanted to be pissed at Frieda, but in his gut, he knew he'd brought this on himself for slapping her around when he was drunk.

He had his phone but no charger, but he knew people could recharge technology at public libraries, so he asked around until he got directions and started walking.

Frieda was anxious. She'd just gotten a text notifying her that Justin had been served with the protective order as he was coming out of jail. So, he was out and likely furious. She notified the school about the protective order, then sent Connor a text. She couldn't get off work every time her life fell apart, but she needed the boys to know their father was out of jail, that he was not allowed to be with them, and that they were not to get into a car with him. It was nerve-racking, but she had no other choice.

Katie received the info, as did the other teachers who had the Tiller boys in classes, and her heart sank. Once his father was out of the house, Donny had turned into a whole new kid in her class. Happy, outgoing, and soaking up everything she taught. She hoped Justin Tiller had the grace to abide by the court order, but he didn't strike her as amenable to rules. Now she was doubly conscious of yet another child in her care whose family issues would make him vulnerable to stress and physical abuse.

When school was out, Katie had Donny under her eye as he moved to the group who would be walking home. She kept watching for Lee and Connor, and when they finally came out and she saw the serious conversation Connor was having with the others, she guessed Frieda had warned him.

Her heart sank as she watched Donny's shoulders slump, and then the way his brothers gathered around him, patting him on the back. They walked away from school, so close against each other they appeared to be attached.

THE NEXT BEST DAY   399

At that point, the principal walked up behind her.

"Some kids have a really tough life," Susan said.

Thor Dooley went running past them, hell-bent for leather toward his daddy, who caught him in open arms.

Evie and Beth were holding hands and skipping as they went to meet Roxie at the curb.

"And some kids don't," Katie said.

"Are you still seeing Sam?" Susan asked.

Katie nodded.

"How do you manage your relationship with the twins...being Daddy's girlfriend on one hand and their teacher on the other?"

Katie shrugged. "The girls manage it for me. At home, they crawl all over me. At school, I am 'Teacher,' and they don't question the authority of the position. They've been that way from the start, and I credit Sam for instilling that respect in them."

Susan nodded. "This job would be a lot easier if parents advocated that from the start, instead of letting their children rule the house."

"Yes, ma'am," Katie said.

Susan wandered off, leaving Katie to finish bus duty.

That night while they were at Katie's making dinner, Sam noticed Katie's preoccupation.

"Hey, honey...is something wrong?" he asked.

"Oh. No. Just a notice we received at school today. Justin Tiller was released from jail, and Frieda has filed a protective order against him. Once he was served, they had to notify the school. He's not allowed to be around the boys. Donny has been a different child since his dad has been out of the home. Then today, I saw the oldest brother, Connor, gathering them up to walk home, and when he stopped and started talking to Lee and Donny, I saw Donny's little head drop. He looked like he was carrying the weight of the world. Kids who come from chaos have such a hard time."

Sam slid his arm across her shoulders.

"I love your tender heart," he said softly. "And I'm glad you told me Justin was released and about the protective order. That paperwork hasn't come across my desk yet."

Katie leaned into his hug, and as she did, the girls came bouncing into the kitchen.

"We want a hug, too, Daddy!" Evie said.

"Yes, a hug!" Beth said.

Sam winked at Katie, then grabbed Evie and held her sideways on his hip.

"A hug like this?" he asked, and gave her a squeeze.

She dissolved into giggles.

"No, Daddy. Not like that," she shrieked.

He put her down and grabbed Beth and threw her over his shoulder and started hugging her little legs hanging down across his chest.

"Then a hug like this, right?"

Beth was giggling.

"No, Daddy! I'm upside down," she said.

He put her down, then stood with his hands on his hips, shaking his head.

"I'm all confused," Sam said.

And then Katie joined in. "Like this!" she said, and picked up both little girls and started hugging them tight.

"Oh! I can do that," Sam said, and wrapped his arms around all of them, and while the girls were poking at each other and laughing hysterically, he stole a kiss from Katie. "Maybe there are other things Miss Katie can teach me," he said.

Katie blushed. "Here, take these little wiggle worms before I drop them. I have to finish peeling potatoes."

"We're wiggle worms!" Beth cried, as Sam took them out of Katie's arms.

"Yes, and you're both going to wiggle on outside and play so we can finish making dinner."

"Can we wiggle in here with you if we wiggle quiet?" Evie asked.

Katie didn't hesitate. "Of course. Go get your coloring books and crayons. You know where they are. And you can color here at the kitchen table until we're ready to eat."

"Yay!" they said, and ran.

Katie glanced at Sam. "They're beginning to sense the connection between us, and it probably makes them a little insecure. I don't ever want to be the cause of that happening. The more they are included, the less threat they will perceive."

Sam sighed. "You are so damn smart about little kids. Every parent should have an early childhood education before they're allowed to have babies. It would save some children from a world of hurt."

Katie shrugged. "Or at the least learn how to function on common sense. And...here they come."

The girls marched into the kitchen, each clutching a box of crayons and a coloring book. And so the evening continued.

But long after the day was over and Katie was lying in bed, trying to unwind enough to sleep, she couldn't get Justin Tiller out of her head.

Chapter Twenty-One

JUSTIN TILLER'S GRAND IDEAS WERE NOT PANNING OUT. He still didn't have a job, but after wandering into a bar and running into Mitch Lewis, an old friend from Borden's Gap, he now had a place to stay. Granted it was on Mitch's couch, but it was out of the weather, and Mitch knew enough people needing day workers for Justin to pick up some work.

But the longer he stayed in Jackson, the more he missed his old way of life. Frieda working. Him staying home with the kids. He was saving up money to get a car. Even if it was a junker, he was sick of being afoot.

———

The days were getting shorter and the weather cooler. There were no more yards being mowed, and Katie often had her gas fireplace going at night.

It was coming up on Halloween, and costumes for sale hung from almost every window in town. The UPS truck was all over town making deliveries, as was the Amazon Prime van.

The girls wanted to be fairies with wings, and have flowers in their hair, and magic wands that could change flowers into pink frogs with googly eyes.

Sam was at a loss, so while the girls were playing in their room, he called Katie. The moment she said hello, he unloaded.

"Katie…honey…where the hell do I find fairy dresses and wings?"

Katie laughed.

"So is that the final choice?"

"Oh yes…fairies with wings and magic wands that can turn flowers into pink frogs with googly eyes."

Katie empathized with the panic in his voice. "Don't worry, love. I got your back on this. I'm a boss at online ordering."

"Oh my God, I owe you big time. I'll bring a credit card right over."

"No…I'll walk over to get it. Just hand it to me at the door, and the girls will never know I've been there. I'll find the stuff and order it tonight," Katie promised.

"Deal," Sam said, and so she did.

He met her at the door with the card and a kiss.

"Just so you know, you continue to become irreplaceable in our lives."

"My dream job," she said, then shivered when a chill wind blew up the back of her shirt, and hurried back across the street.

Looking for fairy costumes became her entertainment for the night as she snuggled close to the fire. Finally, she placed the orders, then got up and dug through her closet for a heavier jacket to wear to school tomorrow. She had playground duty and didn't want to stand in the wind and be sorry she hadn't dressed more warmly.

After packing up her school cart, she began turning out

lights and locking up. She paused in the living room and looked out at the house across the street, knowing one day they'd be doing all this together, then turned around and went to her bedroom.

This life, this house, this job. It was all so familiar now. A far cry from a few months ago when she'd spent her first night here in a sleeping bag, racked with nightmares and afraid of her own shadow.

Sam had been her first visitor, even then offering his help.

She crawled into bed, set the alarm, and then rolled over on her side and fell asleep. Her dreams were troubled, and she tossed and turned without anyone beside her to turn off the panic, then woke up to a whole new day and called it good.

━━━━━━━

Justin Tiller had been in Borden's Gap all day, driving his car around, waiting for Frieda to get off work. He'd parked in the back of the parking lot at Hillbilly Pizza, knowing she'd never spot him in the old Ford Focus he'd just bought or see him through the tinted windows. He wanted to talk to her again, but he couldn't, so he opted to stalk her instead. He wanted to see his sons. He wanted them to see him sober and with money in his pocket. Unfortunately, all of Justin's wants and desires hinged on pride and not love.

Then he saw her car coming out of the employee parking behind the building and saw Frieda at the wheel, and tensed. She looked pretty. And he was horny. They were still married. This should be so easy, just to walk up to her and have a conversation. But hell no. She'd involved the law. He watched her leaving the parking lot, then pulled out a distance behind.

———————

Frieda was tired. So tired. It had been a busy day at work, and she still had to make dinner and wash and dry a load of laundry so she would have clean work clothes for tomorrow. And invariably, the older boys would have homework, too.

"God give me strength," she sighed, anxious to get home.

She was just passing Welby's Grocery and debating whether to stop and get food from the deli, when her phone rang. When she noticed it was her boss, she frowned and answered.

"Hello?"

"Frieda, this is Elton. You left your paycheck behind."

"Oh crap," Frieda said. "I'll be right there."

"No, no… I'm leaving to make a deposit at the bank right now. I'll just swing by your house and bring it to you."

"That would be awesome," Frieda said. "Thank you so much."

"No problem. I'll be there in less than five."

Frieda hung up. "Good man," she said, and gave up the deli idea and kept driving. A couple of minutes later, she pulled up into the drive and parked beneath the carport. When she got out, she looked up the street for her boss's car and paid no attention to the old Ford as it passed.

When she saw Elton's car, she went to the end of the drive to meet him. He pulled up in it and rolled down his window.

"Here you go, girl. You look beat. Get some rest."

She reached in the open window, took the check, and then stepped back and waved.

"I wish, and thanks again!" she called out as Elton waved and drove away.

Then Donny came running out, wrapped his arms around her, and gave her a big hug.

"Hi, Mama. I'm glad you're home!" he said.

Frieda hugged her baby. "Me too, sugar."

They walked into the house together, unaware that Justin had seen everything and put his own interpretation on the innocence of it all.

———————

"Took my boys away from me, and she's already fuckin' around," Justin growled, then gunned the engine and peeled out as he turned the next corner and headed for the bar at the edge of town.

He walked in with his chin up, eyes flashing, ready to get drunk or fight, whichever came first. And as luck would have it, one of his old drinking buddies saw him and waved him over.

Hours later, they dragged him to his car at closing time and put him in the back seat, where he promptly passed out. Then they locked the car doors to keep him safe and tossed his car keys in the floorboard beside him so he'd see them when he woke up.

The imminent approach of a favorite holiday had shattered the focus of Katie's students. Halloween was all about what kind of costumes to wear, and parties, and trick-or-treat time, and all of it had spilled over into everything at school from art classes to what was being served in the lunchroom.

Miss Katie's bulletin board garden had pumpkins in the patch now, and a pumpkin-head scarecrow to keep away the birds. Every day this week, at least one of her students would bring her a Halloween treat. Sometimes a little piece of candy, sometimes a cupcake with orange frosting. And Evie and Beth had brought her jack-o'-lantern earrings from Arnold's Antiques and Gifts. She knew because she'd seen them in there when she was buying Halloween treats for her class.

When the earrings arrived, Katie immediately switched out the earrings she was wearing for the jack-o'-lanterns, and everyone in the class had to look and touch because that's how first graders rolled.

On this morning, Katie was dressed for playground duty, and as soon as the children were finished with their lunches, both of the first- and second-grade classes went out to play.

Katie was glad she'd had the foresight to bring her warmer jacket. Even though the sun was shining, the air was sharp and the wind was brisk.

She and Marcy were talking, but always keeping an eye out for trouble. Kids fussed. Kids fell. Kids came running to tattle on someone. It was just a normal day.

Katie was watching Freddie about to come down the slide, and when she realized he intended to do it on his belly, headfirst, she blew her whistle and pointed at him.

He heard it. Saw Miss Katie shaking her head and pointing, and knew exactly what it meant. He sighed, then came down the slide sitting down.

"Lord. That would have been a headbutt to end all headbutts," Marcy said.

Katie nodded. "If it hadn't broken his neck first."

They looked at each other and grimaced.

And then Katie caught movement from the corner of her eye and saw Justin Tiller sprinting across the play-ground straight toward Donny. Before she could react, Justin grabbed him by the arm and began dragging him away, with Donny crying and protesting as they went.

Katie grabbed Marcy's arm.

"Call Susan. Tell her to ring the bell and get the kids inside, then call the police. Justin Tiller is trying to kidnap his son."

Marcy gasped, then got on their two-way to tell Susan what was happening. Even as the bell was ringing to go inside, Katie was racing across the school grounds.

―――――――――

Donny was scared. His daddy was drunk and shouting bad things about his mama, and telling him that he was going to have to live with him instead. Donny kept drag-ging his feet and pulling hard, trying to get away, but his daddy was holding on too tight.

"Stop, Daddy, stop!" Donny cried. "You're hurting me! You're hurting my arm!"

Donny's cries only angered Justin more, and when his son dug in his heels and leaned backward, Justin yanked him so hard, it lifted him completely off his feet.

The shriek that ensued was heart-stopping. Justin had just broken his little boy's arm. Bone had torn through the flesh, and blood was everywhere. Just as he was about to pick Donny up and run, Justin heard the sound of footsteps behind him and turned, but it was too late to stop Katie's attack.

She launched herself at him like a ninja, chopping at his neck, kicking him in the groin, busting his nose with the palm of her hand, and then she did a complete three-sixty on one foot and took him out with a kick to the chin with the other.

He dropped like a poleaxed steer and didn't move.

Katie ran back to Donny.

He was sobbing and writhing, with his little arm clutched against his chest as she knelt down beside him. The sight of his arm made her sick. Bone was protruding through the skin, and blood was pouring. The injury was so bad that she was afraid to move him. But blood loss from a child this small was dangerous.

She sat down behind him, using her body for a brace, then pulled a bandanna from the pocket of her jacket and held it against the wound, trying to stop the flow of blood.

Even though the pressure was far less than it needed to be, he screamed.

Katie winced, sick that she was hurting him all over again.

"I know, baby, I'm so sorry. Lean on me. Help is almost here."

Donny leaned into the security of her arms and body and came undone in her arms, shaking uncontrollably and sobbing so hard it was difficult to understand what he was saying.

"Daddy…Daddy hurt me, Miss Katie…said bad things…mean things…and he hurt me."

Katie wanted to cry, but one of them in hysterics was enough.

"I know, honey, and I'm so sorry he did that."

"Doesn't love me," Donny sobbed.

"That doesn't matter. Your daddy doesn't even love himself. Your mama loves you. Your big brothers love you. We all love you, Donny. You are such a special little boy."

She saw Susan Wayne coming across the playground as fast as she could, and the look on her face was one of horror.

"Oh my God, Katie! What happened?"

"Justin tried to take Donny. He broke his arm before I could catch up."

"Well, from the looks of Mr. Tiller, you did catch up," Susan said. But when she knelt down beside them to look at Donny's arm, she paled, then touched Donny's cheek.

"I want Mama," he said, hiccupping through tears.

"I already called her," Susan said. She pulled a handful of tissues from her pocket and gently began to wipe away snot and tears.

"Did you call an ambulance?" Katie asked.

"They always dispatch one with a call from the school," Susan said.

And then Katie looked up and saw Sam running toward them with all the help they needed right behind him.

"Thank God," she said. "Sam's here, and so are the EMTs."

Sam had just handed his dispatcher some papers when a 911 call came in. He stayed to listen, and then his heart nearly stopped.

"911. What is your emergency?" Lucas said.

"This is Susan Wayne at the elementary school. We have a parental kidnapping in progress. Justin Tiller just grabbed his son when the children were on the playground and is trying to get away with him. It's a violation of a protective order."

"Yes, ma'am. On the way," Lucas said, and began dispatching the call as Sam took off out the back door.

He jumped in the patrol car, running lights and siren all the way to the school, trying not to panic. He pulled up at the same time the officers arrived, and seconds later, an ambulance arrived behind them.

Sam got out running, heading for the access gate the janitor was unlocking, with officers and medical personnel following.

When he saw Katie sitting on the ground and the principal kneeling beside her, his gut knotted. *Please God, don't let her be hurt...not again.*

And then he saw her look up, and the relief on her face when she saw him made him run even faster. But the closer he got, the more of the scene was revealed.

Justin Tiller was out cold on the ground, and Katie had a little boy cradled against her. Blood was all over both of them.

"Are you okay?" he asked.

"I'm fine. Justin broke Donny's arm. Compound fracture."

"Jesus," Sam said, and then pointed at the man on the ground. "What happened to him?"

Before Katie could answer, Donny did it for her. "Miss Katie drop-kicked my daddy like a ninja. She saved me."

Sam blinked. "Drop-kicked?"

"Black belt. Karate," Katie said.

The other officers were now on the scene, as were the EMTs.

One was checking Justin's vital signs, while the other two EMTs began stabilizing Donny to move.

And then Frieda Tiller arrived, out of breath and pushing through the crowd. Donny saw his mama and started crying again.

"Daddy hurt me!" he wailed. "He wouldn't let go and broke my arm."

Frieda stifled the horror she was feeling and knelt nearby, watching the EMTs frantically working to get him ready for surgery.

"I'm sorry, baby. Mama is so sorry, but it's going to be okay. The doctors will fix your arm, and your daddy is never going to bother you again. I promise. Okay?"

"Okay," he said, and moments later, they carried him out of the playground on a stretcher, with Frieda running beside it.

Unaware of what had been happening, Justin was beginning to come around. He moaned, then rolled over and puked.

"I need a drink," he mumbled.

"Hangovers are a bitch," Ben said as he and Carl dragged him to his feet and cuffed him.

Justin blinked, looking around at the playground, and remembered.

"Dammit all to hell! Where's my son? My wife is an unfit mother. He's coming to live with me." And then he saw Katie and added her to his complaints. "That woman kicked me in the jaw. It hurts like hell. It might be broken." He kept glaring at Katie. "I'll make you sorry for what you did. You don't have the right to keep my boy from me."

Sam grabbed Justin by the cuffs, yanking him so close he could see the pores in Tiller's skin.

"You just threatened a woman in my presence. If anything ever happens to her...for the rest of her life...I'll come looking for you first. So you better pray her life is nothing but blessed, or I will make you sorry in ways you cannot imagine."

Justin gasped. "He just threatened me. You all heard it."

Katie couldn't quit staring at Sam. He'd just become her knight in shining armor.

"We didn't hear anything," Ben said.

"Get him out of my sight. Lock him up," Sam said.

Ben grabbed Tiller by one arm, and Carl grabbed the other. Together, they walked Justin Tiller off the playground. What he'd done today was a guarantee he would not be working this mess out in jail. With his arrest record and the seriousness of what he'd done, this would put him in prison.

Susan eyed Katie's appearance. "I'll get someone to watch your class so you can go home and change. I think your students would freak if you walked in the room looking like that."

"I'll need my keys. They're in my purse, and it's in my room," Katie said.

"Just go out to your vehicle. Tell me where you keep your purse, and I'll bring it to you myself."

"Yes, ma'am," Katie said, then told her where to find it.

Susan started walking toward the building, leaving Sam alone with Katie.

"I'm escorting you to your car because I need to hold you and can't."

"I'm too bloody to hug," she said, as they started toward the outer gate.

"This scared the hell out of me," Sam said. "When I saw you, I thought you'd been hurt. Then I find out you took down the bad guy. Karate? Black belt?"

Katie shrugged. "I got mugged once in college. I didn't like how it felt, being helpless at the barrel of a gun. So I did something about it."

Sam sighed. "You are going to be a kick-ass cop's wife."

She glanced at him then—at his profile and the cut of his jaw and a nose that had obviously been broken at least once—and thought he was beautiful.

"Is that a proposal?"

He paused. "If I thought you'd accept it…hell yes."

"I accept," Katie said.

Sam's eyes flashed as he took a deep breath.

"If you weren't so damn bloody, and I didn't have to go book another bad guy, I'd hug you so big."

Katie laughed from the joy washing through her.

"If I didn't have to go change clothes and take a bath, I'd let you."

Sam stopped, then cupped her face and kissed her anyway.

"That seals the deal, my love. We'll get to the good stuff later. Go. Your boss will be waiting on you."

Katie turned and ran, disappearing through the gate ahead of him.

It took a little over half an hour for Katie to get home, throw her bloody clothes in the washer, and then shower and dress again. And when she started back to school, she had a moment of déja vù. She'd gone back to Saguaro after the shooting to prove to her class that she was okay, and now she was going back to her class here for almost the same reason.

She entered the building at a fast clip, waving at the secretary in the office to let her know she was back, and hurried down the hall to her class. When she walked in and saw it was Susan who was in the room, she was relieved. She would have already made whatever explanations about Donny.

"I'm back," Katie said. "Class, what do you say to Mrs. Wayne for staying with you?"

"Thank you, Mrs. Wayne," they chimed.

Susan smiled. "It was an eye-opening experience. I haven't been behind a desk in years, and never with ones so young. I salute you."

"Were they bad?" Katie whispered.

Susan shook her head. "Not at all, but very informative."

Katie grinned. "Oh…that. Children are like miniature court reporters. They record everything in those little brains and then tell anyone who is willing to listen."

Susan chuckled. "Court reporters. That's a good one," she said. Then she waved at the children and left the room.

Katie turned to the class, glanced at the clock, and realized there was only one more class before the last bell. She also knew the kids had missed their afternoon snack, and they were all a little frantic about Donny, so she went to the mini-fridge, got out a bag of individual packets of already peeled and sliced apples, and set them on a table nearby.

"Everyone get an apple snack and take a seat on the reading rug. We're going to have snack time and story time together today."

"Yay!" they cried.

"Inside voices, please, and don't crowd. There are apple snacks enough for everyone."

While the kids were getting their snacks and finding where they wanted to sit, Katie went to her library of storybooks, searching for one in particular. As soon as she found it, she settled down in her chair in front of her students and held up the book.

"*The Velveteen Rabbit*. Page one."

And she began to read.

The apple slices quickly disappeared, but she'd already drawn the children's imaginations into the story, reading all of the parts with different voices and different inflections of emotion, until even the wiggliest of the wigglers was still.

This time, nobody fell asleep. Nobody moved.

Evie and Beth were holding hands.

Freddie has his back to the wall again, his knees drawn up beneath his chin, enraptured by the story.

Thor wasn't talking about his daddy, but he was sad for the Velveteen Rabbit because it had no daddy.

They were all lost in the story, all the way to the last page.

"The end," Katie said, and closed the book.

Then she looked up. Their silence surprised her.

"That was sad, Miss Katie," Evie said.

"So sad," Beth echoed.

"Sometimes the best stories have a little sad in them, but it had a good ending, didn't it?"

They nodded.

Thor held up his hand.

"Yes, Thor?" Katie asked.

"Donny cried. I heard him."

"I know. His arm got hurt. But the doctors are fixing him and he will get well."

"Who was that man?" one little girl asked.

Before Katie could figure out how to answer that, the bell rang.

Saved by the bell.

"Okay, class. Scrap paper in the trash, please. Don't forget your jackets and backpacks, then get in your lines."

They scrambled to do what she'd asked, and then they were marching out into the hall, past the pumpkins and the scarecrow in Miss Katie's garden, toward the exit.

It wasn't until later, when Katie was on the way home, that she had time to savor the fact that Sam had proposed and she'd accepted. In the grand scheme of unique proposals, it might have had a place all its own, but she didn't care. Today, her future in Borden's Gap, and in the rest of her life, had been sealed with a kiss.

———

The doctors took Donny straight to surgery. Frieda sat down in the waiting room and cried until she gave herself a headache, then called her mom.

Rita was putting groceries in her car when she got the call. Seeing Frieda's name pop up on caller ID made her smile.

"Hi, honey, what's up?" Rita said.

"Mama, Donny is in surgery. Justin came back, tried to kidnap Donny off the playground, and broke his arm. It's a bad break. Bone came through the skin."

Rita moaned. "Oh my God. Our poor baby. What in the world? I didn't know Justin was even in town."

"Neither did we. And if it hadn't been for Donny's teacher, I don't know how this would have played out."

"What do you mean?"

"She ran Justin down and took him out with a karate kick. Like a ninja, Donny said. Then she sat with Donny, trying to stop the blood loss, until the ambulance came. As far as I'm concerned, she saved his life."

"God forgive me, but I hope Justin dies in prison, and that will still be better than he deserves. How can I help?" Rita asked.

"Could you please pick up the boys and just take them home with you? I won't leave Donny."

"Yes, I will. They can just stay with me until you and Donny go home."

Frieda sighed. "Thank you, Mama. I don't know what I'd do without you."

"That works both ways, sweetheart. You're my family. Family sticks together," Rita said. "Keep us posted on Donny. And if you need anything from home, just text me and I'll bring it to the hospital for you."

Frieda's eyes welled. "Oh, Mama, he's so hurt. Justin didn't just break his arm. He broke his heart."

Rita was fighting back tears. "He'll heal, and one day that man will just be a bad memory in their lives. Tell Donny that Granny loves him, and we'll see him soon."

"I will," Frieda said, and disconnected.

Rita managed to get her groceries in the car and took off for home to put them up before she had to go get the boys, crying all the way, while Frieda was sending her oldest son a text explaining what was about to take place.

———————

Cheryl Phillips had just signed a contract for the sale of her house. All she had to do now was find a place for her and Ree to live in Jackson, then pack up their things.

She had both beds and mattresses hauled off and didn't care what happened to them. Raymond had defiled them, and she wasn't taking anything to do with that man into their future.

Ree was still Ree. Quiet. Withdrawn. And leaning toward panic without her mama. But Cheryl knew they were still in their first days of rebirth, and all she could do was hope her little girl would respond to the new, happier environment. She wasn't expecting miracles. Not at first. But she *was* counting on God to make one in His own time.

———————

It didn't take long for word to get around about what Justin Tiller had done, and that the new teacher had stopped an attempted kidnapping on the school playground. Word was that Katie McGrath had taken Tiller down with some karate chops, ending with a ninja spin and kick to Justin's jaw.

The local paper was gathering info for the story they

were doing on the attack. But they only had a police report and the skimpy details the school principal gave them about Katie, so the journalist started research of her own, and what she learned blew her mind. The Katie McGrath who had taken down Justin Tiller was also the heroine from the school shooting in Albuquerque! She began searching for and reading every story about the incident, learning how close Katie came to dying, and that of all the adults shot during the massacre she was the only one who had survived. She had saved her whole class, then gone back for two of her students who'd fallen and saved them by sheltering them with her body.

By the time the journalist ran with that info and turned in her story, she knew she had a scoop no one was going to believe. The next day, the headline in the Saturday issue shocked the town to the core.

HERO TEACHER DOES IT AGAIN

And the story spun out from there.

Katie hadn't been up an hour when Sam called.

"Hey, baby. Have you seen this morning's paper?"

"No. It's still out in the drive."

"Then fair warning. Your secret is out. Somebody at the paper did some research on you. Don't panic. Don't be upset. Wear your truth like a badge of honor. Do you hear me?"

"Oh lord," Katie muttered.

"I said, don't panic. Just read the piece. You shine, baby. You shine."

The call ended. Katie darted out of the house and

down the drive, then ran back like she was being chased and locked herself inside.

When she unrolled the paper, the first thing she saw was the headline.

"So much for burying the past," she muttered, and began reading.

She was halfway through the story when she started to cry, and by the time she was through, she was a wreck. Seeing this in print was like pulling the scab off an old, festering wound.

Susan called her to make sure she was okay.

Then Louise called her to make sure Katie knew she hadn't told.

And then Frieda Tiller called her and began crying, thanking her all over again for being the caring teacher and phenomenal person she was.

Katie was so scattered she hadn't noticed Roxie's car was in Sam's drive until she saw him walking into her yard. She opened the door and walked into his arms.

Sam held her until she had her emotions in check and then stepped back enough to look her in the eyes.

"I'm so proud of you. I can't believe someone as beautiful and as awesome as you loves me…loves us." And then he took a little black velvet box out of his pocket and opened it. "I did this backward already, so I'm starting over. Katie, darlin', will you marry me?"

"Yes, again," Katie said, and held out her hand as he slipped the ring on her finger. "It's beautiful," she said, turning her hand for the single, square-cut stone to catch the light, then threw her arms around his neck. "Thank you for loving me. I am so blessed."

Sam kissed her long and hard, wanting to take her to bed for the rest of the day and knowing that wasn't going to happen.

"Come back with me so we can tell the girls together," Sam said. "And just so you know, I fully expect them to lose their little minds, but in the very best way."

Katie nodded, then took Sam's hand and followed him across the street. The moment they walked in, Roxie was in the hall, grinning at them.

"Well, did you do it?" she asked.

"I did it," Sam said.

Katie held up her hand. "He did it."

Roxie grinned and clapped her hands. "I am so happy for all of you. Now, I'm going to run errands. Anytime you two want to get away on your own for a bit, just call."

Roxie left, and Sam and Katie went to the girls' room.

Sam could hear them arguing over the iPad as they came down the hall, but when they walked into the room, both girls looked up and the argument ended.

"Miss Katie! Are we baking today?" Beth asked.

"Not today," Katie said.

"We have something to tell you," Sam said, and then sat down on the side of their bed, and pulled Katie down beside him. "I asked Katie to marry me, and she said yes."

Chapter Twenty-Two

THE GIRLS' EYES WIDENED. "WHAT DOES THAT MEAN?" Evie asked. "Does she live with us now?"

Katie pulled Evie up in her lap. "No, not yet, sugar. But it means Daddy and I are engaged. See the beautiful ring he gave me? It's like a promise for when we do get married."

Beth scooted in and Katie pulled her up in her lap, too.

"Then you will live with us when we're married?" she asked.

Sam wanted to hug them. They'd already included themselves in the process.

"Yes," Katie said.

"You won't live across the street anymore?"

"No. I'll be right here with you two and Daddy every day. We'll wake up in the same house and go to bed in the same house, and we'll be a family," Katie said.

The girls looked at Sam. "Will we still call her Miss Katie?" Evie asked.

"What do you want to call her?" Sam asked.

Evie looked at Beth and then grabbed her sister's hand.

"We want to call her Mama. Could we please call her Mama?"

"Absolutely!" Sam said.

Katie hugged them close. "I would be so happy if you would call me Mama," she said.

"What do we call you at school?" Beth asked.

"After we're married, I'll be Mama for always," Katie said. "But we have to have a wedding first, and that will take a while to figure out."

"A wedding? Like when the girl wears a long white dress?" Evie whispered.

Katie nodded. "But I'll be needing flower girls for the wedding. Do you know any little girls who would like to do that?"

They raised their hands, just as if they were in school.

"We would! We would like to be flower girls!" Evie said.

"Flower girls," Beth echoed, then added, "What do flower girls do?"

Sam burst out laughing.

"They walk in front of the bride, throwing flower petals in the aisle for her to walk on, and then they stand and be really quiet while the preacher talks."

"We can do that!" Beth cried.

"Do we get new dresses?" Evie asked.

Katie nodded.

"Let's play flower girls!" Evie shouted, and slid out of Katie's lap, dragging her sister with her, and ran out of the room.

Sam looked at Katie. "I think that went well."

And then they looked up and saw the girls skipping past the doorway, throwing pretend flowers in the air and on the floor, then busting a move as they threw them at each other.

Katie laughed. "I cannot wait for this to become a reality."

Sam stood, and then pulled her up into his arms.

"Neither can I."

━━━━━━━━━

The errands Katie ran that day took twice as long because everyone wanted to talk to her. To praise her. To thank her for her devotion to children in general, and for saving Donny, and then they noticed the engagement ring and that started conversations all over again.

By the time she got home, her head was reeling, but not in a bad way. Releasing the secret had freed her in a way she had not expected. And before the weekend was over, they had set the wedding for spring break, less than six months away.

The fairy costumes arrived a few days later, and the twins became obsessed with the wings. At first they'd tried them out just to see how they worked, and then they began wearing them every waking minute at home. They ate meals wearing the wings. They "flew" up and down the hall until Sam was about to lose his mind.

He came out of his office, struggling with the need to shout.

"Girls! We need to talk. Meet me in the living room."

They came skipping into the room with their fairy wings flopping, waving magic wands, and in their minds turning everything into frogs.

"Please sit," Sam said.

"Are we in trouble?" Evie asked.

"Trouble?" Beth repeated.

"No, but there's something you need to know. Halloween is in two days, and if you break your wings before trick-or-treat night, you're both going to be fairies with broken wings because I am not buying more. Understand?"

They nodded.

"Thank you," Sam said. "Just remember, take care of your wings so you can wear them for trick or treat, or you'll be flightless fairies."

"Okay!" they said, and then got up and walked down the hall, reappearing a short time later without their wings and wearing their jackets. "Can we go play on the swings?" Evie asked.

"Yes. Be careful," Sam said, and watched them exit, then walked to the window to watch. They were a royal handful, but he loved them to distraction.

As he was watching, his cell phone rang. He glanced at caller ID, then breathed a sigh of relief when it wasn't the station.

"This is Sam."

"Sam, this is Merle Rollins at Jackson Realty. You have inquired more than once about the house on Rawls Street in Borden's Gap. Are you still interested in it?"

Sam's heart skipped. "Yes, I'm interested."

"Well, I'm sorry to say the owner has recently passed, and his family does not wish to continue ownership and wants to list it. However, if we can reach an agreement with the heirs, I think it would be in your favor."

"I'd want to view it, and I'd want it fully inspected before I'd make an offer."

"You name the day and time and I'll come down and walk you through, and if you say so, then we'll have it inspected," Merle said.

"You tell me when you can come, and I'll meet you there," Sam said.

"I can do this coming Tuesday around noon, or Wednesday morning."

"Tuesday," Sam said. "I'll meet you there at noon."

"Excellent," Merle said, and disconnected.

Sam smiled. This was exciting news. How great would it be to move into that house when he and Katie got married, instead of crowd up in this little one?

He glanced out the window at the girls again. They were playing on the slide and chasing each other like puppies gone wild.

When they were born, he'd thought it the greatest tragedy that his girls would not have a mother, but what he'd come to realize was that they had each other. What they'd never had, they could not miss. They'd never been lonely. They'd never missed having someone to play with. And they'd always had him.

He was still watching them play when his doorbell rang. He opened the door to find Katie on the doorstep with a shopping bag in her hand.

"Hey, honey! You were reading my mind. I'm missing my girl," Sam said, and hugged her when she came in.

Katie let the love surround her, soaking up his presence.

"Where are the munchkins?" she asked.

"I clipped their fairy wings, so they're outside playing. Do you need help with something?" Sam asked.

"I need you, hot and hard inside me. But I'll settle for a cold bottle of pop and the chance to sit with you out on the porch."

Heat swept through Sam like wildfire. "Jesus, Katie. Don't hold back. Now how am I supposed to function for the rest of the day with that thought in my head?"

She ran her finger down the front of his shirt. "You could have a cold drink, too."

He cupped his hands on her backside and pulled her close, letting her feel what she'd done to him.

"I don't think a cold drink is enough to shift my focus, but we'll give it a try."

Katie sighed. "I know. That was a low blow, but—"

"Enough!" Sam said, laughing, and swept her up into his arms.

Katie threw back her head and laughed, and when she did, he nipped the hollow at the base of her throat, then ran his tongue along the spot to soothe the pain.

Then the kitchen door banged against the wall.

"And…here comes the horde," Sam said, and burst out laughing.

"They live here," Katie said. "I'm the one out of place."

"Not for much longer," Sam said. "And I for one cannot wait."

Then the girls came running, tackled Katie around the legs, and they all wound up on the floor, laughing and giggling and wrapped in Miss Katie's arms.

The following Tuesday, Sam was on edge all morning. He so did not want to be disappointed by what the old house looked like inside. He was up to some remodeling, but not a gut job. Either it worked or it would not. And when noon finally rolled around, Sam was on his way to Rawls Street.

The Realtor was already there, sitting on the verandah steps. He stood when Sam arrived.

"Hello, Chief. Nice to finally meet you," Merle said. "Are you ready to do this?"

"Yes, sir," Sam said, and followed the man into the house.

From the moment he saw the grand staircase curving upward to the second floor, the white marble floors and the cherrywood crown molding and the elegant carvings within the mantels above the fireplaces, the house felt right, even familiar. What had Katie called it... *soul memory*.

They kept moving from the grand dining room to a large eat-in kitchen. He would replace appliances, but the woodwork and flooring were stunning, and the library, office, and a downstairs bathroom made it hard to resist.

The four bedrooms upstairs were huge, and part of the space had been made into walk-in closets in three of the four. The master bedroom had its own en suite bath, with a deep, old-fashioned claw-foot tub and a shower to die for. A bedroom that would be for the girls had its own bathroom and large closet, and by the time they started back downstairs, if the house wasn't eaten up with termites and the foundation and wiring and plumbing were up to date and they didn't want an outrageous price for it, he wanted it.

"What are they asking for it?" Sam asked.

"Two hundred thousand," Merle said.

Sam had been expecting three or more and was trying to keep a straight face. "Okay. Call the inspector and get me a report. If it's sound, I want it."

"Excellent!" Merle said. "Like I said, they don't want to mess with it. They know the real estate in Borden's Gap is not going for big-city prices. They chose that number. It was their decision."

Then Sam's radio squawked.

"Duty calls," he said. "I'll be waiting to hear from you."

"Yes, sir," Merle said, and as Sam left the house, he began turning off lights and locking back up.

Sam's hopes were high as he drove away. He wanted to live there with Katie and the girls, and make love and make more babies, and fill that house from roof to basement with so much love that there wouldn't be room for ghosts. Not his. Not hers.

———

Unaware of Sam's intent, Katie was getting ready for Halloween at school. Her students' parents planned the party and brought refreshments, and Katie would be responsible for crowd control.

Because they weren't allowed to wear their costumes to school, Katie had ordered face paint and headbands with animal ears. She'd done it in years past, and by the time parents arrived for the party, all of the kids would have their appearances altered in some way.

And to get into the spirit of the day, she'd painted the

tip of her nose in the shape of a cat nose and painted whiskers on her cheeks and had a headband with cat ears. When she showed up at school, Susan walked out of her office, clapping.

"You are such a fun, amazing teacher. I want to be little again and in your class."

"What can I say? I love my job," Katie said, and hurried to her room.

Marcy saw her coming and threw her hands up in the air and groaned.

"I give up! You're the fun teacher. I am a dud."

Katie laughed. "You are not a dud. And here…I brought some extra stuff. You can have it."

"Oh my gosh! Thank you!" Marcy said. "What all is in here?" she asked as she opened the bag.

"Metallic peel-off stars in multiple colors, and fake eyebrows and mustaches. You just peel off the backing and they stick on…for a while."

Marcy threw her arms around Katie's neck.

"I owe you, kitty kat."

"You could be a bridesmaid at my wedding," Katie said.

Marcy's eyes suddenly welled.

"For real?"

"For real," Katie said.

"Oh my God, I am so honored," Marcy said. "I would love to."

Katie smiled. "Good. Now let's get this stuff set up. I have no hopes of having one sensible hour of lessons today. It's going to be a trick keeping them peeled off the walls until the party this afternoon."

Then she went into her room, stowed her things, and got ready for their arrival. When the students began arriving in Katie's room and they saw her, they went into hysterics. Everybody wanted to touch her ears and couldn't quit looking at her face. Then the bell rang and class began. She got them all the way through lunch and recess, but as soon as they came inside from playing, she pulled out the animal-ear headbands and spread them out on one of the big tables.

The kids went wild. There were all kinds of dog ears and tiger ears, and ears that looked like horses, and ears that looked like pigs. She let them pick out what they wanted to be, and then she set up a video for them to watch about bees and how they made honey. It was as close to a science class as she could get, and then she settled in to painting their little faces to fit the ears that they had chosen.

Evie and Beth both chose cat ears like Katie, so she painted little black noses and whiskers on their faces, and moved on to paint dog faces and horses, and yellow and black tiger stripes and little pink pig noses. The kids were beside themselves, and each time she finished one, she took a picture.

Susan had heard about the paint party, and when she came down to see the animals emerging on the children's faces, she brought a photographer from the local paper with her.

"Miss Katie, you just keep on painting. And children, you continue watching your video. The photographer is taking pictures for the paper."

Katie sighed. Once again, she was going to wind up on the front page. At least this time it was for something fun.

As soon as she finished the last student and took her picture, she sat them down in group fashion and asked Susan to take a picture with her and the kids, then joined the group.

The principal took several and left just as parents began arriving for the party. When the parents saw their children, they had to take more pictures. And then Donny and his mother walked into the party and Katie ran to greet them.

His little arm was in a fierce-looking case, with screws sticking out of the plaster. He was pale and even thinner than before, but he had a big smile on his face and took it as his due to become the center of attention.

"Oh, honey! I am so glad to see you!" Katie said. "Frieda, thank you for bringing him."

"He isn't ready to come back to school yet. The surgery was pretty intense, and we can't take the chance of a fall or playing too rough yet. But he wanted so badly to come that I took off work and brought him."

Katie hugged Donny, and then his mother.

"I am so glad you did. Both of you. Find a safe place to sit, and we'll bring the food and the fun to you."

"Can you paint my face, too?" Donny asked.

Katie smiled. "I would love to. I think there are tiger ears left. Is that okay?"

"*Roar!*" he said.

"I guess that means yes," Katie said, and quickly painted tiger stripes to go with the ears while the parents began laying out the food.

By the time all of the food was laid out, the party was already in progress. The kids played games and ate snacks and were thoroughly sated by the time the last bell rang.

The party organizers had already cleaned up the debris, put Katie's room back together, and taken their children home while Katie was walking the other children out. Once they got out on the front lawn to wait for their rides, Katie's students began strutting their stuff as they mingled with their peers.

Evie and Beth came up behind her, smiling.

Beth did a little pirouette in front of Katie, then threw her arms up over her head.

"Miss Katie, this *was* our next best day!" she cried.

"The next best ever!" Evie added, and they reached for each other's hands and skipped to the curb where Roxie was waiting.

Their joy tugged at Katie's heart. That they were going to become her daughters, that she was going to marry their father and, for the first time in her life, be part of a family was the ultimate gift.

And the next night, when Sam took the girls trick or treating, Katie was with them. The night was chilly, but the girls were too excited to be cold. They were wearing pink, long-sleeved T-shirts beneath their pink and green gauzy dresses. The flower garlands in their hair were pinned down tight, and their little wings bounced as they walked. They each had a trick-or-treat bag in one hand and their magic wands in the other, and they were flinging magic and pixie dust all over the streets of Borden's Gap.

"Girls. Easy on the pixie dust," Sam said. "You don't want to turn everyone in town into a frog."

"Okay, Daddy," they said, and then giggled.

Sam put his arm around Katie and hugged her close as

they walked, while keeping an eagle eye on his two sprites who were just a step ahead.

"This is the best Halloween. I got the best treat of all. I have you, Katie girl."

Katie shivered. "You are my sweet-talkin' man," she said.

"Are you cold?" he asked.

"That wasn't from the cold. It was just another piece of the old me letting go. You fill me up. Every day in a thousand ways, Sam Youngblood. I can't wait to grow old with you."

Sam sighed and pulled her closer. "Love you," he said.

"Love you more," Katie said.

The girls turned around and threw pixie dust on both of them and then danced their way up the walk to the next house with Sam and Katie right behind them.

It was nearing Christmas when Sam signed the final papers for the house on Rawls Street, and in a town as small as Borden's Gap, it was nothing short of a miracle that he'd been able to keep it a secret. But as soon as school was out for Christmas break, he picked a day and told Katie and the girls they were going out to eat.

They were bundled up in coats as he loaded them up in his car and settled in for the ride. But when Sam turned off Main instead of going toward Ronda's Café, Katie frowned.

"Where are we going?" she asked.

"It's a surprise," Sam said.

"We're getting a surprise?" the girls asked.

"It's for everyone," he said, and kept driving.

When he pulled up into the driveway of the old house, Katie's heart skipped.

"We're here! Everybody out," Sam said.

Katie got out, and she and Sam got the girls out of the back seat.

Sam was smiling all the way to the door, and when he pulled out a key and opened the door, Katie was in shock.

"Sam! What did you do?" she asked.

"I bought the house. Come inside, my love. Merry Christmas early. This is ours."

Katie gasped and then threw her arms around Sam's neck and kissed him. The girls were wide-eyed, and for once, both silent. Compared to their little house, it was a castle.

He walked them from room to room, talking about what was getting repainted and what was being replaced. But the elegance of the place was beyond anything Katie could have ever dreamed of for herself.

"I feel like Cinderella. You're the prince, and this is the glass slipper," she said as tears welled and rolled.

The girls had already laid claim to the room that would be theirs.

"Can we paint it pink?" Evie asked.

"I want it blue," Beth said.

"How about we paint it white, you can have pink curtains at the windows and sleep in a blue bed?" Katie said.

"Yes!" they said, and began running in circles in the vast, empty room.

Sam slid his arm around Katie's waist.

"What color are we going to paint the master bedroom?" he asked.

"I think we paint it white and put a red silk comforter on our bed."

Sam laughed and then pulled her into his arms, whispering close against her ear.

"You are already one hot mama, but if you want to sleep wrapped in red, you won't be hearing me complain."

═══════

As soon as the new year had been celebrated, Katie and the girls went back to school, and the house on Rawls Street went under construction.

Katie went by the house every day after school to see the progress, and every night after she went to bed, she dreamed. But nearly always about the wedding, and little flower girls throwing handfuls of flower petals into the air, and seeing the look on Sam's face when he saw her coming down the aisle.

It took her months to find "the dress" but when she did, it was perfection. The flower girls' dresses were long like hers, while the bridesmaid dresses were lilac and the softest green.

When Billy Arnold, at Arnold's Antiques and Gifts, learned she was getting married, he sent her a gift. She opened it on the evening of its arrival, and then wept from the magnificence and the love with which it had been given. An antique silver bracelet that was a single strand of braided silver, and with the gift came the card:

For your wedding…something old.

Katie's world had settled on its axis. She was putting down roots in Tennessee and becoming the woman she'd been meant to be.

Lila and Jack were coming in from Albuquerque for the wedding. Katie needed a maid of honor and couldn't get married without her best friend.

One day led into another, into another until spring break arrived, and it was the day before the wedding. After it was over, the girls would be going to spend spring break with Sam's parents in Nashville, and Sam and Katie were going to honeymoon in Borden's Gap.

They were going to spend their first night as man and wife in their newly renovated house because, as Katie stated, "Since this house has stood the test of time without succumbing to something dire, it bodes well for us to do the same."

———

Morning dawned, bringing Lila and Jack into town from their hotel in Jackson. And once again, Lila was with Katie in a classroom of the Baptist church, helping her pin on the veil. Marcy was fussing with her hair and trying not to cry and mess up her makeup. And both of the girls' grandmothers were in there with them for moral support, while Roxie was getting Beth and Evie dressed. There was so much laughter and chatter, it was like the party had already started.

Lila kept remembering another wedding, and how alone Katie had been except for her. And while she and Katie had not spoken of it, tomorrow it would be a year to the day of the Saguaro Elementary massacre. On that day Katie had almost died, and in this place, she had been reborn.

And then there was a knock on the door. It was the pastor.

"What a beautiful bride!" he said. "What a beautiful family! Are you ready, Katie?"

"Yes, sir," she said.

"My wife will escort you through this maze of hallways. We'll be waiting for you at the altar," he said, and left.

The pastor's wife was all smiles and business as she made sure the flower girls had their baskets of flower petals and Katie's veil was falling properly in the back before she led them toward the sanctuary.

At that point, the music sounded, and Sam, his dad, and Shelly's dad walked into the sanctuary and took their places at the altar, as ushers escorted Roxie, Sam's mother, and Shelly's mother into their seats.

His dad had been the best father a boy could have asked for, and in Sam's eyes, he was still his best man, and Shelly's parents had stood by him all these years. He valued these two men above all others.

Sam glanced up the aisle and as he did felt his father's hand on his shoulder—just for a moment. A reminder that he did not stand alone.

And then the music sounded and Marcy began her walk down the aisle. And then came Lila, a stranger to everyone except the bride. She felt Jack's eyes on her long before she saw his face in the crowd.

And then Evie and Beth appeared in the doorway, all serious and walking exactly as they'd been taught,

dropping flower petals here and there and waving at Sam
along the way.

A ripple of laughter moved across the congregation, and
when it did the girls lost focus. They threw a handful of
petals at the people they were passing, and then they threw a
few up into the air, and tossed some at each other, and then
just before they reached the altar turned their baskets upside
down and emptied the petals into a multicolored puddle.

Sam sighed.

Marcy grabbed them before they ran amok and got
them into their places. They were still waving at Sam, and
he had a finger to his lips trying to get them to be quiet,
when the organ music changed.

There was a pause, and then a thunderous sound
ripped through the sanctuary as all eyes turned toward the
woman standing in the doorway.

Breath caught in the back of Sam's throat, and then he
had to swallow to keep from crying.

There she was…his Katie. Coming toward him.

———

Katie thought she would be nervous, but all she felt was
joy. She thought it would remind her of Mark, but all she
saw was Sam's face, and his girls—their girls—waving at
her and shouting, "There comes Mama."

Katie felt like she was floating. There was no conscious
thought beyond getting to the altar. And then she was there.

She turned to the girls and pulled a single carnation
out of her bouquet and gave it to Beth and kissed her on

the cheek, and then pulled a second carnation out of the bouquet and gave it to Evie and kissed her on the cheek. Then she handed her bouquet to Lila and turned around and reached for Sam.

The rest of the ceremony was a blur. All she remembered was saying "I do" and hearing Sam repeat it. She saw his father take a ring out of his pocket and hand it to Sam, and then it was on her finger.

The preacher pronounced them husband and wife, and then in front of God and everybody, Sam Youngblood kissed her.

It was the best day ever.

And every one of their tomorrows would be the next best day.

Epilogue

THE PARTY WAS OVER. THE GIRLS WERE GONE WITH grandparents. Lila and Jack were on their way back to Memphis. And Sam and Katie had snuck out the back of the church and were already almost home.

The house on Rawls Street was alight through every window, with the light on the front verandah spilling all the way down the steps onto the lawn.

The newlyweds were riding a champagne high, with the taste of wedding cake still sweet on their lips as they got out of the car and ran up the steps.

Sam paused long enough to unlock the door and push it inward, then swept Katie up in his arms and carried her across the threshold, kicking the door shut behind him as they went.

He set her down on the welcome mat to lock the door, and then danced her across the floor all the way to the grand winding staircase.

Then, just as Sam put his foot on the first step, he had a sensation of déja vù that was so strong he lost his breath.

Katie saw the look on his face.

"I feel it, too," she said. "They're just welcoming you home."

Sam shivered, then reached for her hand.

"Welcoming us home, my love. There's a red bed and a lifetime of love just waiting. Are you ready?"

"I was born ready," Katie said, and let him lead her up the stairs.

The End

Keep reading for an excerpt from the first book in
Sharon Sala's beloved Blessings, Georgia series

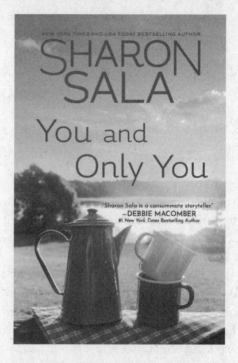

Available now from Sourcebooks Casablanca

Chapter One

Blessings, Georgia
November

LILYANN BRONTE ALREADY KNEW HOW FAST LIFE could change. Her past was a road map to prove it. But on this particular Friday in the first week of November, she experienced one of those déjà vu moments as the Good Lord hit Rewind on the story that was her life.

She was sweeping the front sidewalk of Phillips Pharmacy, where she worked, when she heard the low, sexy rumble of a hot-rod engine. The skin crawled on the back of her neck as a shiny black pickup truck went rumbling down Main Street.

Before she could see the driver, sunlight hit the windshield, reflecting directly into her eyes. At the same time she went blind, she heard him rack the pipes on the muffler, just like Randy Joe used to do when he picked her up for their Saturday night dates. But that was a long time ago, before he went away to war in Afghanistan and got himself killed.

She had no idea who was driving this truck, and when she looked again, it was turning the corner at the far end of the street and then it was out of sight.

For LilyAnn, seeing that truck and hearing the pipes rattle felt like a sign. Was it the universe telling her she was living in the past? Because if it was, she already knew that. Or was it Randy Joe sending her a message, and if it was, what was he trying to say?

As she resumed sweeping, a car drove up and parked in front of Dalton's Fitness Center next door. It was Rachel Goodhope, who ran the local bed-and-breakfast in Blessings. She got out wearing her workout clothes and waved at Lily as she ran inside.

Lily eyed the woman's big boobs and toned body and began sweeping in earnest. Rachel looked good for a woman in her late forties, and everyone knew she liked to stay fit. She was on her third husband, and there was talk he might be getting the boot before long. No one could actually put their finger on what the problem was with Rachel and her marriages. Some said it had to do with her choice of men, while others hinted that Rachel would be a hard woman to please. Still, she obviously saw the need to stay fit in case she was ever in the market for husband number four.

Lily was of the opinion that any woman with a backbone and the nerve to speak her mind should be difficult to please. Her great-great-grandma, Delia Bronte, had put a musket ball through a Yankee captain's hat during the War of Northern Aggression because he had not taken it off his head when he forced his way into her house. Lily liked to think she had a little bit of that in her, as well.

Just thinking about that Yankee intruder and her great-great-grandma's gumption made her push the broom a little harder across the sidewalk. But seeing that truck had set her to thinking about the past, and before she knew it, she was knee-deep in memories long since gone.

———

LilyAnn had been a constant source of pride for her parents through all her growing-up years. When she reached high school, she lost her braces and grew boobs, hitting her stride with a bang. She became an honor student, a cheerleader, and was voted prettiest and friendliest every year by her class. When she was chosen head cheerleader her senior year, Randy Joe Bentonfield, the star quarterback, also chose her for his steady girl. She was over the moon, and her parents rejoiced in the moments in which she excelled.

As the year progressed, she marked another milestone by being named homecoming queen, then another when the announcement was made that she would be the valedictorian of her high school graduating class—two more notches in a high school career on a fast track to success.

But it wasn't until she won the title of the Peachy-Keen Queen that her parents broke out in full braggadocio. Lily felt as if her life could not get any better. But as the old saying goes, once you've reached the top, the only place to go is down.

On the morning of September 11, 2001, two planes flew into the World Trade Center in New York City and another one into the Pentagon. When a fourth one was taken down by the plane's passengers, crashing into a cornfield killing all on board, the world suddenly stopped turning on LilyAnn's axis. It was no longer about her.

National outrage followed the shock as young men and women from all over the country began enlisting in the army, including a lot of the young men in Blessings.

Randy Joe was one of the first to sign up. She cried herself silly, after which they made love. Randy Joe was so full of himself about being a man going away to war that he gave her a promise ring before he went away to boot camp. He came back long enough to have his picture taken in his uniform and then he shipped out, returning a month later in a flag-draped casket.

People said it had been a good thing he'd had that picture taken beforehand because he'd come back to Blessings in pieces, no longer fit for viewing.

His death devastated Lily, but at the same time, it thrust her back into the spotlight. Now she had a new status—the almost fiancée of Blessings' first war casualty. She dropped out of college that year and wore black, which went really well with her long blond hair. She visited his grave site every day for a year, and people said what a faithful young woman she was, grieving for her lost love in such a fashion.

When a new semester of college rolled around, she didn't go back. She was still paying visits to the cemetery, although as time between visits lengthened to weekly, then monthly, people still commented that LilyAnn was such a sweet thing to remember her dearly departed in such faithful ways. And because she'd lost her way and didn't know how to move past her first love or the success of her prior milestones, she took the mantle of bereavement to a whole new level.

One year turned into two and then three, and going to college was something other people did as everything became a blur. Her daddy had a heart attack and died, which turned her mama into a widow, and Lily barely remembered her dreams for the future and had forgotten how to get there.

The worst were the times when she could no longer bring Randy Joe's face to mind. At that point, the guilt would set her to eating a whole pint of chocolate-chip ice cream, just because it was his favorite treat. It didn't revive her memory or renew her desire to move on, but it did pack on the pounds.

The years came and went without notice until Lily was eleven years lost. Now she only visited his grave when she thought about it and had unwittingly masked her emotions with a bulwark of extra weight.

She had no status in Blessings beyond being one of two clerks at Phillips Pharmacy and the daughter of Grace Bronte, the widow who married a man twelve years her junior whom she met on an online dating site and proved all her critics wrong by living happily ever after in Miami, Florida.

Between the loss of Randy Joe and the abdication of her only living parent, LilyAnn had lost her way. She was stuck in a rut: too afraid to step out for fear of getting too close to someone and getting left behind all over again.

Also by Sharon Sala